Praise for
Can Xue

"...e's a new world master among us, and her name is Can Xue."
—Robert Coover

"Can Xue has found not just a new direction but a new dimension to move in, a realm where conscious beings experience space, time, and each other unbound from the old rules."
—*Music & Literature*

"*Vertical Motion* is incredible—short stories that I'd call 'surrealist,' but it's a kind of clear-eyed surrealism, as if dreams had invaded the physical world."
—John Darnielle, author of *Wolf in White Van*

"Funny, bizarre, improbable yet oddly moving, her stories in *The Last Lover* often arise from the mutual fantasies of East and West. They can sometimes bring Kafka, Ishiguro or Calvino to mind. In the end, though, Can Xue commands a truly unique voice."
—*The Independent*

"One of the most raved-about works of translated fiction this year."
—*Flavorwire*

Also by Can Xue
in English Translation

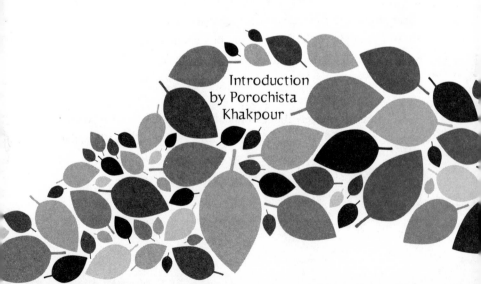

Introduction
by Porochista
Khakpour

Frontier

Translated from
the Chinese by
Karen Gernant
& Chen Zeping

OPEN LETTER
LITERARY TRANSLATIONS FROM THE UNIVERSITY OF ROCHESTER

Can
Xue

Copyright © 2008 by Can Xue
Translation copyright © 2017 by Karen Gernant & Chen Zeping

First edition, 2017
All rights reserved

Library of Congress Cataloging-in-Publication Data: Available.
ISBN-13: 978-1-940953-54-0 / ISBN-10: 1-940953-54-5

Printed on acid-free paper in the United States of America.

Text set in Caslon, a family of serif typefaces based on the designs
of William Caslon (1692–1766).

Design by N. J. Furl

Open Letter is the University of Rochester's nonprofit, literary translation press:
Lattimore Hall 411, Box 270082, Rochester, NY 14627

www.openletterbooks.org

CONTENTS

INTRODUCTION

Porochista Khakpour

In the summer of 2016 I found myself in a place on a 20,000-acre working cattle ranch in the middle of a desolate stretch of northeastern Wyoming: Ucross, Wyoming, population 25. It's an artist residency I've been to twice before, and one could indeed dare call it a part of the old mythos of the American Frontier. There is nothing to do but work. Once a week the residents and I go to a saloon about 25 miles away in Buffalo, where local cowboys and cowgirls play bluegrass. This saloon, part of a hotel called The Occidental, has been a haunt of everyone from Butch Cassidy to Buffalo Bill. That's about the only thing there is to do.

These high plains are where I've done most my writing in the past decade, and it became where I did almost all my reading of Can Xue's *Frontier* this time around. This residency, my own writing escaped me as Can Xue's book demanded more and more of my time. I had thought a few days would be all I needed—I was not a new Can Xue reader after all, and had usually managed to plow through even her most difficult work in a couple days—but this was not the case with this recent novel. In fact, a curious thing began to happen as I read. The further I got, the longer the book seemed to get. It was shocking; the book would lengthen the more I got into it. *This book won't end*, I told a friend, *it's strange, I swore I was two hundred pages in a day ago and there I am today.* Days later, I felt I had made very little progress. It went on like this for quite some time, til my time was basically up.

This is usually a complaint—something taking a long time, a book requiring effort. "Time flying" indicates an enjoyable exploit—this is what you want. But this time around, even this sentiment felt reversed. I didn't want the book to end, and the story, perhaps sensing that, refused to end. Even when it ended, it didn't end. I just started reading it again. I went from the last pages to the first without breath. I had no choice.

One might say, this summer I found myself trapped in Can Xue's *Frontier.*

This of course, would probably not surprise my friend Can Xue. This seems to be part of the fabric of the book. And of course who could put a stunt like this past her—she is China's premier writer of the avant-garde, an experimental trickster, whose very name is not just a pen name but an alter ego—she refers to herself in third person—and so who could possibly put anything past her?

We have been regularly emailing for over a year now, so I thought to write her amid all this. I didn't want to alarm her so I asked a mild question at first, not sure how to explain my dilemma—*this book is lengthening as I read it, not shortening, help me*—instead I said, *So, dear Xiaohua* (what she goes by), *how did you come up with this?*

I should have known this question could go nowhere. She wrote back quickly:

"Like all the works by Can Xue, the idea was from her dark heart. Then the idea (I [Can Xue] didn't know clearly what it was, but I did know it was what I wanted) came out gradually, naturally . . . I wrote and wrote for some time, then someday I found that a great pattern appeared faintly in the work. Actually anything I wrote, am writing, or will write is like this, I'm sure. I call the pattern 'the pattern of freedom.' In *Frontier,* everybody, every animal is a pattern of freedom, and the background is the background of that great pattern of freedom." Her final sign off was appended with a polite "Please feel free to ask Xiaohua anything!"

I did not. I simply sat and stared at the yellow and blue expanse in front of me, the Big Horn Mountains looming faintly like the "purple mountain majesties" of American patriotic verse, and all the high grass interrupted only by an occasional creek, prairie upon prairie only punctuated by blackbirds, bison, rabbits, deer, antelope, a turkey or two.

The pattern of freedom. Was this freedom? Was freedom expansion instead of contraction? Was freedom in its essence eternity?

After all, frontier by definition meant "the extreme limit of settled land beyond which lies wilderness," that I knew. So what were the borders of the frontier? No one could know, most likely, I decided. The minute the borders are set, it's possible the thing ceases to be a frontier.

.

I came to Can Xue about six years ago. In 2010, I was teaching a World Literature intro class at an arts college in Santa Fe. I had chosen Daniel Halpern's international reader *The Art of the Story* (2000) as one of my principal texts. Most of the writers I had heard of, but there were a few I didn't know so I went about reading those carefully. One was Can Xue, whose story "The Child Who Raised Poisonous Snakes" was definitely the most bizarre story I had ever read. This is saying something—I have a big appetite for the bizarre. When I taught it a few students got the bug like me, but most were confused and traumatized by it. I was secretly happy about that—I wanted her to myself. I imagined a weird cult all around the world of her admirers, her allure completely lost on normals. Occasionally I'd ask people about her and nine times out of ten they had no idea who I was talking about. But when they did, it was instant cult camaraderie.

In 2015 I got to know her. I was on the jury for the Neustadt Prize for Literature—some call this "the American Nobel," and it comes with a hefty award—and it was obvious to me who I'd pick for my nominee. The best part was we had to inform the person we were nominating. It happened that I was writer-in-residence at Bard College, where Bradford Morrow first published Can Xue in the States, in Bard's journal *Conjunctions*. All I had to do was write the managing editor, my colleague, and ask her for Can Xue's email, and there we were, emailing all the way until now. Can Xue was honored by the nomination and especially by the invitation to the States which came with the award—so much so that when she did not win (she was close), we decided she should still come. And so we schemed, and indeed she is due to come to the States in October 2016, not far from the American publication date of *Frontier*, in fact.

Every time Can Xue has a book out in English translation, it's yet another opportunity to see if that cult of Can Xue can expand. And one expects it won't, but I've seen it with my own eyes: those chosen ones really bite and can't let go.

And so how does one introduce her? I always begin with her name. Can Xue's name is a pseudonym that means both "the dirty snow that refuses to melt" and "the purest snow at the top of a high mountain"—and it happens to be synonymous with Chinese experimental literature. She is the author of six novels, fifty novellas, 120 short stories, and six book-length commentaries, with only a half a dozen of her works published in English (she has had five English translators, all of whom she refers to like they are close collaborators and even friends). Robert Coover called her a "new world master," Susan Sontag believed she was worthy of a Nobel, and Eileen Myles has been a longtime fan.

Then there is her *self*, the transmission of her writer persona through interviews. Here is the writer as true iconoclast, the uncompromising original. A choice quote on her process: "I never edit my stories. I just grab a pen and write, and every day I write a paragraph. For more than thirty years, it's always been like this. I believe that I am surrounded by a powerful 'aura,' and that's the secret of my success. Successful artists are all able to manipulate the '*balance of forces*'—they're that kind of extraordinarily talented people." Of course.

As I mentioned she refers to herself in third person, describes fiction as a performance, and claims that all of her works are from the experiments in which she takes herself as the subject. In this sense Can Xue is almost more medium than artist, a vessel rather than a generator, creation being relegated to its perhaps most logical state: the mystical. "In my mind, my ideal readers are these: those who have read some works by the modernist writers, and who love metaphysical thinking and material thinking—both capabilities are needed for the reading of Can Xue." Of course.

She is also of the late bloomer species, one who came to her work well into adulthood, a story I don't relate to but now wish I did: "I decided to become a writer when I was thirty years old. But I think before that I had been preparing for this, actually, since I was three years old . . . After the situation in China changed, all the literary things happened to me naturally. I have been like an erupting volcano ever since." She began writing in 1983 and now is 63—at her peak, it feels like, though it's hard to say when she wasn't at a peak.

Her last novel *The Last Lover* (Yale University Press) won a big translation award in 2015, the Best Translated Book Award, and got her more attention. One might say Can Xue has never quite "broken out" in the U.S., or even China, or anywhere for that matter.

I always say the same thing when a book of hers is about to come out: *it will be interesting what people make of this one.* I'm not even sure who I'm talking about—perhaps my ideal reader—but here I go again with *Frontier*: *It will be interesting what people make of this one.*

•

Can Xue's *Frontier* refers to a place called Pebble Town, the main location of the novel, a sort of dreamlike realm at the base of Snow Mountain, where reality constantly mingles with some other dimension. Through a dozen different characters, we dip in and out of the region, and it's hard to know if we are also going in and out of the worlds of the living or the dead, the dreamlife or the waking life.

Animals abound here, more than in any other Can Xue tale. You have geckos, wolves, eagles, black cats, snakes, black birds, butterflies, parrots, frogs, snow leopards, centipedes, turtles, crows, worms, sheep, pangolins, and cicadas, and probably many more that I lost track of. These animals sometimes operate like humans, other times like all-knowing deities, sometimes as demonic antagonists, other times as saints, occasionally as real entities and often as symbols. Pebble Town, as stony as it might seem, is alive with poplars and wind and all sorts of flora, and it is also quite brimming with fauna. (And sometimes flora and fauna seem like one: "The other poplars were so beautiful and vivacious that they seemed on the verge of speaking.") The humans are never quite alone, always being witnessed or witnessing some other species who is on this ride with them. You are never ever quite alone in Pebble Town. The frontier, as free and expansive and limitless, is always populated just enough. Before you can fully let go and lose yourself, something, some being, something with a pulse, is there to remind you, *you exist.*

The nature of your existence, though, might be up for debate ("Nancy looked bewildered, and—as though discussing a problem with an invisible person—said, 'Hunh. I'm puzzled by lots of things here; they're mixed up. Still, this place is magnetic. Look at that eagle, flying and stopping . . . Everything's in doubt.'"). You could be an abandoned child, you could be the Director of Pebble Town's Design Institute—the region's Kafka-esque Castle of Dubious Employment—who goes in and out of death, you could be the one black man originally from Africa but adapted to this presumably

Eastern land, you could be a couple trying to find your footing in a new land. Time is not quite clear and as some characters note, people don't age in quite the same way.

The beauty of Pebble Town is that everyone expects its lawlessness—or at least the fact that its laws and properties are not to be known. Can Xue very casually writes of its wonders, as if it were as banal as dust: "She sank into memories and told José that she was in an accident in the interior several years ago and was taken to the hospital, where she was pronounced dead. But after a day in the morgue, she came back to life. She was moved into an ordinary room. A young person went to her room every day and chatted with her. As they chatted, the institute director sensed that she'd seen him somewhere before, but couldn't remember where. The young person said he was a vagrant and constantly on the move. He was currently helping out in the hospital. Not until the day she was discharged did he tell the truth: he said he had talked with her an entire night in the morgue and had almost frozen to death. She suddenly found this young person really annoying."

In another section, an anecdote also takes a strangely pragmatic turn, as if Can Xue wants to transform anything mythic, mystical or magical here into something more folkloric, simple, mundane: "Grace's legs gave way and she sat on the floor. She propped herself up with her hands and then grabbed hold of a little feathered thing. It appeared to be a dead bird. This whole room seemed full of dead birds. She saw Lee standing against the wall, afraid of stepping on them. Oh, he was moving away from the wall, apparently intending to exit. Grace said silently, 'Coward—what a coward!' Lee exited, and Grace lay down. Dead birds kept dropping from above. Although she couldn't see them, she could smell the fresh blood. She started thinking back. She recalled that when she was a child, the old woman she called Granny (perhaps not her real granny?) smoked cigarettes. She had a little turtle in her pocket. Grace wanted to look at the little turtle, so Granny pulled it out and placed it in her hand, warning her, 'Careful—it bites people.' One day, it did bite her palm. It was gory, for it broke her skin. She cried. As Granny bandaged it, she kept saying, 'Didn't I warn you?' Grace still had a scar on her palm. When Granny lay in her coffin, they put this living turtle in with her; they put it in her pocket. Afterward, Grace thought about it for a long time: How long could the little turtle live underground if it ate Granny's flesh?"

The book is full of these vignettes and stories within stories, that operate with more autonomy than they would in another book. Reading *Frontier* is not unlike reading the Old Testament, where stories are strung together by some other logic that is not always apparent to the reader, though you are still left with some thematic impression. And the stories have their own arcs and narratives and stand up on their own. But their relation to each other is often the mystery.

But unlike the Bible's eschatological semiotics, the issue here is something more straightforward: the nature of Pebble Town, or the Frontier. Where are we exactly? Is this heaven? Is this hell? Is it earth? A land of the past or present? China at times gets mentioned alongside the Gobi Desert. The placelessness of our destination is what carries this curious tale.

Can Xue seems very interested in this. On the one hand, Pebble Town is everything: "Our Pebble Town is a huge magnetic field, attracting people who are fascinated with secret things . . ." And on the other hand, it is nothing: "When we went to the frontier years ago, we couldn't see the road ahead clearly then, either. Since we couldn't see the road, we just walked. Sometimes we could tell we were walking on flat land, sometimes on rubble. Later, at daybreak, we found we had circled back to where we had started. We had gone nowhere."

In the end, we are left with something like a message in a bottle, a beautiful compelling thing that might, like a frontier itself, take endless readings to crack. I know I haven't done it yet. But like that message in a bottle, the interior is greater than the exterior—the book indeed expands as you go on. I wasn't crazy in finding it only got longer, and I fear that I will have many decades to go before this book gets to its conclusion with me. I guess in the end, I too—sitting here, book in lap, computer on porch, within a still twilight in the middle of this unknowable frontier of my own that I've come to know year after year—am one of the denizens of the Frontier: "Between cracks in the foliage, the steel-blue sky was divulging some information to them. Deep down in their hearts, they understood, but they couldn't say what it was. They could only sigh repeatedly, 'Pebble Town, oh. Oh, the frontier. Oh . . .'"

Note on Names

With Can Xue's permission, we have changed some of the Chinese names to English names that are similar to the Chinese. For those who have read or will read the novel in Chinese, we provide this list.

Sherman – Shi Miao – 石淼

Amy – Ayi – 阿依

José – Hushan – 胡闪

Nancy – Niansi – 年思

Lee – Zhou Xiaoli – 周小里

Grace – Zhou Xiaogui – 周小贵

Little Leaf – Xiao Yezi – 小叶子

Marco – Ma-ge-er – 麻歌儿

Roy – Rui – 蕊

Woolball – Maoqiu – 毛球

Tulip – Yujinxiang – 郁金香

Frontier

Chapter 1

LIUJIN

It was late. Liujin stood there, leaning against the wooden door. The ripe grapes hanging on the arbors flickered with a slight fluorescence in the moonlight. Blowing in the wind, the leaves of the old poplar tree sounded lovely. The voice of someone talking blended with the rustling of the poplar leaves. Liujin couldn't hear what he was saying. She knew it was the man who had recently been coming here late every night and sitting on the stone bench near the courtyard gate. At first, this had frightened Liujin and she hadn't dared to go outside. Time after time, she had peeped out the window. Later on, realizing that this bear-like old man was harmless, she worked up the courage to approach him. He had good eyesight: even in the dim light, his eyes were as penetrating as sharp glass. He was busying his hands twisting hemp. He didn't like to talk with people; his answers to Liujin's questions were always vague: "I'm not sure . . ." He wasn't one of her neighbors; where did he come from? Although he didn't talk with her, he seemed to enjoy talking to himself. His words kept time with the sound of the wind and the leaves. When the wind stopped, he stopped. This was really strange. Tonight, his voice was louder, and pricking up her ears, Liujin made out a few words: "At noon, in the market . . ." Liujin tried hard to imagine the scene in this indoor market: piece goods, gold and silver

3

jewelry, raisins, tambourines, foreigners, and so on. But she had no clue what the old man meant. Even though it was late, a woman was actually singing piteously and plaintively on the other side of the street; the woman seemed to be young. Could she be singing for the old man? But he apparently wasn't listening; he was talking to himself. These days, Liujin had grown accustomed to his voice. She thought the old man looked a little like the poplar tree in the courtyard. The poplar was old, and so this man must be old, too. Liujin asked: Are you twisting the hemp to sell it? He didn't answer. Sleepy, Liujin went off to bed. Before she fell asleep, she heard the young woman's song turn sad and shrill. When she arose in the morning, she saw that the old man had left without a trace—not even a bit of hemp had been dropped on the ground. He really was a strange person. When she inquired of the neighbors, they said they didn't know of such a person. No one had seen him. This made sense, for people generally didn't go out so late. Liujin knew that she went to bed later than anyone else in the little town: she had formed this habit a long time ago. Still, what about the young woman singing? Judging by the direction the voice came from, she seemed to be from Meng Yu's family. That family bought sheep from the pastures, slaughtered them in the market, and sold the fresh meat. With the strange old man showing up in her yard, Liujin no longer felt desolate and lonely in the autumn nights. She felt a vague affection for him, but she preferred not to explore the nature of this emotion.

She had lived by herself in this small enclosed area for five years. Before she was born, her parents had moved here from a large industrial city in the interior. Five years ago, her elderly parents went back to their hometown with many others, but she didn't. Why had she stayed? Why hadn't she wanted to go to the big city? She had some impressions of the city from her father's descriptions of it. These impressions were mostly misty, not very reliable; she had tried hard to synthesize them, but without success. And so when her parents packed their bags and prepared to leave this small frontier town to go back to their old home, she began to feel dizzy. She was even unsteady when she walked. Late at night, for several days before they left, she heard the cracking sound at the riverside: with her bizarre sense of hearing, she knew the sound came from the poplars. These explosions came at intervals until the wee hours. In response to this inauspicious sound, a vague notion gradually occurred to Liujin. When she suggested that she stay behind, her father merely raised his right eyebrow. This was the way he expressed himself whenever something confirmed what he thought. "You're an adult. It's your choice." All of a sudden, Liujin realized that he and Mama had been waiting for her to suggest this: she really was an idiot. So she unpacked her suitcase and put everything back where it belonged. True, she was thirty years old: why did she have to live with her parents? When the train started, her parents didn't lean out the window. She didn't know what they were thinking about. But when the last car was about to vanish from view, she suddenly saw clearly the big city in the distance. To be precise, it wasn't a city, but a large white cloud floating in midair, with mirages in the mist. She even saw the apartment in the tall building where her parents lived. She didn't know why their window was so dark in the strong light. How had she recognized it? Because her mother's old-style pleated skirt was hanging in front of the window. On her way back, she walked steadily. She was returning to the home that now belonged to her alone. She trembled a little in excitement.

At first, Liujin wasn't used to living alone. She sold cloth at the market. Every day when she left the noisy market and returned to the isolated little house, it was dark. For several days in a row, a tiny white wagtail strode hurriedly into her house; the little thing cried out briefly and sharply, as if looking for its companion. After quickly patrolling around inside, it left with a despondent cry. Liujin heard it fly to a tree, where it continued chirping. Had it experienced some tragedy in its life? Sitting under the lamp, she thought about the man who had recently been coming often to the market. He wore glasses, and when he picked up the cloth to look at it, his glasses almost touched the material. Liujin found this amusing. He seemed out of place in the market. He wasn't like the other shoppers, and he didn't bring any shopping bags, either. He was dressed like a farmer from the frontier. Of course he wasn't a farmer; one could see that from the expression in his eyes. He always looked at cloth, but never bought any. Nor did he glance at Liujin. The way he touched the homemade cloth brought about an almost physiological response in Liujin. What kind of person was he? "I'm just looking," he said, as if imploring Liujin. "Go ahead and look as long as you like," she replied stiffly. All of a sudden—she didn't know why—she felt empty inside.

One day, although it was late, the white wagtail hadn't returned to its nest. It was circling beside a thorny rose bush, singing sadly. Acting on a hunch that something had happened, Liujin walked into the courtyard. She saw the bespectacled man from the market talking with a young woman under the streetlight. Suddenly, the woman screamed and ran away. Looking dizzy, the man leaned against a power pole, closed his eyes, and rested. The wagtail sang even more sadly, as if it were a mother who had lost her daughter. Approaching the man, Liujin said softly, "Tomorrow, I'll take out a few more bolts of new cloth with a snow lotus pattern. It's like . . . snow lotus, and yet it isn't." When the man heard her talking to him, he relaxed a little and said "Hello." He turned and looked at her courtyard. Just then, she noticed that the wagtail had disappeared. Without saying anything else, the man left. The way he walked was funny—a little like a horse. Liujin had heard others call him "Mr. Sherman." Maybe her encounters with him at the market weren't accidental. Otherwise, why had he appeared in front of her house today? She also remembered the way the young woman had stamped her feet impatiently; at that time, the wagtail was chirping non-stop. Later, Liujin ran into this man in front of her house several times and greeted him properly, calling him "Mr. Sherman." He always stood there—a little as if he were waiting for someone, for he kept looking at his watch.

Liujin wondered if he was waiting for the young woman. Why had he chosen this place? How strange.

With Mr. Sherman showing up, Liujin had more energy. She worked hard tending her garden. Whenever she had a day off, she went into full swing. She planted many chrysanthemums and salvia along the wall—near the thorny rose bushes that were already there. There were still two poplars, one in the front and one in the back of the courtyard. Now she planted a few sandthorn trees: she liked plain trees like this. She also fertilized the grapes. On one of her days off, Mr. Sherman entered her courtyard. Liujin invited him to sit under the grape arbor. She brought out a tea table and placed a tea set on it. Just as they were about to drink tea, the wagtail appeared. It walked quickly back and forth, its tail jumping with each step. It kept chirping. Mr. Sherman paled and craned his neck like a horse and looked out. Finally, without drinking his tea, he apologized and took his leave. Liujin was very puzzled. It was this bird—perhaps it was two or three birds, all of them alike—that particularly puzzled her. Liujin realized she hadn't seen the young woman again. What was going on between her and Mr. Sherman? Just now as he was sitting here, she had noticed that his right index finger was hurt and was wrapped in a thick bandage. He was dexterous in picking up his teacup with his left hand. Maybe he was left-handed.

By and large, Liujin's life consisted of going from her home to the market and from the market to her home. On an impulse one night, she walked out and took the street to the riverside. The water level was low, and the small river would soon dry up. The sky was high. She walked along the river in the moonlight. There, she saw the corpses of poplars. She didn't know if the four or five poplars had died of old age or if they had died unexpectedly. Their tall, straight trunks were ghostly. At first sight, her heart beat quickly. It was hard to muster the nerve to walk over to them. She startled a few willow warblers: their sharp cries made her legs quiver. She turned around and left, walking until she was sweating all over; then finally she looked back. How could the dead poplar trees still be right before her? A shadow emerged from the poplar grove and said, "Ah, are you here, too?" The sound startled her and almost made her faint. Luckily, she recognized her neighbor's voice. The neighbor wasn't alone. Behind him was another shadow. It was Mr. Sherman, and he was laughing. As he approached, Mr. Sherman said to Liujin, "When one sees dead trees like this, one shouldn't run away. If you do, they'll chase right after you." The neighbor chimed in, "Mr. Sherman's telling the truth, Liujin. You haven't experienced this before, have you?" Even though she was standing in the shadows, Liujin felt her face turn fiery red. Had these two been hiding here long? How had she happened to come here just now? She recalled sitting at the table earlier writing her mother a letter, and being unable to go on writing because her mother's words kept reverberating in her ears: ". . . Liujin, Liujin. There's no way for you to come back to us. You'd better take good care of yourself." Did Mama want her back after so long? She stood up and listened closely for a while to the wagtail's lonely singing in the courtyard. When she had rushed out the gate, she forgot to close it. Perhaps these two men came here often to study these dead trees, but it was the first time she had ever come here.

"Look, the others are flourishing. It's only these few trees: Did they commit collective suicide?"

When Mr. Sherman spoke again, his glasses were flashing with light. Liujin looked over at the trees and saw the moon brighten. The other poplars were so beautiful and vivacious that they seemed on the verge of speaking. Only the few dead ones were spooky. Her neighbor, old Song Feiyuan, rammed a shovel against a dead poplar trunk. Liujin noticed that the tree trunk remained absolutely still. Old Song chucked the shovel away and stood dazed in front of the trunk. Mr. Sherman laughed a little drily. Liujin suddenly recalled how wild this neighbor was when he was home. That autumn, this old man had gone crazy and dismantled the rear wall of his house. Luckily, the roof was covered with light couch grass, so the house didn't collapse. In the winter, he warded off the cold north wind with oilcloth.

"Brother Feiyuan, what are you doing? These trees are dead," Liujin tried to calm him down. A sound came from the river, as if a large fish had jumped up out of the water.

Liujin was three meters away from the men as she spoke to them. She wanted to get a little closer, but whenever she took a step, they backed up. When she straightened again after bending down to free a grain of sand from her shoe, they had disappeared into the woods. A gust of wind blew over her, and Liujin felt afraid. She turned around to leave, but bumped into a dead tree. After taking a few steps around the dead tree, she bumped into another one. She saw stars and shouted "Ouch!" She looked up and saw that the dead tree trunks, standing close together, were like a wall bending around her and enclosing her. Apart from the sky above, she could see only the dark wall of trees. Frustrated, she sat down on the ground, feeling that the end of the world was approaching. It was really absurd: How had she come here? Fish were still jumping in the little river, but the sound of the water was far away. She buried her head in her hands. She didn't want to see the tree trunks. She thought it might be her neighbor Song Feiyuan playing tricks. This had to be an illusion, yet how had he and Mr. Sherman caused her to produce such an illusion? She strained to consider this question, but she was too anxious and couldn't reach a conclusion. Suddenly aware of a strong light, she moved her hands and saw lightning—one bolt after another lit up her surroundings until they shone snow-bright. The dead trees that had closed up around her had now retreated far into the distance. The branches danced solemnly and wildly in the lightning. She stood up and ran home without stopping.

Recalling these events, Liujin felt it was quite natural that the old man had come to her small courtyard. Perhaps it was time for—for what? She wasn't sure; she only felt vaguely that it had something to do with her parents who were far away. She remembered that the year before he left, her father had also twisted hemp. In the winter, he had sat on the bare courtyard wall: he had watched the activity on the street while twisting hemp. Not many people were on the road then, and there were even fewer vehicles. Father twisted the hemp unhurriedly, and—a hint of a smile floating on his face—gazed at the people passing by. "Dad, do you see someone you know?" Liujin asked. "Ah, no one is a stranger. This is a small town." Liujin thought to herself, *Since every person was familiar, then Father must be taking note of something. What was it?* Liujin walked into the courtyard and went over to the wall where her father had often sat. Just then, she heard the sorrowful singing of a bird. The bird was in a nearby nest; perhaps it had lost its children, or perhaps it was hurt, or perhaps nothing had happened. Or was it a pessimist by nature? From its voice, she could tell that the bird was no longer young. Maybe, back then, Father had sat here in order to listen to it. This seemed to be the only spot where one could hear it. What kind of bird was it? She guessed that the nest was built in the poplar tree in back, but when she walked a few steps away, she couldn't hear the bird. When she returned to her original spot, she could hear it again. If Father had made a companion of it in the winter, it must be a local bird. Could it be an injured goose? If a wild goose had been injured, how could it build a nest in a poplar tree? It did sound a little like a goose. Geese flying south sometimes sounded like this. Whenever Liujin heard geese at night, she couldn't hold back her tears. It was clearly a cry of freedom, but it sounded to her like the dread that precedes execution. "The sound is directional. You can't hear it unless you're in just the right place," the old man addressed her suddenly and quite distinctly. The hemp in his hands gave off soft silver-white light. "Where did you come from?" Liujin walked over to him. He lowered his head and mumbled, "I can't remember . . . Look, I am . . ." He broke off. Liujin thought, *What kind of person has no memory? Is there a category of people like this? He is . . . who is he?* She wanted to move closer to him, but she felt something pull at her right foot and nearly fell down. She was greatly surprised. After regaining her balance, she thought she would try once more—but this time with her left foot. She staggered and ended up sitting on the ground. The old man sat there twisting hemp, as if he hadn't noticed. Liujin heard herself shout at him angrily, "Who are you?!"

Though it was late at night, a column of horse-drawn carts ran past. This hadn't happened for years. Liujin had heard that the city was growing, but she'd had no interest in looking at those places. She heard it was expanding toward the east, but the snow mountain was to the east. How could the city expand there? Had a corner of the snow mountain been chopped off? Or were houses being built halfway up the mountain? Liujin had seen snow leopards squatting on a large rock halfway up the mountain: they were graceful and mighty—like the god of the snow mountain. Later, she had dreamed several times of the snow leopards roaring, and at the time, rumbling thunder had echoed from the earth. But even now, she wasn't sure what snow leopards sounded like. Because it was the weekend, she resolved to watch the old man all night, and find out when he left and where he went. After the sound of the horse-carts disappeared, he stood up. From behind, he looked like a brown bear. He crossed the street and headed for Meng Yu's home. Meng Yu's window was lit up. After the old man went in, the young woman, who was singing again, began to wail sadly and shrilly. Liujin heard loud noises coming from the house: Was something going to happen? But after a while it grew quiet and the lamp was also extinguished. After standing there a little longer, she went back to her house and fell asleep. She didn't know when daylight came. The night seemed long, very long.

What had happened that night in Meng Yu's home? Liujin couldn't see any clues. She walked over to his courtyard and saw the filthy sheep. Meng Yu, who was old, was repairing his boots. He was wearing glasses and absorbed in hammering; sweat seeped from his forehead.

"Sir, was the person who went to your home last night looking for a place to stay?" Liujin sat down on a stone stool beside him. Meng Yu looked up at her and shook his head. He put down his boot-repairing tools and sighed deeply. The young woman's silhouette paused briefly in the doorway, and then she went back inside. She did odd jobs for Meng Yu's family.

"As soon as he arrived, it was as if Amy was possessed," he said. Amy was the young woman's nickname. What was the old man's connection to her? Meng Yu said, "Maybe they're from the same town." Liujin had rarely gotten a good look at Amy's face because she always worked with her head lowered. Even at the market, she was immersed in the flock of sheep, as if she, too, were a sheep waiting to be slaughtered. She liked to wear a red skirt. Liujin thought of her as a rare beauty. So, where had the old man gone that night? She had distinctly seen him go through the gate of Meng Yu's home, and then Amy had sadly and shrilly cried out in fear.

Liujin glanced sideways at the sheep. She couldn't bear the doleful expression in their eyes. She couldn't figure out, either, how they had gotten so dirty: it was as though they had rolled around in the mud. This made her hate Meng Yu; she thought he was heartless. He had likely lied to her; probably the old man who twisted hemp was hiding in his home and came out only at night. Maybe he was Amy's father. But everyone said Amy was an orphan. The sheep were still looking at her without making a sound. Liujin thought it would be much better if they bleated.

"Liujin, look, has any unknown person ever come here?"

As Meng Yu spoke, he was looking down, oiling his boots. Liujin thought and thought, and then said, "No."

"Hey, then he must be somebody from somewhere. Let's go inside and sit down, okay?"

When she went through the courtyard and into the house with Meng Yu, the sheep turned around and headed toward them. She held up her hand to ward off their pitiful eyes. His small house was in the old style. Because it was mostly empty, it looked spacious. He didn't ask her to be seated. He was standing, too. Facing the courtyard, Liujin saw a red skirt appear in the flock of sheep: the sheep were surrounding her and starting to utter sorrowful cries. It was wondrous.

"How's everything with you and Mr. Sherman?" the old man asked, turning his attention to her.

"It hasn't made any headway. I don't understand him." Liujin was staring blankly.

"Hunh. You need to be patient."

Liujin didn't know why he said she needed to be patient. Or why he had spoken so assuredly of "everything with you and Mr. Sherman." There was nothing between her and Mr. Sherman. He went to her courtyard now and then for some tea, that's all there was to it. But it was hard to say: maybe there really was something between them. Was Mr. Sherman a bachelor? Liujin couldn't say. Feeling ill at ease in this empty house, she took her leave. When she went out, she noticed the old man staring sharply at the woman clad in the red skirt in the courtyard, and she sensed the strained atmosphere in this neighbor's home. When she reached the courtyard gate and turned around, Amy was pointing toward a sheep with a knife. Liujin didn't dare look and took off hurriedly. Liujin recalled that this family had had a tough time of it. On the outside, they looked docile, even a little weak. She couldn't imagine that they could be so brave inside. Apparently they weren't going to tell her anything. She'd have to wait until late at night and ask the old man.

Just now, when the old geezer Meng Yu mentioned Mr. Sherman, Liujin had felt a little rush of emotion. Over the last several years, she had been involved with all kinds of men. When her parents were still here, she didn't want these men to come to her home; instead, she used to meet them at the Snow Mountain Hotel in the foothills of the mountain. Standing on the balcony, she and her lover could sometimes see the snow leopards drinking from the small brook halfway up the mountain. That was the main reason she chose this place. Once, she and her boyfriend (a geography teacher) went to the wild animal preserve. It was almost dark, and she said to the geography teacher, "I'd really like to be friends with the snow leopards. I get excited when I think of their massive claws. You can leave, I'm staying." The geography teacher then dragged her forcibly out of the wild animal preserve. As soon as they got back to the hotel, she felt a nameless anger rising from the bottom of her heart, and the next day she broke up with him. They left the hotel separately. She had a romantic memory, too: it was about the wild geese. Liujin told her boyfriend, "Most of all, I like listening to geese honking on a clear night." They didn't know whether the geese would pass through here, so they walked to the distant fields and waited. As they walked and walked, Liujin felt that she and her boyfriend had merged into one person. The first few times, they encountered only desert birds. Later, when they were paying no attention, a leisurely cry came from high above. The two of them embraced tightly and shed tears. That man was a stone carver with a wife and two children. It had been years since Liujin had gone to the Snow Mountain Hotel. She imagined that she had become a snow leopard squatting on the large rock.

Snow Mountain Hotel was well-known locally. To attract business, it later placed a cage in the lobby; the cage held a young snow leopard. Although it wasn't large, it looked fierce. Guests passing by the cage were a little afraid. They didn't understand why the hotel owners thought this would attract them. Liujin had also stopped next to the cage and exchanged glances with the young snow leopard. She discovered that communicating with it was impossible because of its vacant eyes. It seemed it couldn't see the people surrounding it. One couldn't be sure what it was looking at. The last time Liujin went there, she found the large hotel had disappeared without a trace. A skating rink had been built where it once stood, but the skating rink had no ice, and the main entrance was closed. She and her boyfriend had to stay in a small hotel at the edge of the city. In those days, whenever she mentioned Snow Mountain Hotel, the person with whom she was talking hemmed and hawed and changed the subject. "Snow Mountain Hotel—did such a hotel actually exist? That's a weird name." Liujin was puzzled; she suspected there was something fishy about this hotel's disappearance. She got in touch with her ex-boyfriend to discuss it with him, but he avoided the subject, too, saying, "Recently, I haven't given much thought to those times." She thought: she wasn't suggesting resuming their old affair. Not at all. Why was he being so touchy? Or perhaps he wasn't touchy: maybe he was simply afraid of talking about the hotel. Had there been a major homicide case there, and the hotel was then destroyed? This speculation horrified her. Once, back then, someone had attacked her in the carpeted corridor in the hotel. He had pretended to spray her in the face with gas. But she didn't fall down; she was just dazed for a second. When she came to, the perpetrator had disappeared. She had told her boyfriend. He said he'd seen this from a distance and had run along the corridor to save her, but when he'd made it only halfway, the bad guy disappeared. Perhaps there was a secret passageway in the middle of the corridor. That night, the two of them held each other tightly, trembling. They couldn't sleep. Snow Mountain Hotel gradually faded from their memories, but the mystery had never been solved.

"May I ask your name, sir?" Liujin asked the old man sitting at the courtyard gate.

The old man mumbled for a while, and then spat out several distinct words: "My name is Meng. Meng Yu."

"How can you be Meng Yu? That's the name of the old man across the street."

"Hunh. That is I."

Liujin recalled that Meng Yu seemed to know something about this man's background. Apparently he was watching out for him. Was he a ghost from Meng Yu's past life? Why did he have the same name? Liujin didn't believe him. She thought this man might be a little crazy. He wasn't twisting hemp tonight. In the moonlight, he was weaving a purse out of colored ribbons. He was good at two crafts. He could weave without looking. Liujin imagined that he was a huge silkworm spinning its own beautiful cocoon.

"So, Uncle Meng Yu, where do you live?" She wasn't giving up.

The words he spat out next became indistinct again. In the distance, Liujin heard a wolf cub trying out its voice. It was a little hoarse and a little hesitant. Inwardly, she cheered it on. All at once, she had an idea: were these two persons actually one person? Right! She had never seen them at the same time. But that one was a wizened old geezer, and this one was strong and stocky. They had nothing in common except for their name. Anyhow, it was hard to say. She hadn't gotten a good look at the old man at the gate, had she? He might have been disguised. She'd heard that the wolf that had disappeared for years was once more active around here. Wolves frequently showed up in this little town. Uncle Meng Yu walked around late at night. Wasn't he afraid? "Wolves," Liujin couldn't help saying. Glancing sharply at her, the old geezer said, "Hunh."

Liujin saw Meng Yu's wife—the woman other people called "Mrs."—pass by. What was she doing here in the middle of the night? She was carrying a bamboo basket filled with fried bread. After setting the basket down next to this geezer's feet, she glided away. Liujin withdrew to the back of the grape arbor and sat down amid the irises. Just then, the old woman reappeared at the door. She yelled, "She's Mr. Sherman's woman. What are you thinking?" The bear-like old uncle stood up and snarled at the old woman. Although Liujin couldn't understand a word he said, her heart was thumping like a drum. It was really scary: she had been trapped by the hunter, and however hard she struggled, she couldn't break free without losing an arm or a leg. How could this old uncle, whom she had never met before, yet felt some affection for, have such a complicated relationship with Meng Yu's family? She wanted to shout at him:

"WHERE DO YOU COME FROM?" But many wolves began howling at once. And then the "Mrs." disappeared. Some raindrops were falling from the clear sky. The old uncle staggered to his feet and headed out. Liujin noticed that he wasn't going to Meng Yu's home. He walked east down the middle of the street. He moved like a sleepwalker. The moon was bright, and another flock of geese flew past. The sounds reverberating in the sky made her think of her parents in the tall building in the industrial city. The letter she received from her mother the day before had said marriage was predestined. Was she hinting about this Mr. Sherman? But Liujin wasn't sure what Mr. Sherman was really like. What impressed her most about him was the way he touched the cloth at the market. That made her speculate that this kind of man must be deeply interested in making love. But her general impression of him was vague: he wasn't like the geography teacher, nor was he like the stonecutter. Liujin didn't know what to think of him; she wasn't at all sure of her feelings. God knows, she had never thought of him in a romantic way. Why did the people around her assume she did? And did this man really think of her in that way?

She bent down and picked up the basket of fried bread and threw it into the trash can. After a few seconds, she even threw the basket in. She was afraid of such things and afraid of everything connected with that family. Could Uncle Meng Yu and the old man Meng Yu really be the same person? How ridiculous. That courtyard was always crowded with sheep and goats. If you wanted to see anyone in the family, you had to squeeze past these dirty animals. And the people in the family seemed to always know all the secrets in this little town. Although they were very quiet, Liujin didn't think the tension in the courtyard had ever relaxed. The house was gloomy inside. She recalled the encounter that night in the poplar grove: What kind of hatred did Song Feiyuan feel for the dead trees?

She returned to her room, where—under the lamplight—she saw her father looking seriously at her from his photograph on the wall.

17

A little animal had stopped on the glass on the left side of his face, so his face appeared to have a dark scar. Oh, it was a little gecko! Liujin loathed mosquitoes and flies, but loved geckoes. Sometimes, she caught geckoes in the garden and brought them back to her room. She called them "the insect cleaners." But tonight, this small thing made her father's face look a little fierce. She whisked the small critter with a feather duster several times, but it didn't move! Such an obstinate little creature. When she sat down, her father was still staring at her. She hadn't looked at this photo for such a long time that she had almost forgotten it. So, had her father not forgotten her, or had she subconsciously not forgotten her father? In the few days before leaving, Father had frequently looked at the garden in a daze, but he hadn't even glanced at her. It was as though he'd forgotten he was leaving Pebble Town. A few days later, he had left without looking back. He hadn't turned around to look at her when boarding the train, either. Liujin thought she must have inherited her father's disposition, so she shouldn't expect—what on earth had she ever expected? "Dad, Dad," she cried out in her mind, a little absently, a little sentimentally. In the blink of an eye, the small gecko dropped to the floor. She walked over quickly, bent down, and picked it up. But it was dead. When Liujin looked up at her father once more, his eyes had clouded over.

She walked into the courtyard again and buried the gecko under the irises. It was after midnight when she finished, yet she was still fully awake. She spied the shadows of several people on the ground. Who were they? Who was standing next to the poplar? No one. There was no one at all. But then whose shadows were they? Several shadows were next to the steps at the entrance, too. In the bright moonlight, the edges of the shadows were sharply focused. How strange. Looking toward the right, she found several more at the courtyard entrance—and they were moving inside. Liujin rushed back to the house and closed and bolted the door. She leaned against the door, shut her eyes, and recalled the scene just now. Then she lay down, but she didn't dare turn the light off. She kept watching the window, waiting and waiting. Those things made no noise. She didn't believe in ghosts. Then what were these shadows? Could shadows exist by themselves? Thinking about these gloomy topics, she felt that the deeper she went, the less control she had. Finally, she could only drop into a whirling abyss.

Holding up the piece of homemade cloth, Mr. Sherman smelled it and then smelled it again, as though he were going to devour it. Liujin noticed that one of his ears was moving. "This design is not readily available. People say that the printing and dyeing process is difficult," Liujin commented.

"Ah, I know. My family does this kind of work!" He laughed, and his glasses flashed with light.

"Oh, I see. You're a professional."

Mr. Sherman was embarrassed. He put the cloth down and hurriedly departed, saying he had to buy groceries. Liujin wondered if she'd said something wrong. He didn't really seem interested in her, so how had the old man Meng Yu reached his conclusion? There was a commotion in the market, and some people surged toward the exit. A child said, "Wolf!" and an adult covered the child's mouth. How could wolves come to such a populated place? What nonsense! Liujin had thought for years that people coming to this market tended to rush around impulsively. Once—no one knew who had spread this rumor—it was said that a certain stall was handing out free soda pop, and people had hustled over there. Many people collapsed from heatstroke, and one person was actually trampled to death by people squeezing past. All day long that day, Liujin smelled disinfectant. Her nausea made her hiccup. When Liujin sold cloth, she usually didn't dare look at her customers. She thought the customers in this market were too mean, and she'd better keep her distance. Now, when she looked up, the market was deserted. A large pool of blood had formed in the circle of chairs in the center of the market where people took their breaks. She didn't know if it was animal blood or human blood. Or was there really a wolf?! Her boss was smoking non-stop. He was in low spirits as he said, "There won't be any more business today. These hooligans!" "Who's a hooligan?" "Who? The people who start rumors!" "What's that blood?" "It isn't blood. It's fake!" He raised his voice sharply and angrily. The shopkeepers on either side of him craned their necks uneasily to look at him. He sat down again dejectedly, and complained to Liujin, "People are sneaky! You might as well go home now."

Liujin had no sooner left the market than she noticed that the people hadn't gone far. They were congregated next to the square, looking on. She was disgusted with their behavior. Among them were many regular customers who came here every day. Why were they so harebrained today? Did they really believe the wolves had come here? Impossible! She deliberately walked into their midst to find out what they were saying. But they weren't saying anything; they just silently made way for her. Wherever she walked, people got out of the way. A little girl called to her.

"Sister Liujin, someone asked me how to get to your house. I told him." This was Xiyu, a harelipped child.

"What did he look like? How old was he?"

"He . . . I'm not sure. He isn't from around here. He kept looking back while he was walking."

Liujin's heart leapt. Could this be a messenger from her father? The person looked comical. He wore green canvas pants, and a "shirt" plaited from elm leaves. He appeared to be only about sixteen years old. Just now, he'd been squatting in the salvia. If you glanced at him quickly, you might take him for a shrub.

"Who are your parents? Your clothes are really funny!" Liujin said good-naturedly.

"I'm not a child, sister Liujin," he said seriously, and then all of a sudden he smiled, revealing small, white, protruding canine teeth. "As for my clothes, I traded with someone at the foot of the snow mountain. I gave him all of my bricks of tea—a full load of tea. I came here from the interior to sell tea."

"My god. What will you tell your parents when you go home?" Liujin wrinkled her eyebrows.

"I like it here so much that I'm not going back."

"How did you know my name?"

"It's a secret. But don't worry. I won't bother you. I just came to take a look at you. Goodbye!"

When he walked off, the elm leaves rustled. He looked really funny. Liujin followed him and watched from the gate: he crossed the street to Meng Yu's home. Was it a coincidence that he also went to Meng Yu's? Five or six cellophane candy wrappers littered the area near the salvia. Liujin thought, *This kid really likes candy!*

While she was deep in thought under the grape arbor, Mr. Sherman entered the courtyard with a basket of groceries. Liujin thought back to the commotion at the market and tried to guess where he had gone then. Mr. Sherman sat down, took off his glasses, and wiped them with a handkerchief. Because he was very nearsighted, Liujin assumed he couldn't see anything without his glasses, but— pointing at the candy wrappers—he asked who had thrown them there. Liujin told him it was a kid whom she didn't know, probably an outsider.

"An outsider?" Mr. Sherman's voice became sharp and unpleasant. "I'm an outsider, too."

Liujin thought this was ridiculous. What was wrong with Mr. Sherman?

"I used to live on the other side of the snow mountain." His voice softened. "Our family dyed cloth. We didn't have a dye-works business. It was only a hobby. Do you understand?"

He put on his glasses and watched Liujin's reaction.

Liujin nodded her head vigorously and said, "I think I understand. I sold out of the cloth you were looking at in no time. What kind of blue was it? I can't remember the word. You must know."

A frog jumped a few times in his grocery basket, then leapt out and away. It had never crossed Liujin's mind that such a gentle man would eat frogs—how strange, how barbaric. As the two of them sat in silence, the wagtail that she hadn't seen for a long time reappeared. Taking small swift strides, it shuttled through the flowers, but it didn't sing. Liujin felt awkward and impolite, so she forced herself to say something, "Your frog . . ."

"Did it run off?" A smile floated on his face. "Then water is flowing underground here. It heard it. Frogs are very intelligent."

He slammed the basket upside down on the ground, and all the frogs struggled to free themselves and hopped off. They were everywhere. He laughed innocently. Liujin felt tense.

"I hear that you not only sell cloth, but help your boss stock it—that you know a lot about the merchandise. The snow mountain has been melting slowly for years. On clear days, I can see the snow mountain better by taking off my glasses. I wonder what sort of myopia I have."

Liujin hadn't realized that this person had paid so much attention to her, and so her heart fluttered a little. His protruding eyes were really a little unearthly. He seemed able to see some things, and was blind to other things. What sort of person was he? Was the young woman—the one who had quarreled with him—his lover? It seemed so. So why did he come here? Maybe he was lonely and just wanted someone to talk with. Just then, the wagtail ran up next to her feet, and Mr. Sherman enjoyed this scene from behind his thick lenses. Liujin even felt love radiating from his eyes, but she warned herself: this can't be true!

He bent over, picked up the basket, and said he must go. "Your courtyard is really nice." He looked greatly refreshed.

After he left, Liujin wanted to find the frogs, but she couldn't, not even one. They were hiding. Liujin envisioned the chorus in this courtyard on a rainy day: she was enchanted by this image. Did his behavior suggest affection, or was this a prank? Liujin could never distinguish between the two. It was like the night in the poplar grove. Mr. Sherman was an unusual person. He said the snow mountain was melting; this was probably true. The climate was certainly getting warmer and the environment was becoming polluted. In the market, she always smelled the rotting corpses of animals. Once, in a corner, someone had swept out a large nest of dead rats. No one had poisoned them; they had simply died. It was scary. Liujin felt that everyone smelled of corpses.

Liujin missed Mr. Sherman. She hadn't thought of him before, though she had known him for a long time. Although she tried hard, she could only recall the twinkling gaze behind his thick lenses. Sometimes, when she came upon Mr. Sherman abruptly, she felt he was ugly and unbearably vulgar. Sometimes, she felt he was manly, gritty, and decisive—making him attractive in an unusual way. Outside the window, the wagtail resumed singing. Liujin thought, *This little bird is a messenger between us.* The scene under the grape arbor just now had struck her heart like a warm current. The woman who did odd jobs for the Meng Yu family started to sing again: "Snow lotus blossoms, the snow lotus blossoms that open deep in the mountains . . ." Her hoarse voice was an inauspicious omen. Where had this beautiful woman come from? Had both of the Meng Yu geezers fallen in love with her? Did both of them want to control her? One day the year before, Liujin saw her appear silently in the flock of sheep in Meng Yu's courtyard. She had thought she was a visiting relative of the family. Somehow, Liujin felt that Pebble Town had a big heart. All kinds of strange people could find places to fit in. Liujin, who had been brought up here, didn't know whether other cities (for example, her parents' large city) were the same. Was this a virtue? Perhaps it was—if she could solve the puzzle about those people.

Liujin bent down next to the girl and asked, "What are you looking at, Xiyu?"

"Your courtyard wall. You don't know that someone has made a hole on it, do you? It was that boy."

"I know. Don't worry about it. I'll give you some grapes to take back with you."

"Thank you, sister Liujin."

The little girl hopped when she walked, much like a frog. The frogs had disappeared from the courtyard without a trace. Or maybe they had gone into the groundwater that Mr. Sherman had mentioned. When the girl reached the gate, she turned around and stood there looking at her. When Liujin asked her what she was looking at, she said someone was standing behind Liujin.

"Xiyu, your imagination is running wild. Who do you see?"

"I don't see. I hear him."

Frowning, Liujin thought this over. When she was about to ask her again, the child had already walked away. She started examining the courtyard wall, looking at it section by section, but she didn't notice anything suspicious. The little girl must have been teasing her. What did she think of Liujin? In her eyes, a thirty-five-year-old single woman must be much too odd. She went back to the house, picked up a pen, and wrote to her mother. After she'd written of some ordinary household matters, she couldn't go on writing. She looked up to see rain beating against the window. Outside, the gorgeous sun shone high in the sky. Where had the rain come from? She walked outside and discovered that the young boy wearing leaves was pouring water on her window with a watering can.

Liujin was both annoyed and amused. She charged up, grabbed his watering can, and berated him: "You aren't selling tea leaves. You've come here to make trouble. Where do you live? What's your name?" The kid didn't answer; he was still staring at the old-fashioned watering can. A mischievous idea struck Liujin. She raised the watering can and poured water over the boy's head. He stood there, unmoving, as she watered him thoroughly. He mopped his wet face with his hand, and looked curiously at the furnishings in her house.

"Go in and change your clothes."

Taking the boy's hand, Liujin went inside with him.

She told him to go to the bathroom and take a bath. She got out her father's old shirt and a pair of underpants for him.

But the child bathed for a long time without emerging. Suspicious, Liujin knocked on the door. There was no answer. She opened the door: he had left, maybe by climbing out the window. The old clothes were still lying on the chair.

Liujin sat down, stupefied, at the desk, and said to the wall in front of her, "Look at how lonely I am." But without knowing why, she wrote in the letter, ". . . Mama, life here is rich and colorful!" She'd been writing that letter for a long time, and she kept feeling she couldn't go on writing. She couldn't picture her mother's face. Who was she really writing to? Had her mother really written back, ever? Inside Liujin's drawer were many letters from her mother. She was convinced that the words didn't convey her mother's ideas, but were from the dark shadow behind her mother—her father—because her mother had never paid attention to her. But the letters were actually in her mother's writing. For the most part, the letters didn't ask about her life, but simply described Father's and her hopes for old age. "Your father and I hope to walk around the city on a rainy day." "We hope to come back to the snow mountain and talk with the snow leopards." "We hope we can melt into a wisp of black smoke in this smoky city." "Today we swam in the river. We wanted to be able to walk on water through exercising." "We . . . we will not vanish, not ever." But words like these were inserted into much longer letters, in the middle of confused descriptions of the city. Only someone like Liujin could extract their meaning. Now and then, she would ask herself: What is this correspondence for? Her parents didn't seem to think of her at all, nor did they care whether or not she married: they hadn't even asked about this. However, another kind of concern showed up between the lines or in ambiguous expressions. Then after all, they still thought about this daughter. What was it that they were concerned about? Liujin couldn't figure it out; she just felt bewildered. So when she took up her pen, she wrote strange words.

When she wrote them, what she thought of were the poplar grove, the filthy sheep, the mysterious woman in the red skirt, and the old man twisting hemp in the starlight. "Mama, I, I am not one person!" Not one person? How many persons was she? She remembered an adventure from her childhood. She and her father had gone to the Gobi Desert. The whole time, they had walked along the periphery of the Gobi. Suddenly, dozens of sand birds dropped from the sky and fell onto their heads, shoulders, and next to their feet. The little things chirped, and pecked their heads and clothes, as if they had a grievance against them. Liujin noticed that in the blink of an eye the golden-red sun had darkened and the wind had picked up. Many people were shouting her and her father's names. That was the first time that she, at the age of twelve, had found herself surrounded by a lot of invisible people. Waving her hands, she vigorously drove the birds away. She felt completely at a loss. As for her father, he unexpectedly left her and walked alone toward the west. An inner darkness struck her: she thought she was going to be abandoned in this rough, barren land. The birds had arrived suddenly, and they vanished just as suddenly. "Hey—" she shouted desperately. Thank God, Father reappeared before long: hands behind him, he walked calmly toward her, as though nothing had happened. Now, as she wrote this sentence, she heard a reverberation at the earth's core. She felt that Pebble Town was a slumbering city. Every day, some people and things were revived in the wind. They came to life suddenly and unexpectedly. That's right. Liujin recalled her neighbors, she recalled her several lovers who were struggling in loneliness, she recalled Mr. Sherman whom she hadn't known long. It was as though each of them had emerged from the earth's core: they came with some features of old times that were incomprehensible to her. Thinking of these enigmas, she didn't know how to go on writing her letter. "The wind blows as usual, the sun rises as usual." As if in a fit of pique, she wrote, "How many more things will emerge from the grottoes in the snow mountain?" With this inexplicable question, she ended the letter. Someone entered the room. It was the girl Xiyu. In profile, there was nothing wrong with Xiyu's lips. How come? And looking again from the front, you still didn't notice anything wrong until she started talking.

"Sister Liujin, have you ever seen Mongolian wolves?"

Liujin noticed the dark hole in her little mouth and turned her head away so that she wouldn't have to see it.

"I, I have to go to the post office," she said as she tidied the desk.

Xiyu climbed onto the desk, and turned her mouth toward Liujin again, as though forcing her to look at it.

"A Mongolian wolf carried my little brother off in its mouth."

"You're hallucinating." Liujin glanced at her and went on, "There aren't any Mongolian wolves here. Mongolia is far away. As for your little brother, I saw him this morning. He was nursing at your mother's breast."

"He was nursing? I was thinking just now that a wolf had carried him off."

She dangled her two thin legs from the desk, and cupped her chin in her hands and worried. Earlier, Liujin had wanted to ask her about the boy wearing leaves. Looking at her now, she gave up that idea. What immense, weighty worries were packed into this little girl's heart? How did she get through each day? But Liujin also felt that the little girl wasn't pessimistic.

"Oh, sister Liujin, I saw them. A lot of them are in your house!"

"Who?"

"Mongolian wolves. Their shadows are all over the wall on this side. One is really large. It's like a hill squatting there."

"I have to go to the post office."

The girl jumped down and ran out. Lost in thought, Liujin sealed the letter and stamped it, but she didn't feel like going out to mail it. This little imp Xiyu had reminded her of something. Liujin had never seen Mongolian wolves, but as a child, she had heard many legends about them—most about carrying off children and bringing them up in a pack of wolves. She wondered if the wolves seen recently in the market had been Mongolian wolves. Had they crossed the snow mountain and come here? The children of Pebble Town were always fooling around on the streets, even late at night. So it wouldn't be surprising if they had been carried off by wolves. Perhaps the older children had been eaten, and the little ones had become wolf children. Liujin found these thoughts fascinating and began imagining the lives of the wolf children.

The letter lay conspicuously on the table. Looking at it, Liujin started connecting it with the wolves. In her imagination, Mongolian wolves also showed up in Smoke City. What fun it would be if her wizened father galloped on a wolf's back. "Dad, Dad, you mustn't get down!" she shouted to herself. This vision gave Liujin some faith in the letter she had just written. She slipped it into her handbag and made up her mind to go to the post office. When she locked the door, something stirred inside the house. *No matter*, she thought. Without turning around, she went out to the street.

After dropping the letter into the mailbox, she ran into a neighbor, Auntie Lu. Auntie Lu was her mother's good friend.

"Why do I always think your mother has come back?" As she talked, Auntie Lu massaged her swollen eyes, as if she wasn't awake.

"She hasn't. Auntie Lu, where are you going?"

"Me? I'm walking all around to have a look. I'm thinking of these children's problems. Those wolves really did come in the night. My granddaughter didn't come home all night. This morning, she rushed in and yelled that she was hungry!"

Auntie Lu disappeared around the corner, and all at once Liujin felt empty. Auntie Lu seemed to think that her mother still showed up frequently. Liujin didn't know what Auntie Lu, who was a local, thought of Mother. The sight of Mother and Auntie Lu wearing headscarves and walking together to work flashed out from Liujin's memory. Back then, Auntie Lu was a little neurotic: she kept turning back to see what was behind her. Why did this old auntie feel that Mother had come back? Was it . . . She didn't dare continue this thought. She felt her words were incomprehensible. She wanted to recall what she had written to her mother, but she couldn't remember a single sentence.

When she was almost home, Liujin saw the woman from Meng Yu's staring idiotically at the passersby on the street. This didn't happen often, since she ordinarily did all she could to avoid other people. Curious, Liujin walked over at once to greet her. "Are you homesick?" Surprised by her own words, Liujin felt awkward. With a slight smile, Amy shook her head. "No." Liujin thought that Amy's Mona Lisa smile could easily captivate men. She asked, "Where is your home?" She was surprised that the woman wasn't evasive and talked on and on. She said her home was on the other side of the snow mountain, and that she had a father and brother. Her home wasn't a regular house, but just a few thatched rooms. The family cut firewood for a living. Woodcutters had nearly disappeared now, but her father and brother loved working deep in the mountain and didn't want to give it up. Back then, her mother worried every day at dusk, for she was afraid that the snow leopards had attacked father and son. It was difficult to imagine how impoverished her family was. Sometimes they couldn't even afford lamp oil. For years, she had thought of coming out to see the world, but she was afraid. This went on until one day Uncle Meng Yu had come to her home, and brought her here.

"You're lonely here, aren't you?"

"No, no!" she vehemently retorted. "I like this place best of all!"

Amy's eyes opened like two flowers, and Liujin saw purity surging up in them. Remembering her shrill sad singing at night, Liujin sensed an even more immense enigma. She didn't know what to talk about, so she said goodbye and left. The whole time, Amy was smiling slightly—a smile with the faint scent of pine trees after rain. Liujin felt that she herself had acted like an idiot.

For no reason, Liujin thought that Mr. Sherman would come, and so she tidied the flower garden. It was odd that she didn't find even one frog. Now she recognized that Mr. Sherman's letting the frogs out was premeditated. Even though they were already good friends and the two of them had drunk tea together many times in her garden, Liujin still didn't have one solid feeling about this man who attracted her. Nor had she dreamed of him. She took note of one thing: whenever guests sat in her cane chair, the chair creaked for a long time. The heavier the person was, the more the chair creaked. But Mr. Sherman was different: when he sat down, he and the chair fused into one. The old, old chair just groaned a little and then fell silent. He harmonized so perfectly with it that it was as though this burly middle-aged man had grown into the chair. Because of this, Liujin couldn't help the deepening affection she felt for him. The grapes had almost all been picked, summer was drawing to a close, and Liujin felt on edge somewhere deep in her soul. But Mr. Sherman didn't come that day. He didn't come until the next day. When Liujin saw him appear at the courtyard gate, she was like the saying "Dry Mother Earth is thirsting for rain." She actually blushed.

"The frogs have gone underground, Liujin." When he talked, a hint of absentmindedness skimmed over his face.

"Really? Here?" Liujin's voice was merry.

"Really. Right under your courtyard. Otherwise, why would I have set them free here?"

"Then, do you know where they come out? What's it like underground?"

"No. I don't know. Maybe from the vent under your house? I'm not sure."

He continued to stand, and so Liujin had to stand, too. They listened to the frogs in their imaginations. As the sky gradually darkened, Mr. Sherman's face blurred. She felt that his arm resting on the courtyard wall was unusually long—like a gibbon's. Suddenly, Liujin thought of her faraway parents, and yearning welled up in her heart. The air vent? A very long time ago, at night, she and her father had actually squatted at the vent under the house and listened; back then, however, it was just like now—they didn't hear anything. Yet, it wasn't that they heard nothing: she and her father heard her mother talking nonsense in the house. Her mother kept stupidly imitating a crowing rooster. Whenever she heard it, she wanted to laugh. Her father was critical of her attitude. Mr. Sherman really wasn't sure where the frogs were. What made him think the frogs were underground? He must have experienced many things that Liujin hadn't come in contact with. She had encountered his unearthliness in the poplar grove. At the time, she had felt that he came and went mysteriously, and that he was very shrewd. Perhaps it was just because of his shrewdness that it was a long time before she felt affection for him. She was a little afraid and meant to keep her distance.

"I really want a garden of my own." As Mr. Sherman talked, he removed his thick glasses and wiped them. The two lenses swayed in the moonlight, gleaming like bewitching mirrors. Seeing this, Liujin's passion for him waned. How could she fathom the ideas of a person like this? Just then, Mr. Sherman laughed softly.

"What are you laughing at?" Liujin was a little annoyed.

"I'm remembering that when I was a child I went barefoot chasing frogs. Frogs were my good friends, but they always teased me."

Then he put on his glasses and took his leave. Liujin remembered that she had forgotten to even give him the tea that she had prepared. What did she know of this man? Only that his family dyed cloth and lived on the other side of the snow mountain. That's what he had told her. Liujin went back to sit under the grape arbor, and finished the cup of cold tea. For a moment, she seemed to hear the sound of water, but it was merely an illusion. Turning around, she saw the light on in her house. Had she turned it on earlier, or had it gone on automatically? She definitely hadn't turned it on, and at the time it wasn't dark yet. She didn't want to think about these things. She was too tired. Maybe she should think of some happy, tangible things. Then, what was tangible? It seemed that the beautiful woman in Meng Yu's home was. That red skirt was so gorgeous, as was that delicate, dreamlike face. That was beauty. And her midnight singing. That, too, was beauty. The magpies and the wagtails weren't out yet; the courtyard was so quiet that it made her nervous. She decided that she would ask Amy some questions next time. Would Amy let her get close? She was so beautiful that she didn't seem like a person of this world. Besides, the murderous-looking atmosphere in Meng Yu's courtyard deliberately kept people away . . . Neighbors, neighbors: What kind of people are you? She felt weary again. The light in the house wasn't terribly bright. It seemed to be covered with a layer of gauze. Liujin assumed some little insects were flying in the lamplight, as usual, and the gecko had probably also emerged. It was another world inside.

Chapter 2

JOSÉ AND NANCY

José and his wife walked out of the Pebble Town bus station and stood at the side of the long cement street. The two of them let out deep breaths simultaneously: they felt they had stepped into a picture of the legendary Crystal Palace. The chilly air was clear and fresh, and under the high, distant, steel-blue sky, the street seemed very wide. The sidewalk was made of pretty, colorful stones. Elms alternated with oleasters, screening the quiet avenue. In the middle of the road, men looking down at the ground were slowly pulling a few flatbed carts. The simple houses were quite far from the road; each house had clumps of greenery out front. José and his wife were a little taken aback as they stood under a tree with their bags at their feet. This small frontier town was beyond their expectations; to them, it felt like a utopia. After a while, the rickshaw from their workplace arrived; it was a pedicab whose driver was a big fellow with a black beard. He helped them pile their heavy luggage into the front, and asked them to take seats in the back. Then he started pedaling slowly and effortlessly. He was a virile man who evidently didn't like to talk much. José and his wife felt it wouldn't be right to talk, so they enjoyed the view of the beautiful town in silence. Pebble Town apparently had only one street because they saw no forks in the road. When the rickshaw reached the end of this straight road, it went up an asphalt path. On one side of the path was a small river; on the other side were poplars. No one was on the road. There were only birds chirping in the trees. After they made a few turns, the river and the poplars disappeared, and a rocky hill stood before them. The driver got down, saying he had to pee, and then he disappeared.

The husband and wife waited and waited on that desolate hill before finally suspecting they'd been tricked. They didn't know how to pedal the rickshaw, but if they walked off and abandoned it, they wouldn't be able to take their luggage. Nancy squatted on the ground and sighed. José thought to himself, *She's always like this; whenever something happens, she sighs.* He hastily estimated that it was almost two miles to the main road, and the road wasn't good. Besides, it was almost evening. They had to leave their luggage behind and get away from here soon. They had to find their workplace. He didn't dare spend the night with his wife in the fields of the frontier. It could be dangerous. After talking it over briefly, they walked away holding hands.

It was hard walking on that path. It was filled with jutting rocks, and they almost tripped and fell several times. Nancy was nearsighted and couldn't easily walk in the dark. She had to hang on tightly to José's arm and let him guide her. It seemed it wasn't just two miles, but maybe more than three or four miles. When they finally got back to the main road, they were too tired to talk. The main road was empty, yet extravagantly lit; they leaned against a power pole waiting for someone to appear.

It was about half an hour before they came across someone. He was dripping wet from walking up from the river. When José went up and made inquiries, he replied, "Didn't you see me? I was watching you from the river all along! The boss sent me. I was afraid of making a mistake, so I didn't call out to you. Everyone from the office is out looking for you."

"But we've left our luggage in the wilds."

"Don't worry. Someone picked it up quite a while ago. You ran into a madman, didn't you? It was a prank. People here are fond of doing that. Follow me—Pebble Town welcomes you!"

The two of them looked up at the same time and saw a flock of geese flying in the deep blue sky. They almost wept.

It was very cool after dark, so even though they had walked a long way they didn't feel hot. They were the only ones on this road. Such a quiet little town.

That night, the dripping wet middle-aged man took them to the guesthouse of the Construction Design Institute. As they entered the room, they saw their luggage. Lying on the bed, Nancy couldn't fall asleep for a long time. She seemed to dread the future. Every few seconds, she whispered into the dark, "It didn't occur to me." José thought his wife was blaming him, but he was excited, even . . . radiant. He liked challenges. He heard someone turn on the water in the next room, perhaps taking a bath. He kept listening; the sound of water continued. He remembered the small river outside the town, and the man standing in the river. Had the man been fishing? But he hadn't been carrying a pail of fish. Maybe many other people had also been in the river; he and Nancy had been concentrating on hurrying along and hadn't noticed. The people of this little town must have noticed every move they'd made. When they were on the desolate hill, they'd felt keenly that the world had deserted them. When José recalled the days and nights on the train, he felt that Nancy had undergone an inner upheaval, because on the train she was longing for small town life and had vowed solemnly and repeatedly that they would never go back to the big city—their hometown. As they neared their destination, she became jumpy. Pointing out the window at one quiet little town after another, she asked, "Is it like this? Does it look like this? . . . What do you think? Will it look just like this? Huh?" Unable to answer, José was perplexed and alarmed. He knew that his wife's train of thought was always unusual. But just now, why had she said that it had never occurred to her? José thought it should have been the other way around: she should have foreseen everything. When they had first seen the little advertisement in the newspaper, they had resolved to give up everything in the large Smoke City and set out for an unfamiliar place. People who could move so far must have thought things through quite thoroughly. What on earth was wrong with Nancy? Had some little setback beaten her down? No, no, her whispers must hold a hidden meaning. Then, what was this hidden meaning? José thought: as soon as he'd reached this small town, everything buried deeply in his past had emerged and slowly unfurled before his eyes—but he couldn't see it well. For example, when the man was pedaling them slowly out of the city this afternoon, a familiar feeling had welled up in his heart. He couldn't say when that feeling had arisen, but it was certainly related to things in his previous incarnation. He'd experienced this before. This made him suspect that it wasn't because of the newspaper ad that they had left Smoke City; perhaps this had long been premeditated. After this, when the man abandoned them, he had felt even more suspicious. Outside, a gale blew up, threatening to rip the roof off. The room suddenly became cold. Nancy snuggled up to his chest, and they wrapped the thin quilt tightly around themselves. A loud shout in the corridor was followed by hurried footsteps. Door after door was opened, and then closed, as if everyone was running out. Outside, one gust of wind was closely followed by another. Then someone blew a whistle, as if in a military camp. The two of them didn't dare turn on a light, nor did they want to get up and see what was happening because they were exhausted from the day. Nancy murmured, "It's really noisy tonight." They decided to ignore everything and go to sleep. And then they really did fall asleep.

José awakened at dawn. After going to the washroom, he went to the now calm courtyard. The courtyard at the guesthouse was several acres large. Some shrubs grew there, but there wasn't a single old tree; the only trees were young, newly planted firs. José reflected that if there had been any old trees, they might have been toppled by last night's gale. The sun was almost out, and he smelled again the distinctive clear, fresh air. The day before, this had almost brought him and his wife to tears. The guesthouse was located on high land. When you looked out, you could see the snow mountain. He could see it well because no fog blocked his vision. It stood there indifferently. José sighed lightly: Ah, so this was the snow mountain! It wasn't completely snow-covered. Only the peak was white, probably because it was so high. People said it was four thousand meters above sea level. For some reason, the middle-aged man who had brought them here the day before was standing in the courtyard washing his face. He placed the washbasin on a block of stone, and wiped his face with a towel until it glowed red. José walked over to him.

"Washing the face is a kind of exercise," the middle-aged man said.

"True, true. You're really fortunate."

José surprised himself by saying this. What had he meant by it?

"You're right. I'm bathing with the chilly breeze blowing in from the snow mountain. Every morning, I stand here and bathe in the wind, and listen to the birds on the mountain and the cries from the snow leopards and the black bears."

"So far from here—and you can still hear them!" José was astonished.

"People on the frontier have good hearing." He laughed out loud. "And so you and your wife can't get lost in Pebble Town. How could you? Huh?"

Although José was sure the man meant well, his laughter made him uncomfortable. And while this person was talking, he never stopped using the towel; he scrubbed his face until it was like a shiny red apple. Ordinarily, José loathed people with this kind of face. And so he took his leave and went back to the room. The middle-aged man shouted from behind, "Why don't you cherish your happiness? And don't do anything rash."

An elderly silver-haired woman had come to their room and was whispering to Nancy. Smiling at him, Nancy said the old woman was the institute's director. José promptly exchanged greetings with her. This woman director had a nice way about her. Looking at her closely, José thought she wasn't very old at all. She smiled a little and said to José, "Just ignore the man outside. He's a little crazy because he was unlucky in love. He's the janitor here."

The director's words startled José. He thought everything here was a little topsy-turvy. Yet, Nancy was composed and didn't seem surprised. She and the woman director seemed to get along very well.

"I've been thinking—you've just arrived. Your apartment is ready for you. Now the most important thing is for you to feel at home, so I'm not going to assign you any work for a while. Just wander around wherever you like. Go have a look around—get a sense of Pebble Town's geographical location."

After she left, José thought for a long time. What did "geographical location" mean? Did it suggest the snow mountain or did it suggest the frontier? And what about "get a sense of"? Looking at him, Nancy laughed, "You're making too much of what the director said. Actually, she's an old mama!" José felt this was even stranger. How had Nancy fused into this environment all of a sudden? Changes in women were unfathomable. She had actually said this eccentric director was an old mama. Then was the madman who had pulled them in the rickshaw a warm-hearted brother? When the two of them had stood on the hill, she'd been utterly discomfited. He had even thought she regretted coming here. But after only one night, she had changed her mind.

They were taken to the top floor of a three-story building. The apartment—a loft with a slanted roof and a large glass skylight—was huge. Sleeping on the large bed was like entering outer space. Ecstatic, Nancy immediately lay down in the center of the bed with no thought of moving. José fetched the luggage, and started unpacking and putting things away. They had two rooms: the living room in front, the bedroom in back. While José was going back and forth moving things around, a continual "da, da, da" sound came from the roof, as though someone were pounding with a wooden stick. And the sound wasn't coming from just one place; it seemed to be in constant motion. "Nancy, listen!" "What? I heard it all the way here!" "Could it be birds?" "I think it's the wind." "How can the wind make a noise like this? It's like a wooden stick pounding." "Probably that's the way the wind is here." José couldn't come up with a response, so he went on dealing with the luggage. After a while, the pounding sound started on the skylight. José stood on the bed to look more closely, but he saw no stick pounding on the glass. He thought, *Nancy's way of thinking has changed so quickly that she might as well be a local! See, she's sleeping contentedly, even snoring.* Then someone came to the door, and José jumped down from the bed at once. The person came in without knocking: it was the jilted janitor, his face still glowing red. Without waiting for an invitation, he took a seat in the living room.

"I need to talk with someone," he said as he looked around.

"I'm busy now. Do you mind?"

"No, no. Go ahead, go ahead. I just need you to lend me an ear. Is your wife asleep? Perfect! I've come to talk about my personal problems. I have a regular job with the Design Institute, but I've never married. Why? Because I have high standards. The woman I fell in love with is a beautiful Uighur. She lives with her family on the mountain. How many years have passed? I can't remember. Who would keep track of something like this? I've seen her only twice. One time was at the market, which was only a little bazaar back then. She showed up with her father. Huh, I know you won't believe this. No one ever did, except for me. Mr. José, are you laughing at me? I see your chest moving. Never mind, I'm used to that. My story always makes people laugh because it sounds crazy."

The janitor was lost in thought as he looked at the wall in front of him. José thought, *It's got to be his memory of this romantic encounter that keeps him active and gives him a positive outlook.*

"My name is Qiming. You may call me old Qi," he broke the silence abruptly.

"I just want to ask: When the wind blows over the roof, why does it sound like someone pounding it with a wooden stick?"

"Ah—good question. That's how things are on the frontier—the intangible is tangible. I have to go to work now."

He got up and left.

Nancy turned over in bed, and shouted, "I saw it!" José looked to see her pointing at the skylight. She looked straight ahead: Was she awake? José sighed inwardly: it was as if she were sleeping in outer space. In the past, when they lived in the interior, their bedroom was closed in: heavy drapes blocked the soot and the light. Back then, he had often joked that these deep blue velvet drapes were the "iron curtain."

José continued putting things in order. A picture frame accidentally fell from his hand and broke into pieces. It held their wedding photo. Now both their faces were a mess. From the other room Nancy asked:

"Who's here?"

"No one. Go back to sleep."

"But I hear a man and a woman."

José hid the picture frame and turned around. Sure enough, a man and a woman were standing there. Evidently, everyone here was used to entering without knocking. He gave a slightly embarrassed smile and said, "Hello." They smiled slightly, too, and said, "Hello," introducing themselves as neighbors. They told him to call on them if he needed anything. Their home was to the east, three doors away. "These three apartments are empty, but you mustn't open the doors by yourself," the man added. José asked, "Why not?" The man frowned and thought for a while before finally answering, "No reason. It's simply our custom here. Maybe because we're afraid a wind will blow the door down." José noticed a white flower of mourning on each of their chests. The man explained that their beloved dog was seriously ill and wouldn't live long. José said, "But it hasn't died yet." The woman answered, "But it will die eventually. If not tomorrow, then next month." They seemed critical of José's attitude. They glared at him and then fell silent.

Nancy had dressed and come to join them. She was wearing a necklace with a jade toad hanging from it. She invited them to sit down. The man and woman hesitated bashfully for a long time, and finally decided to leave. By then, José had almost finished dealing with their luggage and putting everything away. But Nancy didn't seem to realize this. Holding her head and complaining of a headache, she paced back and forth. José asked her what she had seen when she was sleeping. She said she'd seen a crane flying up from the south and circling above the skylight. "Cranes live a long time," she said.

"I didn't like their bravado." She was suddenly infuriated. "Why white flowers? What for? No one wants to die, right?"

"True. I don't like them, either," José chimed in.

José admired his wife's acuity. He thought that even in her dreams, she was aware of the essence of things. The day before they arrived, when they were sleeping in a room in midair wreathed in smoke, she'd said she heard a large bird flying past the window. Was it the same crane? She preferred long-lived animals, and she also raised a little black turtle in their room. But was the crane really long-lived?

"I want to walk around. Let's both go," she suggested.

The entrance to the staircase was to the east. When they got there, José kept staring at the locked door. He noticed his wife smiling a little. This building where they lived was in the middle of the poplar grove. Not far away was the small river, but perhaps it wasn't the same small river? José lost all sense of direction. Nancy walked on the flagstone path beneath the poplars. She was composed, sometimes massaging her temples. Her headache seemed much better. What surprised José was that there wasn't a ghost of a breeze. He recalled that he had heard a bizarre wind in the room, and he swept his eyes involuntarily over the steel-blue sky. But Nancy suddenly bent down, leaned over the grass, and placed one ear close to the ground.

"Nancy, what are you doing?"

"A large group of people is coming across from the snow mountain. José, this small town is going to be overcrowded. We'd better batten down the hatches."

As she spoke, her body writhed in anguish on the ground. Her movement was strange—as if the bones had been pulled out of her body. The weeds underneath her had been crushed and smashed into the ground. Looking at his wife, José felt growing doubts and suspicions. Was it really because of reading an advertisement that they had decided to come all the way out here? Had Nancy really known nothing about this little town before they decided to come here? If that wasn't true, then what was? He sat down on the grass, too, but as soon as his butt touched the ground, he felt a kind of jumping—no, it was a knocking, just like the wind knocking the roof. He leapt to his feet, astonished, and turned to look at Nancy again. She was looking down and snickering.

"What happened?"

"Didn't I tell you? A large group of people is on the way. You haven't gotten hold of yourself yet. You have to stop being so wishy-washy right now."

In the distance, old Qi the janitor was standing in the river. This man seemed to like doing things in the river. He was probably observing them. Maybe this was a task that the institute had given him. José didn't know why the institute would do this. Up to now, the only impression he had of the Design Institute was the white-haired woman director. Nancy wanted him to get hold of himself. What did she mean? He wanted to go and see the Design Institute, that place where he would work for a lifetime. It must be nearby. And so he hailed old Qi. When Nancy asked why, he said he wanted old Qi to take them to the Design Institute so they could look around.

Standing up, Nancy brushed the dust from her clothes and whispered, "Hunh. You're too impatient."

After a while, when old Qi showed up, José made his request.

Puzzled, old Qi rolled his eyes. They didn't know what he was thinking until he suddenly laughed and said, "Mr. José, you were there yesterday. It's where the madman abandoned you."

"But I certainly didn't see the Design Institute in that area. It was just a hill."

"You didn't look closely. Actually, it's not far from there. It has a gray arch, so it isn't conspicuous. Lots of other people can't find it, either. Do you still want me to take you there?"

"Ah, no. I don't want to go now, thank you. I'll give it some more thought."

Nancy stared at him reproachfully and dragged him home. With an understanding smile, old Qi called after them, "That's good."

When they got back to their building, Nancy wouldn't go in. She said the apartment was "suffocating." She'd rather walk around outside. To his surprise, Nancy said that when they were on the hill she had seen the buildings at the Design Institute; they were all unimposing, low, gray buildings. At the time, she hadn't known it was the Design Institute, so she hadn't said a word for fear of being mistaken again. She was right. If they had simply walked in there and found no one expecting them, it would have been embarrassing. As they walked around on the cobblestone path in front of the building, Nancy seemed agitated. Apparently she had something on her mind.

"Nancy, what are you thinking about?" José asked uneasily.

"I'm thinking—ah, José, I'm wondering what kind of people will live in Pebble Town forty years from now? When I think of these things, I get very excited."

"You're looking far into the future. You're like the geese that look down from above: will they be frightened into being unable to fly? I think of things like this only occasionally."

43

But José sensed distinctly that Nancy had some other idea—not what she had just spoken of. What was it?

Upstairs, the man who had been in their apartment stuck his head out the window to talk to the woman, who was heading out the door holding a shopping basket. The man wanted the woman to find a veterinarian named Snake. The woman said, "Okay, okay," bent her head, and raced away. José noticed that she now wore an even larger white flower. As she went past and nodded, they saw her red and swollen eyes. Although neither José nor Nancy liked these neighbors, their melancholy was impressive. Those two seemed to spend the whole day wallowing in a kind of funereal atmosphere—white flowers, black clothing. Seeing them gave Nancy a headache. Nancy liked to think about lofty, distant things; she liked to roam about in the immense, boundless world. She regarded these neighbors as obstacles to her train of thought. José sensed this, too. They didn't notice how lame the woman was in one leg until she walked past. José felt sorry for her. He smacked his head and said, "How come I didn't notice!" "Unh," Nancy responded as if deep in thought. All of a sudden, they both wanted to go upstairs. When they went in, several people came out of the building, racing away with their heads bent.

The man was rather flustered and hurriedly threw something behind the sofa—because José had just opened the door and walked in. Standing up straight and blushing a little, he said, "Welcome, welcome. My name is Lee. My wife's name is Grace. The institute director told me your names."

José saw it. It was a miniature dog with short reddish-brown hair. He didn't know why it was so dirty; it was covered with spots of black grease. It was lying on the ground, panting, its eyes almost shut.

"It used to sleep in bed with us, but it hasn't wanted to do that recently. It's so dirty and sick now. It doesn't want to eat anything. Don't make a fuss over it. If you do, it'll give us trouble when you leave."

Lee invited José and Nancy to come inside and sit down, lest they disturb the dog. The furniture in the apartment was the same as theirs, except for a black quilt and white pillows on the large bed: the combination looked oppressive. It seemed natural for the three of them to go over to the window and look out.

José was astonished because he saw a scene that was completely different from the one outside his window. It was a small garden with palms, banyans, and coconut trees, as well as some other unusual plants. An old man bustled about in the garden. José wondered why he hadn't seen this garden from his window, for their window faced the same direction. And how could these southern plants grow so well in the north? All at once, Nancy's impression of these two neighbors changed. She grew excited and kept asking Lee the names of these plants. She kept tut-tutting as she marveled at them. José said, "Why can't I see this garden from our window?" He had no sooner spoken than Nancy reproached him, "You're talking nonsense again, José. That isn't good." When José stuck to his question, Nancy angrily stamped her feet and went home alone. Lee looked at José sympathetically and sighed. "You're a straight talker. Look at the gardener again. You'll see that in fact you know him." José looked carefully and said he didn't recognize him. Lee said, "Then stop staring at him. He'll get angry. The old geezer is from a southern plantation. Now he stays in this garden and never leaves it. He lives in his memories." Lee drew the drapes. Noticing that they were a dark blue just like the ones in their previous home, José wondered if their neighbors came from the same place they had. Because he hadn't opened the skylight, the room looked gloomy, but this oppressive atmosphere felt familiar to José. And this skinny man—had he seen him before? He asked José to sit on the only chair, while he himself began talking. As he talked, the large white flower on his chest swayed.

"Young José, my wife and I came to this Design Institute more than a year ago. Here, we can't see our future. Of course, we didn't come here to find our future. We just wanted to find an atmosphere, an atmosphere that could constantly inspire us. And in this, we were right to come here. People living in Pebble Town always feel a covert motivating force. Your wife, for example: I believe she already feels it. She's very sensitive. You're a man, and men generally lag behind in this. Let me ask: can you endure a life in which you can't see the future?"

"Probably. I don't know. I'm confused. What's wrong with your dog?"

"It isn't sick!" Lee stood still. In the shadows, his eyes flashed with light. "That's the problem. Nothing's wrong with the little animal, but it wants to die."

Sensing a cold breeze in the room, José shrank back into the chair. Lee noticed this slight movement. The drapes were drawn very tight, and the skylight was also closed. Where was the wind coming from? As José was speculating about this, Lee had quietly gone to bed and covered himself with the quilt. Set off by the snow-white pillow, his long, thin face looked a little dirty. He said he had to lie down because he wasn't feeling well; he had heart problems. He asked José not to be offended. "Now we're one family," Lee added. José stood up and walked lightly to the front room to look at the puppy. He squatted down and stretched out a hand to pet it. But it stopped him with a slight moan. Lee's despairing voice reached him from the other room, "José, when will the fog lift?" When José looked up, he saw that Grace had come back and was standing there looking woeful. Beside her was a grocery basket. In addition to some vegetables, there were a few things wrapped in pink paper—probably medicine for the dog.

"Mr. José, have you seen the garden?" Grace said, looking at him solemnly.

"Yes. So beautiful—"

He was thinking about other ways he could describe the fairyland, but Grace interrupted him.

"The garden isn't there to be admired. It's enough to know that such a place exists right under your nose."

José wondered how she could reproach him just as Nancy did. Women—ah, it was so hard to figure out how their minds worked. He thought of Lee lying in bed, and he suspected that Lee had been ground down by her. With such a serious heart disease, he didn't know what kind of work he could do. Today wasn't a day off, yet they were staying home. They were like people taking extended sick-leave.

Grace dumped the dog medicine into a small ceramic bowl and dissolved it in water from a thermos bottle. She placed it in front of the animal, which opened its eyes right away and stood up. It thrust its head into the bowl and lapped up all the off-white medicine in a few gulps. Grace called out to it softly: "Xiumei, Xiumei . . ." The puppy held its head high, seemingly in good spirits. José thought it was about to start running, but it barked—depressed—once, and then lay down again and closed its eyes. Its ears drooped. "Xiumei, Xiumei—" Grace called patiently. It didn't respond.

"What's this medicine for?" José asked curiously.

"What do you think?" Grace ridiculed him.

José caught what she had left unspoken and felt uncomfortable. In front of this woman wearing a white flower on her chest, he felt as naked as the day he was born. Mumbling vaguely "I have to go home," he went out the door. In the corridor, he straightened his back and took a deep breath. A large white moth flew in from the window on the east side. His heart constricted, and he hid his face in his hands as he rushed home. The moment he got there, he bolted the door behind him. Nancy smiled.

"You've already let it in. It came in before you did. This is the season when white moths lay their eggs."

Pointing with a feather duster at the moth on the wall, she asked, "What should we do?"

What else? Of course they had to kill it, or throw it outside. José despised moths most of all; whenever he saw one, he got goose bumps. But he knew that Nancy would never kill little creatures. Sure enough, she walked over lightly, and wrapped the fat moth up in a newspaper and escorted it out of the room. When she did things like this, Nancy was earnest and agile, with a feminine charm. After washing her hands, she came back. She sat down and told José something strange: she had found her long-lost diary. It had been in the back pocket of the old suitcase. She had written it as a young girl; she had recorded a long dream about escaping from some great danger. At this point, she waved the old brown notebook in her hand. José wished she would talk about the dream, but instead she told the story of the diary.

This diary had apparently been lost quite a few times, and then had reappeared in their home. "Who would touch this thing? It doesn't have any shocking private secrets!" Nancy was puzzled. She had no interest in talking about her dream; she said it was just a "childish description." As José watched, she put the diary back in the pocket of the suitcase, and asked José to help remember where it was. José thought and thought, but still couldn't remember when he had seen this old diary. Just then, something knocked at the window. This happened time after time, and José went over to take a look. What he saw was fog; one corner of it had dispersed, revealing a coconut tree. Ah, this was the garden, wasn't it? But the fog quickly rolled over the coconut tree again, and everything was shrouded from sight. He told Nancy that the weather in Pebble Town was very unpredictable. "That's why I reminded you not to jump to conclusions," said Nancy, glancing reproachfully at him.

This was their second night in the small frontier town. Although it was chilly, Nancy insisted on opening the skylight. As they lay on the wide bed, they felt the building swaying beneath them. Above them a flock of wild geese flew by; their lingering honks were fascinating. "Is it an earthquake? The director told me that Pebble Town has a lot of earthquakes." Nancy's voice seemed to be coming from far away, and the wall reverberated. The past was crowding into José's mind; he couldn't fall asleep. He tried to insert the ill Lee's image into several different phases of his own life, but failed again and again. The more he thought, the more he felt that he knew this man well. Finally, he had to get up and go over to the window. A little fog still hung in the night air, yet a faint outline of the flower garden appeared. José noticed the pavilion in the flower garden. The gardener was lying on the pavilion floor, a black cat beside him. This scene felt unreal. Behind him, Nancy was talking. Her voice still stirred up buzzing echoes. She continued talking of earthquakes, asking him to prepare for their escape. "We can escape to the flower garden." José thought her idea was rather bizarre. In fact, they couldn't find this flower garden—so how could they escape to it? Something suddenly rapped on the window, like thunder. José turned, ran in fright, and threw himself onto the bed. He hadn't yet recovered from his panic when Nancy said, "That was the wind." The sound of Lee's hysterical weeping came from the corridor. What a noisy night.

"Should we help them?" Nancy asked as she turned on the light.

"How? Move their dying dog over here? They would never agree."

Lee was talking about something, and his voice came through distinctly. It seemed to be about the dog, yet it also seemed to be about events in the distant past—something about the ocean. Had he once been a sailor? José didn't want to go out and comfort him. If he did, he might as well forget about sleeping tonight. Lee smelled strange—like sandalwood but also unlike it. Whenever José talked with him, he felt himself withdrawing from the world—and floating like a feather. It was an uncomfortable feeling. He needed to rest now, so he told Nancy to turn off the light, and he lay down again. In the dark, he heard two people weeping. Grace's was sharp and reverberating; Lee's was like roaring and was punctuated by periodic complaints. He mentioned the ocean in his complaints. Nancy cuddled up to José and said in a trembling voice, "The ocean drowned a man's dream." Holding each other tightly, they fell asleep. It was hard to know when the weeping stopped. Later they awakened because their hands were numb. The room seemed darker than usual; after a while, they realized the skylight had closed automatically. How could it close by itself? Was it the wind? Nancy said, "We're at the bottom of the ocean." José reached to turn on the light. Damn, the power was out. When he got up, he felt his feet weren't touching the floor; rather, he felt like a fish swimming. He swam in a circle and went back to bed when Nancy called to him.

It was much darker than usual, and José turned to Nancy to tell her about his decision to move here. He said it was hardly a decision—but more a matter of the conditions being ripe for success. Maybe he'd reached this decision ten years ago. When they had been abandoned on the hill, he had felt something solemn and stirring. Time and again, he repeated these words: "How could I finally fully carry this out?" He realized this was an unanswerable question, yet he couldn't help but raise it repeatedly. "Oh, the frontier!" Nancy responded irrelevantly. José started thinking of the orientation of their house in Pebble Town—that is, what the institute director had called "its geographical position." All of a sudden, his mind was alight with radiance. The entirety of Pebble Town appeared in his mind, and he saw that their house was situated in the northwest corner. But there was a problem with this northwest corner: there was something confusing and dark, like a swamp. Inside it a miniature puppy was swimming energetically toward the bank from the mudhole. It wanted to climb up, but it couldn't. Time after time, it fell back into the water as if something were preventing it from succeeding. He was vexed, and—all unaware—he said, "Is it Lee's dog?" He had no sooner said this than his hallucination vanished, and everything turned dark. Had the two neighbors exhausted themselves with their crying and turned into fish just as they had done? He was trying to imagine the situation in the rooms to the east. When he started doing this, those rooms all dropped. That's right: they dropped into a void and no longer existed. The old gardener was shouting something indistinctly in the garden below. "That often happens." Nancy whispered, "We have to get used to it eventually." José said, "Okay." They tried hard to sleep some more. Before dawn, they struggled between sleep and wakefulness. They dreamed simultaneously of the poplars, though they didn't know this until they woke up. The poplars were a symbol. It was only the light from behind the poplars that made their silhouettes visible. Later, they moved away from each other, each occupying one side of the bed. They slept soundly.

When they awakened, it was noon of the third day since they'd arrived in Pebble Town. After washing up and getting dressed, they went to the Design Institute's canteen for breakfast. On the way, Nancy kept looking back. She said she saw the gardener from the tropical garden. Yet, when José turned around, he saw no sign of him. "You always see something that I can't see." "That's because you're distracted."

The last time they'd come here to eat, hardly anyone else was here. Now the canteen was crowded, and they had to line up for a long time to buy food. After José had stood in line for a while, he noticed that all the employees who'd come here for breakfast looked out of sorts, and no one greeted anyone else. Thus, although crowded, it was as silent as a school of fish. He saw the institute director come out after buying her breakfast. Just as he was about to greet her, the man in front of him backed up and stomped on his foot. "Ouch!" He clapped the other person on the shoulder. But the person ignored him and kept standing on his foot. "What's wrong with you?!" José said angrily. When the man turned around, José saw a heavily pockmarked face. He moved his foot away and whispered, "I'm not being rude. I want to remind you of some things. Don't you know that people are watching you?" José sensed that this man was friendly, and his anger dissipated. He evidently shouldn't have considered greeting the director. Now she was seated alone far away in the back of the canteen, eating her food in silence. Maybe she held a peculiar position in the Design Institute. But what was Nancy up to? How had she gotten along with that old woman? Nancy had bought her food and was sitting at a round table waiting for him. When he carried his food over there, he noticed that no others were sitting at this table, yet the other tables were crowded. "I think things are very well organized here," Nancy said quietly as she ate. She was satisfied. José thought, he and Nancy were becoming more and more distant from one another. Still, no one had joined them by the time they finished eating,. Everyone else was crushed together, and many people even stood as they ate. The director and the two of them were isolated in this canteen.

While they ate, many pigeons were flying outside the window. Some flew in; others perched on the windowsill. The ones that flew in perched on the cupboard. They weren't afraid; they looked curiously at the people filling the canteen. A rather large gray pigeon stood on the director's table, pecking at the bread she held. She was happy: she ate a bite and then gave the gray pigeon a bite. José stared blankly, even forgetting to eat. It wasn't until Nancy nudged him that he came to his senses. Nancy said, "I like pigeons. The director truly has the presence of a frontier woman!" When the director finished eating, she got up and washed her dishes. For some reason, the pigeon followed and assaulted her, pecking at her hair, mussing it, and flapping its wings wildly. Just then, José realized that almost everyone had stopped eating to watch this scene. Qi, the janitor, showed up, set his bowl down on their table, glanced furtively at the scene, and said, "You think this is bizarre, don't you? The pigeons come to deliver messages. Long ago, the institute director's son had an accident in a creek, but his body wasn't found. Someone said he had boarded a small boat and left the city. Back then, pigeons were everywhere in the poplar grove—wild pigeons. Now the pigeons are all pets. When she was young, the director was a workaholic and paid no attention to her son."

As if realizing that he shouldn't have said these things, he stopped talking, picked up his bowl, and moved to another table.

Nancy merely sniffed at what he said. The whole time they were in the canteen, no one else approached them. José wondered secretly how Nancy would feel if it was like this every day when they came to eat. The people in Smoke City had been much friendlier than the ones here. Acting as if she didn't care, Nancy urged him to finish eating. She said she wanted to look for the tropical garden and that she felt sort of sure about its location. She'd gotten the idea from the pigeons they'd seen just now. "Some things hide right under your nose." She pretended to be relaxed as she forced a smile. "I think the garden isn't in the residential area, but outside."

The moment they walked out of the residential area, they were outside the city. Scattered ahead of them were some small farm homes, but the land was desolate: a large area of wasteland overrun with weeds stretched into the distance. Nancy was in a good mood as she walked through the wasteland. She said she had already "smelled" the tropical garden. All of a sudden, José saw the institute director drinking tea in a farm home at the side of the road. What was going on? Did the Design Institute's work consist of drinking tea? The director saw them, too, but evidently didn't want to invite them to enter. Many chickens were in the courtyard. As she drank tea, she fed the chickens. They passed by reluctantly. The woman never called them over. Nancy continued to believe they were near the tropical garden because she smelled the flowers. "And otherwise, why would the institute director be sitting here?" she asked. José was deeply impressed by Nancy's great faith. But at any rate, he couldn't figure out why the garden they saw in front of their window (that close!) could be located two or three miles away in the wasteland in the outskirts. A flock of crows wobbled toward them; like the pigeons, they weren't afraid of people. Maybe all of Pebble Town's birds acted the same.

"José, did you see the gardener?" Nancy asked.

"Where?"

"In the small courtyard of the farmhouse. He flashed past the window and then went in. I think he and the director created the garden together. They chose this neglected open country for experiments so they'd be away from prying eyes. Look, look!"

Nancy blushed. She was pointing at the distant horizon, her index finger in constant motion, as though pursuing a mirage. José thought his wife was really out of her mind. A wind picked up, bringing rain with it. It was bare all around, with no place to take cover. Their only option was to make a run for the small farmhouse.

The door was unlocked. No one was home. They checked every room, including the kitchen and even the pigpen in back. Nancy said the institute director was watching the rain from the arbor in the garden; she had earlier figured out that the director wasn't interested in the Design Institute. As Nancy was speaking, she picked up a coconut shell from the table, placed it on top of her fist, and spun it. José thought the coconut shell was very much like a human head.

"So, what's the director interested in?"

"I don't know; I'm mulling that over."

As they talked, the sky darkened all of a sudden. It seemed a storm was blowing in. José was quite dejected; he had no desire to stay here in the farmhouse, for he wasn't accustomed to the smell of the pigpen. Nancy apparently felt differently: she looked around. She even opened the kitchen cupboard and took out a bottle of rice wine. She sipped a little of it and passed the bottle to José, too, but after two swallows, a fire leapt up inside him. They were both a little dizzy. Thunder roared. Nancy dashed to the window and shouted, "Come, look. Quick!"

José saw the institute director's snow-white hair blowing in the wind. She and the gardener were rushing around crazily. But their silhouettes flashed by for only a moment and then disappeared. Where had they gone? Nancy was distracted. After a long while, she said faintly, "I want to find that garden."

"Wait for me here, José, okay? I'll look for it."

"It's so dark outside—a big storm must be on the way."

"No, it's stopped raining. And we're already here. I have to do it."

With that, she went to the courtyard. She was a determined woman. When she vanished outside the courtyard gate, José heard an enormous noise coming from the east; it wasn't thunder. The quilt was in a heap on the bed, as if someone had just gotten up. Maybe the director and the gardener were actually a married couple. One had lived in the north and one in the south, and they had built this tropical garden here . . . Did the garden really exist, or did it exist only in everyone's imagination? José sat down on a wooden chair, but the chair that had looked so strong all of a sudden became extremely soft. As he sank into it slowly, he ended up sitting on the floor. Sticks and boards lay scattered all around him. He scrambled up awkwardly from the floor and flicked the dust off his clothes. All at once, he sensed that nothing in this house was real. Even the chickens had weird, gloomy expressions. Avoiding the chair, he chose to sit on the bed. The bed was strong and probably wouldn't collapse. But a buzzing sound came from it, as though someone sleeping there was talking. The sound annoyed him, so he went outside.

The dark clouds had dispersed, and the courtyard had brightened. Someone outside was playing the flute. The music reminded him of the open country and mountaintops where flowers bloomed. José was enthralled. For no reason, he assumed it was the gardener playing the flute. He stood at the courtyard gate and looked out. What he saw, instead, was the institute director. Leaning her plump body against a large locust tree, she had stopped playing and had tossed the flute onto the ground. Her head drooping, she looked melancholy in profile. José walked over quietly.

"Ma'am!"

"What do you want, Mr. José? You came to Pebble Town from far away, but this place has changed. The thing you want to find no longer exists. Look—even I am looking for it!"

Her dolorous eyes turned gray and lifeless; her mouth—once resolute—was now drooping.

"But what Nancy and I want to find isn't the same as what you want to find. We only want to find the tropical garden. We saw it once from our apartment—the place you arranged for us to live . . ." He was speaking a little incoherently and didn't go on. The institute director didn't answer him. She was gazing toward the sky. José sensed that her thoughts were no longer in this world. Her lips were trembling, maybe silently reciting some words. The gardener's sinister face appeared from a spot five or six meters behind her. Bending over, he was picking something up from the shrubs. As José was about to greet the gardener, the geezer turned his back and ignored him. José realized abruptly that this person wasn't very much like the gardener: the gardener was a little older than this man, and his air was like that of an outsider. He was definitely a local. He stood up, a small lizard in his hand, and headed toward the farmhouse. José was about to follow him when the director spoke from behind.

"Don't go, Mr. José. He appears and disappears mysteriously; you can't catch up with him. He catches these critters in this wasteland all the time, so he can transport some fresh blood to his garden.

"Where on earth is that garden?"

"You can see it everywhere. But I—I'm feeling ill."

Sliding down along the tree trunk, she sat on the ground. Scratching her chest, she repeated, "I'm really feeling sick." When José asked if she wanted help, she shook her head and wheezed. José picked up the bamboo flute. He was puzzled that such a crude thing could produce such a lovely sound; she was really talented. She stretched out her hands, asking José to help her up. Her hands were so cold that he shivered. They returned together to the small farmhouse. José was thinking of Nancy, so he kept looking in all directions, but he didn't see her. She was nowhere nearby.

"I'd really like to see the old man's garden," José mustered his courage to say.

"He won't take you there because he isn't a local. He—he speaks a strange dialect that no one understands. He and I communicate through pantomime."

Still talking, they went inside. The gardener was sitting there silently smoking a pipe. He was looking down, not at them. He was a hairy man; his face was covered with a gray beard. José thought this person was certainly like a local, so why did the director say he wasn't? As soon as she entered the room, the director made straight for the large bed and lay down on it. She was acting as though these two men were her relatives. An idea suddenly crossed José's mind. Was it possible that he himself was related to the director? If not, then why had he dashed over here—so far away—the moment he saw her tiny advertisement? And then there was this gardener: perhaps it was the same with him. After finishing his pipe, the gardener began cleaning the house. He dusted the furniture with a rag. José noticed that the chair that had caved in beneath him had been restored to its original state—and now looked sturdy again. Curious, he pressed down on the chair with both hands; the chair didn't sink at all. And so he cautiously sat down again; this time, nothing happened. Two minutes later, José thought to himself that it wasn't right for him to sit in this room: What if those two were husband and wife? He stood up, about to leave, when the director spoke from her bed, "Mr. José, don't go. Wait for Ms. Nancy to return."

"Will she come?"

"Hunh. When she doesn't find it, she'll be back."

"Won't she find it?"

"Of course not. Where would she look? Where, I ask you? Haha haha . . ."

She began laughing hysterically on the bed, not at all like a sick person. This scared José. As she laughed, the gardener made a face. It was the ugliest expression José had ever seen. His face crinkled, and his gray weed-like beard hid his features until they virtually disappeared. It was disgusting. All at once, José thought these two persons had duped him and Nancy. They were using some tricks to scam them with a tropical garden. And Nancy—with her wishful thinking—was still struggling inside the net they had cast. All at once, an incident floated up in José's mind: one day, years ago, Nancy had been in high spirits as she told him that she was going to the wharf to meet her auntie. Her aunt lived in Manchuria. Aunt and niece had never met one another, so the aunt had brought many gifts. Nancy blushed excitedly as she looked again and again at the photograph and asked him, too, to look at it carefully. When the ship pulled in, several passengers disembarked. But no auntie. He was terribly disappointed, but when he glanced at Nancy, she didn't seem to mind at all. She was still glowing, filled with the vitality of youth. All the way home, she told him how delicious the Manchurian salmon tasted. José was surprised to be recalling this incident at this moment: Could the incident from the past be connected to the situation now? "Oh, Nancy, Nancy," he sighed.

When the institute director stopped laughing, she whispered to the wall. The gardener seemed angry: he was pointing at José, and strange sounds came from his mouth. José couldn't understand even a word of what he said. He raised his hands and made a chopping motion toward his own neck; a fierce light shot from his eyes. José was standing next to the window, not sure whether to stay or go. Suddenly, he saw Nancy. Just like the director, Nancy ran across with her hair flying, as if being chased by something. She ran over to the large locust tree where the director had stopped. After a while, Nancy's shouts rang out in the courtyard: "José! José!" José walked out and saw that Nancy's back was to him; she was braiding her hair. He walked over hastily.

Nancy's face was covered with bloodstains. The cut near her mouth was still bleeding. She smiled a little, revealing blood on her teeth, but she wasn't perturbed.

"I was ambushed by a pack of mad dogs. I picked up bricks to hurl at them. Damn, they bit my face—I won't get rabies, will I? Maybe they weren't mad; maybe they were just wild. Oh, José, I saw that garden and also the somber gardener. I saw them through the dog's eyes when it pounced at me. It was so large. I squatted low, and it placed its heavy front paws on my shoulders . . ."

An unusual light flashed from Nancy's eyes, and her face turned purple from the blood surging up.

"How could that garden—that garden—have appeared in a wild dog's eyes!?" she shouted loudly. She was hoarse.

Just then, the institute director and the gardener stuck their heads out the door, but Nancy was distracted. She didn't notice them. She implored José wretchedly to take her home soon.

All the way, she leaned heavily on José, like a little girl suffering from a serious illness. It was just under two miles, but they walked a long, long time. Finally, José could no longer keep going. Every now and then, they had to sit down on the ground. José worried: Why had Nancy become so weak? If the dog had rabies, would she die? When he thought of the crazy dog, he suddenly found the energy to run. Putting Nancy on his back, he raced along.

When they finally reached the residential area, he was about to fall over from exhaustion. Nancy had gone to sleep on his back. Her face was still purple. He set her down on a bench at the side of the road. He intended to ask the apartment manager where to find a doctor. He had no sooner stood up than he saw Lee walking over. He told Lee what had happened.

"Did this happen at the farmhouse over there? Where it's so desolate all around?" As Lee spoke, he began laughing. "Don't worry; they weren't mad dogs. They're dogs raised by our director. She indulges those dogs and lets them run around in the wasteland all day long. And so they seem to be wild."

The rock in José's heart dropped to the ground. He greatly appreciated Lee. But why had Nancy's face turned purple? He couldn't understand that.

"That's because your wife was too excited. Just think about it:

she was in the wilderness, running, and besides, she saw the dog's strange eyes."

"So you know about the dog's eyes?!" José was startled.

"It's no secret. Anyone who has ever come into contact with those dogs knows—our institute director is no ordinary woman."

Just then, Nancy suddenly came to and said, "Lee, don't you dare talk about her behind her back! I heard everything."

At midnight, when José and Nancy were in bed, the skylight was suddenly automatically propped open. They heard wild geese flying by. Hollow and lonely feelings welled up in both their hearts. Nancy whispered, "The frontier is so beautiful."

Chapter 3

QIMING

Although Qiming was thirty-nine, he didn't feel old at all. He had no skills; from the time he was young, he'd worked as a janitor in the guesthouse at the Design Institute. Everyone knew him. Sometimes he was a little melancholy, but generally speaking, few people were as optimistic and confident as he was. Qiming had never married; he lived in a simple cabin behind the mailroom of the guesthouse. It was as if the institute administrators had stuffed him indiscriminately into this crude dwelling. But Qiming was quite satisfied with his place. Material life meant nothing to him. For example, he was single, but his heart swelled with erotic dreams. He felt he'd had a lover all along; it was just that they had never lived together. It was because he had a lover that he felt so young. Who could love as he did? Everything he did, he did for the beautiful woman of his memory. He had last seen the Uighur beauty years ago. He still recognized her—of course! The slim girl from back then had now grown up to be a stout housewife, but what difference did this make? Qiming's yearning for her blazed even more. Aware that someone was staring at her, the stout woman set her satchel down and began dancing with other aunties on the avenue. Qiming stared like crazy. Too bad he didn't know how to dance. He could only watch from the sidelines. He heard one of the dancing women say in words that he understood: "That guy is awfully ugly, like a savage." His goddess began laughing uproariously. She flung out her arms and jabbered loudly. After Qiming went home, he was too excited to do anything for the rest of the day. Years had passed; yet, whenever he recalled that meeting, his face burned. The scene hadn't faded at all. He even imagined that he was holding the beauty tightly and spinning around with her. It wasn't a Uighur dance, but a dance he had invented. Sometimes others called him Grandpa. Discontentedly, he thought to himself, *Am I old? No, no way! My life has just begun! Is it fair for a person to be called Grandpa just because he's unskilled?* He felt more energetic than ever before. Ha, it was time for him to take a wind bath again. He filled a basin with water and, facing the wind blowing over from the mountain, he wiped his face. Then he scrubbed his torso. The guesthouse was great. No one in this quiet place fussed about his activity. While the breeze dried him off, Qiming returned to the time of his youth. His family was a large one; he had eight siblings. They lived at the seaside in the south and made their living as fishermen. He was only thirteen then, but he had gone out on the ocean many times with his father. He loved his life of freedom. He didn't know why his father had to send him away. He remembered that day: a man who looked like a cadre came to their poor dwelling and took a seat. His father said this person was Qiming's "lucky star," and then made Qiming go with him. His brothers and sisters saw him off with envious glances. And so he traveled with that person to this small town in the north—all because he couldn't disobey his father. Back then, this place was truly desolate. The so-called town was no more than some simple buildings scattered around the wasteland. There were no roads or public facilities. Though there was a little electricity, power outages were frequent. You had to light kerosene lamps. However, as Qiming saw it, this wasn't a problem because he was used to an even poorer life at home. At first, he did heavy labor. When the officials asked him what he was good at, he said he had only been a fisherman. But this place had no fisheries, and so he worked on constructing buildings, repairing roads, reclaiming land from the river, transporting coal, manning the furnace, and so forth. One day, the Design Institute director noticed him and asked him to work as the guesthouse janitor. That's when he settled down. He was twenty-two then, and he had no idea why the institute director had chosen him. He thought this sharp-eyed woman was imposing. Finally, after becoming the janitor in this quiet place, he slowly came to understand Pebble Town—and why his father had sent him far away.

One time when outsiders came to visit the Design Institute, Qiming saw the Uighur beauty who would change his life. She wasn't wearing her minority dress; for some reason, she was wearing a drab grayish outfit. But her plain clothing couldn't cloud her stunning beauty. Qiming couldn't stop staring and tagged along behind her. This playful girl actually broke away from her group and led him to hide behind the rockery. They sat on a cobblestone, watching little birds hopping here and there, and watching the poplars dance in the sunlight. It was so beautiful—like a fairyland. But this stunning beauty couldn't speak his language, so he could only ogle her and caress her elegant hands over and over. Finally, the tour group had to go back. Their bus stopped outside the gate. When the people passed the rockery, the girl jumped out like a fawn and rejoined the group. This, then, was Qiming's fleeting encounter, and this encounter had shaped his life. Later, he saw her once more in the market: she was with her father. She seemed to have forgotten him. He followed her all the way to her faraway home—at the big mountain over there. He didn't dare go in because several large dogs guarded the entrance. The next time they met each other, she was already a married woman. Later, he saw her several more times, almost always with her family. He rarely saw her alone. But Qiming wouldn't give up: this woman could set his heart afire. What more could he possibly want? He couldn't sleep at night in the narrow bed in his humble home: he spent a lot of time meditating. He liked this feeling: it made him feel special—a man destined to pass his lifetime in solitary meditation. His father had been farsighted!

When Qiming bathed in the wind and thought of his family, he didn't feel sentimental. In his memory, his poor home became sweet. He recalled how sad his three sisters were when he left. They had tears in their eyes—Father had warned them not to cry. Their rough hands had reddened from the freezing cold water. Their noses—congenitally flat—made them look rustic. Qiming had turned around at once, because he felt like crying, too. Then he said farewell to his mother's grave: he placed his young face on that stone marker—and all at once he felt his mother's warmth. There had been much human warmth in Fish Village and in that ugly three-room adobe house. He could see seagulls from the entrance to his home. Whenever he saw them, the idea of leaving home for distant places rose vaguely in his mind. How had Father known this? Although he longed for his faraway hometown, he didn't plan to go back for a visit. Partly because he reveled in this aesthetic faraway feeling, he was afraid that any bold action would destroy his spiritual pleasure. Another secret reason was that he had obeyed his father's will in leaving home in the first place; it wasn't his own choice. On the way, indignant and grief-stricken, he vowed over and over to never go back. Now, more than twenty years had passed, and as Qiming reflected on this matter, he started to question his views. Was it all about Father's will? Now, he liked everything here so much, and he was self-sufficient and content with his life. It was that one migration that had brought him everything! Just think, if his father hadn't been so astute and hadn't entrusted him to that cadre (this was of course his father's long-range plan), what would his life be like now?

The newly-arrived young couple were completely bewildered, especially the man. Qiming could see this, because he used to feel the same. Who wouldn't be puzzled by Pebble Town's strange ways? Back then, besides feeling gratified, he was also puzzled and uncomfortable—until the incident that changed him. Qiming's "incident" was, of course, the appearance of the Uighur beauty. Before that, when he was working in construction, he frequently felt so confused that he didn't want to go to work. He would sit at the riverside for several hours looking at the tamarisk trees. The foreman was a folksy middle-aged man. He squatted down, clapped Qiming on the shoulder, and said, "You can't go back, son." He told Qiming to look up at the sky. Qiming did—and saw only a goshawk. The sky was so high, and its color held no gentleness: it was completely unlike the sky at the seaside. The foreman told him to take another look, to look more carefully. So he looked up again—and suddenly realized what had puzzled him. He stood and quietly followed the foreman back to the work site. It was such a wondrous feeling: the foreman was terrific. Before this, he had paid no attention to this old man, though he had seen his family. His three children wore ragged clothes, but the children's eyes were composed and bright. Like him, they worked in construction. They weren't the least bit bewildered, probably because they were locals. Having had all these experiences, when Qiming saw José and his wife abandoned by the crazy guy on the hill, he understood completely why they felt rattled. After a few days, he sensed that Nancy was somewhat like the locals. He sensed, too, that José was stepping into his role, even though he didn't understand the role. José was a little impatient. So what? The tranquil frontier would help calm this young man. The reason Qiming took note of this couple was that they reminded him of himself when he had just arrived on the frontier.

After he finished work that day, he rested on the rockery cobblestones. In the haze, he sensed a sheep approaching him, a red cloth tied around its neck. It was a domesticated sheep. After smelling his hand, it knelt down beside him. Qiming was fighting in his dream with a kid with whom he often played back then in Fish Village. This kid threw him to the ground, stepped on his chest, and looked down at him. But as soon as the sheep knelt beside him, the kid above him disappeared. He struggled to open his eyes and saw Nancy sitting next to him. He blushed and stood up in embarrassment. He said, "Hey, I was dozing." Nancy looked bewildered, and—as though discussing a problem with an invisible person—said, "Hunh. I'm puzzled by lots of things here; they're mixed together. Still, this place is magnetic. Look at that eagle, flying and stopping . . . Everything's unresolved." Qiming thought to himself, *This young woman who has just arrived has already become a Pebble Town local.* The transformations in the world were so rapid. He heard they were from Smoke City. What was a smoke-swathed city like? Nancy was still sitting on the rock. The wind blowing here had reddened her pale, delicate face. She looked at him, and yet she didn't seem to actually see him. So Qiming couldn't decide whether to talk with her or not. Except for his goddess, he hadn't been this close to a woman for years. He was a little nervous. Nancy quietly pulled some weeds and deftly plaited them into a chain to wear on her head. Qiming's heart throbbed, and nostalgia rose in him, but he couldn't remember the scene across from him. So he did his utmost to imagine the scenery in Smoke City. Was it similar to the misty mornings in Fish Village? People often bumped into each other at such times.

"Ms. Nancy, are you getting used to this place?" he asked a little hesitantly.

"Mr. Qi, when you first arrived, did you see the snow leopards come down the mountain? Someone said more than one hundred of them are walking around in the town."

Qiming didn't dare make eye contact with a woman whose eyes were so abnormally bright. He thought to himself, *How could eyes like this be produced in a smoky city?* He was torn: he wanted to leave, but he also wanted to listen to this woman.

"No. But it's said there are a lot of them. For a while, everyone was talking of the snow leopards coming down the mountain."

"So it's just a legend," Nancy asserted.

"It's a legend," he agreed.

When Nancy said "legend," she looked absolutely absorbed. All at once, Qiming felt her expression was familiar. Where had he seen it? Perplexed, he glanced at her. But she stood up and removed the chain of weeds from her head. She said, "Just now, I saw how happy you looked as you were dreaming, and so I assumed you had seen the snow leopards coming down the mountain. You see, I like to make inferences, don't I?"

After she'd been gone for quite a while, Qiming finally remembered where he had seen the absorbed expression on her face. It was in a mirror—no wonder it seemed so familiar. He was stunned.

Qiming didn't contact the young couple for a long time, but he did take note of their activities. This was instinctive; he had no idea why he did it. He noticed they were always wandering around: it was said that the director hadn't given them any work. Qiming snickered to himself: what work could they be assigned to do? They would just go on waiting. He heard that they were both engineers. But this town had already been built, so construction design engineers were no longer needed. This Design Institute was merely an empty name. He had witnessed Pebble Town's construction, but José and Nancy had arrived only long after it had been finished. They were a new generation: how could she have the same expression as his? This Nancy woman must be unusual; no one should take her lightly.

When he first arrived at the Design Institute, the director had been like a mother to him. She often came over to see how he was doing, often sat in the dark in his little cabin and talked with him about the snow mountain. Sometimes, she came to his place as soon as she arrived for work and chatted with him right up until lunchtime. They didn't do any work. She consoled him, "It doesn't matter. I'm the institute director." Qiming was greatly astonished by her behavior, and also happy. He considered her his mentor. But later on, she didn't come to see him, nor was she concerned about him. She no longer seemed aware of his existence. So years later, Qiming still lived in temporary housing, while his workmates had moved to more comfortable apartments long before. Had he been forgotten? In the beginning, Qiming felt aggrieved, but the longer he lived in the small cabin, the more he realized the benefits of living here. Every night, he felt he was sleeping in the embrace of mother earth. And so he rested well. When he arose the next morning, he was in high spirits. Second, this kind of house was like a public place. He didn't even bother to lock the door; anyone could walk in uninvited. Nothing seemed to be a secret, yet everything was mysterious at the same time. Take the blocked-up wall out front, for example: it seemed to be made of brick, but after noon, it became adobe. And the next morning, it was restored to brick. After being here only two days, he spotted this mystery and told the director about it. She patted him on the shoulder and said, "Young man, you have very good prospects." His rooftop was made of cement tiles. Sometimes the sunlight streaming through the countless broken holes brightened the room, and sometimes the holes disappeared and the room darkened. Of course it was dark most of the time, especially when he had guests. Nancy had come over once. She had sharp eyes. She glanced back and forth in the dark and could see everything. When she moved close to talk, Qiming felt a long dormant urge awaken in him. In that moment, even the Uighur girl's image faded. He marveled at the heat emanating from Nancy's body! Qiming thought that the moment she entered, she had fused into one with this room. It was miraculous. What had this young couple's lives been like in the faraway Smoke City? Was the ocean there?

The day that Nancy's daughter was born, Qiming was building a grape arbor in front of the guesthouse. He murmured to himself, "She's put down roots here." Then he saw José rush to the hospital, the institute director beside him. Soon, a cold wind blew up. Qiming put away his tools and went inside, where he brewed himself a cup of tea and sat down to think about this incident. Time had passed so quickly. The day he had been fishing in the river and the young couple lost their way seemed like yesterday. Qiming called their daughter (he firmly believed it was a girl) "Daughter of the Frontier." He thought, after this little girl—who had inherited her mother's heat—after she grew up, he would tell her about the ocean. It was yesterday that he'd gotten `word that his father had died. The person who came to tell him was a sallow-faced man with whom he had played when they were children. He had stood awkwardly in his room and hadn't spoken about his father, but about his own arthritis. It was as if he had traveled thousands of miles just to tell Qiming this. He said he wouldn't go back, because their fishing village no longer existed. He wanted to stay at the Design Institute.

"They have to take me in! Hunh," he roared suddenly with great confidence. His eyes were fierce.

Qiming thought this guy was ridiculous. Was he a little crazy? He didn't quite believe the news he had brought; maybe he was talking nonsense.

"Tell me more about my father's death," he pressed him.

"Oh. He had an odd disease. He fell asleep and didn't wake up. But before he fell asleep, he gave me this."

He took an old watch out of his pocket and gave it to Qiming. *Father always had this on him.* Qiming's hand trembled as he took the watch. He told the other man not to be upset; some place would take him in. Everyone could find shelter in this Pebble Town, especially people like him with no home to return to.

"It's true that I no longer have a home. There was a tsunami. Don't you read the newspapers?"

Actually, Qiming hadn't read a newspaper for years. Pebble Town had a superiority complex, and everyone who lived here was soaked in this atmosphere. Outside events never interested them. He rarely even thought about his own family.

"I hopped a passing freight train to get here. They threw me off, but I hopped on again. This happened several times."

"How did you know which train was coming to Pebble Town?"

"Do you mean those coal trains? I could tell just by looking at them!"

Hands behind his back, this man, named Haizai, stood in the middle of the room, staring at the opposite wall. Qiming thought apprehensively, *Will he discover the secret in this room's wall?* But Haizai laughed again and dropped his gaze. He had spent several dizzying days on the coal train to get here. Why wasn't he at all tired? And he wasn't dirty, either. Qiming asked Haizai if he wanted to rest on his bed. Haizai kept refusing, insisting he wasn't tired. He was focused on finding a job right away. He'd better deal with this before dark, and then he could move into an apartment of his own. His luggage was stored at the train station. He need only move it over here. Qiming had a sudden thought and said, "Why not wash dishes in the canteen?" Several others working in the canteen had done just that—hanging on there at first without being formally hired. Anyhow, most of the apartments were vacant. One could simply move in. At the end of the month, he would automatically get his monthly wages. It was said that the director gave no attention to minutiae: she simply paid everyone who was there. Haizai listened, his expression unchanging. At last, he said, "That's what I thought, too." Qiming was surprised. Haizai continued, "I got here yesterday, and walked around, getting the lay of the land." Qiming was even more surprised. This person, his childhood playmate: How come he talked just the way the Pebble Town residents did? He had completely lost the simplicity of Fish villagers. Had he just begun to change or had he changed long ago? Before Qiming had worked this out in his mind, Haizai waved goodbye and departed. He took buoyant and decisive steps. This encounter had occurred only yesterday.

Qiming remembered Haizai's father was an illiterate guy, a real fisherman who was at one with the ocean and the shoals. In the past, Qiming had looked down on him and his family, because Qiming's father was educated and moved to Fish Village only after coming upon hard times. Now in Pebble Town, these distinctions weren't important. Haizai—this uncouth person—seemed even smarter than he was, and was genuinely optimistic. At this point, he walked out of his room, a little puzzled. It was quiet outside. Only two guests were sitting under the sandthorn tree playing chess. Qiming watched for a long time without seeing either of them make a move. They were simply dazed, looking up at the sky. A little curious, Qiming strode over to take a look.

It was a man and a woman, both getting on in years. Resting their coarse, weather-beaten hands on the table, they were merely making a show of playing chess. When they saw Qiming, they hailed him. They seemed quite humble.

"We're going to stay here a long time. We're special guests." The old woman's lips were dried up, and it seemed hard for her to speak. "The institute director invited us."

"You're very welcome here. We like having guests," Qiming said.

The old man struck the ground with his cane and shouted, "Don't take her seriously. She talks nonsense. We didn't get a personal invitation. We simply saw a small ad in the newspaper and decided to come. The ad gave the institute director's name and said that she invited everyone to come here for a tour! We've walked all around this area. It's quite desolate."

He stood up, a little agitated. He looked at the sky, then at the ground, then suddenly turned around and picked up a large chess piece. He thumped it down and said, "Check!"

A slight smile appeared on the old woman's wrinkled face. She seemed excited, too, but she controlled herself. She moved a piece so quickly that Qiming didn't see which one it was. Then she stood up and asked Qiming, "Is it true that lodging is free for all the guests here?"

Startled, Qiming began to stutter. He said he wasn't sure; this wasn't part of his job. The old man approached him and whispered,

"The gardener here is from our hometown. He used to raise poppy flowers in the garden, and then he was convicted for it. I saw him yesterday. He hasn't aged much. Why are people here so young? Huh? Look, he's on his way over!"

But Qiming saw only a small tree swaying in the wind. These two people annoyed him. He took his leave impatiently. Qiming had noticed a phenomenon here for years: everyone who came to Pebble Town took on certain traits that made them just like the people already here. At first, people weren't so much the same, but after a few days, they were talking just like the locals. Qiming sometimes felt fragile. At such times, he wanted to confide his feelings to a person from his hometown in the dialect he'd spoken as a youth. Just now, when he saw Haizai, he'd felt this way. But, apart from his name, nothing about Haizai reminded him of his hometown. In fact, he was more like a Pebble Town resident than he himself was. How come? Perhaps when one left home, one automatically became another person. Back then, he experienced this, too. After going with the cadre on cars, trains, and several other modes of transportation, he gradually hardened his heart. The person Qiming admired most was the institute director. He couldn't say why. Even though she'd had nothing more to do with him after settling him into this shed-like cabin, Qiming still appreciated her. He sensed an invisible solicitude being transmitted from her every day. And so every time this nominal Design Institute took in more newcomers, he gasped at the director's generosity. She had even gone to the hospital with José to visit Nancy and their newborn baby! What a terrific woman!

The two elderly people had left, but the chess board was still set up on the stone table. Maybe they would return after a while. The good news about Nancy giving birth to a daughter had invigorated this place. The wind was blowing continuously from the snow mountain. It was so cool, so refreshing! What was his precious goddess doing now? Harvesting grapes? Qiming took out his watch and listened: oh, it was running so forcefully. It ticked vigorously as if to demonstrate its power. Qiming felt it was strange. Maybe this watch was his father, and now his father was finally with him.

Haizai didn't appear for days, nor did he go to work in the canteen. Qiming thought, *Maybe he went to work on maintenance for the city. It was easy to blend in there. Anyone could go.*

One day, however, José came back from the hospital and made a special point of asking him about this. José said that while he was resting in a hospital room, Haizai had shown up. He introduced himself as Qiming's fellow villager and said that he'd arrived in Pebble Town only a few days before. He was working in the hospital. When José asked what kind of work he was doing, he answered, "Helping out in the morgue." He told José that deceased people here were much different from those in the interior or on the coast. Here, the corpse didn't stiffen and could be moved easily. He liked this work quite well because the pay was good. As Haizai was talking, the institute director came by. As soon as Haizai saw her, he sped away rapidly as though he'd seen a ghost. Had he known this woman in the past? José asked the director if she knew this person. She sneered and said, "Naturally." She sank into memories and told José that she was in an accident in the interior several years ago and was taken to the hospital, where she was pronounced dead. But after a day in the morgue, she came back to life. She was moved into an ordinary room. A young person went to her room every day and chatted with her. As they chatted, the institute director sensed that she'd seen him somewhere before, but couldn't remember where. The young person said he was a vagrant and constantly on the move. He was currently helping out in the hospital. Not until the day she was discharged did he tell the truth: he said he had talked with her an entire night in the morgue and had almost frozen to death. She suddenly found this young person really annoying. As for him, he knew his place and left. Long after leaving the hospital, the institute director still couldn't shake off her depression. Later, she gradually found relief in her daily routine.

"The institute director and I have recently become close friends, and we talk about everything with each other," José said with feeling.

Qiming was astounded by this story. After mulling it over, he asked José, "Did the institute director tell you what she and Haizai talked about that night in the morgue?"

"She said she couldn't remember. She's been plagued by this question the last several years."

Qiming's thoughts drifted: he thought of his father. *What was it like for his father as he neared death? Was it the same as the institute director's experience in the morgue? What had Haizai talked about with him?* All at once, an image of the fishing village swaying in a storm appeared in his mind. He felt a little dispirited and forlorn. But that feeling passed very soon. He still wanted to talk with Haizai.

When he went to the hospital to look for Haizai, Nancy had already brought the child home. The morgue was separated a little from the hospital rooms. Many flowers were growing at the entrance, where a guard sat sunbathing. Qiming explained why he had come.

"Oh, you mean that volunteer. He said he was going to take the day off. He's a great help to us. It isn't very often that someone wants to do this kind of work," he gave a thumbs up as he praised Haizai.

"Is he really a volunteer?"

"Yes, that's why we respect him so much. He told us he would work only as a volunteer. He didn't want any wages. All he wanted was three meals a day with us. What a wonderful person! Do you want to come in and look around?"

Qiming sensed that this furtive middle-aged person was constantly taking stock of him, and he was disgusted. He promptly turned down his invitation. Even after walking a long way from the hospital, he could still smell Lysol on his body. He wondered if Haizai had been in the morgue just now. When he thought of him working as a volunteer in the morgue, he couldn't help but laugh. Apparently he had chosen this work in order to talk with the dead.

But this kind of communication must be tough. He could achieve his goal only with someone like the institute director who wasn't really dead. Qiming recalled that Haizai had been a very stubborn kid. He was so obstinate and so inflexible that he offended almost all the villagers. He had probably traveled to many places and kept doing this shameful thing. Qiming sank into dark memories. This was his new practice—remembering a life he had never experienced. As he walked, he thought about this, and the more he thought, the colder he felt. When he reached the guesthouse, he was shaking all over. He figured he should go home and lie down and rest until he recovered.

"Old Qi—old Qi, is something wrong?" Sun Er, from the mailroom, caught hold of his arm and shook him hard.

"Don't—don't worry," he managed to say.

Sun Er chortled for no reason. Qiming struggled free of him, and even though everything was blurry in front of him, he groped his way into his room, removed his shoes, and got into bed.

No sooner had he lain down than he had a sudden recollection. It was a rainy night. He'd been sleeping peacefully, but was awakened with a start by the sound of rapping on the wall. Was it a thief? It was really pathetic if someone had to come out and steal during a downpour like this. He gradually became aware of a sliver of light entering the room. What on earth? He sat up to light the kerosene lamp beside the bed. The first match he struck didn't catch. When he struck a second match, someone grabbed his hand, preventing him from lighting the lamp. Just then, Qiming noticed the sliver of light widening. A wall was moving, and he smelled the weeds and shrubs. Was he in the open country? The person who grabbed his hand spoke, his voice sounding as if it came from a vat. It was unpleasant.

"I want to create a tropical garden here. What do you think? I tried it, but tropical plants won't survive here. But we can build a greenhouse in the air. Don't you see? It's absolutely unobstructed. It's ideal for a tropical garden. I'm a southerner, wandering around this place. Can you identify my accent?"

Actually, aside from the unpleasant buzzing quality, his accent was the same as the local people's.

"But my house wasn't originally built in the unobstructed wilderness," Qiming protested.

"So what? Living here, young man, we have to be flexible. Hunh. Can't you tell what my accent is? I'm from the southernmost place."

Qiming wanted to ask him something, but the sliver of light suddenly disappeared. Maybe the wall had come together again. The person disappeared in the dark. The next morning, it was still raining. He forgot all about this incident.

Now although he wanted to think this incident was a dream, it certainly hadn't been a dream. It was simply an incident that he'd completely forgotten. When he had talked with that person back then, he'd been absolutely clear-headed—a little as if his body had been in another space. Was that person the Design Institute's gardener? Qiming thought he hadn't conversed with the gardener before. The gardener was taciturn and a little arrogant. No doubt that person was one and the same; he *had* conversed with him. This person did build the tropical garden of his dreams here: Qiming had heard several people talk of his flower garden, but he hadn't seen it yet. He wondered if the gardener knew Haizai in the past. How were they connected? Why had Haizai said the gardener was also from Fish Village? Also, he hadn't approached this taciturn guy for years, and now as soon as Haizai arrived and mentioned him, he finally remembered talking with him on a rainy night about the garden— the garden that, even now, he still hadn't seen. What kind of garden was it? Several people had spoken of it, but they disagreed on where it was. Some said it was on the east side; some said the south. Others said it was inside the Design Institute; still others said it was on a hill in front of the Design Institute. Someone else said the gardener's tropical garden was halfway up the snow mountain. Later, Qiming saw the gardener again, but the gardener was cold to him, giving no sign that he knew Qiming.

Another week had passed since he remembered his brief conversation with the gardener. One night, Qiming really did dream of the tropical garden. Many poppies were growing outside the garden, and one huge banyan tree nearly occupied the entire space. It wasn't like a tree, but more like the devil. He walked around amid the aerial roots—so dense that the wind couldn't penetrate them—and thought he would never be able to extricate himself. He felt, too, that the aerial roots had turned into countless frosty hands that were grabbing and pinching him.

After arising in the morning, while wind bathing under the poplars, he saw Nancy appear with her newborn daughter. The baby had a mass of black hair, unlike a baby's hair, but more like a four- or five-year-old's hair. Once more, the phrase "Daughter of the Frontier" surfaced in Qiming's mind. The post-partum Nancy walked daintily. Qiming was surprised: How could someone who had just delivered a baby wander all over? He remembered that he had once almost told Nancy of the Uighur beauty. Nancy vanished from his view. Qiming gazed at the snow mountain and sighed deeply.

In the morning, he was sweeping the conference room. He climbed up on the windowsill to wipe the glass, and after a while looked down. He was astonished to see Haizai sleeping on the lawn below. He jumped down from the windowsill and ran downstairs.

"Why are you sleeping here?"

"Someone chased me. The dead are struggling for territory against the living people."

Flicking the dirt from his body, Haizai stood up. He looked relaxed. Qiming noticed that his right hand was bleeding. When he sucked the wound, he looked intoxicated. Qiming asked what was going on, and he said he had bit himself while asleep and that he had done this to stay alert. All of a sudden, a thought occurred to

Qiming: Could this man have killed his father? He felt a little sick. He invited him to his small room, but Haizai didn't want to go, saying this style of house was too stuffy. He didn't like the Design Institute any better: he had now found a more interesting place to go.

"You mean the hospital morgue?" Qiming asked.

"No, no, no. That's only a cover."

He put on his hat and said he was leaving. Qiming purposely teased him: "Our institute director intends to give you a job."

"I'm grateful to her, but I already have a job. This is a beautiful city. I think I'd like to live here after retiring. It never crossed your mind that we'd see each other here, did it?"

As he watched him depart, Qiming sighed, "He's really a carefree vagrant."

When he returned to the conference room, he saw the director sitting in the empty room thumbing through a notebook. She motioned, indicating that he should sit next to her. Her head bent, she made many marks in her notebook with a fountain pen. Qiming was uncomfortable sitting there wondering what the woman would say to him. Was it about Haizai? Just now, he had boasted to Haizai. But the director couldn't have heard him: she couldn't hear anything so far away!

After quite a while, she closed her notebook and let out a scarcely perceptible sigh. Qiming noticed that her white hair had recently turned wispy, and her plump face seemed more wrinkled. She covered her face with one hand and kept saying, "I'm getting old." Qiming recalled that this conference room hadn't been used for a long time. Perhaps the director had abandoned her job? Just then, she looked up and said a little ruefully, "Oh, Qiming, my life is really tough. I've always been cornered. Just think, if someone knows all your secrets and even what you would do in the future, knows all of that better than you do—because you're not at all sure what you'll do in the future—what's the point of living? It might be tolerable if that person lived far away from you, but he doesn't! Instead, he keeps sneaking back and forth in front of you to remind you of his presence. What can you do?"

"Are you talking of Haizai? I'll talk with him and tell him to leave. I knew him when we were kids." Qiming wanted to help out; that's why he spoke this way.

But the institute director shook her head, not wanting him to intervene. She looked even more worried.

"What's wrong with you, Qiming? That's just silly. So he's your childhood companion—what does this have to do with the present? He's a completely different person now! You mustn't drive him away; that wouldn't be at all good for me. Oh, God, who can understand me?"

Qiming sat there blankly, unable to think of anything to say. He sensed that he was still too immature—far removed from understanding the director. Just then, she changed the subject and asked about the Uighur woman.

"Since the time I saw her dancing next to the road, I've never seen her again. I've gone over to the snow mountain twice. I've stood on the slope gazing at her home in the distance. Her children are grown up now," he replied earnestly.

"Qiming, you're really fortunate. You've never taken a detour. Do you like living in this room?"

"Yes, I do! I've seen miracles here. One night, a wall . . ."

But the director turned around. As she looked at the window to the east, the hands of a burly man grabbed onto the window frame: he seemed about to climb into the room. Qiming wanted to get up and take a good look, but the director pushed him back into his chair. They waited and waited, but the man below never showed his face. Qiming sensed that the director knew who he was, but why did this man want to hang from the window? Was he courting the institute director in this way? Qiming was curious, but he didn't dare ask. The director stared at the man's hands until they disappeared. Qiming thought this was a prank. Exhausted, the director bent over the front row of chairs. The notebook fell from her knees. When Qiming picked it up for her, he saw one colored page inside with a sharp arrow drawn on it. The director looked up and thanked him. She'd been crying: her cheeks were still wet. She pouted like a young girl and wiped her face with a handkerchief.

"Qiming, you don't think I ignored you, do you? It's just the way I am. I have too much to do, but I do think about you. Over time, you've carved out your own path. As for me, I'm halfway to my grave. I want to simplify my life. That person just now—you saw him, too. He goes to extremes. He wants to vanish completely from this world. Do you think that's possible? Hunh."

Qiming thought privately that it was the gardener hanging on the windowsill. Was he a spider-man? He was so arrogant that he must have hurt the director's feelings. Qiming felt spiteful toward him because the director was such a nice person.

When Qiming and the director went outside, they saw Nancy carrying her baby again under the newly planted fir tree. Once more, he thought this woman was a little abnormal: How could she be walking around after just giving birth?

"Look at how pretty they are. The child has really beautiful hair."

"Sure they are. This is the frontier," the director smiled. "She's Pebble Town's child."

The director looked vivacious, her spirits renewed.

Qiming finished cleaning the conference room. He looked down from the window several times. Each time, the director was conversing with Nancy. The child at her breast didn't cry or fuss. José merely watched from the entrance. Qiming realized that José had become mature and sober: he was now burdened with worries. This was a generation that had taken root on the frontier! Had he taken root here, too? Qiming wasn't sure. He had neither children nor relatives here. What he had were only some wispy feelings, but wasn't everyone here the same? Everyone bustled about for fanciful things they couldn't grasp, so they understood each other. It was said that the institute office was going to move from the suburbs into the city, because the employees had been complaining that the area was desolate—too removed from social life. They wanted to move to a more populated place. Qiming could absolutely understand this. A larger population would mean more communication. All kinds of subtle things were transmitted through the crowds. It was especially true in Pebble Town. Here, everyone revealed some message when speaking, even though the one speaking was unaware of it. Yet, Qiming was able to grasp these messages. This was why he found it agreeable to live in the city. What would it be like if he lived in the desolate suburbs? Qiming shut his eyes and tried hard to imagine it; he supposed it was a little like life in Fish Village. Naturally, people living in small enclosed places always wanted to escape to the outside world. After all, hadn't he and Haizai both come to the frontier?

Sometimes Qiming had insomnia at night. At such times, he didn't feel at all alone. He wandered through the small town, and rested in one warm, dark hideout after another. He thought of how lucky he was! He was grateful to his father, but he wasn't interested in going home to visit him. He'd rather keep his memories of his father. Sometimes, he wandered for an entire night, sleeping for a while only at dawn. The next day, he began work as energetically as ever. Occasionally, he would get out of bed at midnight and sit for a while next to the flowerbed at the guesthouse, looking up at the stars and thinking of his Uighur beauty. The stars in the north shone particularly brightly. As he watched them, his heart would tremble for a long time, as though something inside him had been opened. He would soliloquize, "People living in this small town are so fortunate!" Sometimes, as he was immersed in these feelings, a cool wind blew over from the snow mountain: that wind would lift his emotions to high tide. A lot of children were running through the rosebushes, shouting, "Aigury! Aigury!" Aigury was his beauty's name. When he went back to his room, he would sleep soundly. In his dreams, Pebble Town and Fish Village were mixed together, and he was mixed together with his childhood. There were some doors in that scenery, but those doors didn't open to any place. He would involuntarily run to a doorframe and stand inside it, distractedly recalling stories of his life. In these stories, his figure was blurred, sometimes like a child and sometimes like an old man. Yet the background was always snow lotus flowers and calliopsis. No ocean, though. In his dreams, he asked: Where has the ocean gone?

One dreamless night, Qiming was awakened by the baby's crying. At first, he thought it was a cat in heat, but he gradually realized it was the baby. The infant was next to his door! He got out of bed at once and opened the door: in the moonlight he saw the baby wrapped in pink. He looked out and saw Nancy sitting silently beside the flowerbed.

"Nancy!"

"She's crying—crying all the time! What can I do? José has gone to buy some medicine," she whined.

The baby girl made even more noise, and Qiming held her and lifted her up in the air. One, two, three! But it did no good: she was still crying loudly.

"The doctor says there's nothing wrong with her. But why does she cry? I think she hates me."

Nancy held her head and squatted on the ground.

"Nancy, she's such a treasure, and her crying is so full of life! Even the snow mountain can hear her. Go ahead and cry, cry. I like listening to it!"

Qiming lifted the baby up in the air five or six more times, and she eventually stopped crying and began to smile.

Nancy jumped up and said, "Oh, she likes you! This little monster likes you! God, no one else can do anything with her!"

"Sure she likes me. She's a child of our frontier, isn't she? Nancy, you've done us a great favor. She's fine now. She's sleeping. You can go home and get some rest, too."

A long time after Nancy and the baby left, Qiming still felt emotional. He had never held a baby before. Just now, with the baby in his arms, a strange sensation had come over him. He could still see the baby's smiles, and something was growing within him. He felt a little aching—an aching filled with expectation and wonder. He said to himself, "This is a person, a new person, who was born not long ago. My God . . ." Just now as he had lifted her up, he had seen the ocean in her tiny face. In the same instant, somewhere nearby, a desert bird had chirped "dididi" incessantly. He had never imagined that a new life could so unsettle him. Was it because she was Nancy's daughter and the mother's warmth had been transmitted to the infant? On this dark night, this mother and daughter had appeared at his door. It happened so naturally—yet how had this happened? The baby was much like her mother, a bundle of warmth. Ah . . . Qiming was lost in his thoughts.

As he lay in the dark, what was eddying in his mind was not the beauty Aigury, but the skinny Nancy and the baby in her arms. He did his utmost to banish this vision and said to himself repeatedly, "This woman is but a migratory bird." But the baby? The baby was different from the mother. The conflicts between them had already appeared. When he first arrived in Pebble Town, he had longed to fuse with this land. Because of this, he even deliberately harmed himself. He thought that being injured could deepen his emotions. The baby's continual crying—was this also to deepen something? He turned over, and his hand bumped into the watch beside his pillow. He took hold of it, and after a while, he saw the ocean and the baby's face. "Dididi . . ." His face was hot, his heart throbbing. The sudden change in himself scared him.

"Haizai, how the hell did you run out?"

"I didn't run. I walked and walked under the water, and when I surfaced I had reached another province."

Qiming and Haizai were talking in the shed of the convicts' labor camp. This was a labor reform unit from another province. They were helping with afforestation in Pebble Town. The shed was filthy. Dirty socks and underwear were everywhere. Haizai was content here. He was smoking a cigarette in a leisurely fashion. Qiming told him he had looked for him at the hospital's morgue. Haizai said he probably would have continued working in the morgue if he hadn't encountered the institute director there. "It wasn't for me, but for her sake, that I left the hospital. Who would want to be lying there like a corpse?"

A young convict entered. His hair stood up and his gaze was fierce. As soon as he came in, he made a lot of noise. It was clear that he didn't like Qiming sitting there. Qiming considered leaving, but Haizai kept him from getting up by pressing on his knee. All of a sudden, the other person picked up a brick and threw it at his back; the impact sent Qiming rolling to the floor. He shouted "Ouch, oh ouch!" Luckily, he wasn't badly hurt.

"People here are violent," said Haizai from above him.

"Why didn't you let me go?" Qiming complained, "It's all your fault!"

"You idiot. Once you came here, you couldn't leave. If you had run, he would have chased you and killed you. It's better this way. You may hurt a little, but you're safe now."

Haizai started laughing. Qiming didn't think it was at all funny. He heard heavy, hesitant footsteps outside the work shed. Several people were walking back and forth at the entrance, as though they intended to come in. Qiming's nerves were taut. Haizai finished smoking and said he had to go to work and wanted Qiming to go with him. He handed him a shovel. Qiming's back hurt, and he couldn't stand up straight, so he used the shovel as a walking stick.

When they went outside, the convicts stared at them from both sides. Qiming was afraid they would throw bricks at him again, and so he cringed, trying to hide his head and face in the hollow of his shoulder. Just then, Haizai ordered, "Hold your head high!" Qiming looked up and saw that the others had turned their backs.

When they reached the poplar park, Qiming asked Haizai if they had to dig a hole. Haizai said no. He said they had brought the work tools to throw others off. He found a grassy spot and lay down, his hands pillowing his head, staring at the sky. Qiming asked, "Did those people want to hurt me?"

Haizai laughed and didn't bother to answer.

"Is this the work you found? Are you a volunteer?" Qiming asked.

"Yes. Qiming, when your father was dying, what did he wish? Do you know?"

"Tell me."

"I don't know, either. I looked into his eyes, but I couldn't figure it out. I knew he was very worried. Then, he gave me that watch."

"Oh, the watch! I can guess a little now," Qiming cried.

All at once, he remembered the "dididi" sound in the middle of the night. He had always found that sound exciting. He noticed that Haizai's eyes had softened and were even a little too affectionate. This vagrant was staring at the gray-blue sky and worrying. Qiming took the old watch out of his pocket and looked at it carefully. This was a good watch, even though the copper plating had broken off. The hands still ticked vigorously. When Qiming was a child, his father tried to commit suicide once. At the time, he didn't understand what had happened in his home; he just knew that everyone was unusually quiet, even walking on tiptoe. His father, his neck wrapped in a bandage, lay quietly in bed, and asked Qiming to read him a section of their family history every day. Qiming remembered that the family history mentioned this watch. It was said that his grandfather had taken the watch from the body of a dead prisoner of war on the battlefield. Back then, dead prisoners weren't buried, but just rotted outdoors. At that time, Father lay in bed for two months. He took the watch out frequently and looked at it. Pride showed on his face. Sometimes, Father would rub his head and say, "Son, you must do your best to remember those blurry past events." Of course Qiming didn't understand, but Father said this time after time, and he remembered it. Father was seventy when he died: in the fishing villages along the seacoast this was a long life. He had lived a long time! Had he really considered ending his life on that long-ago day? If he had, then why hadn't he succeeded? He certainly wasn't indecisive. Of all the people Qiming had known, he was the most resolute. Qiming asked Haizai, "Was my father in pain when he died?"

"Are you serious? I think he was at peace. He died without suffering. He didn't have any strange disease."

"That's what I thought, too, but I needed to hear you say it."

Qiming lifted the watch, and a curassow appeared in the direction the watch pointed to. When he moved his arm, the curassow moved in the same direction. He turned around so that the watch would point in the opposite direction—and the bird quickly flew in that direction. When he slid the watch into his pocket, the bird disappeared into the high clouds. Below, Haizai was talking—but in a low voice, and he couldn't hear what he was saying.

The two of them stayed in the poplar park until late that day without eating any supper. When they parted ways, Haizai was a little sentimental, telling Qiming that it would probably be hard to see each other in the future because his labor reform unit was moving to another city. He also said that he had wanted to stay in the hospital, but the institute director had made him abandon that idea. At first, he had felt that Pebble Town was the best place for him, but this was the institute director's domain, and he couldn't contend with her. So he had to get out of the way. "She'll never make peace with me in this lifetime."

Shouldering the two shovels, Haizai took off dejectedly. And Qiming once more circled around among the flowers. When he left the park, the old gatekeeper stopped him. The old man asked how Haizai was related to him, and seeing the old man's seriousness,

Qiming told him. The old guy sipped his tea and said slowly, "There's something wrong with his mind. He comes to the park every day, pretending to be coming to work. After he gets here, he lies on the grass. Before long, an old woman shows up. As they chat, they begin quarreling, and the old woman hits and kicks him. He covers his head with both hands, but doesn't retaliate. Each time after the old woman finishes beating up on him, she leaves, but he continues squatting there for a long time. The old woman hasn't come the last few days, yet he still has. I suspect that today is his last time here. What do you think is wrong with him?"

Qiming thought to himself, *This old man is more a spy than a gatekeeper.* And so as he departed, he said loudly, "True, he's a little crazy. You'd better be careful."

"A madman! Haha, a madman! A madman has come to the park again! This happened before, too!"

He leaned out the window and shouted at Qiming's back. Then he turned and asked his wife to join him in taking a look. So the old woman also squeezed in at the window to watch Qiming. They shook their fists at him.

Qiming started to run, anxious to leave the nightmare behind. By the time he reached the guesthouse, he was sweating all over. He felt weak.

Chapter 4

SHERMAN

Sherman was an orphan who had grown up in an orphanage in the interior. When he was old enough, he left and went to many places before finally settling down on the frontier. A well-off family near the snow mountain adopted him. Later, he enrolled in a school that taught spinning. He dropped out and started working, not as a spinner but in the Pebble Town park archives. It was a cushy job. Since it didn't matter if he went to work, he often stayed home. He, his wife, and daughter lived in the parks' apartments—poor quality two-story buildings. They lived on the second floor. The roof leaked every year when it rained.

Sherman's wife was a gardener. She had been a beauty, good at singing and dancing when she was young, and was still pretty even now. The other day when Liujin saw Sherman arguing with her, Liujin thought she was a young woman. In fact, she would soon turn forty. The couple started fighting not long after their daughter was born. Sherman's wife turned their home into a battlefield; Sherman couldn't do much about it. One day when he got home, he didn't go in immediately, but looked through the window. He saw his wife sitting in their shabby home, moaning constantly in pain. Deeply touched, Sherman went in right away, but without letting him ask her anything, his wife stood up and silently did the housework as if nothing was wrong. Sherman asked, "Were you feeling unwell just now?"

"No. I'm fine."

Her head high, she went into the kitchen. She sang while washing the dishes.

Sherman thought his wife was unfathomable. He couldn't even guess what she was thinking most of the time. As the years went on, Sherman felt more and more that it was impossible to understand her. Yet it was this very woman whom he'd fallen for at first sight years ago at her auntie's home. Last year, after their daughter moved out, life at home was even more hellish. Sherman spent less time at home now.

Then where could he go? He couldn't bear to stay in the archives because several young people considered his office their teahouse, going there to talk, drink tea, and smoke. Sherman enjoyed melting into crowds of people, so he began frequenting the market. He didn't buy anything, but just roamed around to kill time. In the market, he became aware of the unpredictable swings in public emotions. People in the market were strangers to each other, yet whenever they became excited by the same thing, they could turn violent, even barbaric. Ordinarily, though, each individual was wrapped up in his inner concerns; no one was interested in talking with strangers. When Sherman moved around in the bustling crowd, he always heard a weak moan. The intermittent sound was everywhere. Sometimes Sherman sat down in a corner for a moment and concentrated. The more he listened, the more puzzled he became, because at such times he felt that everyone was moaning, but each one was doing his utmost to suppress this sound. Sherman looked up and took stock of these people's faces, but doing so didn't tell him anything.

He became acquainted with Liujin by accident. One day in the market, as he fingered the locally woven material, he ended up talking with her about dyeing cloth. The young woman didn't talk much, but she listened attentively. As they stood beside the dry goods, the noise in the market vanished, and in that brief moment, Sherman saw an eagle above the cliff. He said to himself, "Her parents can't be locals." One time in her small courtyard (such a relaxing, beautiful courtyard!), he asked if she had heard weeping in the market. She said it wasn't weeping; it was a moan that came as people struggled against something huge, "such as a tiger charging down from the hill." She winked at him as she said this. This woman was a much different type from his wife. She was also mysterious, but she didn't spurn others. Sherman was captivated by her. He schemed for a long time before placing frogs in front of her small courtyard. But, later on rainy days, he didn't hear the croaking he expected. The frogs had vanished. Sherman was impressed by Liujin's formidable willpower. Back then, he wasn't sure what Liujin thought of him. She seemed to welcome him, but Sherman thought things weren't that simple. And so, although he liked this woman a lot, something always held him back.

When he didn't feel like going home, he frequently sat in the poplar park with Song Feiyuan. Sometimes they sat there until dark, like two vagrants. Feiyuan was instinctively violent. Sometimes he would ram his head against a poplar until he bled. Sherman delighted in seeing this. It was because of this that he often spent time with him. He certainly didn't expect Liujin to appear in this place. The young woman acted a little crazy. She dashed around as if in a realm of nothingness, blind to anything in her way. Seeing she was about to fall, he alerted her, but she wouldn't listen and finally she did bump into something and fell down on the ground. After a while, she sprang to her feet and ran off, as though being chased by a ghost. He recalled that under the faint moonlight, Song Feiyuan had said huskily, "Someone else is coming." This was a strange comment. At that time, he had just become acquainted with Liujin, and he wasn't sure what Feiyuan meant. Did Feiyuan think that Liujin was coming to the poplar grove for the same reason? However, they didn't run into her there again.

Sherman frequently referred to his wife's thoughts as "lizard tongue," for her tongue never stopped at a certain place. She never had just one idea at a time; each one contained many other ideas. He knew she didn't intend to be like this; rather, it was instinctive. Their relationship over the last many years hadn't exactly chilled, but it was depressing. Sherman often told himself, "My wife is a huge mountain pressing down on my head." His spiritual connection with Liujin rekindled his vitality. When he talked with her, he could sense a silent snow leopard making its way between them. At those times—even though he was myopic—he could see irises in the dark. Sometimes, while talking with Liujin, he could suddenly understand one of his wife's ideas. He thought, *There are so many hidden paths in a woman's mind.*

He still slept in the same bed with his wife, and late at night, in spite of themselves, they would have sex and pull one another into a tight embrace, as though wanting to melt into one another's body. But as soon as the night was over, she wrapped herself up again in steel armor. Sherman had tried hard to probe her mind, and then he gave up and became a little numb. However, he couldn't quite manage to be "estranged" from her, so he always sensed a protracted war in their home—especially after their daughter moved out. One night, as they were having sex, Sherman suddenly began shaking from cold and he immediately withdrew. He struggled all night as if in an ice hole. He called out to his wife many times, but she didn't respond. Not until the next morning did he realize that rain was leaking through the roof, soaking the whole bed. He was surprised that he had slept there all night. His wife said, "You wouldn't get out of bed. I went over to the other room and slept by myself." When they had the roof repaired, he was overcome by fumes from the tar, and he lay there thinking he would die. He couldn't open his eyes; everything around him was spinning rapidly. He was in the swaying white light. Unexpectedly, he heard his wife shout "Sherman!" He felt a little gratified. When he recovered, his wife also returned to her usual ways. From the bed, Sherman looked at her from behind and wondered, *Has our relationship ended up this way because she's also an orphan with unspeakably dark experiences?* But in the beginning when she told him she was also an orphan, he had been so happy! Alas, childhood! Did that early, innocent part of one's life determine one's whole future? Sherman wanted to calm down, but this was impossible. Every now and then, they would fight furiously. They never had long, confidential talks. Neither of them was accustomed to that. Sherman wasn't good at expressing himself in words, and his wife Yuanqing—although she was good at singing and dancing—had never told him what she was thinking, either.

Song Feiyuan was a vendor of roasted mutton. He and Sherman had known each other for several years. Song Feiyuan didn't like to talk, either, but the two of them did understand each other.

"How are we going to spend the day, friend?" Song would say to him.

Then—in spring, summer, or autumn—they would go to the poplar grove. In the winter, they would go, instead, to a small bar and drink. Song Feiyuan was the only local who was chummy with him. Sherman often sighed: this person was so sincere. He lived at the end of the avenue where Liujin lived. His shop was on another smaller street. Sherman didn't notice for a long time that Liujin also lived there. He frequently saw Song Feiyuan walk out of his adobe house, which was partially crumbling to dust. He would stand at the side of the street and look in all directions, like a helpless child. His business didn't open until evening, so he could spend the day loafing with Sherman. When Sherman called out "Feiyuan," his face lit up, as though he had found the meaning of life. He didn't like other people to go into his dilapidated house, but Sherman had seen his two children and his wife. His impression was that they behaved furtively, like groundhogs. Sherman concluded from this that he had no one at home to fight with. Was this why he had knocked down one wall of his home?

Next to the dead poplar tree, Feiyuan told Sherman that his childhood dream was to become a soldier.

"I was always holding a wooden club and thrashing around pretending to be in a battle. My mother encouraged me. Luckily, she died young; otherwise, she would be upset about my becoming a vendor of roasted mutton."

"What's wrong with selling roasted mutton kebabs? I think that's great!"

Sherman burst out laughing, and so did Feiyuan. They weren't often so happy. They looked at the sky together. They both liked the frontier sky. Sometimes they looked at it for half an hour without speaking. Sometimes they saw a single goshawk in the sky; sometimes they saw nothing.

If they had enough time, they walked around Pebble Town. By the time they had circled the town once, it was dark. When they rested in a teashop, Sherman would start falling into a trance. He felt like a vagrant in the interior. When he walked, he took off his glasses and the snow mountain appeared before him, and one by one, leopards and bears did, too. He glanced sideways at Feiyuan, who was just walking ahead. So he told him to look at the snow mountain. Feiyuan said nothing about it was new to him. He wandered there every night, and couldn't be any more familiar with it than he already was. Sherman did his best to imagine "wandering there every night," but it made him dizzy. Each time they circled around the town, they observed the same episode—an old man starting a campfire right in the middle of the road. The fire only smoldered, and they choked on the thick smoke. They bypassed it and walked out to the fields, but couldn't help looking back at that man. He was an old man, who was bent over when he walked—his head nearly bumping the ground. The man stood absentmindedly in the thick smoke; the melodious sound of a flute came from behind him. Because they ran into him so often, Sherman felt he should speak to him.

"Do you live near here, sir?"

"Yes, right over there." He pointed to the wasteland behind him. "There are quite a few wild dogs here. You have to be careful in the suburbs."

Feiyuan told Sherman that this person was creating a smoke screen—to cover up the garden behind him. The sound of the flute came from there. Sherman wanted to look at the garden, but Feiyuan didn't. He said the garden seemed near, but if you walked toward it, you'd never reach it. He had tried this a long time ago. Sherman asked about the wild dogs, and Feiyuan answered, "Wild dogs? They're his dogs!" Sherman was puzzled. Why hadn't he seen the garden? The next time he ran into the old man, he pushed through the smoke screen and took a good look, but he still saw nothing. Feiyuan laughed at him for "trying in vain." He didn't understand. Feiyuan said, "Not everyone can see it." This incident made him glum, but he believed Feiyuan was telling the truth. He sighed to himself, "Pebble Town is really a wonderland!" He recalled that when he first came to the frontier, his adoptive father brought him to Pebble Town for sightseeing. It was deep in the autumn, and very cold, but quite a few barebacked men were standing under the poplar trees, facing the snow mountain and letting the wind blow over them. His adoptive father told him these people were wind bathing; people said this could prolong one's life. Pebble Town residents loved competing to see who would live longer. This made Sherman think: Pebble Town didn't have a large population, but there wasn't one secluded place. There was no way to find a desolate place to be alone, because someone was always already there—this old man, for instance. Sherman couldn't even see what he was doing all year long in this desolate area because he hid everything from view with that strange smoke screen.

Feiyuan worked in his shop until late at night. Actually, there wasn't much business at night, but he liked working then. Sherman kept him company on one occasion. Everyone else had already gone home when an old woman dressed in red entered and sat at a table. Lowering his voice, Feiyuan told Sherman that she had cancer and wasn't allowed to eat mutton. She came just to chat with him. He and Sherman sat down across from her.

"Today is the thirtieth anniversary of my coming here. When I was young, I worked on a tramp steamer." She spoke easily, and her color was good.

"A tramp steamer!" Feiyuan was a little surprised. "How did you keep track of time on board?"

"Not easily. All the days were the same—the sun rose and the sun set. There was no way to keep track of time. Calendars didn't help much, either."

"Ah, ah . . ." Feiyuan opened his mouth; he didn't know what to say.

Sherman felt that he and Feiyuan were acting like idiots in front of this old woman. Especially him. He had no idea what he should say to her.

"This friend of yours: is he also counting the days?" she asked kindly, but Feiyuan was flustered and began to stutter.

"I don't know. Perhaps. Is he? No, no, that's not right. I should say, yes . . ."

When the old woman took her leave, the black cat in the shop howled at her.

"I don't think she'll die anytime soon," Sherman said.

"Oh—" Feiyuan mused for a moment, then said, "She cried just now. She comes here late at night to cry. The day she came to Pebble Town, she was carrying a small suitcase and squinting at the sky. Back then, I was still dreaming of becoming a soldier. Oh, it seems just like yesterday . . ."

Sherman definitely hadn't seen her cry. Feiyuan suggested that they sit beside the street for a while. He turned off the light and moved the chairs outside. By then, no one was out, and this little street had fallen asleep. Breathing the night air, Feiyuan's figure seemed to be diminishing, and his voice came from far away.

"Sherman, have you counted?"

Overcome by drowsiness, Sherman struggled to say, "Not yet. But I will!"

When they parted ways, the dew had already fallen. Sherman felt his way home through the dark and did his best to make no noise. The bed was empty. When he lay down, he heard a strange, obscure sound. It was terrifying. He had heard it a long time ago when he had stood on the ocean floor to get away from the head of the orphanage. He turned on the light and got up. There was nothing out of the ordinary in the room. He saw that his wife Yuanqing was sleeping in another room, the room that had been their daughter's. She slept soundly, snoring lightly.

Sherman dressed and went to the kitchen to cook noodles for the two of them.

"Where did you go? I haven't slept the whole night. It's really frightening," she said, her eyelids drooping.

"What are you afraid of?"

"You mean you didn't hear? There's a strange sound in this room!"

She stamped her feet furiously and went to work without eating. Sherman locked the door behind her and ate his breakfast.

Just then, the sound came again, though only faintly. If you didn't concentrate, you'd miss it. Sherman looked down from the window and saw a group of kids jumping rope. When they swung the rope, it whooshed. So was this the noise he'd heard? No, no, it wasn't.

After eating, he went back to sleep, letting that sound keep him company. It wasn't as frightening in the daytime, after all. He woke from a trance with a start. A thought came to him: Was this the counting time that the old woman had spoken of? It appeared that he was her opposite: when he had stood at the floor of the ocean to escape the search of the orphanage head, he counted the time; as soon as he climbed ashore, he forgot it. This is to say: only when you remember this sound does this sound appear. Maybe his wife Yuanqing was skilled at this, and so she finally grew frustrated with him. He said to himself, "Sherman, Sherman, you've idled away too much time." Feeling regretful, he went back to sleep.

After awakening, he still remembered this incident, so he looked for Feiyuan in the afternoon.

"The old woman is gone. Last night at the tumor hospital. She didn't suffer."

"She was beautiful," Sherman sighed.

"Yes, there are many beautiful women in Pebble Town. When she arrived, however, she looked ordinary. Her face was dark. But her eyes were charming in a special way. The longer she stayed here, the more beautiful she became. Oh, these women."

Sherman was touched by Feiyuan's words. It occurred to him that his wife was beautiful, too, as was Liujin. He wasn't sure where his relationship with Liujin was heading.

The afternoon sun shone on Feiyuan's face. His thin, dark face was unusually alive. Sherman thought the blood of ancient soldiers ran through his veins.

After they ate at Feiyuan's small shop, customers started coming in. Sherman sat to one side helping him make mutton kebabs. While absorbed in this work, he heard that sound again. He looked up at Feiyuan. Feiyuan was stupefied; he was like a stone statue enveloped in a fog of light blue smoke. After a while, "the stone statue" finally began to move, but only stiffly. Sherman thought this was simply interference from that sound.

Feiyuan quietly told Sherman: the person sitting on the third seat on the left is the old woman's son. Like his mother, he doesn't come to eat mutton kebabs. But he doesn't come to chat, either. He wants a cup of clear tea, and then he looks out the window. Sherman thought the middle-aged man was quite composed, as if contemplating a problem. He wasn't at all like someone whose mother had just died. He puffed on a cigarette and then slowly spat out the smoke.

Seen through the smoke, his face looked longer. "He burrowed into a crack in a cliff on the ocean floor," Feiyuan said. Sherman quietly asked Feiyuan, "Where does he work?" "On a tramp steamer. On the ocean. Where else could it be? He took his mother's place. He's been here a month."

That night, when most customers had left, that man was still sitting there looking outside.

"You and your mother never came here together," said Feiyuan.

"Ah," he said. "The past few years, she regarded this place as a city on the ocean floor. That's what she told me two days ago. I told her that I'll live here, too, after I retire. But she said, 'No, no. Every place is the same.' Sitting here, I keep thinking that she might walk in at any moment."

He looked intoxicated, and he reeled a little when he stood up. Sherman thought, *Perhaps he's in the water?* After he went out, Feiyuan told Sherman, "His feet have really broken free of the ground. What a forsaken man!"

At that moment, Sherman sensed profoundly that Feiyuan was damned good at living, and that was why he had chosen to open this small shop. He even thought he might open one, too, after he retired. When he walked through this small street and made his way home, the moonlight and street lamps suddenly faded away. In this short time, his feet actually broke away from the ground. But very soon, his feet dropped onto the ground again. When he looked up, he saw lights on in his home—and the silhouettes of his wife and daughter swaying at the window. He bumped into someone in the dark. When he heard his voice, he realized it was the son of the deceased old woman!

"I want to go inside your building," he said softly.

"Oh! I'd really like to invite you to stay in my home, but my place is just too small," Sherman said, a little worried.

"No. I'm not used to being in other people's homes. I just want to sit for a night at the foot of the stairs. It's so late—it's dangerous to walk around, isn't it? Yesterday, Mama told me there were sharks in the neighborhood."

Sherman hurried into his house. Mother and daughter turned to him in astonishment.

"There's someone downstairs," he said. He surprised himself by saying this.

It didn't occur to him that mother and daughter would ask in unison, "Is it that sailor?"

"Yes. How did you know?"

"I told Mama just now." His daughter Little Leaf said, "I've known him for a long time. He's pathetic; he doesn't fit in anywhere."

Yuanqing looked a little anxious. She urged her daughter to go with her to the other room to sleep, and so they did. They closed the bedroom door, but kept a small light on.

When Sherman lay down, he heard the strange sound again. This time it seemed particularly clear: it was in the dining room. Accompanying that sound was his daughter Little Leaf's crying for help. Sherman leaped up and ran, barefoot, to the women's bedroom and rapped on the door.

"Little Leaf! Little Leaf!"

As he knocked on the door, the light in their bedroom went out, and he heard Little Leaf's sleepy voice.

"Don't shout at me, Papa. Don't make so much noise . . ."

Sherman was shamefaced as he went back to his room. In the dark, he thought of the shark. Could the shark be making this noise? Was that person still downstairs? How was he going to get through this night? His daughter Little Leaf was so grown up. When she was little and he held her in his arms, she stared straight at him with those beautiful black eyes and never cried. Her eyes weren't like Yuanqing's; she wasn't nearsighted, either. Who did she look like?

Recently, a lethargic young person had been coming to Sherman's office. As soon as he got there, he would hide in the shadows behind the file cabinets and rest, as if exhausted. After dozing for about half an hour, he would jump up and go back to work. He was the new electrician. People said he was "weighed down by the past." This was what his colleague Zhao had told Sherman. He had never joined in the mischief-making of the other young people in the office. The chair behind the file cabinet had become his designated seat.

"Marco, are you sick?" Sherman asked with concern.

"No, Uncle Sherman. I'm fine. Just tired." He smiled in embarrassment. "Sometimes it's really hard for me to keep my eyes open."

Sherman asked Zhao what it meant to "be weighed down by the past." The colleague replied that Marco had bizarre hallucinations: he thought he had been transformed into another person. He had moved from his home and cut himself off from his relatives; it was as if he didn't even know them. He used to have a girlfriend, and then he broke up with her, too. Because of this, the girl had become a kind of lunatic. Marco wasn't unaware of the trouble he caused others. Sometimes he was lucid. At such times, he went out wearing odd clothing, a red toupee, and sunglasses. No one could recognize him. Zhao somehow saw through his disguise and confronted him. To Zhao's surprise, Marco actually lied to his face, claiming to be an overseas Chinese returning home, and said that he would stay only temporarily in Pebble Town. When Zhao mentioned his ex-girlfriend, he squatted down abruptly and wailed. Then he wiped away his tears and told Zhao he had to go back to Holland right away.

Whenever Marco arrived, Sherman felt heavy-hearted. Each time, he wished he would leave soon. Sherman wondered if it was possible for a person to transform himself into another person while asleep. In just half an hour, the young guy fell sound asleep, snoring open-mouthed. Sherman didn't know, either, why he was so heavy-hearted. Was it because he couldn't transform himself? The other young men fastened clothespins on their ears, and crawled around on the floor, but—who knew why?—they didn't disturb the sleeping Marco. Zhao crawled over and told Sherman sorrowfully that he would also like to go to Holland—but where was Holland? He had no idea. And so all he—and the rest of them, too—could do was to crawl on the ground, crawl and crawl some more. It might have looked like fun, but actually they did this to release their inhibitions. When Sherman heard "release their inhibitions," he glanced sideways again at these people. He couldn't help but laugh. Later on, he asked Marco very seriously what Holland was all about. Marco said that his family used to be very poor. When he was still an infant, a Dutch woman had adopted him and taken him to Holland. But when he was three, his adoptive mother had sent him home. People said he'd gotten into trouble there, and the adoptive mother no longer wanted him.

"What's Holland like?" Sherman asked.

"I don't know. Every day, I try to remember, but I can't remember anything about that country. That isn't right, because I lived there three years. Damn. It's as if I'd never been there."

Feiyuan also knew about Marco's situation. He looked down on Marco and called him a "white-eyed wolf"—a heartless, ungrateful person. He also said that Marco's adoptive mother saw through him and that's why she finally sent him back. Feiyuan's verdict: "This person is dangerous."

"Then I shouldn't have any contact with him, should I?" asked Sherman.

"Contact? Contact is fine. It's good for you to have contact with him."

His daughter Little Leaf, however, actually came to his office looking for Marco. When—thick as thieves—the two of them sat talking in the dark behind the file cabinet, Sherman grew nervous. He couldn't hear what they were saying. He considered leaving, but that didn't seem right. That day, none of the young people showed up. It was just the three of them in the room, and his daughter didn't seem to mind his being there.

On the way home, he told Little Leaf, "People say he's a white-eyed wolf."

"True. I've heard that, too! I like white-eyed wolves. They're the kind I really like! Pa, I'll be with him, and later on, I probably won't come home much. Even if I come home, my heart won't be there. Haven't you ever wondered why Marco was hanging around your office? It's because I told him to. Whenever he complained that his workplace was too noisy, I suggested that he rest in your office. Ah! Just look at that sailor!"

The sailor blocked the entrance to the dormitory, spreading his body out like the "大" character. Whenever people went in, he immediately dodged to one side and then went back to blocking the space with the "大" pose. Little Leaf started laughing and said, "He's imitating a curtain." Sherman thought this guy's trick was quite amusing. But he also thought, *If no one comes through for a long time, it will get tough for him. A person can't maintain that pose very long. Perhaps he was trying to make up for something he missed during his life on the ocean.*

When they went through, the sailor didn't move. Little Leaf lowered her head and forced her way through.

"How are you doing today, young man?" Sherman joked with him.

"This place is great, so passionate," he replied earnestly.

Then he sighed and his arms sagged.

"I have to go. The ocean is calling me. This lost child has waited too long to go home."

In just a few days' time, Sherman noticed that Marco's face had been strewn with straight lines that looked like knife cuts. Were these caused by dehydration? If he hadn't seen him earlier, he'd have thought he was an old man. His clothes also looked old, covered as they were by a layer of dust. Yet his mother had been an elegant woman who had dressed with exquisite taste. An idea flashed through Sherman's mind: this place was his mother's maritime space, it wasn't his. He was wasting time staying here so long. Upstairs,

Little Leaf called to Sherman, as though she had something urgent for him to solve.

"Marco and I have decided to quit our jobs and become gardeners." She looked intently into her father's eyes.

"That's good. You're young. Changing jobs is a good idea."

"We'll take lessons from the old gardener. You won't see us for a while. Ah—that kind of gardening! There's no way I can describe it to you. After seeing it once . . ."

As she was speaking, she left the room and went downstairs. Sherman fell into his chair, a campfire appearing in his mind—along with thick smoke filling the sky. Once more, he felt deeply that life in the small town was infinitely intriguing. His daughter was going off to do things he hadn't done.

After Little Leaf and Marco resigned from their jobs, they disappeared. Sherman and Yuanqing went to Little Leaf's rented apartment, where the landlord told them she had moved out some time ago. When they got home, Yuanqing regretted having gone and said they shouldn't have looked for her. "What good does it do?" Sherman thought Yuanqing knew the ins and outs of the whole thing.

He made up his mind to go with Feiyuan to find the old gardener and have a talk—partly because he was uneasy about Little Leaf and partly because he was curious. He wanted Feiyuan to continue his last conversation about the garden. He felt unconvinced.

When he went to Feiyuan's shop, Feiyuan was stocking goods, so he helped out, too. After the mutton was all put away, it was four o'clock in the afternoon. Feiyuan vacillated. Taking stock of Sherman's face, he asked, "Do you have to go now?"

"Of course. She's my daughter," Sherman rebuked him.

"Oh, that's right. I forgot. Let's go."

When they reached the old man's place, they saw no campfire. It was a foggy evening. They could see some indistinct shapes ahead of them. They looked like houses, but they weren't. Getting closer, they discovered several large wooden boxes arranged along a small river. Why hadn't they seen this river the last few times they'd come here? Sherman put his head inside one box and saw bedding and a few bowls inside. Just then, Feiyuan called to him.

"The gardener's in the sixth box. He's sick. I certainly don't want to disturb him. Just think. He's ninety years old."

"Can we help him?"

"Who can help him in this desolate country? Don't be silly."

Feiyuan sounded dismayed. He didn't hide his discontent with Sherman. He said they'd better hurry back to the road, so they wouldn't lose their way in the dark. Sherman wanted to look at these boxes some more, but it was so dark that when he stuck his head in, he could see nothing. Although he didn't want to do so, he agreed that they had better leave. After walking a while, he looked back and saw a figure next to the river. Was it Little Leaf? Ah, it wasn't just one person; others also emerged. They formed a line. The small river was dark and a little dirty. Sherman had noticed earlier that it wasn't like a frontier river.

Feiyuan walked ahead and urged Sherman to hurry. He said it would soon be totally dark. If they waited any longer, they wouldn't even be able to find the road. Sherman thought quickly and said, "Okay. Leave me here alone. I'm not afraid of losing my way. I have nothing to worry about." Having said this, he felt much more relaxed. Grumbling something, Feiyuan walked off into the distance. Sherman turned and walked back to the river.

Now, apart from the glistening river water, he could see almost nothing. Sherman groped his way slowly toward the riverside. He recalled there were some poplars there. The boxes weren't far from the poplars. He stretched out his hand and felt a tree trunk, and then another. Great!

"Little Leaf! Little Leaf!"

When he shouted, he heard alarm in his voice. No one answered him. A campfire began to burn. It was like the earlier one, smoldering and producing dense smoke. Sherman covered his nose with a handkerchief and walked past the dark fire. After a few steps, he bumped into a wooden box and nearly fell. He felt his way to the opening of the box, bent over, and went in. Inside was bedding. And something hard—a flashlight. He fiddled with it a few times; the battery was dead. He heard the moan of an old person. Ah, someone was here! Smoke from the campfire floated in with the wind. The acrid smell made them sneeze. The old man looked outside and said, "Wonderful, great!"

"Are you the gardener, sir?"

"Don't ask that. When you arrived, the dogs didn't bark, did they? You must smell familiar, so they didn't bark. Listen: that large fish is swimming past again."

Sherman also heard the fish swimming. It was strange: it didn't make a sound, so how could he hear it? But he did. The big fish swam slowly, as if conducting an inspection. When Sherman heard the fish, something warm and strange sprang from his heart. A hairy creature approached. It was a dog, and it definitely wasn't little.

"It's your dog, sir."

"Did you smell it? It ate a corpse again."

The dog kept sniffing Sherman from head to toe. Sherman wondered if it was trying to decide where to bite him.

"Do I smell like a dead person?" he asked the old man.

"Well, a little."

While they were talking, the dog suddenly jumped out of the box—in response to shouting outside. Sherman raised himself up enough to look outside and saw that the campfire had turned into a large bright fire, which was reflected in the river. Although he'd heard someone shout, he couldn't see anyone. It seemed those inhabitants of the boxes were in the river, or in a cave. Sherman climbed out of the wooden box and walked toward the campfire. It looked close, but he walked a long way before reaching it. He tripped over something underfoot: it was a person lying on the ground. Three others were with him, all lying on their stomachs. The person told Sherman to lie down as they were doing. He said, "Otherwise, the fire will incinerate you." After Sherman lay down, he asked the man if he had seen Little Leaf. After laughing for a moment, the man said that Sherman was "behind the times."

All of a sudden, the wind shifted direction, and tongues of flames licked them. Sherman saw that the others kept their faces close to the ground, and so he did, too. Soon, the fire had burned the weeds around them and moved past them. Sherman, however, just felt a little hot, and his rubber shoes smelled terrible from being burned. The person next to him stood up, as did the other three. They warded off the smoke with their hands, as if looking at the stars, but no stars were in the sky. Except for the fire, it was dark everywhere. That old man said, "We should go back." Sherman asked where they were going. The man next to him said, "Where? Home. Everyone here lives in the heart of Pebble Town. Look at the shooting stars in the sky. We plan to call this place 'Garden of Shooting Stars.'"

But Sherman didn't see any shooting stars. However, the word "garden" reminded him of some other things. The others made their way into the wooden boxes at the riverside, leaving Sherman standing alone watching the fire. The fire slowly burned out. Several dogs came over and sniffed at his legs, but they didn't bite him. "Dogs, ah, dogs, am I dying?" he kept repeating.

He walked back and forth along the river, listening to the large fish swimming. At dawn, he finally heard Little Leaf calling him. She and Marco scrambled up from the riverbank and walked over.

"Where did the two of you spend the night, Little Leaf?"

"Ha! Papa, we were busy with the durian trees. It's the first time we'd seen that kind of tree, and we were so excited . . ."

Suddenly, a filthy dog pounced on her. She shouted "Ouch!" as she fell. She stared straight ahead, like a dead person. Marco kept shouting at her and lightly patting her face. Sherman also shouted at her. After a while, she finally revived, and the color returned to her face.

"Where did it bite you?" Sherman asked immediately.

"It didn't. That wasn't a dog. That's, that's my auntie."

"Your aunt? You have no aunt!" Sherman said sternly.

Little Leaf began laughing and said, "Oh, I forgot. You and Mama are orphans. What does it mean to be an orphan? Marco, do you know?"

Marco shook his head blankly and rolled his eyes, looking distressed. Sherman asked if they could take him to see the garden. They held out their hands and said no, because "It's broad daylight now."

"Oh, so the garden isn't supposed to be exposed to light," Sherman said, purposely acting scornful.

"No, no," Little Leaf said. "The sun shines everywhere in the garden. It's just that in the daylight, you can't find it. Give it a little thought. Durians and bananas aren't native to the frontier."

"But I saw the gardener."

"Did you? Actually, it isn't his garden. It has nothing to do with him. That's his wishful thinking. Papa, why haven't you gone home yet? There's no place for you to rest here. Everyone here sleeps during the day. Go on back."

Sherman thought it was because he had disturbed her that his daughter urged him to leave. What did she want to do? She didn't say. She and Marco hustled him off to the road and then turned and ran back. Sherman was too tired to keep his eyes open. He'd better go home.

By the time he woke up back at home it was afternoon. Yuanqing was back. She asked him sullenly what he had said to the sailor downstairs, because he had mocked her and wouldn't let her pass.

She put a paring knife in her satchel; only then could she charge past his blockade. She blamed Sherman and Little Leaf for thinking only of themselves and leaving no way out for her. And if the man blocked her way again, she would have to fight him to the death.

"I didn't say a thing to him. He's nuts. He thinks he's a curtain. You're not the only one he blocked. He blocked everyone," Sherman pleaded.

Yuanqing sneered. Just then, a bird flew in through the window and fell to the floor. Sherman bent down and looked. It wasn't a bird; it was a rooster. It was dead. He wouldn't have thought that a rooster could fly this high!

"See? We'll all end up like this rooster. Little Leaf is smart—she found a way to leave this place."

As his wife talked, it occurred to Sherman that Little Leaf had discussed this with her mother.

"The roof leaked again last night. The repairs didn't do any good. So I simply set up a tent in the room."

Sherman had already noticed the tent. He felt a bit uncomfortable.

They ate their meal in silence. Sherman wanted to go out. Yuanqing held him back, telling him to drive the sailor away. Sherman agreed.

But he looked everywhere downstairs without seeing a sign of him. A neighbor told him the sailor had returned to his ship. Before going, he had bade farewell to many people in the building and asked them to let Sherman know that he would come back to see him next year. "Your wife Yuanqing hacked at his hand. Did she hate him that much?" the neighbor said, staring at Sherman. Sherman blushed. He noticed that the neighbor hadn't talked about her "temper," but about "hate." Sherman was imagining what Yuanqing looked like when she hacked the sailor with a paring knife. His eyelids twitched. At home, she didn't even dare kill a chicken.

He went back upstairs and asked Yuanqing, "Did you really cut him with a knife?"

"I did, because I had no other way to get into the building. I aimed for him each time, but the knife only cut through air. Why did such a strange thing have to happen to me? Just tell me that!"

At the end, she was screaming, as if fighting with Sherman. Sherman covered his ears and escaped downstairs.

A long time after this incident, when Sherman had nearly forgotten it, he saw the sailor again. The sailor had lost so much weight, and his gray hair and beard hadn't been cut for such a long time, that he was hard to recognize. He sat in Liujin's garden drinking tea. When Sherman spotted him there, he wanted to walk away, but Liujin greeted him loudly and invited him to join them.

The sailor's eyes were dull, and he was preoccupied as he held a cup.

Liujin said, "He's leaving tomorrow. I went with him to his mother's grave. It's unlikely that he can live here as his mother did. He's tried it."

In the shadows of the trees, Liujin's face looked thin. Sherman thought she was something of a stranger. What had she been doing recently? She called the sailor "Axiang." They seemed to have known each other a long time. When Liujin said "he's tried it," Sherman recalled that this person had pretended to be a curtain downstairs.

How strange! Although the three of them were sitting there, as in the past Sherman still sensed a snow leopard walking back and forth under the table.

"What's new with the project in the foothills of the snow mountain?" Sherman asked Liujin.

"They say they've built a new city that's connected with ours. It's hard to imagine."

As she spoke, Liujin drew back, as if she felt a wind blowing over from the snow mountain. Sherman thought to himself: *Why hasn't that bird come out?* His gaze fell to the sailor's wrist: he saw the scar. A large watch hid it, but one could still see the deep mark from the knife. Why had Yuanqing done this? What was she afraid of? Sherman thought this person was actually very gentle—not the kind of person you had to take a knife to. So Yuanqing must have gone crazy. Why had Yuanqing been so afraid that she'd gone mad? In his mind's eye, Sherman saw his wife wielding a paring knife and ferociously hacking at the man in front of him. Just then, the sailor looked at him, and Sherman felt himself tremble a little. Suddenly, he heard the loud sound of a frog croaking, but only once. And he couldn't be sure where the sound came from. Was he hallucinating?

"Axiang, do you have pets?—such as turtles, guinea pigs, white mice, and the like? While at sea, these animals could tell you the correct time," Liujin said.

When the sailor heard this, he stared straight ahead, apparently daydreaming. Sherman thought, *Liujin is good at talking; she's an invaluable treasure.* He smiled a little. The snow leopard squatted at his feet, warming his insteps. He didn't hear what the sailor said because he was mumbling. Then he stood up, said goodbye, and left the courtyard.

"Sherman, where do you live? This is a small town, but somehow I sense that you live far away. Maybe across the snow mountain?"

As Liujin spoke, she was also listening. Sherman wondered if she was listening for the frog.

"I do live quite far away. My roof leaks. It's been repaired several times, but never satisfactorily. But because of Axiang, I became more optimistic, and so even I would like to see him off."

"Tomorrow is a day off. Let's both go," Liujin said.

"Okay, but don't wait for me. If I'm not there by nine o'clock, just go ahead without me."

Liujin thought Sherman was strange. She really was listening for the frog. She found only one and dug a ditch near the irises so that it could squat there.

Sherman was thinking as he walked. When he had almost reached Feiyuan's small shop, he made up his mind: he would not go with

Liujin to see the sailor off—because he was too ashamed to show his face. At this moment, he suddenly understood Yuanqing's crazy behavior: at the gate to their building, the sailor had been acting as an invisible obstacle that he and Yuanqing couldn't cross over. That explained why Yuanqing took a knife along to deal with it. She was a courageous woman. But this was from his and Yuanqing's viewpoint. What significance did the sailor see in all of this? Ah, ah! So many webs were woven together! And what about Liujin? It seemed she hadn't met any obstacles she couldn't get across. She was a heroine.

As soon as he entered Feiyuan's small store, Sherman froze in amazement, because the sailor was sitting at the third table facing the window. He should have noticed Sherman, but he didn't because his gaze was fixed on a certain place. Sherman evaded him and went into the kitchen in back.

Feiyuan frowned, pointed outside, and said softly, "He wants to go, but I'm worried that he'll have an accident. I don't want to see him have an accident right after leaving my shop, as his mother did. He's still young."

Sherman placed the roasted mutton kebabs on a plate and carried them out to the customers. The sailor was waving something away with his hands. Sherman thought he was driving away fingerlings. Had they blocked his line of vision? Or was his mother in the dark corner across the way? Feiyuan was calling him, "Axiang, Axiang." Axiang opened his mouth, revealing two rows of snow-white teeth. It was the first time Sherman had noticed how sharp his teeth were! How could anyone have teeth like this? Could he have gone to a dentist and had his teeth sharpened this way? Sherman was so nervous that he almost dropped the plate.

"Just take a look at his teeth," Feiyuan said, frowning. "This is the crux of the matter. I feel I should apologize to his mother. My heart aches."

"His mother wouldn't blame you."

"Of course not. But I . . . but I . . ."

Feiyuan's jaw dropped: he was stunned at what he saw over there. Axiang was raising a bloody hand. He was bleeding from the scar that Sherman had seen before. What was he doing?

Taking a bandage that Feiyuan gave him, Sherman hurried over to dress the wound for him. While Sherman was doing that, Axiang's whole body started to shake as he bent over the table. Sherman asked if he was leaving the next day. Axiang nodded his head decisively. He had injured himself on purpose. Why? As a reminder of Yuanqing wounding him?

He propped himself up and looked at Sherman. He seemed to have something to say, but he held back. Sherman encouraged him to say what was on his mind.

"Can you take me to the hostel?" he asked bashfully.

He leaned on Sherman and, dragging his feet as though intoxicated, walked outside.

His room was in the hostel's basement. He explained that this was the only kind of place he could afford because he had stayed too long and run out of money. He said it wouldn't turn out well if he went back, because his skipper wanted to kill him. "He would throw me directly into the sea." That's what he said about the skipper. That dark, gloomy room was filthy. Another person was staying there, too, snoring in the other bed. Axiang asked Sherman to sit on a recliner. He himself slouched on the bed and smoked.

A glow flashed in the corner of the dark room, making the atmosphere strained. Axiang said it was a mini alarm that he had bought with the intention of taking it to the ship. "It will keep me alert. It just lights up instead of making a sound. It's exactly what I was looking for.

"Living on the ocean, your nerves are numb. Everything has lost its meaning. If you don't have a way to stay alert, it can be really dangerous."

Raising himself up a little, he pointed at the man in the other bed and told Sherman the man had been sleeping three days and three nights. He was also a sailor. He seemed to have broken down. Axiang went on to say that he would board the ship the next morning, but his biggest worry was not knowing if the skipper still wanted him. The skipper wouldn't tell him, because he loved to ambush people. If he were suddenly thrown into the sea as shark food, he would narrowly escape death. One of his shipmates had experienced this: he had somehow managed to climb back onto the ship; now he was a cook. Axiang still remembered the way this cook had looked when he climbed back onto the ship. He was bleeding: a shark had bitten off a third of the sole of his left foot.

"My mother also worked on this ship. I replaced her. I was twenty-two before I boarded that ship. Before that, I took care of my ill father. Working on the ship was my lifelong dream. Can you understand that kind of longing?"

The alarm light in the corner went out. A smothered cry for help came from the corridor. Sherman got up and headed for the door, but was unable to find it even after groping a long time. Where had the door gone? Frustrated as he leaned against the wall, he called softly, "Axiang! Axiang!"

Axiang had disappeared. Sherman felt all over the empty bed. The man in the opposite bed sat up. He was eating something.

"Hey, buddy, don't bother looking for him. He works the night shift. He lied to you about being a sailor. He kept telling me that, too. In fact, he works in the produce firm behind this place. All year long, he wears that old sailor uniform. To each his own."

Sherman stood up and asked why he couldn't find the door. The other person laughed.

"This room extends in all directions. Just pick up your feet and you'll be outside." Sherman tried it, and sure enough, he walked outside. Behind him, an alarm went off like crazy. He looked back. The whole building was in chaos; people kept running out. Sherman strode quickly to the street and saw Axiang approaching him, laughing uproariously.

"I bought a train ticket. Sherman, we won't see each other again. Can't you see me off?"

He was a bit dirty, but the smell of fresh grass mixed with flowers wafted from him. Sherman couldn't help but take a deep breath and draw that scent into his lungs. What did "won't see each other again" mean?

Sherman wondered if Liujin was this person's lover. Would there be a scene if she saw him off alone tomorrow? He felt discouraged about his future, and slightly queasy. He accidentally stepped on a passerby's foot. The person swore at him.

Sherman had been awake for quite a while but didn't want to get up. A lot of little things were clamoring and fluttering in the air. The window clattered as it was blown by the wind. All of this made him fearful. He asked himself, "What am I afraid of?" But his voice scared him even more. Was he sick? He had lived this long without ever being sick. He heard Yuanqing talking with a colleague in the other room. At first, he heard only a buzzing sound. Then suddenly a sentence leaped out: "Our daughter Little Leaf is an extraordinary woman!"

Yuanqing looked exuberant. She went out the door talking with her colleague.

Now Sherman remembered the orphanage head's words. At the time, he had been sitting on the bed worrying. The man was conducting a bed check. In the moonlight, the man's face looked like that of an old monkey. "Sherman, Sherman, if you run away, you can never come back." After saying this, he stood at the door for a long time before leaving uneasily. Now these words reverberated in Sherman's ears. He was cold all over. It seemed he really was sick. His mouth even smelled sour. He was tired. Back then when he had run from the orphanage all the way down to this place, he hadn't felt this tired.

In his dazed state, he saw a little grayish-blue bird hop onto the table from the window. It was chirping. Ah, a bird! He felt feverish. His head heavy and his feet light, he walked to the room in front to drink some water. The bird followed him. Sherman thought, *It would be splendid to spend my remaining days with this bird! How long would the bird live?* When he was about to fall asleep, the bird chirped again and again, and Sherman felt grateful as he drifted off.

Downstairs, Yuanqing described Little Leaf's circumstances to her colleague. She gestured a lot, but this didn't help much to make her points clear. Her colleague opened her eyes wide in surprise.

"She's a happy-go-lucky girl. Have I told you that? She—ah, she dares to go anywhere. And she's the same wherever she is. She's doing much better than I am—for example, in those places where ghosts come and go."

She laughed shrilly and then strolled again hand in hand with her colleague in front of the building. They were close friends, so they talked about everything.

"Did you say that Little Leaf has gone to the riverside? There's a gangster mob of beggars there."

"It might be the riverside. It might be the mountain. Are they any different? This child isn't like either Sherman or me. I can't explain it, but anyhow, she's different."

She stopped walking and stared at that little bird that had run out of the building. She had seen this bird many times. She had no idea why it always ran and never flew.

Chapter 5

THE BABY

Qiming tossed the baby into the air three more times. The little girl chortled.

Early one morning, Qiming saw that the baby had been placed in the grass. When he picked her up, he found she was wet—either from her urine or the dew. He thought this was Nancy's fault. He didn't understand how a woman could be so hardhearted. When he looked up, however, he saw her holding her head as she paced in the small lane. She seemed to be in unbearable pain.

"What's the baby's name?"

"Liujin."

"Oh, what a pretty name! It will remind people of Pebble Town. She's wet, Ms. Nancy."

"I know, I know. Oh, I have a splitting headache. Am I going to die?"

As she talked, she turned away. Qiming had to continue holding the child.

Later, he took the baby to her home, where a startled José opened the door.

"Oh, old Qi, old Qi, I'm so grateful to you. Did she chuck the baby aside? She finally cast her away! I was worried and was about to go looking for them."

He started frantically changing the diaper. The baby was unusually quiet.

When Qiming left the building, a cold wind blew him sideways, and then he heard the baby's loud, clear crying. It didn't seem that such powerful wails could come from such a little baby. While she was crying, the snow mountain appeared in front of Qiming, as did a snow leopard squatting under a tree with a young woman. Her hair was black, but he couldn't get a good look at her face. At the time, Qiming didn't yet realize that this baby girl would captivate him for a long time. He felt distracted on his way home.

He saw Nancy in the distance. She was talking animatedly with the institute director. Had she recovered—or hadn't she ever been sick? She showed no regret about leaving the baby behind with Qiming. Was that because she trusted him completely? Qiming detoured, avoiding the two of them. He had a lot of work today, but the incident involving the child had disturbed him. Because this kind of thing had occurred several times, Qiming now felt something akin to a father's love for this baby. He had also noticed that when Nancy was with the baby, she was really miserable. There must be a knot in her heart that she couldn't loosen. Otherwise, what mother wouldn't adore this pretty, healthy baby? Qiming was sorry that such a warm woman didn't love her child.

Standing in the pavilion in the middle of the garden, Nancy talked with the director. Qiming overheard their conversation when he was tidying up the garden. The director seemed to be urging her to go to work, but she hadn't made up her mind.

"When I gave birth to her, I saw the garden—the banyan tree was so close that I could stretch out my hand and grab the aerial roots. I thought I might hurt this child, but once I left her, my legs went weak."

"You need to go to work. My dear, what you need is work. Then everything will be fine."

The director patted Nancy's thin shoulders in a motherly way.

They were talking loudly, so Qiming heard everything. He also saw a bird with a long showy tail land on the pavilion's railing. The bird wasn't at all afraid of the women. Qiming, who had lived so long in the guesthouse, had never seen such a beautiful bird. It had probably flown over from the snow mountain. Nancy was pretty, but her beauty wasn't the same as that of the goddess he loved. Nancy's beauty was scented, but the woman he adored had only color and form, like a painting on a wall.

Qiming heard Nancy agree to go to work. The director said she would work far away so she didn't have to come home every day. Once a week would be about right. The two of them left the pavilion arm in arm; Nancy was crying. He heard the last thing she said:

"She's a wisp of smoke I brought from my hometown."

Qiming thought, *It's awful if she thinks of her own daughter in this way. She must have been seeing her former self in her baby. Is she really going to completely change into another person?* After tidying the garden, he headed over to work on the sewer in the backyard. The fallen leaves had stopped it up. As he made his way over there with his tools, Grace—looking like a ghost—came up carrying a paper bag. She shot furtive glances in all directions. When she reached Qiming, she pulled hard on him, wanting him to squat down with her in the shrubs. Qiming wasn't pleased. She opened the paper bag and took out a small carton. She said that her dog was inside that carton, and she wanted to bury it in the garden. She asked him not to tell anyone from the institute.

"If they find out, that'll be the end of me," she said as she dug a hole with a small iron spade.

"Is it that serious? Then why did you tell me?"

"Old Qi, who can keep a secret from you? You're the eagle here."

She placed the small carton into the hole, cried softly for a short time, and then covered it with dirt. Qiming felt that her soul was joining her pet in the earth.

"Ms. Grace, you have to take care of yourself." Qiming frowned as he looked at this skinny woman.

"My health isn't important. Old Qi, if your living space shrank, getting smaller and smaller, so small that it couldn't hold even a coffin, what would you do?"

"What?" Old Qi was at a loss.

"I'm talking about that baby. She cries day and night. Lee is very sick. He hasn't gotten out of bed for a week. What a strange baby! Just when Lee fell ill, the dog died. The dog was afraid of that baby. I could see that."

"Ah, the baby. It's a really adorable baby."

Qiming noticed Lee entering the guesthouse. The man's face was pallid and his hair disheveled. His clothing looked ragged, and he glanced in all directions. Qiming turned and looked back: Grace had tamped down the earth so there was no trace of what she had done. Qiming was still watching closely when Lee appeared in front of him.

"Old Qi, do you think we'll have a snowstorm tonight?"

Lee sat on the ground, as if too exhausted to move any more. He also pressed his hand into the left side of his chest, and said he wanted to lie down here and get a whiff of the wind from the snow mountain. His eyes were dull, as if he were dying. Then he lay down on his stomach, his face pressed on the ground. Qiming asked if he wanted help. He said no. Then he said, "I'm listening to the dog barking."

Because he still had a lot of work, Qiming left him and went into the guesthouse.

Lee breathed the wind for a long time and still didn't want to get up, but a large flock of crows showed up, jumping back and forth. They defecated next to his head and made a mess of the grass. A group of visitors also arrived. He heard some old people walking toward him and crying out in surprise. He knew they misunderstood his lying on the ground, so he sat up at once. They asked "Do you want some help?" Lee shook his head wearily, but they persisted in asking. Finally growing impatient, he shouted: "That garden has sunk into the ground. You can listen to it, but you can't see it!"

"What? Just listen? Can't we see it?"

"Did we come for nothing?"

"Doesn't the sign say, 'garden in the air' . . ."

The old people were chattering and asking questions, but no one answered them. Later, they took some bread out of their bags and started eating. They grumbled that they shouldn't have come. After eating, they threw their bread wrappers one after the other at Lee. He stood up, wanting to leave, but they held him back. They didn't want to let go of him until he told them where the garden was. Being pushed and pulled, Lee broke into a cold sweat. His vision blurred. He said weakly, "I'm getting sick."

"Really?" they asked.

One of them said he had seen the garden in the air, and so the old men and women left Lee behind and headed in the direction the man pointed out. Now, Lee really couldn't see anything. He squatted and touched the ground with both hands to keep from falling. After a while, he heard José talking and the baby crying. Hadn't he come to the garden to get away from the baby? Lee heard the old people surrounding José and the baby, tut-tutting and admiring her. They used such words as rose, lemon, orange, evening primrose, durian, ginkgo, and so on. Lee thought it sounded as if they were describing the baby, but what were they really thinking? Could the baby be the garden in the air that they were looking for? He thought back to the spiritual agony caused by José's baby when he was at home. After a while, he felt much better, and he could see again. He saw the group of people walk away from the entrance. When he turned around, he bumped his head on the banyan's aerial roots; he warded them off with his hand. The air rippled with the strong scent of the plants, and in an instant he felt refreshed. The pavilion was behind the banyan. Someone was standing in the pavilion and looking out.

"Old Qi!!" Lee shouted loudly.

But he couldn't hear his own voice; he heard only the baby's crying. He gestured, but old Qi turned his back. When he looked again, the small pavilion seemed to be hanging in midair. He couldn't see the grass under his feet, although when he took a few steps, he could still feel himself trampling on the ground. He made up his mind to go inside the building and meet up with old Qi. He would ask him to clarify some things. When he headed in that direction, the small guesthouse retreated. He stopped and looked all around, but a vast expanse of whiteness had settled everywhere; he seemed to be standing in a void. A strange bird was making a drilling sound. Even though Lee covered his ears, he could still hear it.

Qiming stood in front of the window in the guesthouse auditorium and said to Grace, "Look, your husband is still really energetic." Below, Lee stood in a bosk, seemingly smirking. He was standing right on the spot where Grace had buried the dog. Grace stared nervously at her husband and answered Qiming, "He's unstable." No sooner had she said this than a gecko appeared on the windowsill. Grace screamed; she thought a snake had bitten her right hand. But when she looked more closely, she saw only the gecko. It was about two feet away from her.

"Ms. Grace, are you sick?" Qiming asked. He also saw the gecko.

"I think my husband is at a dead end. What do you think, Mr. Qi?"

"I think there's no need to worry. Your husband can't be at a dead end. The frontier is so broad. Listen! There's a long-life bird—two of them! Ha, Mr. Lee has heard them, too!"

Grace also saw two small celadon-colored birds. It was the first time she'd heard this bird called "long-life bird"! She thought Qiming was quite humorous. She thought she and Lee had been wearing white mourning flowers for such a long time and now the dog had finally died. What if the dog had also been a long-life dog?

"There are a lot of long-life things in the city, aren't there?"

"Yes, so you needn't worry about Mr. Lee. He's far from the end of his life. He's crying softly. That's because he's happy."

A continuous explosive sound came from afar. It was from a construction project on the snow mountain. Grace said, "They're going to implode the snow mountain. I'll have no place to hide at night."

Nancy had been working in the office for three days—just reading the files because the institute hadn't assigned any specific work. Her office was on the second floor. From the window, she looked out on the rocky hill outside the wall. On it were weeds, and a small black-colored bird hopped in and out of the weeds and sang shrilly, like porcelain being smashed on concrete. Now and then, one or two people walked past the hill, gleaning scraps.

When the sun was setting, the gleaners walked faster, as if in a panic—as though they had reached the end of the earth. The person in the section office next to Nancy's told her that this rocky hill was called the gate of hell. She recalled that she and José had gotten lost here; it still felt spooky. Back then, she had certainly seen the Design Institute, but she had thought it was some abandoned houses. At twilight that day, as the sun was setting, these houses had looked very shabby. Nancy had been terrified at the sight of them, so she hadn't mentioned them to José. Now facing this rocky hill, Nancy's emotions rose and fell as some strange thoughts popped up.

First, the institute director: Nancy felt that she and the director had known one another well before she had come to Pebble Town. She had simply forgotten this. Maybe the director had been her teacher, or maybe she was the mother of one of her colleagues. She was very sure that they had spent some time together. Nancy was dismayed that she'd completely forgotten this. The feeling was accentuated when those little black-colored birds all returned at dusk to the thicket on the rocky hill. At times like this, she sensed clearly that there were many empty spaces in her memory, and each one of those spaces must have held the most amazing incidents of her life.

Next, her precious daughter Liujin: she had fled from Liujin, left her behind with José, and hidden here because she couldn't stand the baby's crying. And because of the baby's gaze. Her daughter was so little, and yet her gaze was so bright—not like a baby's gaze. Nancy had grown up in Smoke City and was accustomed to people's blurry expressions. And so when her eyes met her daughter's, she felt hollow inside, as if she were going mad. Her daughter's crying was kind of strange. She didn't seem to cry because of feeling uncomfortable. Rather, her crying sounded threatening. José was infinitely patient in taking care of their daughter; he never stood up to her will. In the apartment, he scurried back and forth waiting on her, and this annoyed Nancy. From time to time when her resentment rose to a certain level, she would purposely carry her daughter outside and place her on the ground. Her daughter was clever. At first, she continued crying, and then she would calm down on the ground. Nancy realized that her large eyes could even follow the birds in the sky; she was a really precocious baby. As she sat in the office thinking of her daughter, all at once she felt that this baby was an abyss, a quagmire, and she herself was sinking into it step by step. Each time she sank a little more, she felt she was drowning. She had given her daughter such a pretty name: Had she hoped it would help to control the evil?

She also had a strange feeling about her husband. Previously, while in Smoke City, she'd been close to him. They were frequently on the same wavelength. Their first day here, she felt her husband's train of thought slowing down on this rocky hill: he seemed to have grown a shell and wrapped himself in it. When the crazy man had abandoned them on the hill, she had squatted on the ground and sighed—not because she regretted coming here, but because a feeling of loneliness had surged up within her. Yet, José thought it was regret. She knew, too, that José's train of thought wasn't static; it was simply that she couldn't penetrate it. Now, she watched these little black birds fly up from the thicket and disappear into the clouds without a trace. She felt disconsolate. She still couldn't make up her mind about one thing—would she face retribution for discarding her baby daughter? She consoled herself that in any case José was there with the baby, and that would preserve her indirect relationship with her daughter. In this transparent city, it was best to keep personal relationships indirect.

Just then, Nancy looked up and saw the large gecko on the ceiling. The geckoes here were huge! It had apparently been here for a few hours.

"Ms. Nancy, it's time to quit for the day."

It was a black person speaking. He smiled a little, revealing bright teeth. When Nancy had first arrived, she'd been startled when she ran into him because she hadn't imagined there'd be an African black person at the Design Institute—and one speaking her language. The black person's name was Ying. Slender and handsome, he was about thirty years old. He showed up at Nancy's office several times a day; he seemed to be the timekeeper. Sometimes he said, "It's an hour and fifteen minutes until quitting time." Sometimes he said, "Look how fast the time is flying. We've been working for two hours." Nancy couldn't figure out what he had in mind. Once she had gone to his office and seen a lot of skulls hanging from the ceiling. Ying had the curtains drawn. The room was dark and terrifying. He was drawing a blueprint by the faint light of a reading lamp. He looked a little fierce, like a black leopard, but when he looked up and saw Nancy, he smiled kindly and affably.

The canteen was some distance from the office; they walked there together. Now and then, Ying bent down to pick wildflowers. He told Nancy he had lived in Africa since before he was eight, tramping from country to country. The institute director's father had adopted him and brought him here. Unfortunately, the old man had died soon afterward.

"As soon as I came to Pebble Town, I became fanatically interested in studying. I studied and studied and became the person I am now. Who would think that I used to be a vagrant child?"

Ying also said that nighttime was the hardest for him. He felt that his black body had disappeared, yet he could hear the African drums of the ancient mother earth. Sometimes he went out to the fields and bayed at the moon like a wild animal.

"Why are you named Ying?" Nancy asked.

"The old man gave me this name. It's lovely, and I like it. Do you?"

"Mm. I'm imagining how it would feel if my body vanished."

Nancy slept in a small room next to the office. Now she started having insomnia. She walked to the dimly lit corridor: a cracking sound was coming from the office. She pressed her ear against the tightly closed door and listened; it sounded like skulls bumping against each other. She had seen only the black man's office. Could skulls be hanging in every office? A small animal scratched her on the instep. She looked down: it was a gray kitten. When she picked it up, it meowed loudly. It sounded like her daughter. She let it go at once, her heart pounding. She remembered the director's warning: "Don't leave the room." On a night like this, the Design Institute, which was built on the rocky hill, seemed like a giant grave. She even saw some rats, holding something like meat in their mouths and scampering quickly along the wall. She returned to the room. She had no sooner sat down than she heard her daughter's crying again. Ah, it turned out to be another kitten—a black one. Its blood-red mouth was wide open, facing her. Nancy's mind went blank. Her hand shook as she opened the door and let the kitten out.

Sleeping in the office, Nancy had particularly deep and wild dreams, as though she were walking in a no-return grotto heading to the earth's core. She stopped from time to time to ask herself: Had she always been longing to come down into the depths of this place? There were no small animals in the grotto. She couldn't even hear her own footsteps. And yet lights glimmered faintly in the distance.

Three of these lights alternately ascended and descended as though dancing. When she walked ahead, she felt lighthearted—ah, at last she had broken free! She'd broken free at last!

One afternoon, as she stood on the hill enjoying the breeze, she suddenly noticed José standing and holding Liujin in some couch grass in the distance. Liujin seemed to have grown a lot. She even had little braids. Why didn't he come over here? As she ran over to them, the wind blew harder.

"Nancy, Nancy, stop! The baby will cry!" José shouted.

And then, she heard the shrill crying. Nancy suddenly dropped to her knees as if her legs were broken. She saw José leaving.

Ever since Nancy had abandoned the baby, José had brought her up alone. The rhythm of his life had changed completely. Except for asking Grace to watch her when he went shopping, he didn't leave her for a moment. He noticed that Grace was afraid of the baby—as though the baby weren't a baby, but a little animal that would bite people. But José had no other option. After leaving his daughter in the playpen next to Grace, he ran down the stairs. He was uneasy as he shopped, always afraid that the sulky Grace might mistreat his daughter. Luckily, nothing like that had happened. But it was plain that Grace didn't want to hold the girl.

Liujin was growing up remarkably fast. When she was only three months old, she ate the same food as adults. José chopped meat and vegetables and boiled them in rice gruel for her. She ate happily—and she ate a lot. The baby didn't sleep much, so he was busy all the time. The two of them fell asleep and got up at nearly the same time. Over time, his daughter cried less often, and José no longer felt as stressed out as before. But it was still stressful to make eye contact with her unusually bright eyes. He sensed reproach in her gaze. One morning after they got up, Liujin pointed at the drapes and screamed time after time, just like an older child. José walked over and opened the drapes. Outside, the sky and the earth were spinning: he nearly fainted.

He couldn't get a good look at the memories that his daughter had been storing up. He wanted to observe them calmly, but he couldn't. His life had become a muddled mess.

One day, he pressed his cheek to his daughter's, and told her about his life. As he did so, his daughter babbled. Was she interacting with him? Or simply speaking her own language at the same time? José was telling his story in the voice of another person—an ephemeral wispy youth who liked to sit on the roof and play with his pigeons. As the wind tapped on the skylight, he talked and talked in a thin voice, his daughter babbling along. The various sounds converged into something a little like a lullaby. But his daughter was so excited that probably no one would be able to put her to sleep. José thought perhaps Nancy had been pregnant with her for many years, or maybe she'd been born while they were still in Smoke City. She certainly wasn't like most babies. She was even capable of narrating. It would be wonderful if he could understand her stories. Then when he looked at her eyes, he wouldn't be nervous. After he transformed himself into a youth in his stories, he felt some knots in his heart had been untied. Once more, he had prospects in his life. He even saw the possibility of communicating with his daughter. He got the housework out of the way quickly and bathed little Liujin. Then he went on telling his stories.

The baby's days began filling with happiness. Whenever José bent down to pick her up and tell stories, she kicked her little feet happily in the cradle. And so father and daughter, faces touching, kept on talking. The baby was still babbling broken syllables, but with time they became more and more focused and enchanting. These snatches of syllables stimulated José's thinking. Bit by bit, he felt he no longer controlled his own narration: more and more blanks appeared in his stories. He loved this new narrative style: these stories filled with blank spaces were both simple and a little hard to explain. In the past, he hadn't known he could tell stories this way. Afterward, even when he was doing housework, recalling the happy moments gave him great pleasure. He realized that his daughter was his invaluable treasure. Naturally he also knew that his daughter would grow up and have her own language. What would his communication with her be like then?

José needed to straighten up the cradle, so he placed the baby on the bed. After a while, he heard her kicking hard and shouting, "Bagu! Bagu . . ." José turned and saw that the skylight had been opened, though he didn't know when. The blue sky was full of birds. He'd never seen this before! He ran to the window and saw numerous birds covering the entire skylight. The scent of birds suffused the room. His daughter was even more upset and kicked without stopping. Her little face was red. José picked her up and brought his cheek next to hers. Suddenly he heard her say very clearly, "Mama." That's when José remembered that Nancy had been gone for ten days. He was a bit hurt. At the same time, he understood a little: what Nancy had left behind in the home wasn't her daughter, but herself—a past self of hers. And through caring for the baby, he had entered his wife's past. The birds slowly scattered, and the baby calmed down and stared with big solemn eyes.

"Mr. José, I saw Ms. Nancy. She says hello," Lee looked at him from the doorway.

"Ah, is she okay?"

"She looked fine. She said she can't leave the Design Institute. If I were she . . ."

José wondered what he wanted to say. This Lee's life was so difficult: How could he compare himself with Nancy? Nancy was healthy, except for being a little jumpy. Lee wasn't aware of what José thought of him. After looking for a while at the sky outside the skylight, he said to José, "These are all resident birds: their nests are in the poplar grove at the riverside. Their gatherings are regulated by an indescribable impulse. When I can't sleep, I think about their habits and paint pictures in my mind. Many birds are also on that hill, although it's another variety—black-colored. Ms. Nancy probably sees them every day. Is it good or bad for Pebble Town to have so many birds?"

José sensed that Lee was in a better mood, for he had said so much all at once. Could this be related to the death of their pet dog? How was the little dog connected with this family? The baby kicked him in the chest and said, "Bagu."

"Your daughter can talk! Wow! She's so adorable now! She fits in with our life here. Mr. José, I'm going over to the Design Institute soon. Is there anything you'd like me to tell your wife?"

"Just tell her we're fine, and tell her to take care of herself."

As José said this, he was kicked again. His daughter seemed to be giving him confidence, appreciating what he was doing. Or could this actually be Nancy admiring him? José beamed at this thought. He opened the drapes again and saw the bright, clean, blue sky; the birds had disappeared into thin air. If their scent hadn't lingered in the room, he would have forgotten them. From the apartment to the east came Lee's loud singing. This man was so strange. José remembered seeing the tropical garden at his place. Beginning last night, José felt he was at the center of the world. Now this feeling was even stronger. Could it be that everything revolved around him? Indeed, what kind of person was "José"? He heard Lee sing of a tortoise, and José trembled. Pebble Town residents really had many things in common. Their ideas and intentions were usually similar. At the end of José's field of vision were some vague contours: Was this the snow mountain? In the daytime, people talked of the mountain, and he could see it from a distance, but he hadn't been there even once. It was a locale that he absolutely did not understand. Could it be connected with his daughter's life? In Lee's song, the tortoise died, and José calmed down a little.

A long, long time ago, he and Nancy had stood on the iron bridge visualizing their future. They lived simple lives then, and they based all of their plans on the present reality. Although they weren't very content with the present, still—shrouded in the heavy smoke—the contours of things softened a lot. Oh, how the smoke had disguised the realities! Nancy couldn't see the truth at first, either. "I have some knots of past events in my mind that I can't untie." Nancy often said things like this. Now, he heard his daughter babbling at his chest, and he sort of understood what Nancy meant. He said, "As soon as that person pushed the window open, the smoke flowed into the room. He—he heard the people running below, and shouting . . . This building he lived in was swaying. How could this be? Well, it's true. Baby, he's dizzy from all of this. He recalls the iron bridge, and as soon as he does, he gets even dizzier." After he said this, he suddenly understood what he had not understood before. His daughter kept saying one syllable, "Poo, poo, poo . . ."

With his daughter in his arms, he took old Qi's pedicab over to the hill outside the Design Institute. On the way, his daughter's silence frightened him and he considered returning home. Her eyes looked dull, no longer like the eyes of an older child: they seemed to have regressed to the look of a baby. Did she know they were going to see her mother? Not knowing which office building Nancy was in, he hesitated as he stood on the rocky hill. Qi walked up to him and said she must be in the third building.

"She'll be sad that you've come here," Qi added.

Qi hadn't said a word the whole way here, and now he was actually saying something like this. José started to regret having come. He told Qi that he wanted to go back. Smiling slightly, Qi asked him to get into the pedicab. Just then, an old woman gleaner charged over to José, brandishing a twig and shouting slogans. José ducked at once, and the woman charged past. Beside him, Qi said, "I saw Nancy." José asked where Nancy was, and Qi replied that he couldn't say for sure. Anyhow, he had seen her—that's the way things were on this rocky hill.

All kinds of feelings welling up in his heart, José returned home with his daughter at twilight. He made up his mind not to go to

Nancy's workplace again. On the way home, Qi had told him that the institute director had probably made this arrangement. He went on to say that the director always had the interests of others at heart. No one was more concerned about others than she was, so one had better simply accept her arrangements, and in the end, something good would come of it. Listening to him, José recalled the first time the director had spoken of Qi to Nancy and him: she had described him as "a lovelorn janitor." So he, too, deeply acknowledged the director's greatness.

When he went to the market to buy noodles, he saw a wolf. No kidding—a wolf! It was huge—about the size of a pony—and standing next to the cabbage. No one walking past paid any particular attention to it. It was as if everyone thought it was a painting. Of course it wasn't a painting: it turned its head now and then and looked disdainfully at the whole scene. It also opened its mouth now and then, revealing buckteeth. Could it be a domesticated wolf? José had never seen one before, but he'd heard that wolves could be tamed. José didn't dare stare at it, for fear that it would sense his presence. He went around to the side where general merchandise was being sold, for there was an exit there. An old woman kept walking beside him, and now she started talking with him.

"A wolf came here a few times in the spring, but this is the first time a wolf has shown up in the market."

"Aren't any of you afraid?" José asked.

"Sure we are, but being afraid does no good. Everyone knows that. My legs are shaking, but what can I do? I can't outrun a wolf. And it's huge."

"It seems it doesn't want to eat anyone."

José wasn't very confident of this, and the old woman walked away without answering.

After leaving the market far behind, José kept looking back. He was still refuting the old woman—why did people have to go to the market? Why didn't they go to some smaller shops instead? Weren't there several of them in this town? But he felt vaguely that this was a weak argument: the wolf's might said it all.

When he had just reached the foot of the stairs at his apartment building, he heard his daughter crying. He raced upstairs, taking the steps two at a time.

"I thought something had happened to you," Grace said.

"Huh? I'm fine," he answered as he picked up his daughter.

Not until they were back in their own home did his daughter stop crying. José was preoccupied with thoughts of the wolf. He really wanted to tell his daughter about this. Opening her big eyes and looking at him, his daughter seemed to want to tell him something, too. Did she want to talk of the same thing? The dark rocky hill appeared in José's mind: on top of it was a view of an enormous wolf from behind. Grace probably knew he had run into a wolf, and that's why she'd spoken as she had. "Sweetheart, wolf. Sweetheart, wolf," he kept repeating to his daughter. Then he set her in her cradle and started to cook.

That evening, three birds were quarreling on his windowsill. They made three different sounds. José named them "time birds." He couldn't turn off the light because his daughter would cry if he did. He had to leave the light on all night. He woke up during the night, and saw that wolf's silhouette on the wall. His daughter was staring at the silhouette. The moment he made a sound, the silhouette disappeared. The "time birds" sang merrily outside. A bird that he had named "Future" sang even louder in a drawn-out tone, attracting José's attention. When José opened the drapes, they flew off.

Grace was knitting a sweater in her room, depressed. The baby's crying disturbed Lee too much. She used to think he would die of it because of his serious heart trouble. Now things had taken a turn for the better. Her husband was not only still alive, but he was feeling much better. So why did Grace still feel depressed? Even she couldn't explain it. For some reason, she felt vaguely that her husband's condition was an omen of approaching death. She understood very well that her husband's disease was incurable, and she knew how serious his condition really was. Even during their honeymoon, he'd been sick. He'd had this disease for more than twenty years.

As it happened, José's daughter was crying hard on the night their dog died. Lee had taken the last of his heart medicine. Gripping his chest, he half-lay on the bed and moaned. Grace urged him to go to the hospital, but he kept shaking his head. Grace wondered if he was planning a joint funeral for the dog and himself. Would he expect her to take care of it alone? But before daylight, the child suddenly stopped crying, and Lee dozed off. He slept a very long time, not awakening until the next night. After getting up, he ate a large meal, and groped his way through the dark to go outside. Grace was mourning their dog and paid no attention to her husband. She recalled only that he strolled around all night, and when he came back in the morning, he was covered in mud. That was unprecedented: he seldom went out at night for fear of falling down.

"The sound of the baby's crying reaches the farthest corners of the city—I walked around in order to find out. There's a two-story stone building holding many coffins. I stayed among the coffins. Grace, tell me: Why does the infant life beside us stimulate us so much? The baby girl inspires me greatly."

As Lee went on and on, Grace stood in front of the window and looked straight out from there: she saw an elm tree with many birds' nests in it. The radiant sun shone on the exuberant green leaves. Red wildflowers grew beneath the tree. The scenery outside their window was thriving with vitality. Grace felt the tide of life blowing against her face. Instinctively, she dodged away from it and retreated to the shadows beside the drapes.

Now, sitting in an armchair knitting a sweater, she recalled this incident. She thought one of the frontier's major characteristics was that the scenery outside exerted tremendous pressure on people. Every time before a major incident occurred in her life, the scenery

all around was filled with particularly intense intimations of it. She
had seldom experienced this when they lived in the interior. On the
nights when the baby cried so hard, a gale blew up. Each time she
sat up at midnight and turned the light on, she saw some dead twigs
poking through the curtain, reaching toward her on the bed. She had
no way to escape. Lee, though, didn't move: his body had stiffened,
as if he were dead.

Yet, in general she liked the scenery here. She and Lee used to
be melancholy. They had high expectations of life, but their vision
was always dull. The air and water on the frontier seemed to have
cleansed their spirits. This cleansing stimulated their desires and
enhanced their spiritual realm. When Grace was out walking, she
sometimes suddenly stopped in her tracks, listening to all kinds of
birds singing sweetly. She felt she was in a wonderland that she'd
never been to. There were many birds here. Grace plunged into
strange recollections.

Formerly, she and Lee had lived in a southern city. Later, every
few years, they had moved a certain distance to the north and settled
in a city there. This had gone on for more than ten years before they
finally decided to take the train to this northernmost place, Pebble
Town. Thinking back on those roller-coaster years, as well as the
several cities they had temporarily settled in, Grace sensed that something had been manipulating them all along. One night, in a city in
the interior, they had walked on a small street whose lights were out.
Lee had said to her, "Why do we always move north?" At the time,
Grace was gazing at the stars in the sky, and all at once a noiseless
glacial zone appeared in her mind. Lee had gone on, "I think the
most magical animal in the world is the penguin." Grace was too
startled to say a word. What made their thoughts move in the same
direction? But in the end they couldn't reach the polar region, and so
they had settled in this frontier town. The winters here were long and
frigid, but with central heating they didn't feel the glacial cold inside.
Here, Lee got considerable relief from his heart disease. More than

once, Grace had thought Pebble Town was their final destination. It wasn't likely that other places would have air like this and stillness like this. This was the best place they could ever find to live in this nation. Maybe it was because of this that Lee finally brought home a puppy, a miniature dog. Before this, they hadn't had pets and hadn't grown plants. When the puppy had just arrived, Grace wasn't sure she could take care of it; she felt quite conflicted. After a while, though, she considered it a member of the family. But the puppy didn't thrive in their little family. It was always "hanging by a thread." Gradually, Grace changed from being aloof toward it to sharing both joy and suffering with it. She worried about it all day long and took good care of it. But in the end, it mocked them by dying prematurely, leaving them with ghastly memories: it had been sick many times, and each time it twitched all over and foamed at the mouth.

Grace had some vivid memories of every city where they had lived. For example, Bell City had long, narrow, unfrequented streets. The shops at the sides of the roads were closed most of the time. Some drunks sat under the canopies in front of the bars. It was a sleepy city. Mountain City was built on a mountain slope. Living there, one had to climb the hill almost every day. This wasn't good for Lee because of his heart disease. He almost died several times. However, sitting in the revolving restaurant on top of a ten-story building, they surveyed Mountain City, and—one by one—their innermost desires were revived. And then there was Star City. During the season when the sweet osmanthus bloomed, the suffocating fragrance made people fidget all night. In Cotton City, you couldn't see any cotton; steel structures were everywhere . . . but what did any of this prove? These wafting memories couldn't be grasped or penetrated. The farther north they went, the less Grace could tolerate the face she saw in the mirror: it was not at all what she wanted to look like. Later, she became apathetic: she didn't care what she looked like. Once her brother came to see her and said, "Grace, Grace, you still look so young! How come?" Did she look young? She wasn't sure. The face in the mirror reflected her decline. In her dreams, she went to Match City, where she had once lived. She was actually lost in this square place. But when she asked directions, she realized she no longer understood the dialect there. It seemed to be the dialect of a remote and backward place. She understood almost nothing. Pebble Town gave her other memories. Some of them resolved the riddles from before, but most were dark holes that were even harder to penetrate. For example, the puppy: Wasn't it a dark hole in Lee's and her lives? What was the sickly Lee's motive for buying the little dog? When she recalled this, she suddenly heard the baby's laughter coming from the corridor. Such an odd baby—laughing like an older child!

"Grace, you're the picture of health today," José said cheerfully.

"Why don't I think so? You take such good care of the baby. Ms. Nancy certainly doesn't worry at all."

José looked perplexed. He thought the woman's words hid other meanings. When he went home, he was still trying to guess what she meant.

When Qiming saw José appear next to the flowerbed with the baby, a hot current rushed from his heart to his face, and the hand with the broom trembled a little.

He washed his hands and tidied his clothing, then walked toward José and the baby.

"Baby has grown some more. Her eyes remind me of the trumpet shells in my hometown."

José handed his daughter to him, and he lifted her over his head. The baby chortled so loudly that people standing in the road outside the guesthouse could hear her. She was already sturdy. She lifted her little arms high.

"I hear that as soon as you pick her up, she starts laughing," José said contentedly.

"Mr. José, Baby and I were brought together by fate."

The happiness falling on him was so sudden: carrying the baby,

Qiming circled around the flowerbed several times. He kept lifting her toward the sky. Her merry laughter filled the flower garden.

Finally, though wishing he could go on like this, Qiming returned the baby to José.

"How about your being her adoptive father?" José said.

"She's truly an active baby."

Qiming used his sleeve to wipe away the tears spilling from his eyes and sighed emotionally. Just now, when he had lifted the baby toward the sky, he had clearly seen a sail and mast. A boat with an invisible hull sailed into the clouds.

"How many years have passed?" he seemed to be asking José, yet also asking himself.

But José responded, "Now I understand the director's goodwill."

José and the baby had left quite a while ago, but Qiming was still drenched in sentimental happiness. He had made up his mind: he would visit this child often at José's place.

Qiming wondered if—in separating Nancy from her child—the director was showing that she expected even more of her. A woman could certainly change in that old, somewhat gloomy building overlooking the barren hill. She would become even more of a Pebble Town resident. It seemed that ever since the day they arrived in Pebble Town, his life had been bound up with theirs. Back then, as he stood in the river, he had been really curious about the two young people struggling ahead on the road across from him. As he swept the floor, Qiming thought back to these events. After sweeping the walkways, he leaned on the broom as he used to do and gazed at the distant snow mountain. And so he remembered that it had been a long time since he'd thought of the goddess in his heart. Before he realized it, some impurities invaded his pure imagination.

He returned to his room, filled a basin with cold water, and began once more to wind bathe.

"Hey, Qiming, do you want to go back to our hometown to visit?" Haizai had emerged from somewhere.

"No. I think it's impossible. Wasn't there a tsunami there?"

"Hunh. The village is gone, but traces of it are left in the land. I guess those traces can be found here, too, so we might as well look for them."

Haizai grimaced. Qiming asked if he would stay this time—if he wanted to grow old in Pebble Town. Haizai didn't answer. He looked around and asked if he could lie down on the bed.

He took off his shoes and got into bed, saying he was terribly tired and really had to rest for a while. Then he would take Qiming to see his hometown. While still talking, he suddenly began to snore. Qiming thought, *The "hometown" he spoke of probably isn't far from here.*

Qiming locked the door and walked out to the street. He was afraid the director would see Haizai, and he knew she wouldn't be happy. He bought eggs, green onions, and flour, intending to make pancakes for Haizai. But unfortunately, the director spotted him. Noticing his purchases, she smiled and said, "The demons that climbed out of the abyss can't be driven away. We'd better take care of ourselves."

The director followed Qiming home. Haizai was still snoring. The director bent down and peered at Haizai's face. She turned and sat on a small bamboo chair that Qiming provided. Suddenly, she bent her head and buried her face in her hands. Qiming was stunned: Why was the well-respected director—so smart and strong—acting like a little girl?

It was a long time before the director looked up. Qiming saw that she was perplexed.

"Qiming, do you still recognize me?" she asked.

"Of course. You're our director." Qiming's heart pounded, and his voice shook.

"That's good. I thought you wouldn't recognize me. Just now, I went back again to that hospital in the interior. I was lying on the table in the operating room. Outside the window, the yellow sand was billowing. The doctor gave me a face transplant."

Exhausted, she massaged her eyes, and then looked up. She asked Qiming to feel her forehead.

Her forehead was ice-cold. Qiming stopped himself from crying out by clapping his hand over his mouth.

The director's voice seemed to be coming from a crack in the wall when she said, "You're startled, aren't you? This is what happens to me whenever the past crosses my mind."

She had no sooner spoken than the loud, clear sound of a child's crying came from outside. Qiming opened the door, and all at once the room brightened. He noticed that color had returned to the director's face. José was carrying his daughter and walking by from the flowerbed. The director stood up. Looking determined, she was once more her usual self. She strode quickly toward José and his daughter.

Haizai woke up.

"I crushed and killed a little girl with my wheelbarrow. The mountain road was so slippery that I couldn't stop."

Huddled in the quilt, he sat on the bed and stared wildly at that blocked-up wall. Then he ordered Qiming to close the door because the rays of light would make him "go on a rampage." "I'm not accustomed to an environment that's too transparent," he said.

He arched his back and walked along the wall, sniffing as he went. Ignoring him, Qiming began to cook. Each time a pancake was finished, Haizai snatched it and ate it all, saying he was starving. "For the past several days, I've neglected my physical needs." Qiming finally used up all of his flour, but Haizai was still hungry. Qiming was a good cook: the aroma of onions and eggs permeated the small room.

"I've slept and I've eaten. Ha! Now who's telling a story?" Haizai said as he wiped his mouth.

He said someone was telling a story in the garden outside the gate. He had listened intermittently: the story seemed to be about a goose flying south. He asked if Qiming had heard it. Qiming opened the door and looked outside. When he came back in, he said no one was outside. There were two birds in the garden. Haizai still insisted that someone was telling a story; maybe it was the man with the child. Haizai said a strong homesick feeling dominated the story. As he talked, Haizai sniffed again at the wall. He looked anguished.

"What do you smell, Haizai?"

"My hometown. This is quite an unusual wall."

"Yes, it can change irregularly, and at night it can disappear."

Haizai sat down on the bamboo chair and told Qiming that he had traveled through more than half the country and at last he had come here. He felt he had indeed returned to his hometown. Wasn't this true? Qiming said he felt the same way, and so he had settled down in this small town. He didn't want to go anywhere else. After saying this, he immediately recalled his goddess. At this moment, he really wanted to talk with Haizai about this beauty, but he didn't know what to say, so he kept repeating a silly remark, "The frontier women are really beautiful, really beautiful, really beautiful. Nowhere else . . ."

At night, the two of them went to the poplar park again; they vaulted over the low fence to get in. When they jumped down, they startled some birds. Qiming was relieved that the old guard hadn't been awakened.

Haizai lay on his stomach on the grass and wanted Qiming to do so, too. As soon as Qiming lay down, he heard people talking. They spoke with a southern accent: they seemed to be quarreling about something. Their voices came from underground. If you placed your ear close to the ground, you could hear better. Haizai whispered to Qiming that this was the old guard's family. When he had first come here, he had realized that this park belonged to that family. In other words, in the daytime it belonged to the visitors and at night it belonged to the guard's family. "After midnight, they go back to the hill in the south. That's their family's tea plantation, and it's wreathed in mist most of the year." Just then, some animals appeared under the dim yellow street light in the distance. They were rather large—one, two, three—and even more of them. Haizai said they were southern tigers. They didn't attack people, so one needn't be afraid. Qiming asked, "Why don't they? They did when they were in the south." Haizai began laughing. He laughed so loud that it startled the tigers. They stopped in their tracks. Qiming was shaking all over. At the same time, the family that was underground began arguing even more vehemently. The southern tigers apparently heard this, too. They couldn't seem to decide where to go. Then they walked toward Qiming and Haizai. There were probably at least six of them, making no noise as they walked on the grass. Haizai urged Qiming to lie on his stomach, too, without moving, and said it would be best to close his eyes if he didn't want to be upset. This advice was ridiculous, but under the circumstances Qiming did shut his eyes. In no time, the tigers did step on his back. Though this hurt, it wasn't life threatening. He counted: probably three of them walked over his body. They disappeared over the other side of the fence. From underground came the sound of the family crying, and all of a sudden Qiming heard his father's voice in the midst of the weeping. The voice was loud, yet he couldn't understand what Father was saying. In the end, Qiming got tired of listening.

"Qiming, Qiming! Quiet down!" Haizai said, "Why did you call your father?"

"I didn't say anything, did I? What's going on?"

"Hunh. You summoned the tigers back. Luckily, they don't eat people here."

When Qiming noticed that they had appeared under the street-light again, he opened his mouth in alarm. Now he dared to observe them. Qiming had never seen tigers before. The closest one was looking at him; the expression in its eyes greatly resembled that of Nancy's baby. Would its voice also be like the baby's? Under the tiger's gaze, Qiming started feeling feverish. Lying beside him, Haizai began bickering with the father he had just heard. Father's tone was persistent; Haizai sounded desperate. But it was hard to hear what they were arguing about. Qiming pinched his face hard, struggling to stay awake. His father seemed to be referring to the watch, blaming Haizai for losing it. Haizai started crying and explained himself, saying he had buried the watch in the safest place—at the bottom of the ocean. Nobody would be able to reach that trench. Qiming was startled when he heard this. He felt his breast pocket: the watch was still there. The voices were slurred; he didn't know what they were arguing about. Looking up, he saw that the tiger's eyes had become two green flames, perhaps because it had walked from the streetlight to the recesses of the poplars. The other tigers had disappeared. How beautiful the tiger's eyes were! Why didn't Nancy like such eyes? Qiming began sweating: his clothes were drenched. He turned aside, avoided looking at the tiger, and muttered, "I want to go home . . ." His muffled voice sounded like thunder. Haizai jumped up and rebuked him, shouting: "It's midnight. Who brought the baby here?"

Qiming stood up, too. Side by side, the two of them walked ahead, following the faint sound of the baby's crying. They went through the grass, the flowerbed, the poplar grove, and the dark bosk. Just then, they saw another grassy area stretching to the horizon. The baby's crying was coming from some place ahead of them.

"The old guard's kingdom is truly immense!" Qiming sighed emotionally.

"Shhhh. Don't make a sound. Damn!"

As Haizai cursed, they saw the fence, and the baby's crying faded away. An iron door appeared in the back. They went through it and left the park. Then Haizai headed in a different direction with his head down, and Qiming went home alone. When he passed through the deserted Culture Plaza, the bell was ringing non-stop. But it was midnight, and he was the only one who heard it.

Chapter 6

LIUJIN AND ROY

This summer, Liujin's life was a little upended. She wondered if this was related to the Snow Mountain Hotel being torn down. Often when she was alone at home, memories of the hotel would suddenly surge up for no reason and upset her. She had named that hotel "Tumulus." Occasionally, she wondered how her relationship with Sherman might develop in the future. The Snow Mountain Hotel wouldn't be in the picture. Back then, she was so young, and her memories related to the hotel were so vivid—as vivid as leaves in sunlight . . . But now, this obscure, shapeless relationship with Sherman was insubstantial—like a loose gossamer floating in the air. The long summer would end soon. The little wagtail hadn't appeared for three days; it must have gone somewhere else to play—maybe to the neighbors' courtyard, where many sandthorns grew. Walking past, Liujin heard the hullabaloo of birds singing, and stopped for a moment. Loneliness rose in her heart. Deep down, she still feared being irrevocably involved with this person whose background was murky. Once, he had put a lot of frogs in her courtyard, but they had all vanished without a trace. Thinking of this made her uncomfortable.

Liujin tossed and turned in bed in the dark. She heard a muffled explosion coming from the direction of the snow mountain. She thought, *The snow leopards must be terrified and running for their lives on the mountain.* The sad, tragic scene made her close her eyes tightly, but she couldn't stop her mind from racing. The night before, she had asked Uncle Meng Yu, "What was Pebble Town like forty years ago?"

The old man paused in his handiwork and looked up at the sky. Then he pointed at her chest, bent his head again, and continued twisting his rope. Liujin was very confused, but she still gained a hazy enlightenment. Standing in the curtain of night, she thought it over repeatedly: bit by bit, some events from the past came into focus, and she thought she was one step closer to the answer.

It had been a night just like this. Her insomniac father—as always—had moved a rattan recliner outside, placed it under a tree, and lain there looking up at the sky. In her dreams, Liujin heard an animal howling—each sound more shrill than the last one. She awakened with a start. Feeling her way in the dark, she walked out of the bedroom, through the living room, and outside. She stared at the courtyard and saw five black animals circling her father. The moon was unusually bright. Her father's head lolled to one side. He was sleeping. All at once, Liujin felt terrified and helpless. Was her father dead? She screamed: "Pa—Pa!" Those animals (it seemed they were bears) turned around and looked at her. Liujin retreated hastily behind the door and prepared to close it. Luckily, it wasn't the wild animals that approached her. It was Mama. Her mother was barefoot; she wasn't even wearing slippers. She asked Liujin if she was hungry. "No. Mama, look at Papa!" she said. Mama took her small hand and led her back to her bedroom. As she settled Liujin into bed, she said, "You're growing up." She tucked her in and left the room. Liujin gaped at the shadow of the tree swaying on the wall. The animals howled again. A bloody scene of her papa's neck being snapped came into her mind. It was a long time before she fell asleep.

"Does your neck hurt, Papa?"

"Oh, a little. When I sleep on the rattan recliner, there's this pressure on my neck. What is it?"

Liujin was ten years old then.

Staring at Uncle Meng Yu's strong, rough hands, Liujin was reminded of the animals in the dark night. Had the animals in Pebble Town run down from the snow mountain, or had they emerged from underground? After she grew up, she encountered all kinds of animals numerous times in the Snow Mountain Hotel. As time passed, she got used to seeing them. All of a sudden, Amy's stirring singing came from across the street. Uncle Meng Yu was working with his head bent, and made no response. Perhaps the singer was no longer Amy, because the voice was mixed with a masculine quality. When you listened a little longer, you became even more confused.

There were seldom birds in Liujin's garden. She noticed that the nests in the poplars had been abandoned. In the past when she came home from work, these little creatures greeted her. Even at night, one or two skipped around in the flowerbed or under the trees. And then, only the wagtail was left. Now, not only had the wagtail vanished, but so had the gecko.

"Uncle Meng Yu, I think you're a local."

The old man stopped working for a while—a long while, and then went back to twisting the rope. Liujin walked away and bumped into a person in the shadows of the fence. The person took hold of both of her legs. Liujin bent over. She recognized the big eyes: it was the boy who'd worn leaves. He said, "Liujin, I sneaked in. The old man sitting at the entrance didn't let me in. Will you sit here with me for five minutes?"

Liujin sat with him on the grass below the fence. The boy hugged her arm to his chest. He was excited, but said nothing. Liujin stroked his round head.

"You're like a hedgehog."

He giggled.

"Where are your clothes that were plaited from leaves?"

He still said nothing. He just rested his head on Liujin's arm, as if he wanted to go to sleep. After a while, Liujin withdrew her arm, stood up, and said, "I have to go in. What about you? Why don't you come in with me? You don't have anywhere to spend the night, do you? You can sleep on the hearth in my kitchen, okay?"

The boy sat unmoving, so Liujin went into the house by herself. When she reached the steps, she turned and saw Uncle Meng Yu leave the courtyard. She left the door open and turned on the light in the living room because she thought the boy might want to come in. If he did, he could sleep on the couch. Just as she was about to go into the bedroom, the boy entered the living room. He turned off the light and sat down on the windowsill. When Liujin drew close to him, she heard the sound of a flowing brook. Liujin asked what this noise was. He said it was the sound of his gut squirming.

"My name is Roy. I gave myself this name. Back home, I had another name."

"Do you have to work at night, Roy?" Liujin asked, patting the boy's shoulder.

"Yes. I work the night shift. I don't have a specific job. The job I've given myself is to look at pedestrians' eyes. There are many pedestrians on city streets at night. I wander among them. One after another, I look at their eyes and ask, 'Do you see me?' None of them does. But I still have to ask because it's my job."

Liujin sighed softly. She thought of the wagtail. The boy's words made her tear up. Whose child was he? She looked at his hands through her blurred, teary eyes. A white fluorescence came from two of his fingernails—the index finger and middle finger of his right hand.

"You see better in the dark. Is that right?"

"Yes, I was trained to be this way. My family used to live in a grotto. My father was a hunter. We were quite well off. Father wouldn't let us turn on lights. He wanted us to train our eyes, and so I had a lot of practice. I saw you crying just now."

"I see. Then tell me about these two fingernails." Liujin held up his hand.

"I don't know. I didn't always have them, but then I did."

Just then, Liujin heard a bird flapping its wings. Had the wagtail returned? She asked Roy if he saw a bird. Roy said the sound came from his tummy.

"I want to sleep. Roy, are you going to spend the night on the windowsill?"

"I'm on the night shift. I have to go out after a while. Hey, Liujin, your room is crowded with people!"

It was after midnight when Roy left Liujin's house. The soft sound of the door closing awakened Liujin. She put on shoes and dashed outside. She followed him at a distance. After taking the main road for a while, Roy turned and headed toward the train station. He was tall and walked rapidly. Liujin had to jog in order to catch up with him.

The lights were on in the train station, but no one was there: it was silent and even a little eerie. Roy walked to the end of the platform, raised his arms, and cried out loudly. Liujin hid behind the square pillar and observed him. When he had shouted seven or eight times, Liujin heard a subtle roar. She thought it was an illusion because she knew there was no midnight train here. The sound quickly vanished. Liujin thought, *It's definitely an illusion.* Roy was still shouting—shouting himself hoarse, and the roar sounded again. It was real. After a few seconds, a whistle blew, and the train rushed past in a cloud of smoke. Liujin saw Roy wobble and almost fall off the platform. Her heart sank. But nothing happened. The train slowed to a halt, and many people surged out of the car. Liujin had never imagined anything like this. Was it because it was a holiday? The entire long platform was filled with people, and Roy was being jostled. All of them knew where they were going. He was the only idler, and he was always in other people's way. Liujin saw him stay resolutely on the platform, craning his neck to take stock of the passengers who were walking with heads bent. They frequently pushed him roughly away. Liujin shouted at him a few times, but her voice was drowned out by the noise. Although she clung to the pillar, the passengers hurrying past jostled her, too. It was unbearable. These people were dashing around madly! Were they all in an urgent hurry? Finally, she was pushed over. The one at fault was actually an old woman, and the suitcase she was carrying also hit Liujin in the back, as if she were attacking Liujin. When Liujin fell, she thought she might be trampled to death. But no one stepped on her. They all strode over her as they passed by. Liujin was surprised all over again—how could the train hold so many people?

A long time passed, and then she heard Roy whispering to her. By now, hardly anyone was left on the platform. Roy crouched beside her, a large garland around his neck.

"Are you hurt, Liujin?"

"Tell me, Roy, how did you summon the train?" Liujin asked him sternly.

"I don't know." Roy narrowed his eyes and stared into space.

"You come to the station often, don't you?"

"Yes. Liujin, these passengers didn't recognize me. It's depressing. But today, they gave me this garland. Look—they're irises."

"Who gave them to you?"

"I don't know. I was pushed over, and when I got up again, I had this."

By now, the platform was deserted. Roy supported Liujin and headed for the exit. It was unusually dark away from the platform. Even the passenger cars melted into the darkness and became invisible. Liujin thought, *It'll probably be light soon. Where does this boy stay in the daytime?*

"I sleep in the park," Roy answered, as if he had heard her question.

"The poplar park?"

"Yes. No one there would drive me away. I know the old gate-keeper there."

The lobby was unlit, and the two of them felt their way out. When they finally reached the exit, an enormous sound came from the darkness behind them, as though the door to another world had closed. They discovered that they were illuminated by the bright streetlights. Liujin was surprised to see that Roy's garland had withered, as if the flowers had been picked two days earlier. She asked Roy about this. He smiled a little absentmindedly and said, "Maybe they've been baked like this because of the fire on my body. In the dark, sparks explode when I pound my chest."

"Do you sleep well in the park?"

"Yes. The sun thaws me out. The old man is over ninety years old. He keeps me company. He's lonely."

They were going in opposite directions, so they parted at the station's entrance. Liujin stood under a lamppost until darkness swallowed the boy's shadow. She realized that, in spite of herself, she kept silently calling, "Roy! Roy!" even after he had walked far away. He had made too great an impact on her. Why did a person like this exist?

"Have you seen this child?" Liujin asked Sherman.

"No. When you talked about this just now, I kept puzzling over it. This boy, this Roy—did he come from that tropical garden?"

"Oh, the garden! I know what you mean. My parents told me of it. It's the very most illusory place. The boy Roy, however, is a real person."

"Hunh. Maybe an imaginary thing has sneaked into our daily lives. I'm not sure. I've been to the riverside, a dirty river. There you can see what your parents told you about."

Although Sherman was drinking tea calmly as he sat in the rattan chair, Liujin sensed his panic. It was because of the topic they were discussing. For some reason, Liujin's yearning for this man was ebbing. She was looking in all directions, searching with her eyes for the bird. But she was dimly aware that the bird wouldn't reappear. She felt both regretful and relieved. The wind was cool, carrying the smell of the snow mountain with it. Liujin took a deep breath and thought of the riddle of the snow leopard. In spite of herself, she spoke of what she was thinking: "The question of Roy is the riddle of the snow leopard."

Sherman looked a little flustered. What kind of woman was she? He had never figured her out, and he probably never would. But there was one thing for sure: both of them were puzzling over the same thing. The stars in the night sky were so beautiful—beautiful and large. You couldn't see a sight like this in the interior. Looking at this night sky, they couldn't discuss anything. Although neither spoke, each one heard the other's silent sigh.

"When I was a child, I often got into trouble, so the orphanage cook would put me on the high hearth with my legs dangling in the air. That's how I grew up. You can see how wretched my childhood was."

Liujin saw Uncle Meng Yu arriving early at the courtyard. He sat on a stone stool at the entrance. He hadn't brought his basketwork. This was unprecedented. Sherman stood up and took his leave, saying, "Liujin, I'd really like to sit here forever. It's like sitting halfway up the snow mountain!"

Liujin saw him off. She noticed the two men taking stock of each other for a second. Uncle Meng Yu's face was in the dark, Sherman's in the light.

After Sherman left, Uncle Meng Yu took a small birdcage out from under his overcoat. When he placed it on the ground, Liujin saw the white wagtail. Was it the one she was missing? She squatted down and opened the door of the cage. The little bird ran out. But it didn't run far: it jumped back and forth around them.

"His mind is filled with thoughts of death," he suddenly said very clearly.

Liujin was startled. She had never heard the old man utter such clear sounds. She was familiar with this way of speaking—filled with vestiges of the past and reminding her of her parents.

"Who are you speaking of?"

"Hunh. Who else?"

Although it was still warm at the end of summer, Liujin felt ice-cold all over, and her teeth were chattering. She felt as if she were on top of the snow mountain. She looked down: the little bird had actually gone back into the cage of its own accord. This bird must be hers: the old man had actually domesticated it. She said she had to go in because she was cold. The old man said nothing, but just looked at her from the shadows.

After Liujin went back inside, she took heavy winter pajamas out of the cabinet and put them on. From the window, she saw Uncle Meng Yu bend down and pick up the birdcage. Then he put it back inside his big coat. She looked down and opened a drawer: lying inside was her mother's most recent letter. She had read it once during the day. Her mother told her that her father's insomnia was no better. Recently, he had found a new interest: after midnight, he would go downstairs and stroll the smoggy streets. He would do this until dawn and then come back and sleep. When he came inside in the morning, he was always carrying something. He would put it on the table and then go to sleep. Mother saw that these were their household objects from long ago—long before they had gone to the frontier. They included a lampshade, a shoehorn, a ruler, a bonsai plant, and a copper wind-bell. Mother asked Father where he had found these things. He said that in places where the smog was the thickest, he would scratch a few times in the air and grab one of these things. After doing that, he could sleep. If he couldn't find anything, it was tragic—because if he didn't sleep, he would periodically think of committing suicide. "My willpower is weakening by the day," he said.

When Liujin reread this letter, she felt a little gratified—as she had many times before. She recalled that Father sometimes hadn't slept for an entire week when they lived here. But now, nostalgic memories could draw him into dreamland: this was great! It was late at night when she finished reading the letter. The old man had left long ago. With no small animals visiting, this home was depressing. In spite of herself, she scratched in the air a few times, but nothing was there. She was a little frustrated with Uncle Meng Yu. Why did he have to take her bird? Had he meant to make her courtyard desolate? Recently, Amy had grown even prettier: her beauty was overbearing. Liujin felt that her dark eyes spewed fire. In the market courtyard, Amy hid among sheep and made no sound. For some reason, Liujin thought she was carrying a knife. She seemed to have a backbone of steel. How much had her relationship with Uncle Meng Yu and Grandpa Meng Yu evolved? Liujin couldn't imagine. The activities of the people in the house across the street were growing more and more mysterious.

She had gone to bed and turned off the light earlier, but now thinking of what Uncle Meng Yu had said, she couldn't sleep. The more she thought, the more she stewed. So she got dressed and walked out past the courtyard.

Sherman sat under the light next to the street, looking at his hands. He brought his left hand up to his myopic eyes, then moved it a little farther away, then brought it closer, then away. He kept repeating this.

"Sherman, are you crying?"

Liujin moved closer to him and sat down, and Sherman hugged her. All of a sudden, Liujin was alarmed that she actually felt no desire at all. What was wrong with her?

"I'm not crying, Liujin. It's something inside me that's crying. I saw him. He's a white person, and he blocked my path! See, Liujin, everything is dark. Only this small spot where we're sitting is light! But it will gradually darken, too."

Sherman released her and stood up. He tottered ahead without looking back.

Liujin went back inside. She slept soundly. When she woke up, she saw Roy sitting on the windowsill and drinking water directly from her thermos. Liujin was moved by this and got dressed quickly and made the bed. Outside, the sun shone brightly.

Roy drained the thermos, wiped his mouth, and said, "Liujin, I think someone recognized me yesterday, but he wavered."

"What kind of person?"

"So tall that I couldn't see his eyes. I saw his eyes only when he bent over. Then he straightened up again. I think he must be as tall as a two-story building. When he was walking in the crowd of people, I couldn't see him. Alas, I missed my chance."

Liujin called him into the kitchen and gave him goat's milk and pancakes. He ate quickly—like a small animal. When they drank tea, Liujin asked where he bathed every day. He said, in the brook. He had two changes of clothing. He paid attention to personal hygiene. Moving closer to Liujin, he asked, "Do I smell?"

"No, it's just the smell of a leopard's coat. When you're asleep, your skin probably reveals the pattern of a leopard's skin," Liujin said, smiling a little.

"Really? You really think so? And then does it disappear as soon as I wake up? I'd really like to see it!"

He stood and picked up a watering can that he had placed behind the door. He lifted it very high and sprinkled Liujin with water. She dodged out of the way and ran into the living room, grabbing a feather whisk-broom and chasing him. When she caught up with him, Roy squatted and held his head in his hands, letting her whip him. Liujin swatted at him until she was tired, then dropped the whisk-broom and sat down, and asked, "Roy, have you seen the tropical garden?"

"I don't know what you're talking about, Liujin."

"I'm speaking of banyans, durians, lichees, and mangoes."

"Unh. Yes, I've seen them. And a green bird."

"Where?"

"Inside myself. When I'm asleep, these things probably appear on my skin, too."

Liujin wanted him to talk of these things, but he stood up, saying he had to be going because he still had to work that day. He said he'd be in the poplar park if she wanted to find him: he slept in the sun under the trees every morning. When it rained, he slept in the mailroom at the park.

He walked out into the sunshine. Liujin looked at his receding figure for a long time.

When Roy walked into the market, the people there stood motionless. In Roy's eyes, they were like the coral trees in the ocean. Circling around these coral trees, he arrived at the courtyard in back. It was filled with sheep moving restlessly about. Roy felt dizzy and nearly fell.

"Kid, how dare you rush in here!"

A woman wearing a red skirt emerged from the herd of sheep and grabbed him by the arm.

"Don't move! It's dangerous. Take another look—are these sheep??" Her tone was stern.

Roy stared: sure enough, they weren't sheep. They were snow leopards. They were entering the market rapidly from that entrance.

"Don't move and you'll be okay."

After a while, the courtyard emptied out except for one leopard. Roy saw the woman in the red skirt confront the leopard with a knife. When the snow leopard charged at her, she deftly dodged away and cut a long bloody hole in the wild beast's flank. Snarling, the injured leopard charged out of the gate, leaving a lot of blood behind. Roy stood there staring.

"Those people are all motionless," she said, pointing at the market. "They're used to this. If you hadn't charged in here, you wouldn't have seen what was happening today."

She carefully wiped the blood from the knife and put the knife into the leather sheath at her waist.

Finally, Roy made eye contact with her. He asked hesitantly, "You—do you know who I am?"

"Of course. As soon as you came in, I could smell you. What are you planning to do now?"

"I want more people to know who I am."

"You stubborn kid. Aren't you afraid?"

"No."

"Then hold your hand out!"

He held out his left hand. The woman took out her knife and traced a line in his palm. Blood gushed out, but he felt no pain. Amy knelt down, took his hand in both of hers and sucked for a while. The bleeding stopped. When she looked up, her mouth was covered with fresh blood, and Roy felt nauseated in spite of himself.

"You're afraid," Amy said.

"I'm not."

When he walked out the gate, he felt top-heavy and unsteady. The people who'd been motionless like coral had now come back to life. When he made his way through the crowd, they pulled and grabbed at him and he nearly fell several times. But they helped him up. "I'm Roy! I am Roy!" he shouted as he struggled ahead.

Sherman was standing outside the market's main entrance. He shouted, "Roy! Roy! I know who you are!"

Roy elbowed his way to the entrance. In his eyes, Sherman was a red-eyed beggar in rags. He extended his left hand to Sherman, and for a few seconds Sherman looked closely at the cut on his palm. Then he looked Roy in the face. At the same time, Sherman was scowling—recalling something.

"Did you ever sleep under the bridge, Roy?"

"No. I haven't even seen a real bridge. After running away from home, I've slept wherever I could."

Sherman kept saying "strange." He went on, "You look a lot like the boy who sleeps under the bridge."

"You're mistaken."

Dejected, Sherman dropped his gaze and looked at his feet. He was ashamed. By then, Roy felt re-energized: taking long strides, he walked into the stream of people on the street. Holding up his injured hand, he kept approaching all kinds of people, hoping that more of them would recognize him and talk with him. The strange thing was: with the cut on his palm, many people seemed to know him. Everyone nodded and waved at him. But still, no one wanted to chat with him. The moment he opened his mouth, the other person would dash away.

Roy saw that an old man standing next to the street was watching him. When Roy noticed him, he motioned Roy over. The old man had a thick, long, snow-white beard. A little grayish-blue bird stuck its head out from the beard and chirped twice in Roy's direction. When Roy saw the little bird, tears spilled from his eyes. He said, "Grandpa, where does the little bird want to go? I know this bird."

The old man took the bird out and let it stand on his own palm. The bird flew into midair and then dropped sure-footedly back onto his palm. When the old man took an exquisite little birdcage out from under his coat, the little bird flew into it.

The old man motioned to Roy to take the bird.

When Roy carried the birdcage toward the park, some new ideas bubbled up in his mind. Today all at once he had become acquainted with three persons. It was truly an extraordinary day. When he reached the park, he hung the cage on a small tree, and the bird began chirping continuously, sounding rather forlorn. Standing there transfixed, Roy started weeping.

"This is a bird king," the old gatekeeper whispered in his ear, "I've seen it in many places."

"It remembers things I've forgotten." Roy wiped his tears away with his sleeve.

The door to the cage was open the whole time, with the bird perched inside making no sound. Roy had a faint recollection of

Liujin's living room and thought, *With so many people jammed in there, is it possible that one of them would carelessly trample the little bird to death?*

"It's the bird king. It has entered our human lives. It . . ."

As the old man talked, he walked into the distance. Roy watched him go into the little mailroom. A triangular red flag hung from the room's window; it blew in the wind. Roy chanted the old man's name, "Grandpa Pu, Grandpa Pu . . ." He looked up and saw the bird again. The bird seemed to be asleep, for it didn't mind at all that the wind was blowing; it enjoyed it.

Every night, some people roamed around in the park. Roy knew that some of them came from elsewhere, as he did. He could tell how worried they were just by looking at them. He didn't strike up conversations with them, for he didn't like to break the silence in the park. When Grandpa Pu stayed in the dark with him, he didn't like to talk, either. At times like this, Roy raised the hand with the fluorescent fingernail and waved it back and forth in the air. At first, he thought that Grandpa Pu had the same superhuman vision that he had, but Grandpa Pu told him he couldn't see anything. At night, he relied on his hearing to distinguish things. Those warm recollections calmed him down. Roy felt that his train of thought was blending in with the little wagtail's—and reaching toward the dark abyss, while the setting sun shone simultaneously in another world.

"Amy, do your sheep change into leopards overnight?"

"Sometimes, Liujin."

Liujin saw many colors alternating in Amy's perplexed eyes.

"Your boy came looking for me."

"You mean Roy. Is he my boy?"

"He looks a lot like your little brother. Not in appearance, but he does resemble him in some ways. In what ways? I've been trying to figure that out ever since I saw him walk out of your courtyard."

When Liujin threaded her way through the stream of people at the market, she was still thinking about what this woman had said. When she thought about people considering Roy her son, a warm current coursed through her veins. Her boss was arguing with someone at the yard goods counter. As soon as he saw Liujin, he turned away from the other person and came over. He told Liujin that some robbers were in the market: one bolt of cloth after another had gone missing. He had stayed at the counter all night the last few nights, but hadn't noticed anything unusual. Yet, when he checked his inventory in the morning, bolts of cloth were still missing. "What on earth is invading us? Liujin, what do you think?"

Liujin hesitated. She had a thought, but she shouldn't voice it because it would sound like nonsense. And the boss didn't really want to hear what she thought. She could see that her boss was tangled up in his own stubborn ideas, that's all. Without answering him, she set down her purse and began straightening the counter. She heard the boss still chattering behind her: he didn't seem worried about his losses. He was merely puzzled. Liujin, though, was a little worried: she was afraid of losing this job. She had worked here more than ten years. She had no intention of losing her job: very few people in Pebble Town were unemployed. The boss would never suspect her of stealing, would he? Didn't he keep watch at night? Liujin's real idea was that a kind of force was able to make worldly matter completely disappear. One example was the frogs that Sherman had put in her courtyard. Curious, Liujin turned around and took a good look at her boss's back. He was drinking tea and looked extremely lonely. It was as though she were seeing him on his night watch.

After arranging the yard goods, Liujin was surprised to see Amy standing on tiptoe at the side gate of the market, hailing someone. Then Roy made his way through the crowd. He was taller than almost everyone else, so Liujin could follow him with her eyes. It was Roy whom Amy had been hailing. Finally, the boy walked up to the counter, where the boss confronted him immediately.

"Did you steal my cloth?" the boss asked Roy outright.

Liujin's face flushed with anger, but Roy was calm. He said, "No."

"You're a nice boy. You shouldn't hang out in the market all the time. This is a dangerous place."

Roy bent his head and smelled the bolts of cloth. With his red face and narrowed eyes, he looked even more intoxicated than Sherman. He looked as if he had drunk several large bowls of rice wine. As if talking to himself, the boss muttered at the side, "Dumb boy, really stupid. Where did he come from?"

"I ran away from home," Roy said. "I want to see the world. Sometimes I do steal things, but not cloth."

Liujin's gaze swept over the crowd. She saw Amy brandishing her flashing knife at the side gate. Who was she struggling with? It looked as though a disembodied blast had knocked her backward.

"I'll take one bolt of the orchid pattern," a familiar-looking customer said.

After Liujin measured the cloth, she noticed that Roy had walked away. The boss came over and told Liujin that Roy couldn't leave the market because some things were happening just then. "Like a fly, he has smelled blood." This disgusting analogy made Liujin blush again. When the boss took his teacup to the back room for a break, he suddenly cried out in fear and fell to the floor. Liujin rushed over immediately, but saw nothing. The boss's lips were purple. Liujin asked where he hurt, and he strained to say, "The customer who bought the orchid patterned cloth . . . Be careful."

That day, Liujin kept asking herself, "What happened? What happened!" The market wasn't chaotic, nor were wild animals walking around: there were just some strange omens. Amy, the boss, and Roy all seemed to be rehearsing, yet she couldn't see what they were rehearsing for. When it was time to leave work, Sherman showed up. He looked emaciated and old. When he reached out to touch the cloth, Liujin saw that even his hand had shriveled. He said apologetically to Liujin, "I've lost my usual tactile sense." Liujin sensed his inner tension, and thought something was on the verge of happening.

Sherman was carrying an empty basket. When they left the market, Liujin asked why he hadn't bought anything. He said he sensed he couldn't take home any of the things in the market today; if he did, there'd be trouble. At that point, he turned around again and swept his eyes over the deserted hall. Then he continued walking ahead. Just then, Liujin heard footsteps, frenzied and loud: many people were walking around the market. Liujin recalled what the boss had said about Roy. She stopped in her tracks.

"Are you waiting for the leopard to come out?" Sherman asked.

"Unh."

Although the two of them were standing shoulder to shoulder, Sherman felt a sudden attack of loneliness.

"I'll go on ahead, Liujin. I'm sorry I let you down. And the sun has set; it's cold everywhere. Take good care of yourself, Liujin."

Then, taking the small path on the right, Sherman walked into the distance. Liujin stood there, feeling a bit surprised: What was wrong with Sherman? Had he seen something? She certainly hadn't. She looked back again. The market was still deserted: Roy wasn't there, and neither was the leopard. But she could still hear footsteps—frenzied and loud. Was there a fight going on inside?

"Amy! Amy!" Liujin shouted in the direction of the deserted hall.

No one answered. Only an echo rippled forth.

Not until Liujin had walked straight past the plaza did Roy catch up, gasping for breath.

"Liujin, I killed the leopard!"

"How? What did you kill it with?"

"With a knife the person handed to me. I dumped the knife inside the market. I didn't dare carry it out. Look, I'm covered in blood . . . Oh!"

He let out an odd scream. But Liujin didn't see any blood on him. She thought, *He's having a wild hallucination.* For years, this market where people came and went kept triggering hallucinations. Was this why she didn't want to lose her job and leave this market? In front of them, Amy's shadow flashed past and then disappeared. She had gone into a beauty parlor. Roy told Liujin he had seen Amy stab herself several times with the knife, yet she was actually all right. Now and then, they stopped walking, attracting sidelong glances from others passing by. Roy said the street was deserted and he was afraid. He was accustomed to walking in a stream of people. Liujin consoled him, taking his hand and saying repeatedly, "I'm here. I'm here for you." His gaze fell briefly on Liujin's face and then slid away. His gaze was unfocused. Liujin wanted to take him home with her, but he refused. He kept wandering aimlessly. Liujin followed him to the vegetable market. A waxy-faced fellow was closing the gate there. Roy approached him, lowered his head, and asked the man if he recognized him. The fellow looked up. "Aren't you Axiang's workmate? Axiang has gone away."

Liujin recalled seeing Axiang off. At the time, the train station was packed with people. Axiang had told her he was going out to buy some fruit and then had vanished in the crowd. Liujin had waited and waited. She waited more than an hour. By the time the train pulled out, he still hadn't reappeared. Liujin believed he had boarded the train.

The fellow was hostile as he took stock of Roy and Liujin. He said, "Ever since Axiang left, many people have inquired about his whereabouts. What was the point? You didn't treasure him when he was around and felt regret only after he left. What an immature attitude toward life."

He locked the gate angrily with his brass key, and then—to make sure it had been securely locked—he pulled hard on it, and the gate boomed loudly.

Ignoring them, he walked off. In fact, Liujin recognized this fellow, for she often bought vegetables from him. She hadn't known, however, that he also knew Axiang, because Axiang had often said that he didn't have a single trustworthy friend in the city. Just then, Roy seemed to come to his senses. He suggested going to Liujin's place for dinner. He said he was exhausted: not only were his eyes tired but his tummy was empty. So they took the path beside the vegetable market and returned to the main road. It was dark, and the streetlights were on. Just then, both of them realized that the other was breathing deeply, and they started snickering. Roy said a strange sound was coming from the grove next to the road. He asked if she could hear it. Liujin looked in the direction he pointed toward and saw some fog. Moving closer to Liujin, Roy said, "I have the bird king. It's in the park. It's the one that's yours." As he talked, Liujin saw the dead poplar tree—so dark, so dazzling—pointing stiffly at the sky. Liujin shivered.

They drank milk tea and ate crackers in Liujin's home. Sitting at the table in the kitchen, Roy looked drowsy. He asked Liujin to turn off the kitchen light. Then, in the dark, he raised both hands: all of his fingernails emitted a fluorescence. Liujin drew one of his hands to her cheek: it was ice-cold.

"You little devil, where did you put my bird?"

"It's wherever the cage is. Right now, it's in the park."

He stood up all of a sudden and moved ahead along the wall.

"Liujin, these things are crushing me so much that I can't breathe."

Roy's whole body was glowing. With each step he took, his body lit up.

"Roy, Roy! Is something wrong with you?"

"Yes. No—no, nothing's wrong! Don't come over here. I feel great!"

Liujin reached out to touch him, but she touched something viscous. Roy said it was excreta gushing out of his system, and this was what was glowing. Each time after it glowed, he had to take a bath and wash his clothes. Otherwise, he would smell. Now he had to go back to the park, because his change of clothes was in the old gatekeeper's home.

When he was gone, Liujin—at her wits' end—kept drinking tea. Her courtyard was now exceedingly quiet. She sensed a familiar, warm thing moving away from her—farther and farther away. A letter was lying on the table: it was from her mother.

". . . We saw the long-life bird—the one that your father and I saw in Pebble Town's park. Its feathers are green, its tail long. We rarely go to the roof of this building, but yesterday was a particularly nice day: there was no wind and less smoke than usual. And so we rode the elevator up. We stood on the roof garden and looked into the distance. Your father said he could see your snow mountain! And then it flew in. It flew in from the north and lit at our feet. We turned its feathers over and quickly found that mark. Your father and I gave this all our thought. What did this signify? The bird didn't look at all aged. We couldn't see how old he was, but he must be older than you. When it flew away, your father said, Our era has passed; a new era has begun. What is the new era? Did he mean Liujin's era? When you were a baby you cried non-stop all night long. Even the snow mountain was moved by this . . ."

At the bottom of the stationery, Mother had drawn the bird, but it wasn't the long-life bird described in her letter: it was, instead, the little wagtail! Liujin came closer and looked again and again at that bird; terror rose from the bottom of her heart. Her parents had probably not gone up so high merely to view the scenery. They couldn't be considered old: compared with the old people in Pebble Town, they were still young. But what was meant by that bird? Nothing more than that their era had passed? Liujin's memory held some odd stories—stories her father had told her. But no matter how she tried, she couldn't remember on what occasion her father had told her these stories. For example, she recalled her father speaking hoarsely of a miniature dog. That dog was unusual. Anyone who saw it would feel world-weary. Father had also told a story of a boy who always stood in the brook and fished, but what he caught weren't fish: they were his childhood playthings. He gave those playthings to Liujin. They were all rather peculiar: an old umbrella spoke, an old slipper, and so forth, as well as one living thing—an old tortoise. As Liujin remembered these events from the past, she was immersed once more in her father's world. From the time she was little, she had known it was a world of constant disturbances. In Father's world, the place below the banana tree was not a shady place for rest; rather, it was a place where ghosts lingered. She had never met anyone like her father, who would spend most nights deep in thought. Had he been born this way, or had he changed only after Liujin was born? Whenever Liujin had padded sleepily into the courtyard wearing little slippers, Father had patted her head and said, "Shhh!" He stood in the shadows of the poplars, and Liujin knew he was lost in thought. Countless nights of experience told her this. It seemed that, from the beginning, she had been worried for her father, because she thought his world held many dangers.

Now, looking at that bird drawn on the stationery, Liujin sensed her long dormant misgivings being revived. It was as if her parents still lived in this building. Liujin couldn't lose herself in thought all night long. When she thought of something, she would think and think and then fall asleep. She supposed this was because she lacked her father's iron-clad logic.

Liujin glued the stationery with the drawing of the bird onto the wall in front of the desk. She thought, *Maybe someday that long-life bird will even fly back here.*

Chapter 7

LEE AND GRACE

L ee and Grace had come to the Design Institute a year before Nancy and José. While living in Mountain City in the south, they too had seen the recruiting ad, though the ad wasn't the main reason they had come to Pebble Town. This couple had long dreamed of once again escaping their old lives. Grace was a little lame in one leg—a result of having polio as a child, but she was born with a steely will: whenever she made up her mind, she never turned back. In addition, she was instinctively pessimistic. It seemed that she had pursued hopeless things her whole life. Maybe that's why she finally chose Lee, who had a heart condition, to be her husband. She saw the newspaper want-ad from Pebble Town's Design Institute and told Lee about it. After a short discussion, the couple decided to head north.

They took along only a few changes of clothes, as though leaving for a short vacation, then locked up their home and went to the train station. That day, as they stood in the aisle of the train car, Lee felt that many new things were growing inside his body and weakening him as they pressed down on his innards. He even wondered if he would die on the way. As the train kept moving forward, however, an unknown airflow started roaming around in his chest, and because of it, the pressure he felt gradually slackened. He even felt a curiosity he hadn't felt in years, as well as some sentimental feelings. His will to survive gradually strengthened. On the third day of the train ride, he looked at the snow mountain through the window. Grace saw some tombs halfway up the mountain (Lee didn't know how she could see them from a distance). They both felt the excitement of approaching their destination. Lee's head began to spin, and he immediately closed his eyes and lay down.

"Lee," Grace whispered. "The car ahead of us is on fire. It can't stop. Luckily, we're sitting in the caboose. Did you hear an explosion?"

He hadn't, and he couldn't open his eyes because of his dizziness. He was nauseated and shivering from the cold.

"Who opened the window? This is the winter wind from the snow mountain," Grace was still mumbling.

He heard people's footsteps and the sound of luggage being moved, as well as low curses. What were they doing? Perhaps they would escape. Would he and Grace perish here? He wanted to speak, but his lips were quivering and he couldn't get a word out. Those things that had been growing inside his body now changed into ice, extruding his innards. He started to wheeze.

"Lee, Lee, you have to bear up."

Grace held his hand. Lee thought her hand was even colder than his: it clamped down like icy pliers. He wobbled more and more. He wondered if he was dying. All of a sudden, he felt the icy pliers clamp down on his neck. The train lurched, nearly throwing him from the sleeper to the floor. All at once, he was clear-headed.

The train stopped, and the car filled with smoke. Everyone got off. Leading him along, Grace groped for the exit. When she found it, she jumped down with him in tow. They landed together next to the tracks and couldn't move for a long time. Lee noticed that the fire in the forward section was dying out: neither passengers nor firemen were there. It was as if the train had been abandoned. He and Grace were lying in a thicket of tall weeds. No one paid any attention to them. This wasn't a train station, and it wasn't an inhabited place, either. There was no sign of the train's engineer. Lee tried to move, and groaned in pain in spite of himself. Had he broken a bone? Beside him, Grace groaned and mumbled, "The snow mountain wind is really cold."

"Where were the two of you at the moment the train stopped?" Someone in a railway policeman's uniform spoke in a rasping voice from above. He nudged Lee with a club.

"We were in the car. Then we jumped out and got hurt," Lee heard Grace answer.

"Get up and come with me. We received a report of theft on the train."

Grace had already stood up. Lee didn't think he could move and asked the policeman to help him. The policeman bent down and yanked him up. Everything went black before Lee's eyes, and he almost fainted from pain.

"Hunh. We've already searched your home in the south. Who travels like this? You brought no luggage. Did you just lock the door and leave?"

Shoving Lee, he walked toward the front of the car. Next to them, Grace kept saying, "It's so cold, so cold."

Lightheaded, Lee and Grace walked a long way. Then the officer took them into a dark room. Telling them to wait on a worn-out couch, he locked the door and left.

Grace said to Lee, "It's better here—away from the snow mountain wind." Tapping the cloth wrapper on her lap, she seemed rather happy. Their changes of clothes were packed in the cloth wrapper. Lee was surprised: even under these conditions, she hadn't chucked away that wrapper! His legs hurt a lot, so he lay down on the sofa and pillowed his head on Grace's leg.

Grace combed Lee's sweaty hair with her fingers, and muttered, "Everything's fine, just fine . . ."

"What do you mean?" Lee asked.

"We've arrived at our destination. The snow mountain, the wind. Pebble Town is just ahead!"

"But we're locked up here."

"Don't be silly. People can't be locked up in one place."

Gingerly, she placed his head on the wrapper, stood up, went to the door, and pushed it. It opened. The sun was so bright that Lee couldn't open his eyes. With a surprising strength, Grace carried the cloth wrapper in one hand and supported Lee with the other. Limping, she quickly walked outside. Lee remembered they went through the waiting room, passed the canteen (businesspeople gaped at them), and finally reached a tearoom. Grace said she was thirsty: she wanted some tea.

Several people were in the tearoom. They were dressed in black, sitting at tables, heads lowered, conversing in low tones in a northern dialect. The moment they saw Lee and Grace enter, they stopped talking. The proprietress poured scalding hot tea into their cups from a large, long-spouted teapot. The two of them sat in a secluded corner that held a small square table with a screen in front of it. Drawn on the screen's glass was a strange long-tailed bird. And written there were the words "long-life bird." As soon as they took their seats, they realized that the glass screen shielded them: no one could see in. Still, Grace remained nervous. She stood up and looked out, sat down again, and then told Lee to look, too. When he did, he was stunned: the policeman stood in the doorway, a pistol in his hand. But Grace didn't seem concerned. As she sipped her tea, she spoke in an exaggerated loud voice. Lee was frightened. Lee warned her in a low voice to behave herself. The proprietress came by to refill their cups.

"So what?" Grace raised her voice. "Aren't we in Pebble Town now?"

The plump proprietress raised her eyebrows and nodded admiringly. "Yes—oh! Pebble Town welcomes you!"

Lee thought the woman's northern accent was really lovely. He got up again to look at the policeman. By then, the policeman was sitting among the other customers, his pistol on the tea table. Grace whispered in Lee's ear: "Now you're free." When she said that, Lee's pain vanished. Was that because of the tea? He felt refreshed and relaxed enough to actually stretch his back.

"Lee, Lee, we're going to settle down in this new place. We'll walk by ourselves from here to our new home."

Grace's voice was choked with sobs. Lee was a little surprised.

"Lee, tell me: are we . . . still the same people?"

"I don't understand."

"It's best if you never understand. Lee, you're really lucky. Go and take another look at those people."

Lee stood up again and peered through the screen. He saw the customers being tied up. They formed a line against the wall, looking down at their feet. Holding his pistol, the policeman walked back and forth, sometimes threatening a person by holding the pistol to his head. A girl, maybe a shop worker, approached Lee and poked him. She said, "Don't be too surprised. This kind of thing happens every day. These people are illegal immigrants."

All of a sudden, the policeman shoved the barrel of the gun into an old man's mouth. Lee saw him pull the trigger, but he heard no sound, nor did he see the old man topple over. They were deadlocked.

The girl pushed Lee; she wanted him to return to his seat. She was unusually strong, and Lee almost slipped and fell. From behind, she grumbled, "This nosy stranger, snooping around—" Lee laughed. The girl said sternly, "Don't laugh—shame on you!"

For some reason, Lee blushed. Muddleheaded, he went back to his seat. He was surprised to see Grace resting her head on the table. Lee thought, *These few days, Grace has been exhausted looking after me.* He was worried about her health. If she broke down or anything else happened to her, that would be the end of him, too. For years, he had survived only because of her. Although she had one bum leg, she had boundless energy and could work miracles whenever she chose. One time on the street, they were run down by a large runaway truck. It was only because she had pressed down hard on him that they saved themselves in the space between the tires. Afterward, Lee asked how she'd been so calm. She said she didn't know: it was instinctive. While Lee was drinking tea and mulling things over, Grace awakened. She tittered.

"Grace, what's so funny?"

"You. The way you're acting is very funny. We're here—we're at our destination. Why are you still nervous?"

Grace stood up and took the cloth wrapper, and dragged Lee out. When they passed in front of the policeman and the people who were tied up, Grace held her head high and limped along. After going through a large coal shed, they reached the street.

"It's so high! So dizzying!"

"Are you talking about the snow mountain, Grace?"

"Uh. I'm saying there's no turning back. It's just like the time we were under the truck."

Although Lee was tired, he still looked excitedly all around, because he was breathing the air of freedom for the first time in days. They were going to the Design Institute guesthouse, which was in the city. Someone pointed out the direction, and they took the path between the poplars. After walking almost a mile, they still didn't see the guesthouse. They came to a construction site with an oil-cloth tent next to it. Someone was sitting on a long bench drinking tea. Lee and Grace walked in and sat down, partly to rest and partly to make inquiries. A woman whose hair was wrapped in a brown scarf told them that this place under construction was the Design Institute's guesthouse.

"We knew you were coming. The director told us to make up your bed. Look—it's so comfortable! You guys are so lucky!"

As she spoke, the woman smacked her palm on the wooden bed in a corner of the tent. The bedding was a new black-and-white fabric with an annular pattern. It made Lee think of ominous things. Grace put her cloth wrapper on the bed right away and sat down on the edge of the bed. She looked excited. She kept saying, "See, look, this is our new home! Ah! . . ." The woman asked if she needed anything else. Grace said no, because she thought everything had been taken care of perfectly. The woman said she would leave then. Later, if they had any problems, they could seek her out. Grace said, "There won't be any problems!"

Lee said to Grace, "There isn't even a place to bathe here. I stink." Grace replied in astonishment, "Didn't you see the little river? Where there are poplars, there must be a river."

Later on, they opened the cloth wrapper, took out some clothes, and went to the river to bathe. The river water was a little too cold, but they still had to scrub themselves clean. As they were bathing, someone on the bank called their names. The man seemed really vexed: Who was it? They finished bathing in a hurry and hid in the shadows to dry themselves and put on clean clothes. By then, the man had appeared before them.

"I'm old Qi. The director told me to take you to the guesthouse. Come along."

Though not young, this ruddy-faced man overflowed with a youthful spirit. His gaze was as lively as a child's. Lee was puzzled: How did the director know them? And what was the guesthouse all about? Maybe he'd find out later, Lee thought.

Carrying the cloth wrapper, they followed old Qi to the work site, went through it, and reached a remote, quiet woods. Lee saw Grace's eyes fill with longing. Soon, they arrived at the guesthouse at the end of the woods. It was silent inside. The guy led them around the flowerbeds and shrubs, and into the building. They went up to the second floor and entered a room. The only furniture was a bed in the center. The bedding was exactly the same as the bedding on the bed under the oilcloth tent—black-and-white cloth with an annular pattern. That pattern made Lee dizzy, but Grace liked it a lot. Touching the bedding, she kept saying, "Great! It's nice . . ." Someone in the corridor outside called for old Qi, and he left.

"It's just like coming back to my ancestral village," Grace said, "though in fact, I've never been there. I've only heard Mama talk of it."

She repeated that she really liked the pattern on the quilt. She unfolded it and placed her face next to the pattern. Just then, old Qi returned to the room. Noticing Grace's enthusiasm, he said, "Just now, it was the institute director who called me. She told me to look after you. It's beautiful here, isn't it?"

"Gorgeous!" Grace's voice rang out.

But Lee was wondering why the director hadn't made an appearance.

"Our director is a woman. She cares about everyone who comes to her. But sometimes things occur that she can't handle satisfactorily. Then she asks me to help. For example, just now someone was making trouble at the work site. Naturally, as soon as something like this happens, someone tells the director and she sends me to the scene. The work site is terribly vulgar—with the people working there like a tumultuous mob. They're bad influences on others. Once you get involved there, you'll never get out again. This place is different. The director hopes you'll stay here. The director didn't come in because she has a headache. She doesn't look very presentable with an ice pack on her head. She's always putting an ice pack on her head. She's one tough woman."

Lee visualized an old woman with an ice pack on her head—and shivered. Grace asked him what was wrong. He said he was cold. Old Qi was still talking.

"My name is Qiming—the same as the name for Venus. Perhaps I was transformed from Venus. Haha!"

The director called "Qiming, Qiming" again from the corridor, so Qiming got up and left. Grace rushed to the door and looked out. She saw the director covered completely in a black robe. As the director walked, she spoke quite intimately to Qiming.

Grace sat down on the bed again.

"Little did I think," she said, looking blankly ahead.

"What?" Lee asked, still feeling fearful, though he wasn't shaking as much as before.

"This old woman has been manipulating us the whole time," Grace said, frustrated.

But she soon pulled herself together. She straightened the bed and told Lee to lie down. She said she was going out for a while. He should go ahead and rest. Probably because he was so tired, Lee fell asleep as soon as he lay down.

Grace came to the newly trimmed flowerbed and sat on a stone stool to enjoy the breeze. This was a plateau. She looked out: she could see as far as the snow mountain. She saw the tombs halfway up the mountain ready to move—like awakening beasts. She looked back on these exhausting few days, and in spite of herself, all kinds of feelings welled up in her heart. Yes, this was their final destination. What more did she want? Her legs hurt, but hope surged in her heart. She thought, *Maybe the director has her finger on everyone's pulse.* This wasn't a bad thing at all: it meant that someone was taking care of her and Lee. Earlier, when they jumped down from the train and lay in the weeds, she had thought that the air here was really good for Lee's heart condition. Later, the policeman showed up, and she felt more happy than afraid. She simply pushed the door open and then held her head high as she walked past the policeman. She felt absolutely confident. Now she stood up and looked all around. The guesthouse really was located on a high plateau. Looking down at the highway, she felt suspended in midair. Maybe this used to be a small hill. After it was flattened, people constructed these buildings.

"Ms. Grace, how are you getting on in Pebble Town?" Qiming walked over and asked her.

"Excuse me, old Qi, may I ask how you know our names?"

"Ha. Good question! Think back for a moment. When you bought your tickets, didn't you have to show ID? A person's movements are always tracked!"

Grace couldn't say anything for a moment. This man was so rude, so shameless! But perhaps he was telling the truth. If he was, then there was an intangible web, and she and Lee had inadvertently been caught in it. No, it definitely wasn't inadvertent: everything could be said to have been deliberate. She calmed down and said with a smile, "The air here is great. I like Pebble Town."

"Does that mean you don't mind the way we welcome our guests?"

"No. As long as it's a good thing, what difference do the methods make?"

Her eyes grew brighter, for all at once she saw a bird on a stone tomb in the distance.

"Mr. Qi, may I ask if you're a local? If not, why did you come here? Sorry, if you'd rather not answer, you don't have to."

"I'm happy to answer, Ms. Grace. I came to Pebble Town in pursuit of love. And I got what I was looking for, so I settled down here."

This was hardly what she expected to hear. Looking at this rough, ruddy-faced man, she thought to herself, *Things in Pebble Town are so incredible!* She said, "Then your beloved must be very special."

"Yes, she's an exceptional beauty. She lives near that mountain."

"Oh!"

"Ms. Grace, I have to go now. Let me know if you and your husband have any problems here."

Grace was a little distracted as she watched this rather clumsy form depart. She sensed something gushing up from the ground beneath the flowerbed and the guesthouse. The stone stool seemed to sink a little when she sat on it.

When they woke up under the brand-new quilt, the sunlight was so strong that they couldn't open their eyes. Grace had forgotten to draw the blinds the night before. She walked over to the window and looked out: the sky was bright and clean. It was so light! The rising sun was showing just half its face: a gleam of rosy golden light flashed on the horizon. Even though the mountain was quite far away, it appeared to be right in front of her. How strange this was.

"I dreamed last night of a man-bear. From behind it looked like a bear, but it spoke a human language," Lee said.

"Maybe it wasn't a dream. Maybe Qiming came in," Grace turned around and said.

Lee shivered when he heard this. Could Qi be a brown bear? He circled around Lee all night long. While Lee was standing in the pavilion, Qiming appeared for a while in the distant poplar grove, and the next moment he turned up behind the garden rockery. When Lee walked out of the pavilion, he saw Qiming again, waving from the lobby of the guesthouse. And when Lee lay down on the grass next to the flowerbed, he looked up and saw Qiming leaning down beside him. He was talking to him. Lee couldn't hear everything he said, but he faintly heard him repeating "long-life bird." Lee saw clearly that he was a bear, yet at the same time he knew it was old Qi from the guesthouse. This was what puzzled him. Now, Grace was saying that Qiming had come here. How could this be explained? Lee was dubious. He walked over to the window and took several deep breaths. The scenery outside made his heart, long covered with dust, bubble over with joy.

"Nothing you see here is actually what it appears to be."

Grace raised her left eyebrow, as if thinking of something.

"Do you think this is like our ailments?" she asked him.

"Do you mean the thing inside us and the thing outside us are the same thing?' Lee was perplexed.

"Lee, Lee, we've finally broken out!"

Grace's dark face flushed a little, as though she were intoxicated. Just then, a woman in the corridor called for Qiming. Was it the director again? Grace drew the curtains at once, turned around, and made the bed. The two of them stared at the door. In the corridor, the director talked loudly with Qiming, but it seemed she didn't intend to come in. Lee wondered if this director was obsessed with cleanliness. What arrangements would she make for him and Grace? Last night, she had invited them to dinner. The many dishes were all wonderful, and candles were lit for the occasion. The other guests were Qiming and two men who did odd jobs. Qiming said the director would soon join them and they could start without her. They ate in silence. It was a little depressing, and as it happened, the director never did show up. Qiming had whispered to Lee that the director was "injured spiritually" and was in therapy again. Lee asked about the treatment. Qiming said the process was simply sleeping while standing in an empty room. He added that if Lee was interested, he could go with him to have a look and to talk with the director. Grace urged Lee to go.

The room in question was next to the bathroom. Qiming walked ahead with Lee close behind. Since he knew the way, Qiming could find it in the dark. They entered the room. Lee saw a person in white standing against the wall. Qiming said, "This is the director." Qiming told Lee to touch the director's clothing, saying this would make him feel more at ease. Lee did this, but he didn't feel any better.

"She's sleeping. If you want to ask her something, go ahead."

Lee's question was about the director herself. So he approached her and said, "Director, why aren't you ever willing to see me and Grace?"

The director gave a strange laugh, scaring Lee so much that he retreated a few steps. Qiming criticized Lee, saying he shouldn't have bothered the director with a question like this, because she wasn't yet well. And it wasn't a good time for her to meet a stranger, because she had a big ice pack on her head. Although she wasn't awake, even in her dreams she could distinguish annoying questions from non-annoying ones. Lee's question annoyed her, so she had only laughed. After telling him this, Qiming asked Lee to touch her white clothing again. He said this would make the director sleep more soundly. He went on to say that the more soundly she slept, the better her recovery would be. And so Lee touched her clothes a few more times. He thought this method was really strange.

"Do you also have psychological problems, Mr. Lee?" Qiming took Lee by surprise.

"Me? I have no idea. Maybe. I do have a serious heart condition." Lee was a little flustered.

Qiming said time was up and they had to leave. They felt their way through the dark and walked out of the room. A fierce bird in the bosk called out to them. It gave Lee goose pimples. After seeing the odd way the director slept, Lee's esteem for her diminished greatly all at once. Instead, he felt sorry for her because of her suffering.

Grace waited for Lee in a completely dark corner. She grabbed his arm and asked urgently, "How is the director? Is she in danger?" Lee answered that from what he had seen, she wouldn't be in danger. Grace said, "I see," as if disappointed. After a while, Grace said the director was sleeping like a "zombie." As she talked, Lee felt an evil wind blowing on his face. Then Grace bent to catch something. It took several tries before she finally grasped it. She looked at it in the light. Lee saw that it was a little black-colored bird. When Grace let go, the bird flew away.

"This is a wagtail; a wagtail is the bird of destiny. It shows up when people are paying no attention, and it goes into hiding when someone notices it."

Lee asked how she knew, because they had never seen this kind of little bird before. Grace didn't answer. When they walked to the moonlit lawn, Lee saw more than a dozen of these birds running there. As soon as they approached, the birds flew into the bosk.

"I've known this kind of bird for a long time. Before I knew you."

As Lee listened to her, he gripped her ice-cold hand, as though if he let go, she would slip into a dark cave and never emerge. Muddleheaded, he muttered, "Together, we can deal with—"

"If you think they're in the bosk, you're wrong."

Grace dashed to the side of the bosk and kicked the bushes for quite a while, but no birds flew out. She turned around and sat down on the grass with Lee. She complained, "Things are always like this here. Once they disappear, they can't be found again. I've tried many times. I think the birds and flowers here are merely props."

Lee wondered why Grace was in such a bad mood. But she wasn't downcast. She was deep in thought. Once more, she thought of the director's being like a "zombie." She felt this was infinitely significant. The next time she saw Qiming she intended to ask him about this side of the director.

"Are you sure that you touched only the director's clothing?" she asked.

"Absolutely. It was white poplin."

"I don't know why, but I don't think it was she. No, it must have been."

Lee wondered what Grace really meant to say. Just then, the bosk grew noisy again. Little birds chirped continuously. Grace walked closer to the bosk. She stood there listening attentively for a long time. Looking at her gaunt profile in the moonlight, Lee recalled the past when she had searched for something on the winding paths in Mountain City. Grace could hear the summons contained in Mother Nature; he couldn't. Grace loved the wind because it brought messages to her.

In a place not far from this couple sat Qiming, implementing the responsibility that the director had given him: watch over this newly arrived couple. What the director had said was simply "pay attention to," because she hadn't arranged work for them yet and had made no demands of them. She seemed to be treating them as guests. Since they were the director's guests, he still had to "pay attention to" them. When he noticed Grace observing the birds, he was moved.

"Ah, I can tell now. There she is!" Grace said.

"Who?" Lee was startled.

"The director—who else? She's the person you just saw. I figured it out by listening to these birds talk. The truth is that the director is with us, but actually, she's also cutting wheat on the land in her home village. Oh!"

"That's a good way to put it, Grace. Let's go back to our room."

Hand in hand, they reached the guesthouse. A dim light shone in the corridor. As they walked upstairs, they felt lightheaded. Someone had put a ladder on the second floor landing. Lee stumbled and nearly fell. After he steadied himself, he looked up and saw a large white thing poised on the ladder. It was a person!

"The director is standing on the ladder," Grace whispered in Lee's ear. "Look at how beautiful she is. Be careful, be quiet. We mustn't startle her."

They went around the ladder and cautiously entered their room. Lee was afraid of bumping into something in the dark. He kept groping with his hand.

"Who?" Lee jumped.

"It is I—old Qi. Good night."

The moment he entered the room, Lee fell into bed. He'd been so frightened that he almost got sick.

He lay there, wanting to ask Grace to pour some water for him, but she had disappeared. The door stood open, and a faint ray of light from the corridor illuminated the small area there. Everything else was in darkness. Some small black animals flooded in; they were much like that kind of small bird. Oh—so many of them. The moment they entered the room, they seemed to disappear. Lee tried his best to call out: "Graaaaace . . . Graaaace . . ."

But he couldn't get a sound out. He thought anxiously, "Am I dying?" His heart was still beating, but arrhythmically: it beat a few times and stopped for a while. He pulled medicine out of his shirt pocket and took a few pills. After a while, the symptoms eased, and his feeling and strength returned. He started reflecting on the fright he had just experienced. He felt surprised by old Qi's and the director's weird behavior. What on earth was this old Qi doing, and what kind of mission had the director assigned him? Maybe Grace knew, or maybe she didn't completely understand and was trying to figure it out . . .

Grace bent down to check on Lee. She held the hand that he extended. She put some sand-like things in Lee's palm, and told him this was bird feed which she had bought at the market.

"You can try to feed them. Then they won't leave you."

"But I don't want them hanging around me—they make me jittery."

"You'll be okay after you get used to it. Lee, trust me. Scatter this bird feed."

Lee scattered the bird feed next to the bed and heard the birds pecking at it. Grace rushed to the window and leaned out, as though she wanted to fly. Worried, Lee propped himself up. Grace turned around. Her voice sounded as if it was coming from a grotto, echoing in the tiny room. "I see a large banyan in midair—the tree of the south."

Lee wondered why these strange little birds were connected with the banyan tree. Once more, he felt a puff of gas reverberating in his chest. He opened his mouth and said loud and clear, "Oh—" Feeling completely recovered, he even got out of bed. Grace went over and helped him right away, and walked with him to the window, where they faced the large fluorescent banyan. They heard the ringing of the aerial roots colliding in midair. The tree was filled with the chirping of the wagtails.

"Lee, these are the birds that you just fed."

"But I didn't see them fly away."

"They're everywhere. Sometimes they hide themselves; sometimes they show themselves."

While Grace spoke, the banyan tree blurred and then—bit by bit—disappeared. The moonlit night sky seemed to be urgently asking them something, but what was it? When Lee gave voice to this question, Grace said she was pondering this. Perhaps it was nothing that one could get to the bottom of. Such things did happen. For example, they had survived being run over by the truck. There were so many questionable things that couldn't be explained. Lee wanted to turn on the lights and look for the little birds in the room, but Grace stopped him, "Once you turn on the lights, it will be another world." And so they felt their way to bed in the dark.

They didn't fall asleep for a long time. Lee didn't sleep because he wanted to listen closely for those birds; he thought they were still in the room. And Grace didn't sleep because she wanted to remember an adventure she'd had in a shop in Bell City. Though she tried hard, she couldn't remember it. She knew only that it was an adventure. The words "Why are the dishes flying in midair?" crossed her mind. Just then, the ladder in the corridor collapsed with a bang. Lee and Grace jumped out of bed and raced to the corridor.

The ladder had collapsed, and the director had fallen onto the concrete. In the shadows, the beam of white light was more dazzling than usual. Not until they bent over and stretched out their hands did they see that this wasn't a person at all, but a piece of white cloth. How ironic it was! "Didn't the dream come true just now?" Grace whispered. But Lee thought Qiming had played a trick. What had he been up to? They heard someone going downstairs. The footsteps were loud, sounding defiant. Grace shouted down, "Old Qi, leave us a way out, will you?"

Her voice echoed on the stairs. It was eerie. From high up on the wall came the sound of beating wings. The birds! They both smelled danger, and they held their heads and ran back to the room.

They latched the door and went back to bed. The night became even longer than before. Lee sensed that Grace's inner darkness was spreading toward him, as though it would enfold him—yet also as if it would keep him out. This was a new darkness, one he was unfamiliar with. He said to himself, "Grace—what a woman!" For a moment, in the depth of darkness, he felt that he and Grace had become one person. But in the next moment, an iceberg separated them. Grace was guarding her dark shadow and staying on the other side of the mountain while he trudged in the snow with his pant legs soaking wet. In the past, when they lived in Mountain City, Grace supported him whenever he walked uphill; she was with him almost all the time. Now that they had arrived here, did she really want to go her own way without him? He wondered if this was an omen of his bleak future. He had never seen wagtails before coming to Pebble Town. Here, they were everywhere—a little overpopulated. Grace was apparently interested in learning more about their habitual nature, but these birds made it hard for him to breathe.

The footsteps were still sounding on the stairs. Maybe it wasn't Qiming; maybe it was the worker on duty at the guesthouse. He seemed to always be going down; it never ended. Lee didn't think he was going down to the first floor, but to an abyss. Normally, departing footsteps would grow softer and softer, but this noise was uniform—not too close and not too far away. He asked Grace about this. She said it was the sound of his heart beating: even she could hear it. Lee climbed out of bed and pressed his ear to the door. Someone was walking out there for sure. It definitely wasn't his own heartbeat that Grace was hearing. He listened a while: the sound didn't vary. All he could do was lie down again.

After going through that interminable night in the guesthouse, Lee was uneasy about everything in Pebble Town. When he walked on the cobblestone path, he would take a few steps and then stop and stamp his feet—checking to see if the ground was firm. Before long, they moved into an apartment building. They were the only ones living there; the other apartments were vacant. They usually bought groceries at the market and cooked at home, but sometimes they ate their meals in the canteen. After they settled into their apartment, Lee felt much better. The pure air on the frontier enabled him to breathe easily. As a result, his heart condition improved. He could also engage in more activities. Now he often went out alone, sometimes staying out for a long time. He no longer depended so much on Grace. If she wasn't there and he fell sick again, he calmly took his medicine and lay down until he was better. He did this successfully several times.

Their bedroom was on the third floor—the top floor, which was slanted. At first, they kept the skylight open all day. Later, when Lee began feeling dizzy, they closed it and nailed it shut. Grace was the first one to see the flower garden. It was early morning: she slipped out of bed, walked barefoot to the window, opened the heavy drapes—and all at once she saw it. It was a miniature flower garden hanging in midair in the distance. Tropical plants greeted the breeze. It gradually moved closer—until it was right before her eyes. "Whoa—whoa . . ." Grace couldn't stop marveling at the scene before her. She stood transfixed.

"Grace, what's wrong with you? What are you looking at?" Lee sat up and asked.

"It's the scenery at Cloud City, where I've never been. It's the southernmost place. My God!"

They stood side by side, embracing each other. They were excited and on edge. This tropical scene so close to them made their life—never very concrete—even more illusory. Yet both of them felt an unusually strong desire to live. Tears spilled from the corners of Lee's eyes. He kept saying, "Grace, Grace, I can't believe we're finally here!" Grace fixed her eyes on the palm trees; she felt her heart might stop beating. In a trance, she heard Lee calling her. She answered him time after time, and dug her fingers into his flesh. But he didn't hear her, nor did he feel her. Then, struggling free of her arms, he turned and walked from the room to the corridor. A little worried, Grace pulled the drapes and went back to bed. She heard Lee talking with someone. It seemed to be Qiming. Mingled with their voices was a woman's voice. Was it the director?

Lee returned after a while. He had seen the director. She had exhorted the two of them to "observe their geographical position."

She was a profound woman. Lee went back to bed. The scene just now had tired both of them. Grace joked that they were now like two corpses in delicate shrouds lying in a large coffin. She was holding Lee's hand. Lee was amazed that her hand—always cold before—was now radiating heat. Even her fingertips were hot. Unable to sleep, they sat up and looked at the black-and-white pattern on the quilt. Grace said the director must be using the design of the quilt to hint at her expectation of them, but she couldn't figure out what that expectation was. Lee said he couldn't, either, though he was sure the director meant well and must have a training program for them. But if so, he didn't have the foggiest idea what the program might entail. Lee said, "Everything will be all right as long as we follow the director's instructions. Even though her words are sometimes unfathomable, we can do what we understand her to say." Although their discussion was inconclusive, they did feel better and better. They got up and decided that, from now on, they wouldn't open the drapes on a casual impulse to look out at the scenery. If they wanted to look at it someday, they had to mentally prepare for it. Now they understood why the drapes were so thick, and even double-layered with the top part on rollers. This was to keep illusions out. They had never before used such high-quality drapes. Grace thought this building still held numerous secrets for them to explore. Maybe they simply needed to get through each day rhythmically, and the director's expectations of them would eventually be actualized. What she needed was the power of persistence. Had she already found it? Maybe she already had this power without knowing it.

"Lee, listen: many things are hitting the window. They're like birds."

Lee had already heard them. He was excited. He opened the drapes a crack and saw dazzling sunlight. He let go of the drapes at once. He suggested that they explore this whole building and complete the mission the director had assigned them.

They went to the corridor and opened the room next door: a cloud of dust choked them and they sneezed repeatedly. After the dust settled, they got a good look. This room had a bed just like theirs, with a quilt in the same odd black-and-white pattern. A layer of dust covered the quilt. Lee walked over to the window, intending to open the drapes, but the pulley was broken. And so although the sun was out, it was like midnight inside the room. Because he'd pulled the drapes, the dust soared again. Lee couldn't stand it and fled. As he stood next to the door, he heard the melodious sound of a flute coming from outside the window and saw Grace standing motionless in the dust.

"Grace?" he shouted.

Grace didn't move. The room was so dark, and yet the dust looked pink. Lee felt as if he were suffocating. He wondered how Grace could breathe.

"Grace?" he shouted again.

The music from the flute stopped. Grace walked out slowly, looking frazzled.

"No, we don't need to look at the other vacant rooms. We've figured it out," she said.

"What did you figure out, Grace?"

"I can't say. With time, you'll understand. Take another look at the door to the right. There's a huge cobweb on it, but the old spider has left. You'll understand that."

They went down to the second floor. Lee was observing Grace. She didn't have a speck of dust on her. He was surprised: Just now, she'd been standing for a long time in the dust, hadn't she? Grace opened the door to the room on the west, and they walked in. This apartment had three rooms, all vacant. The floor was thick with dust. Judging by the air, this apartment had never been occupied. Because there were three connecting rooms, and there was no light, it was even darker. They had to feel their way around. They sensed they were stepping on some soft objects, but they couldn't see what. They were nervous, afraid a disaster would befall them.

Grace's legs gave way and she sat on the floor. She propped herself up with her hands and then grabbed hold of a little feathered thing. It appeared to be a dead bird. This whole room seemed full of dead birds. She saw Lee standing against the wall, afraid of stepping on them. Oh, he was moving away from the wall, apparently intending to exit. Grace said silently, "Coward—what a coward!" Lee exited, and Grace lay down. Dead birds kept dropping from above. Although she couldn't see them, she could smell the fresh blood. She started thinking back. She recalled that when she was a child, the old woman she called Granny (perhaps not her real granny?) smoked cigarettes. She had a little turtle in her pocket. Grace wanted to look at the little turtle, so Granny pulled it out and placed it in her hand, warning her, "Careful—it bites people." One day, it did bite her palm. It was gory, for it broke her skin. She cried. As Granny bandaged it, she kept saying, "Didn't I warn you?" Grace still had a scar on her palm. When Granny lay in her coffin, they put this living turtle in with her; they put it in her pocket. Afterward, Grace thought about it for a long time: How long could the little turtle live underground if it ate Granny's flesh? As she remembered this, she touched her stomach: three dead birds were stuck to it. She whisked them off. Two more landed on her chest. Another struck her forehead. Lee was calling her from the doorway, but she didn't want to move. The smell of the birds' blood reminded her of the unresolved riddle from her youth. She didn't intend to solve it. She just enjoyed pondering it in the dark. After a while, Qiming showed up, too, and called to her. She had to get up. When she walked toward the door, her lame leg was worse than usual and she nearly fell down.

"Ms. Grace, why are you so pale?" Qiming asked.

Qiming held a large photograph of the director wearing white clothing, her white hair floating. Grace didn't answer Qiming. She glanced at the photo out of the corner of her eye. She appeared to be uncomfortable. Qiming said he wanted to frame it and hang it at the end of the corridor. Curious, Lee held the photo up high and took it to a spot with more light. He was shocked at what he saw.

"Some birds are hidden inside," Lee said.

"You have very sharp eyes." Qiming started laughing. "I'm going to hang her here. Then you won't have to be afraid of anything. The director protects everyone."

Squatting on the floor, Qiming put the photo into a frame and then climbed a ladder and hung it up. Lee and Grace went downstairs hand in hand. Lee asked Grace, "Do you like having the director's protection?" Grace answered, "Sure, what's wrong with you?" It was a slight rebuke.

When Lee stepped onto the cobblestone path, he felt the ground floating. When he bent to pick up a leaf, he doubted it was a real leaf. He leaned against a poplar tree and felt the tree trunk falling apart behind him. He asked Grace what the director's protection consisted of. At this, Grace sank into deep thought. They snuggled together on a bench under the poplar, and for a moment they were silent. One by one, the strange things that had occurred since their arrival in Pebble Town appeared in their minds. They sighed with emotion. However, for the moment, they couldn't see any connection between those incidents.

Wildflowers blossomed everywhere. Besides the little birds gamboling about, ratrabs—Qiming had told them the name of the little yellow-furred animal—frequently appeared along the way. They looked a little like rats and a little like rabbits, but not quite like either. Sometimes they stopped on the cobblestone path and watched Lee. A strange light beamed from their black eyes. Whenever Lee met their eyes, his heart beat regularly, as though he were joined with the mineral resources deep underground. Grace commented that the animals' bodies contained gold mines. Fish were jumping in the brook beside the poplar grove. One by one, they leapt out of the water. A spectacle like this was seldom seen in the interior. Lee thought,

Even the fish are impulsive here. Grace was still deep in thought. Suddenly she said, "If we can get to the bottom of one thing, then everything else clears up, too. Am I right? Lee, last night, I dreamed of gold mines, but I couldn't recall it after I woke up. When I saw the ratrabs' eyes, I remembered it. Look, Lee, that flower is called salvia. The one next to it is calliopsis. Ha! In fact, we're living in the flower garden. We can see the snow mountain from our window. It's all because of the director's protection, isn't it?"

Lee wanted to say "yes," but he wasn't sure. It was quite pleasant to sit under the poplar tree with Grace's hand in his, enjoying the frontier view all around. But soon Lee heard the faint sound of dogs barking—a large pack of dogs barking menacingly. Before long, he saw Qiming dash up, chased by the feral dogs. All of a sudden, Qiming fell to the ground. Two big dogs snatched the shoes from his feet and ran off. All the other dogs scattered, too, and quickly disappeared. The barefooted Qiming was like a drowned mouse as he walked up to them. He looked thoughtful. Lee didn't understand why the dogs had run off with his shoes. He was going to ask, but Qiming spoke first. "Ha, they think the shoes are my feet! Isn't this curious?"

"These dogs are really mean. They're menacing!"

Lee shrank back from the cold wind blowing in from the snow mountain. Beside him, he heard Grace say some inexplicable things, "Mr. Qi, what you saw were dogs, but what I saw were some falling leaves! Lee and I have to keep from falling here, isn't that right, Mr. Qi?"

Qiming didn't reply. It seemed his soul was no longer present. Turning, he headed toward the guesthouse. Lee stared at his bare feet. Whenever he stepped on the fallen leaves, the leaves were silently pulverized. He walked with a light, smooth gait. Lee imagined the minerals underground dancing in time with his footsteps. A ratrab skipped over to their feet. They blushed, and their hearts beat faster. Neither of them dared to look at the little animal. It scratched their feet and ran off again. Between cracks in the foliage, the steel-blue sky was divulging some information to them. Deep down in their hearts, they understood, but they couldn't say what it was. They could only sigh repeatedly, "Pebble Town, oh. Oh, the frontier. Oh . . ."

When the poplar leaves turned golden yellow, Lee and Grace entered the underground mines. That was during the last part of the night. A girl in black appeared in their bedroom, and they followed her out. As Lee felt his way ahead in the tunnel, he was full of doubts: "Is this Grace? Are she and I dreaming the same dream? Is this possible?" They walked and walked, and the black-clad girl's footsteps disappeared. They could hear only the echoes of their own footsteps. The ground was bumpy. With each step, they had to lift their legs high. Lee couldn't figure out how Grace kept her balance. He wanted to talk, and he tried, but nothing came out. It seemed he really was dreaming. Then he pulled Grace along, and the two of them sat down. Lee sensed that Grace was saying something, although it wasn't clear what. Some fragments of sentences crossed his mind— all related to a quartz mine. Lee touched the wall of the cave: yes, it was quartz. He was overcome with excitement and a little afraid. It was wonderful to dream with Grace. Why hadn't they ever done this before? But the tunnel might collapse, and they might be smothered to death. In the quiet, Lee started whenever he heard a suspicious sound. Each time, Grace did her best to pull him back down. Grace was so calm that Lee thought she was meditating—communicating with the quartz all around them. Although Lee was excited, he certainly couldn't communicate with the things around them. When he touched the hard ore, his heart seethed with a bizarre excitement, but he didn't understand why. He heard his wife say something strange: "Sleep tight. It's okay."

So was he awake? Lee wasn't sure. From somewhere above came another sound—the crackling of quartz. It was obvious that the ground was gradually sinking. After a while, the sinking accelerated.

At first, Lee was going to scratch the wall beside him, but he couldn't. His hand slid, and his mind was fuzzy. Just then, he remembered what Grace had said: "Sleep tight. It's okay." He closed his eyes right away. In the dark tunnel hallway, he saw several bright spots.

Grace couldn't hang onto Lee. She looked on helplessly as he fell, and later wondered if this was his good fortune. She sat down and exhaled. She brought her feverish face to the hard stone, and stared guardedly into the tunnel. Several spindly human shadows wobbled and glimmered with light. She coughed noiselessly a few times and stamped her feet. She actually heard echoes from underground. Grace felt intoxicated, her thoughts galloping ahead. She opened her eyes in the billowing yellow dust and identified those mobile shadows. As she was doing this, she kept visualizing herself as a baby in diapers. Once more, she shouted noiselessly for Lee. She walked to the edge of the chasm and stretched out her lame leg to test its depth. She remembered that when Lee was lying under the truck, he had whispered, "We won't die." She had forgotten these words right after hearing them, and hadn't remembered them in all these years. Now they had come to mind again.

"Here I am, Ms. Grace!" Qiming's voice echoed in the cave. "Above us is the snow mountain. Didn't you guess? In the morning, we'll be blown by the wind from the snow mountain."

Grace thought Qiming's voice contained a wealth of experience.

Chapter 8

LIUJIN, HER PARENTS, AND THE BLACK MAN

The year that Liujin was ten, the Design Institute assigned her family to a bungalow with a small courtyard. One Sunday, they happily moved in. Two young poplars were growing in the courtyard, and disorderly weeds stood three feet high. In the beginning, Liujin hated their new home because of the many mosquitoes and because of strange animal sounds at night. When it turned dark, she withdrew inside, not daring to go out. From the window, she saw some suspicious black shadows moving through the weeds: they looked a little like foxes or birds. She heard her parents walking softly in the adjacent room, discussing something. They were apparently very pleased with this new home that they'd been looking forward to for a long time.

José did a great job tidying up the courtyard in only two of his days off. Besides cleaning out the weeds, he planted a few flowerbeds and planted vines next to the fence. This resulted immediately in fewer mosquitoes. Strange birds still hooted at night, but the sounds were less terrifying. No longer panicky, Liujin began exploring her new home. The courtyard was large, and the backyard even had an old well. Liujin craned her neck and looked down into the well; this gave her goose bumps. People said the water wasn't safe to drink. She saw a gecko on the red brick wall next to the main entrance. It looked as if it had lived more than a thousand lonely years. Liujin touched it, but it didn't move. For a second, Liujin wondered if it was dead. But after a while, it began crawling slowly: it crawled from the wall to the ground and then into the house. Once in the house, it climbed the wall again—straight up to a corner of the ceiling. There, it stopped. Liujin thought it was absorbed in its own reflections.

"Liujin, Liujin, it's time to do your homework!"

Mother spoke to her from outside the window. Through the glass, Mama's face looked distorted—short and broad, a little like a tea urn. While Liujin was doing her homework, the bird on the poplar in front distracted her. What kind of bird was it? It wasn't an owl, even less likely a crow. Maybe it was the same one she'd heard at midnight. How she wished she knew for sure! Mother didn't seem the least bit sentimental. She was a strong-willed woman, always acting in accord with her own strange principles. When they lived in a third-story loft, she had never fussed about the sounds made by large birds on their skylight. She was no different now. She seemed to be used to strange phenomena. Though Liujin was young, she had sensed this long ago and admired this side of her mother.

Although the weeds had been pulled, the dark animal shadows still traversed the courtyard. From a crack in the curtains, Liujin peered at a lonely little animal, and her heart thumped. She wondered where it slept. If it didn't sleep, did it go from this courtyard to another, and then to the highway? Or could it sleep while it was walking? As she was mulling over these things, Liujin felt chilly air on her neck, as if an evil spirit were aiming a knife at her back. She put away her schoolwork and hung her backpack from the clothes rack. Hearing a sound in the courtyard, she opened the curtains and took a look. She saw her father bending down, looking for something along the fence. Then he apparently found it, for he held something up high and shouted.

"What did you say?" Mother yelled from the window.

"It's the gecko. It slipped out again. It should stay inside."

Liujin thought this was an odd notion. But after thinking it over, she felt it made sense. This home once belonged to the gecko. Her family had invaded its home. The door creaked again: Father was entering. He set the gecko down inside the house. Liujin went into the dark living room. She shouted "Dad," but no one answered. She looked inside her parents' bedroom; it was dark, too. She didn't think they could have fallen asleep so quickly, for they'd been talking just now. Out of curiosity, she pushed their bedroom door open. In the dim moonlight, she saw the quilts folded neatly on the bed. Mother lay on the rattan recliner, her head to one side. She seemed asleep.

"Mama!" Liujin shouted.

"Huh? Aren't you asleep? What do you want?" Nancy asked hoarsely.

"Where's Dad?"

"In the kitchen. There's a hole at the base of the wall there. Maybe a fox made it."

Liujin felt her way to the kitchen. No light was on there, either. Her father was sitting on a small recliner.

"I couldn't sleep, anyhow, so I'm keeping watch here. I want to see if anything sneaks out through this hole."

"Dad, you must mean *comes in*."

"No, I meant what I said—sneaks out. There are some weird creatures in this house. I'm not sure what they are."

Liujin sat down on a stool. She and her father were worried. The wind poured in from that hole. They shifted their position in order to shelter from the wind.

"On a windy night like this, they probably won't go out," Father said.

José glanced absentmindedly at his daughter, who was sitting beside him. He noticed that his little girl was growing quieter over the years. Too quiet for her age. Sometimes he wondered if her previous impetuosity now had truly disappeared. As he watched, his daughter's shadow began wobbling and separating into a few parts.

When he looked hard, the parts took the form of a person again. Liujin's body could break up in the dark (perhaps he was only hallucinating). He'd seen this happen several times, and each time it surprised him. Why had she cried all night long when she was a baby? Was she scared? José's insomnia gradually worsened. Somehow Liujin became aware of her father's nighttime activity and began keeping him company. José sighed: a daughter was close to one's heart. A boy could never be the same.

"Dad, how big is Pebble Town?"

"We circled around it one time, didn't we?"

José thought, *Liujin worries too much. She can't be easily reasoned with.* Now, for example: his answer didn't satisfy her and even made her a little angry. After saying nothing for a while, she returned to her room and went to sleep. How big was Pebble Town, really? Could she be sure of its size just because he had taken her around it once? José couldn't understand his daughter. He had seen her lying next to the granite well twice, listening attentively at its opening. She had also sat for half an hour next to the well and absentmindedly gazed down into its depths.

In the summer, José kept his word and took Liujin to the snow mountain; they traveled by car. Once in the frozen region, Liujin stood there numb and unmoving as if going crazy. Her reaction had been over the top—beyond José's expectations. He quickly led her down into the needle-leaved forest. While walking there, she wasn't aware of the little animals that jumped back and forth in front of them. Only the two eagles circling in the sky could attract her attention, because she was afraid the eagles would pick her up and carry her off. Halfway up the mountain, she asked about the snow leopards. She was walking ahead of José. Gazing at her gaunt form, José kept saying silently to himself, "Daughter, my daughter . . ." He kept saying this, even though his heart ached. He felt that the snow mountain was becoming much less mysterious. Was this because of Liujin? What an unfathomable little girl.

After his daughter left the kitchen, José opened the window and looked out at the house across the street. The light there was still shining. The family were local tenants. They had a foible: they hardly ever turned out the lights at night. If there was a power outage, they lit a kerosene lamp. Did they work at night? Recently, in an energy-saving move, street lamps weren't being lit, so that family's home had become the only source of light in this large area. It made José's imagination run wild. These people were in the sheep-butchering business. They purchased sheep from out of town and sold the meat to the market. The husband was the most somber person José had ever known. One day, José saw him crossing the street. When he reached the middle of the street, a medium-sized truck rushed across, but—as if deaf—he didn't deviate from his exasperatingly slow pace. The truck screeched to a stop and almost hit him. For several days afterward, José, who had witnessed this, felt extremely lightheaded: he staggered when he walked. Outside, the wind was howling, as if Pebble Town were giving vent to rage. In his mind's eye, José saw Nancy and Liujin as they slept, and for a moment he felt a rush of sentiment. What did the people over there think about this strong wind? Ever since he began having insomnia, Nancy had slept really soundly. Now and then, she would talk to him as she dreamed. Although she couldn't hear his answer, she continued conversing with him from a deep valley. José was deeply moved at times like this. But in the daytime, Nancy told him that she wasn't sleeping, she was awake. She felt she hadn't slept in a hundred years. When José thought of this, he saw Liujin's small figure in front of him.

"After we moved to this bungalow, the wind has been even stronger. Is it because there's no cover anywhere around us?"

"Liujin, you mustn't think of such things. You have to go to school tomorrow."

"I didn't mean to, Dad. The wind woke me up. Should I cover my face with a scarf when I go to school?'

"Don't be silly, the wind will stop before dawn. It always does."

"Okay." Liujin seemed reassured and returned to her room.

He didn't look at that hole, but he sensed something—maybe shadows, maybe rats—sneaking out of the house through it. He named these little things "the native residents." He thought they should be classified the same as the gecko. What was genuine sleep? Living in this kind of room, could he catch some genuine sleep? Nancy was concerned about Liujin's health, particularly her sleeping. Neither of them knew what to do about it. Liujin still seemed healthy, though. Maybe she slept better than most people did. She frequently said, "I slept like the dead." Her manner was odd for a child her age.

Not until the wind gradually died away did José go back inside and sleep. First, he lay on the recliner in the living room, and every once in a while went to the window and looked out. In the courtyard, the animals prowled in silent solitude. They were probably only shadows, yet José preferred to think of them as real animals. He didn't go out for a better look. He had tried before, and they had always vanished the moment he opened the door.

Liujin looked out the window. Her father was standing under a poplar talking with a sturdy middle-aged man. The man seemed aware that someone was peeping at him, and retreated behind the poplar tree. Liujin couldn't see his face, but guessed that it was dirty and travel-stained. When José went back inside, Liujin asked who that was. José said it was a vagrant who had come by to panhandle. He had given him some change. José said all of this without looking at Liujin. Instead, he looked at the wall in front of him and kept moving about restlessly.

"He can't be a vagrant, can he? You seem to know him well."

José was taken aback by his thirteen-year-old daughter's acuity. But he didn't feel like talking about it, so he said nothing. Liujin wasn't pleased with her father—because the man seemed familiar, and yet she couldn't place him.

"Some people and some things have vanished from my memory," she grumbled to Nancy.

"That's impossible. They'll always be there," said Nancy.

As time passed, Nancy felt more reassured about her daughter. She thought, *Despite so many hardships over the years, coming to the frontier was the right thing to do. Liujin is truly one hundred percent a child of the frontier.*

Liujin was happy with her mother's answer. She picked up the watering can and went off to water the flowers. As she walked into the courtyard, she suddenly noticed that the vagrant hadn't left: stepping out from behind the tree, he glowered at Liujin. Liujin was afraid and stopped in her tracks. But the man quickly exited the courtyard. Liujin followed him to the gate and saw him climb into a small broken-down truck and drive away in a cloud of smoke. As Liujin watered the flowers, she unconsciously repeated the words her mother had said: "That's impossible. They'll always be there." She was startled, as she realized that her tone of voice was precisely the same as her mother's. What on earth? She had always thought she wasn't at all like her mother, and sometimes even thought she was the opposite.

"I saw him. Hunh," she said to Dad.

"I don't understand. Maybe you're the one he came here for." José was disconcerted.

"What do you think? Don't you know?"

"No, I really don't."

Liujin looked regretfully out the window. Then the old black cat appeared in her line of vision, and her expression softened. With one leap, the cat landed on the windowsill, and Liujin rushed to find some dried fish. When she returned, she saw her dad go out the gate. The black cat solemnly ate the dried fish. It had always been a well-behaved cat.

"Mama, who is that man?"

"I didn't see him, but I think he's probably an old friend of the family—the one we lost track of."

"Oh?"

"He left a long time ago without saying goodbye."

Liujin waited for her mother to say more, but her mother walked away. Was she hiding something that was hard to talk about? She sat in front of the window and smelled the black cat. That smell always reminded her of the forest and the animals' dens. The cat's eyes were apricot-yellow, and its fur was lovely. Liujin guessed it belonged to this building. She was agonizing a little, because she couldn't remember when and where she had seen that middle-aged man. He stood there, one hand resting on the tree trunk. He talked at length with her father. Liujin faintly heard him repeat one word: "Roses . . . roses . . ." Was he talking of the roses in their courtyard? Years ago, when she had just been born, many black people had come to Pebble Town. And then they had left. She had heard Mother talk of this. But this person clearly wasn't black. Father had stopped up the hole at the foot of the kitchen wall. Even so, when Liujin stood in the kitchen at night, she felt the wind blowing against her feet, frigid air rising from her soles.

She walked to the backyard, bent over the well, and looked in. This well was very deep—much deeper than the many others in this city. One time, Liujin thought that the prowling animals had emerged from here. Of course, she had no proof. Her mother called for her, but she felt aggrieved and didn't answer. The incident today had left her in agony. She shouted down into the well. The gigantic resounding roar scared her. She retreated rapidly and closed her eyes. When she opened them again, the black cat was disappearing silently around the end of the courtyard wall. Just then, she saw her mother looking all around, and so she stood up and shouted, "Mama, do we still have that small duck that I played with when I was little?"

"What?"

"I used to have a toy—a little duck that could float on the water."

"Oh! You do remember, after all. It was probably tossed out long ago. We couldn't save everything."

Liujin thought Mama was certainly looking for her, and yet she pretended she hadn't been.

"The man said something about roses, but I couldn't hear the rest of what he said."

"Oh."

They went inside together. Nancy told Liujin to clean sand from the mung beans. Liujin did this until she was dizzy; she couldn't concentrate. After Liujin had washed the beans, she slipped out to the street. She strolled for a while and then turned at the fork in the road and went to the riverside. It was a great day, and the river water was clear. Liujin drew two deep breaths, and then was startled: not far ahead, her father and the vagrant were talking as they stood shoulder to shoulder in the river. The middle-aged man was striking the surface of the water with a willow branch. Viewing them from behind, Liujin sensed that the two men were close.

"Dad—Dad!"

José turned around in surprise and saw Liujin. Leaving the other man behind, he stepped out of the water and onto the shore. Liujin saw that the other man was still standing in the river, looking up at the sky, absolutely carefree. José sat on the grass and put on his socks and shoes. He made a face and didn't look at Liujin. He was angry.

"Mama said that maybe this person is an old family friend."

"You mustn't follow me around all the time."

"I don't, Dad. I saw him leave in a truck. How can he be back here?"

"That's the way he gets away from prying eyes and ears." José burst out laughing.

The man was still looking at the sky. Liujin thought, *With neither clouds nor eagles in the sky, what's he looking at? Still, the sky in this season is the softest blue, perhaps because there's a little moisture in the air? Who is he?* Liujin wished her father would tell her himself, because after all she was already grown-up. There was nothing he couldn't tell her.

José seemed to hesitate, but finally he spoke.

"He used to adore your mama. But one day he left all of a sudden."

"Then, were they lovers?" Liujin's expression turned serious.

"I'm not sure. Maybe. There's no way to know what's in another person's heart."

"Dad, I want to go back."

"I'll go with you."

"No. You stay here. See, he's waiting for you."

At first, Liujin walked away quickly without looking back. Her father didn't catch up with her. She was very depressed, because she couldn't remember a thing about this man. She saw the black cat on the riverside with a sparrow in its mouth. It was gruesome—the most hideous scene she had ever seen. She felt she shouldn't have asked her father these questions, but—like a silly girl—she had.

Like other kids, Liujin went to school every day. There, she learned all kinds of things. But for some reason, she wasn't interested in school life, and it left no impression on her. Although she was gradually learning more and more, and getting to know her teachers and classmates better and better, in the bottom of her heart she wasn't interested in school. The school at the end of the poplar grove occupied only a little space in her mind. She much preferred working in her family's courtyard, or going for walks in the suburbs, or watching people fish in the river. She also liked spending time with her father. The two of them had once gone by car to the Gobi Desert. That experience left a deep impression on her. She matured a lot during that summer vacation.

It seemed that the medium-sized inn next to the Gobi Desert had something that manipulated people's moods. Father and daughter got up in the morning and had breakfast in the restaurant where a breeze was blowing. They listened to birds singing outside the window; it was as if they were in a utopia. Then they went outside for a stroll. Sometimes they returned at noon, sometimes at dusk. When they came back at noon, it was very hot in the inn. All the guests lay on bamboo recliners in the corridor panting for breath. The waiters' sweat rained down; they walked back and forth, their heads wrapped in white towels. If someone accidentally dropped a plate or ran into a cart, everyone flew into a rage. Liujin saw a waitress stick a fork into a woman's back. Liujin was so frightened that she hid behind her father and didn't dare make a sound. She and her father took turns going to the bathroom to shower. Then they changed into black robes provided by the inn and lay in the corridor as the other guests did. Liujin was adapting and fell asleep soon in the torrid weather. At night, the inn was like an ice house. Despite their heavy quilts and robes—and even padded slippers—they were incredibly cold. The faraway sound of a woman weeping continued intermittently throughout the endless cold night. Liujin struggled and struggled and finally fell asleep. She dreamed several times that she was frozen stiff. Although they were in the same room, she didn't know if her father was asleep or not. He lay motionless in bed. One night, he suddenly had an odd idea and took Liujin out to the courtyard. Liujin saw their shadows on the ground: they looked like ghosts. Her mouth was numb from cold; she couldn't speak. She wished they could return to their room soon. But her father seemed to be looking for someone. After finding him, he stood next to the flowerbed and talked with him for a long time. Because the person's face was hidden by a black cotton hat, Liujin couldn't see him. On the way back, she nearly lost consciousness; Dad pushed her from behind.

Later, a long time after they returned from the Gobi Desert, Liujin was still unable to come back to earth. In the daytime, she often asked herself, "I was dreaming, wasn't I?" She frequently forgot to do homework. In school, her teachers criticized her, and everyone gaped at her, but still she thought about other things.

She asked her dad about the person with the invisible face at the inn. Her dad said it was the inn's owner, who had also emigrated from the south. He had worked with him. Later on, he'd had problems at home, and had abandoned everything and gone to the Gobi Desert. His inn was so special that it was well-known throughout the country. People came from far away to enjoy the unusual experience there.

"There's a place in the Gobi Desert: as soon as people walk into it, they get burned. The people lying in the inn's corridor had all been burned. The owner uses an herbal ointment to help them recover quickly," José said.

Liujin asked why they hadn't gone to that place. It must be really interesting. José said, "Because you're still too young." Liujin wondered why children couldn't go there. Then she told José that she didn't want to go to school; she wanted to stay home. This shocked him for a moment, but he quickly responded that this wasn't a good idea. "You may be in school and not in school at the same time. You shouldn't be all alone. That can't be good for you." As José said this, he himself wasn't at all sure of it, because he didn't know, either, what was better. They dropped this subject without reaching a conclusion, and Liujin never brought it up again. She gradually mastered her father's maxim: "You may be in school and not in school at the same time." Her various teachers seemed to be urging her in this direction, for their lectures grew increasingly boring. Sometimes they ended their lectures by repeating two or three sentences again and again. As she listened, Liujin finally understood, and so her thoughts flew to a certain faraway southern city. She learned how to think in the midst of crowds of people. Thus, her teachers' mechanical teaching midwifed her imagination.

In the dusk one day, the gecko fell from the doorframe to Liujin's feet. Liujin picked it up and placed it at the base of the wall. She turned around and asked Nancy, "Is it looking for something, too?"

"I think so. Are you?"

"Me? I think I'm still too young."

Nancy began laughing. She motioned for Liujin to look at her father sitting among the rose bushes, with his head propped up heavily in his hands. "Your dad is at the riverside watching the steamboat," Nancy whispered to her daughter. Liujin thought her dad looked a little nervous, and she felt nervous, too. What was that? Nancy patted her on the shoulder and pointed overhead. There, the gecko was stuck, motionless, to the ceiling. Maybe it was lying in wait for mosquitoes. Liujin was sure this little creature felt the urgency, too.

Liujin had gone to the Design Institute once and stayed for a day. It didn't leave a good impression on her, and she never wanted to go again. The first day of summer vacation, Liujin weeded the courtyard in the morning. While she was concentrating on her work, a woman entered the courtyard. Saying nothing, she stood to one side observing Liujin. She looked approving. Liujin wondered if this person was a relative. The woman sat down on a stone stool and said slowly, "This is a great courtyard; it has everything. Don't you ever think of going out and looking around?"

"Where?" Liujin asked, perplexed.

"The place where your parents work. It's very interesting."

"What would I see there?"

"Ha! It's a wasteland, with countless little black birds in the weeds—the kind of bird that comes and goes, filling the sky and earth. Many black people walk out of the office building. They are very kind and gentle people. Day after day, they keep getting lost in the wasteland. When the setting sun lengthens their shadows, they grow anxious and scurry around."

"Do you mean the Design Institute is in the wasteland? That isn't very far; I can get there by bus."

After this odd woman left, Liujin changed her clothes, went out, and boarded the bus.

She got off at the entrance to the Design Institute, but she didn't want to go in right away: those gray buildings looked boring. Strolling on the hill overgrown with weeds, she noticed green snakes and little black-colored birds, but not nearly as many birds as the woman had said. Walking downhill, she came to some flat land. She stood there and looked up: she saw one black building after another. How had these buildings turned black? She looked again at the weeds underfoot: they were all dried up. The feathers on the little black birds seemed scorched. Overcome by fatigue, she suddenly longed to go home.

When the middle-aged black man walked down from the slope, Liujin was bending over tying her shoelaces. She saw him when she looked up. She had never met a black person and couldn't help feeling a little on edge. The black man smiled: his teeth were very pretty.

"Every year, fewer and fewer birds come here. That's because of fires. See these dried-up weeds: every few months, they ignite spontaneously. That's not unusual in a wasteland. Your ma wants you to hurry home."

Liujin wondered if the black man might also panic at dusk. He seemed so unflappable. How had Mama known she was here? Had the strange woman told her?

"But now I want to hang around and see some more. Do you know why—when you look up—these buildings turn black?"

"The buildings are simply black. We used to call them the black buildings. Over the years, they turned gray because of the wind and sun. Still, when you look up from the foot of the slope, you see their original color."

Liujin looked and looked again at the "black buildings," and a chill arose from the bottom of her heart. As the black man walked next to her, he kicked the bosk. He said poisonous snakes hid there, and if you kicked a few more times, they would run off. He asked Liujin if she was afraid of poisonous snakes. She said she was: Snake bites could kill you, couldn't they?

"If you're afraid, you should spend more time around them," he said earnestly. "My name is Ying. This was once the name of a snake. Ha!"

Without giving it any thought, they returned to the entrance of the Design Institute. Liujin noticed that the buildings had turned dark gray again, and the sky was the same color. The place where her parents worked seemed lonely. The windows were all closed. And she didn't see anyone coming out of the buildings. If it was a rule that you couldn't leave during office hours, then why was Ying outside?

The bus arrived, and Ying asked if she would take it back. He apparently wanted her to leave. Liujin wondered why.

"I have to take responsibility for your personal safety," Ying said.

Saying that she wanted to look around a little more, Liujin hurried off in another direction. Ying caught up with her right away. She asked why he kept following her. His answer caught her off-guard: he said he did it for her mother.

"In the last ten years or so, your mother and I have been discussing you constantly. It's the only topic she likes. She's—she's a remarkably good mother!"

Liujin thought this black man's words were ridiculous, because she had never thought her mother was particularly caring. On the contrary: she felt she had been quite estranged from her mother ever since she was little. What made him say she was a remarkably good mother? Her words alone? Did her mother brag about herself? Liujin frowned and sat on a clump of weeds. She didn't understand why her mother had wanted to discuss her. The scenery was disheartening enough, and now this odd black man had brought up an annoying topic. She was a little angry. The little black birds flew back in a flock and lit on the clumps of high weeds. Liujin hadn't ever seen birds living in weeds. Could they be the "weed chickens" that people talked of? Where did they hide in the winter? Here, even trees were sparse. Just then, a snake emerged, a little black bird in its mouth. The little bird was shrieking. The odd thing was that, after a while, the snake spat out the bird. The injured little bird lay on the ground, gasping for breath, and the snake returned to its hole. The black man Ying squatted down with Liujin and looked at the bird. He fed it a tiny pill that he took from his pocket. Then he placed the bird in the clump of weeds. He told Liujin that he always carried this kind of medicine to cure snake bites. He also asked Liujin to look down the hill. She did, but the view was hazy. A person with a white headscarf was walking out from the fog. The black man said: That's a rag-picker who's been circling around this office building for more than ten years.

"What can she find outside the office building?" Liujin asked.

"We throw things out the windows so she won't starve. And I even threw out a bronze mirror to surprise her and make her happy. Rag-pickers are so hopeless."

Soon, the woman drew closer. Ying led Liujin over to the shrubbery, where they squatted low to conceal themselves. The woman raked a stick back and forth through the weeds for a long time. Then she began hitting a snake. She struck with ferocious assurance, time after time, until the snake stopped moving. Liujin got a good look: this woman must be a farm worker—the veins stood out in her sturdy hands, and her eyes looked dull. She stepped on the snake for a while, then moved ahead.

Not until after she had walked away did Ying and Liujin emerge from their hiding place and go to look at that snake. It wasn't dead; after a while, it slowly slithered into the weeds. Ying followed it with his eyes and said, "It couldn't have died, could it? The animals here all have nine lives." Liujin asked, "Why did that woman want to hit the snake?" Ying replied, "Because she's desperate." He went on to say that her life was very hard because it wasn't every day that she could find a bronze mirror. Liujin was nonplussed. She looked up at an eagle. The eagle had been hovering for a very long time; it must be exhausted. Or was it desperate, too, because it had found no place to alight?

"Then was my mama also desperate?"

"I don't think so. She's never lost hope—just like you, young lady."

Another bus pulled up. Liujin decided to board it and go home. When she said goodbye to Ying, he looked sad, as if Liujin were going to meet death. Liujin turned around and ignored him.

The black man ran behind the bus, waving and shouting, "Liujin, come back again!"

Complicated feelings about this black man surged up in Liujin's heart. In her young imagination, black people were the world's strangest race. Ying made her think of her great-grandfather, whom she had never seen: she imagined he was an ancient person standing behind a curtain with only his feet showing.

By the time she got off the bus and walked into her small courtyard, her mother had returned and was in the kitchen rinsing soybeans.

"Mama, I've been to the Design Institute."

"Ha. It isn't very interesting, is it? Children don't usually want to go back there."

"Ma, I think Ying is like my great-grandfather."

"He . . . he's the guardian of the Design Institute!"

When Liujin watered the flowers with a watering can, she recalled once more the birds and snakes on the hill. She ached from pity. What did the birds do when it snowed? Could they go into the office building to escape the cold?

The sun set behind the mountain. It was hot and stuffy in the house. Liujin rested next to the well. Just then, she heard water. Looking into the well, she saw water rolling and splashing. She thought, *This kind of place is so volatile.* Even though she was so far from it, she could still feel a slight tremor. The moment she turned around, she saw her dad: he had been standing behind her for quite a while. Pointing toward the well, she asked him to look. José said with a laugh, "I saw this a long time ago. This well is just as restless as you are. People from the Hygiene Bureau have come by numerous times and said this well needs to be filled in. We'll probably have to do that."

José's comments made Liujin lose interest in observing the well. Dismayed, she stood up and walked into the courtyard. Nancy had set up a small square table there. They began eating. They were all sunk in their own thoughts. No one mentioned the incident from earlier that day. Although they lit mosquito coils, the insects attacked relentlessly. They bit Liujin's legs several times. All of a sudden, José stood up with his bowl in his hands. Although Nancy and Liujin followed his line of vision, they saw nothing.

"What's wrong?" Nancy asked.

"I was mistaken. I thought it was the director, but actually it's the bag lady. Like the rest of us, the rag-pickers live in the city. They're locals. I didn't know this until today."

José's remarks made Liujin think of the hill again. She was agitated as she thought of the green snake and of those black office buildings. Her mother had told her just now that Ying lived in an office building, and so he was familiar with everything there. Would he let the birds enter the building during the winter? She needn't worry about the snakes: they could certainly stay in underground holes.

At night, her sleepless father stood talking with someone outside Liujin's bedroom window. He and the other person apparently had a limitless supply of topics. Liujin kept waking up. Each time she awakened, she heard them talking in stifled, yet fervent, tones. Later on, she couldn't stand it and walked to the window and opened the curtains. She saw Ying, the black man. In the moonless night, Ying was a dim shadow: only his head swayed in the air. Liujin thought, *He's so agile. How wonderful to be a black person!* Ying was trying to convince her father of something, but her father kept shaking his head, seemingly not daring to trust this wisp of a man. Liujin saw Ying slap his own head in a moment of desperation. He opened his mouth, revealing snow-white teeth. But her father still shook his head in sorrow. Liujin heard him mention his insomnia and say, "I've had this problem for years; it's incurable." Liujin didn't know if Ying saw her. He was facing in her direction, but she couldn't hear what he was saying.

The animals came from near the ancient well—five of them. They quietly formed a line behind these two men. Liujin thought they were a little like wolf cubs. As Ying said goodbye to Father, Father hung his head and said nothing. Then Ying turned around and left. The five little animals followed him out of the courtyard. Had Ying brought them here? Now Liujin was full of admiration for Ying! She put on her slippers and headed outside, following him all the way to the road. She shouted at the slender figure in the distance: "Ying! Ying!"

Ying stopped but didn't turn around. The five little animals made sounds that Liujin had never heard before—like children's laughter. Ying kept going in the direction of the Design Institute.

"Liujin, let's go back," José appeared under the street lamp, his voice sad. "That person isn't on the same track as we are."

Liujin looked at her father; she didn't understand what he was saying. He was so exhausted. Liujin thought, *Perhaps it's only strange people like Ying who don't have to sleep.*

"Dad, did this person want you to leave home?"

"What a bright kid you are. That's exactly what he said. He wanted me to go with him to the Gobi Desert, rent a house at the edge of the desert, and look for gold mines there. I thought, that's his work, not mine."

"Huh?"

"This man, Ying, is linked in thousands of ways to his native Africa."

Hands behind his back, José walked back and forth in the courtyard. Although he looked wan and sallow, he didn't want to go inside and rest. Why? It was dark. Only some light from the window occasionally illuminated him. Liujin looked at him and felt heartbroken. She thought, *Dad isn't old yet, so how has he fallen into this hellish life?* José urged Liujin to go in, saying he would follow her shortly.

After Liujin went to bed, she kept listening for her father, but never heard him open the door. She roused herself when it was barely dawn and immediately sensed something wrong. She ran out and saw her father sitting with his back against a poplar, his head at an angle. Had he actually fallen asleep?

"Dad! Dad!" Liujin shouted.

"Oh, is it morning? I've been thinking about Ying's suggestion. Your mother . . . she was also considering it. And then we fell asleep. Hey, this Ying is just terrific! And he's been our friend for more than ten years."

Liujin noticed that her dad's forehead was a little lined: it looked like butterflies or tree leaves, and made her imagination run wild. But when he yawned, the lines vanished. When Dad mentioned Ying, Liujin's expression turned somber. She would have forgotten the scenery at the institute if Dad hadn't talked of the black man. Just then, José stood up and slapped the dust off his body. Looking furtive, he asked Liujin where her mother had gone. When Liujin said Mother was home, he wanted her to go and look. Liujin ran over to Mother's room, but she wasn't there. The quilt on her bed had been folded neatly. Behind Liujin, José chuckled.

"Your mother is working in a garden now!"

Liujin asked where it was, and José said, "Hard to say. You just know it when you get there." If she was interested, she could ask the director.

"You can see that kind of garden many times in a lifetime. In the past, when we lived in the apartment building, we frequently went to visit the next-door neighbors, opened the heavy drapes in their bedroom, and saw the garden—in midair. Your mama has never forgotten it."

Just then, the curtains moved, and Liujin screamed from fright. José dashed over and flung the curtains open. They saw the black cat, and Liujin laughed in embarrassment.

"We have to go to the Gobi to look for gold. The cat is doing it right here," José said.

It was bright outside, and the sun's rays stung José's eyes so much that he murmured, "It's too light."

While Liujin sat alone in the house, she thought of Ying and of Africa. What a beautiful scene it would be at dusk if those tall, slender black bodies dissolved, leaving only some heads dancing in midair, and drums began sounding, and African lions towered in the distance. If Ying had been born in such an open place, why wouldn't he be homesick? Liujin's mother had said that Ying had been at the Design Institute for years: the director's father had brought him here. Liujin wondered if she were Ying, and the desolate scenery near the Design Institute jogged her memory, would she be reminded of Africa? If so, this was probably the main reason Ying stayed there.

The black cat returned to the windowsill. Its black fur also made Liujin think of Africa. She pressed her cheek against its fur. The animal's smell was bewitching. The other night, the five little animals following Ying were animals that she had never seen before. What were they? What an interesting person Ying was! He had the air of a king strutting about on the road with five strange animals following him. She heard the director talking with her mother in the living room at the front of the house. They seemed to be arguing a little. Liujin didn't much like the director: this old woman with snow-white hair had gained everyone's respect—that was what Liujin didn't like. Liujin wasn't sure how she should act around this woman who was her parents' boss—and, from what people said, their benefactor, too. She had run into her on the street, and the old woman had patted her head. She had looked puzzled and surprised. This angered Liujin.

"Sweetie, I've brought you a present!" the director shouted.

Liujin hurried to the living room, where the director was holding up a crook-necked bottle with many little fish in it. Some had died from lack of oxygen. The director put the bottle on a table, and because the water vibrated, some fish fainted. Most of the fish were dead. Liujin ran into the kitchen and brought back a basin of water, into which she dumped the fish from the bottle. Some slowly revived. Liujin told the director she didn't understand why she had packed the fish in a crook-necked bottle. The director explained that she was doing an experiment related to execution reform. Nancy smiled, but she didn't enter into the conversation. When the director left the room for a while, all the fish died. Nancy speculated that perhaps it was because of bleach in the running water. As she stared at the dead fish, Liujin started hating the director.

When she went back to her room, an idea jumped out of her brain: Had the director sentenced Ying to life imprisonment? As she considered this, she grew more and more excited. She came up with all kinds of ways that Ying could escape.

"Dad, did the black man really ask you to look for a gold mine?"

"Of course not. He urged me to go, that's all. As for him, I think he doesn't want to go anywhere. He only wants to 'guard'—in other words, keep watch over the Design Institute's land."

"Oh!"

Liujin's heart sank: there was no justice in the world. Everything was the opposite of what she thought it should be; nothing made any sense. She certainly didn't intend to go to Africa to see for herself, but she liked to experience Africa vicariously through Ying. For a long time now, she had felt that the Design Institute's old director was a masked despot. When she had patted her on the head, she wanted to howl. Liujin had never understood anything about the Design Institute—not the people and not the work, either. From the time she was old enough to understand things, she had listened closely and observed. Sometimes, Dad would explain a little to her, but his explanations frequently drew her into deeper, more complicated, and darker entanglements. He seemed to take pleasure in this. But Liujin wouldn't play along. When she couldn't figure things out, she gave up. She simply stopped thinking about it. Ying was one of these issues. Ying impressed Liujin with a sense of intimacy. She was especially enthralled that night when she saw the five little animals following him. Yet, today Dad had said Ying was simply doing his job. Did everyone in this institute have a specific responsibility? Were her dad and mama also just doing their jobs every day? How lighthearted the director seemed while she was killing those tiny fish!

Looking at the back of Liujin's head, José thought to himself, *Although my daughter is thin, her hair is luxuriant!*

The two of them didn't talk as they reached the courtyard. José placed the dead bird in the bottom of the deep hole that he had dug. He would plant a grapevine over it in the future. The bird was probably an owl. He had no idea how it had died. When they saw its corpse below the fence, ants were already crawling all over it. José said some people in this neighborhood shot birds with BB guns; they shot cats and dogs, too.

"Do they do this at night?" Liujin asked.

"Yes. They're sharpshooters. When I turned around, I sensed they were aiming at the back of my head. Hunh, these guys!"

José smoothed the ground and sat on the stone bench, deep in thought. In the kitchen, Nancy was cooking porridge; the aroma spilled all around. José saw his wife appear briefly at the door; she had probably come to take the stool inside. It was time for her to prepare the vegetables. Just then, José heard people talking inside.

"Last year's garlic bulbs are hanging behind the door," one voice said.

José asked Liujin if she heard the voice. She shook her head and said she heard only a cat—the adorable black cat inside. Then she said abruptly, "I don't want to follow in your footsteps."

José answered with a smile, "But you're still a daughter of the frontier."

"Hmm."

Irritated, Liujin lay down next to the well. Although the well was already filled in, Liujin could still hear the deep subterranean water whenever she concentrated. She was at school the day that the well was filled in. The moment she got home, she knew something was different. The courtyard was extremely quiet, and no one was inside. The air smelled of fresh earth. A picture frame had been newly hung in the living room. It held a photograph of her maternal great-grand-father. Liujin had seen that photo once before—pressed in a book. It was yellowed, a remnant of a past life. These two things—the well being filled in and the photo being hung up—occurred simultane-ously. Liujin felt this was quite odd.

Liujin sensed the earth moving at the well's opening. Startled, she jumped up at once. Oh! A pangolin! Had this ugly thing been buried by mistake, or had it squeezed in? As soon as it emerged, it took off in a hurry. Liujin leaned close to the opening and stared blankly at the small round hole. She thought of another possibility: the well had once been this ugly thing's home. Hadn't she suspected this before? How many animals were at the bottom of this well?

"You don't have to follow in my footsteps," José said from behind.

Liujin smiled in confusion, not knowing what to say. She and her dad had recently drifted apart. She remembered that when she was a little child, she and her dad had been so close that even when she went to the public toilet she wanted him to wait for her at the door! Liujin noticed that her dad was a little aloof, a little dejected; perhaps he was pondering some personal problems—or maybe he was inten-tionally drifting apart from her because of some plan? Whenever Liujin thought about this, she felt chilled.

"Is the director an old friend of yours and Mama's?"

"Unh. It seems that when your mama was a child, the director was her school principal. But your mama doesn't remember this. Is it important?"

"Is it? I don't know. Maybe not."

Liujin looked at the well opening again. Strange, the hole that the pangolin had squeezed out of was now nowhere to be seen. José told Liujin, "This is probably because of the viscosity of the mud here." As he said this, Liujin gave him a puzzled look. He was a little embarrassed.

"Actually, I don't know, either," he said, disconcerted.

A woman was singing on the road, a song of sorrow. José told Liujin that she had once been their neighbor. After her husband died, sometimes she was lucid, sometimes insane. She always sang songs that her husband used to sing. She seemed quite pathetic, but actually, it wasn't necessarily so.

"Why?" Liujin asked.

"She's a self-satisfied person. She takes things lightly."

"Oh, I see. You told me that they once had a dog."

Liujin also wanted to sing on the road, or even on the mountain, but she had never done this. She sat at home and thought about Ying. After a while, the faint rumble of thunder rolled over from the east.

Nancy said to José, "This girl is very ambitious, and she has been ever since she was little. I'm not worried about her, though."

José glanced at Nancy's profile and thought back to the days of living on the third floor of the apartment building when Liujin was just a baby. He whispered to himself, "How did they heal the breach between them?" He felt there had always been a tacit understanding between Nancy and their daughter.

He and Nancy had also discussed going back to visit the interior. José still had an uncle in Smoke City. The moment they broached this subject, they thought of the hardships of travel and realized they weren't likely to go. In fact, aside from the travel itself, there was another big obstacle: Liujin. Wouldn't Liujin—with her bright eyes and her sensitive respiratory tract—have problems in an industrial city with smoke curling around all day long? They couldn't be sure about this. Their daughter had grown up in the clean Pebble Town, where no air pollution existed, and so although she was a sensitive and delicate child, she had never been seriously ill. If they suddenly went somewhere where you couldn't even open your eyes, they weren't sure she could handle it. After discussing this several times without coming to a conclusion, they dropped the matter. José felt vaguely that Nancy had a bigger plan, but he couldn't guess what it was. But it would surely become clear with the passage of time. There were moments—he didn't know why—when he also wanted to see life's hidden secrets. But the bright, shining Pebble Town didn't give him an answer.

After Nancy said "I'm not worried about her," José didn't look too pleased. In a split second, the image of "Grandma Wolf" crossed her mind. Had she been playing Grandma Wolf for more than ten years in her relationship with Liujin? Maybe it hadn't actually gone that far, and maybe Liujin didn't hold a grudge, and so although their relationship was rather tepid, basically there was no rift in it. This girl was particularly adept at understanding people and was particularly independent. Nancy felt that even she couldn't match Liujin in this. When she was still a baby, Nancy had left her alone on the lawn several times; later, someone else would pick her up and take her home. José referred to this jokingly years ago. Liujin had laughed—as though her dad were telling a story about someone else. Liujin's composure surprised Nancy: she wasn't much like other children her age. Her feelings had long ago pierced the complicated world of adults. Sometimes she was like people who had gone through a lot. Now Nancy could look calmly into her daughter's eyes because they were no longer as dazzling as they were when she was little. Some hazy things appeared in her gaze, softening it a little. Still, Nancy was sometimes skeptical: Could it be because she had lived on the frontier a long time and had become accustomed to the brightness and intensity of this place? *Liujin, ah Liujin*, sighed Nancy.

José hadn't been wrong in his guess: Nancy really did have a hazy "plan." What it was, he hadn't yet ascertained. Often when she finished her daily routine and sat down, she gazed at her daughter's back, and some scenes popped out in her mind. All the scenes had the same background—a large gloomy room, a thirty-some-year-old woman sitting under a dim light in a corner, embroidering butterflies. This was Liujin, wasn't it? Nancy felt chilled; she didn't dare hold onto this thought. One time, she called Liujin over to her and asked if she had learned how to embroider. Liujin said she had studied it in school, but hadn't really learned how. She couldn't embroider well. When Liujin answered, Nancy seemed to see her thoughts and so she hadn't pursued this. Later on, she made a point of buying some high-quality thread and bringing it home. But Liujin didn't touch it.

When José had trouble sleeping, Liujin often didn't sleep, either. When Nancy awakened, she went to the window and looked at the two forms—one large, one small. Generally, they weren't talking, but just sitting in the courtyard, each one perhaps wrapped up in his or her own concerns. At first, Nancy was worried that Liujin would also have insomnia, but later she discovered that Liujin slept soundly. Nancy had always been ashamed of her parenting—she'd always felt that Liujin was closer to her father. But recently, José had begun to be reclusive and wasn't even slightly interested in his daughter. And so Nancy began paying more attention to her daughter, but Liujin's attitude toward her didn't change.

"Mama, when the wind blows hard, does it blow away the smoke in Smoke City?"

"It can't. The smoke comes not only from chimneys; it's the very air itself in Smoke City. It doesn't matter what the weather is like or where one walks: haze is everywhere."

As Nancy was speaking, Liujin thought of cats, because Dad had said that there were many cats in Smoke City. She thought, *Probably it's only cats' eyesight that isn't affected by the smog.* Liujin had always thought that cats' eyes were a mystery—the pupils changing suddenly from large to small, green fire in the dark. They apparently could see through to everything. Dad had also told her about a cat that had passed through the marble pillars of the hall. She'd heard that story since she was little.

Nancy took stock of her daughter, whose head was bent as she shelled peanuts. She was shaken by the child's questions. All of a sudden, she felt filthy, and sour sweat seeped continuously from her pores. More than a decade had passed, and nothing had yet been concluded. The rejection rooted in her bones, the malicious spurning—all of it was still present, and she had nowhere to flee. Sweating, she paced back and forth in the room like a trapped animal. She loathed herself.

"Peanuts grow underground. No one knows this," Liujin said, looking up. She showed her a large peanut.

"Liujin, Liujin, I do know that. I tell you, little one, I do know that."

She was suspended in midair. Even on tiptoe, she couldn't touch the floor. She strained to remember that day in the guesthouse of the Design Institute: Where had she fallen? She remembered the wind blowing in from the snow mountain and rubbing her face raw. It had hurt. She had shed tears the whole time, unable to stop. José . . . back then, José hadn't helped her up; instead he had lain on the floor with her. As for her daughter, did she really know everything? Sometimes she was sure she did; other times, she didn't know. Back then, her daughter's crying in the middle of the night had assaulted her brain, and so she had finally left her daughter on the ground. Night after night, she had run, and run—run for a long time before stopping and looking. She saw that she was still in the same place.

Chapter 9

LITTLE LEAF AND MARCO

The wooden boxes were arranged in a long line next to the jet-black river. Little Leaf's box was the largest one. You could tell from the dark color that these boxes were quite old. They stuck roses into each corner of the box. The roses were weird: even though they'd been out in the sun day after day, they still looked fresh, as if rooted in the ground. Early in the morning, someone shouted from the riverbank: "Little Leaf! Lit—tle—Leaf . . ."

Little Leaf and Marco climbed drowsily out of the wooden box. When they were wide awake and looked across the river, they saw no one. Marco said it had to be the person from Holland, who had come to urge him to return to that country. Because he knew Marco wouldn't listen to him, he had shouted for Little Leaf, instead.

Nights on the riverbank were terrifying: it was as if the violent wind would blow the boxes into the river at any moment. Mixed with this strong wind were many howling wolves. The two of them were accustomed to this environment. Sometimes Marco lit a candle. Watching the flickering light, he told Little Leaf stories of Holland. "Mama, ah . . ." he often lamented. Little Leaf wasn't nearly as calm as Marco. She trembled when the wolves howled. When Marco told his stories, she couldn't see his eyes. This upset her. Although Marco's eyes were open, his pupils were invisible in the candlelight.

During the day, they worked in a large restaurant on the riverbank. Those who dined there were mostly also migrant workers from the countryside. Some of them also lived in the boxes on the riverbank. Little Leaf was a waitress, while Marco did odd jobs. The work was tiring, but at the restaurant they saw some people and things that aroused their interest. A stolid old man showed up every day for his meals. After examining him closely, Little Leaf concluded that he was more than seventy years old. But his clear eyes looked very young. He didn't eat much—a small bowl of noodles was enough. And sometimes he ate nothing, asking only for a glass of water. At such times he apologized to Little Leaf, "I'm too old. My body can't handle too much food."

Marco told Little Leaf that this man didn't live on the riverbank; he lived next to the main road leading to the snow mountain. He had built a temporary wooden house in the white birch forest there. Marco had stayed overnight in that house once. Marco also said the old man had been a temporary worker in a lumberyard. "Where's he from? It seems I've seen him before." As Marco said this, he looked quite distressed. Little Leaf suspected that the old man was somehow entangled with Marco's past.

Another regular customer was an old woman dressed all in black—even wearing a black headscarf. When she sat down at a table, she made almost no sound. Every time, she ordered a bowl of soup and a small bowl of rice. She ate unobtrusively. After finishing, she lingered a while, absorbed in her thoughts. One time, when Little Leaf was clearing the next table, the woman suddenly spoke up, "There ought to be a clock here." She blocked the light with one hand.

"Oh, I'll tell the manager. But maybe it's intentional? Nowadays, people all wear watches. Hey, that's exactly right. Everyone . . ." Little Leaf broke off, realizing she was babbling.

The old woman forced an ear-piercing laugh, and then stopped laughing and stood up and looked at the picture on the wall—a framed, crude oil painting. Little Leaf had never been sure what the picture depicted: it could be a sail, or it could be a butterfly. She leaned close to the old woman and looked at the painting with her. The old woman said softly, "It's the clock, all right."

From then on, Little Leaf kept noticing this woman, and she also started paying attention to this painting. In the past this painting had been inconspicuous, but now it was disturbing. Furthermore, every time she passed it, she heard a tick-tock sound. It did indeed sound much like a clock. On the wall about four or five meters away from this painting was another picture—a mediocre painting copied from a photograph of a sandthorn that looked as if it were sick and dying. These were the only two pictures in the entire dining room. When Little Leaf walked past the sandthorn, she could hear nothing, and didn't sense anything disturbing. Yet she couldn't pass by without glancing at it a few times. Why? The tables beneath the oil painting belonged to the old woman. She always sat at one of two tables. One time, she revealed her wristwatch—a large and heavy navigation watch. It looked more like handcuffs. Little Leaf was surprised that she wore a watch and yet complained that there was no clock in the dining room! She wanted to ask her if she worked on a tramp steamer, but she was too timid. The woman herself brought up this subject later. She said that she had worked on a tramp steamer. After she retired and came to Pebble Town, she had hallucinated: she had thought the "she" who had worked on the steamer had died of cancer. And so she wore mourning garments and moved to an old house on the riverside. She spoke somewhat impulsively and grabbed Little Leaf's hand, letting go of it only when she finished telling her story. That day, the clock tick-tocked particularly distinctly—and the sandthorn in the oil painting turned colorful and full of vitality.

The old man and the old woman didn't seem to have anything to do with each other, but for some reason Marco kept insisting they were friends. When Little Leaf asked why he thought so, he said he had seen them together in a coffee shop in Holland. "They weren't so old then."

One time, dogs caused a disturbance in the restaurant. A skinny man burst in with a pack of dogs. He ordered food and drink and sat there eating. The vicious-looking animals roamed back and forth in the dining hall. One by one, the angry diners slipped out quietly, and the waitresses took cover behind the door. Then the dogs jumped onto the tables and made a big meal out of the food left by the customers. They also broke a lot of dishes, making a huge mess. Marco and Little Leaf were very excited that day: they had seen these dogs before and thought of them as old friends. The two of them walked back and forth in the dining hall, their hearts filled with indescribable longing.

All of a sudden, a large wolf-dog pounced on Marco, knocking him to the ground. Actually, he fell of his own accord—and quite readily, too. Marco was holding the dog's neck; the dog stepped on his stomach and made eye contact with him. Marco was panting and anxiously looking for something in the dog's eyes. The skinny man came up and berated the dogs. He dragged the wolf-dog out with one hand and kicked it in the haunches. Wagging its tail, the dog looked at its master and left grudgingly. Marco clambered up and scuffled with the man. The man started to return the blows, and then stopped, saying, "I'm dying." His face turned paper-white and dripped cold sweat. Frightened, Marco helped him sit up against the wall. After quite a while, the man said, "My father died before I was born. I have a serious congenital heart condition."

"You won't die, will you?"

"I'm dying. But what will happen to the dogs? Who will they belong to . . . belong to . . . ah!"

He rolled his eyes, struggled a few times, and then gradually revived again.

"Who are you?" he asked Marco weakly.

"I'm that Dutch dog."

By now, the dogs had all left the dining hall. There weren't any outside, either. No one knew where they'd gone. Little Leaf dashed up and said that something had been stolen from the kitchen in the back: a large slab of beef had disappeared right under her nose. The manager had reported it to the police. The moment the man heard this, he stood up and limped out.

He walked unsteadily, but didn't stop. And thus he disappeared from everyone's line of vision. The manager said, "I know him. He always goes to a lot of trouble for these dogs. They're his life."

One day as they sat in the kitchen at break time, Little Leaf and Marco saw the stolid old man planting something in the wasteland. He dug a hole with a rake, took a seed from his pocket, and buried it in the hole. Then he took a few steps forward and dug another hole . . . The wasteland had sandy soil that didn't hold water, and so hardly anything could grow in it. What had the old man planted? "It's something that dropped from a human body," he later told Marco. But what he took out was seed-shaped—a little round, grayish-blue thing. How could something like that fall out of a human body? Later, the old woman showed up, too, and helped him plant. They were busy for a long time. Marco said to Little Leaf, "I told you they were together, didn't I? They used to come to dine separately and pretended they didn't know each other. In fact, they always communicate with each other."

The next day, the two reappeared. They had sown the entire wasteland with that thing. Supporting each other, they stood taking stock of the results of their work. They didn't look at all happy; they looked melancholy. The old woman in mourning covered her face with her hands. They couldn't tell if she was crying. Little Leaf's curiosity got the better of her and she wanted to go over for a better look. Marco held her back. He thought that in Holland, the two of them had owed one another a lot. Now they were paying each other back. Marco knew everything.

One moonlit night when Marco wasn't present, Little Leaf ran over to the wasteland by herself and raked open a hole. After searching a long time, she found a grayish-blue seed. She examined it in the moonlight. From any possible angle, it was nothing but a stone—round and smooth and very hard. There were also vein lines on it. She buried it and raked open another hole, where she found a similar stone, maybe a little flatter and a little brown-colored. Such a large stone couldn't have come from a human body, so why had he said that it had? After reburying the second stone, Little Leaf panicked and ran the whole way back to her living quarters. When she reached the box where she and Marco lived, she noticed several people craning their necks and looking at her from the other boxes. Marco said bitterly, "You're really headstrong."

Late that night, Little Leaf screamed because she distinctly felt her body falling apart—falling apart into many little pieces. Only her head remained intact. And her mouth was still able to scream. Her head floated in midair. She saw Marco busying himself in the wooden box, holding up a candle, picking up those little fragments (who knows why there was no blood?) and piecing them together. He did this conscientiously, inspecting everything carefully lest he miss something.

"Marco?!"

"Oh, baby, I'm here."

Little Leaf was worried: Would Marco bury these little pieces in the ground? Marco urged her to go to sleep, and—in midair—Little Leaf closed her eyes. But she couldn't sleep. In a haze, she again saw Marco bustling around. Somewhere, a cuckoo bird was calling: it was midnight. She didn't know what Marco was doing. Suddenly, her hand felt very weak, like an infant's. She tried to grab a glass from the table, but she couldn't. She heard Marco talking.

"I came home and didn't see you. I just knew that you'd gone to the wasteland and turned over those seeds. You had to relive that person's experience. I've just figured it out. The gardener raised the cuckoo bird. See: he has raised just about everything here. He raised those China roses, and they all blossomed as large as basins."

Then the candle went out, and Marco continued bustling around in the dark. He seemed to be sewing. Was he sewing those fragments together? If he had buried a few small pieces in the ground, what would have happened? She heard him say, "This is Holland's border." His voice was a little eerie.

Little Leaf couldn't fall asleep until the first rays of dawn entered the box. She slept in through the day and didn't go to the restaurant. While she was sleeping, their neighbors saw two older strangers circling around her box numerous times—taking careful stock of it. The neighbors saw the old woman lift a large black watch toward the sun and wind it up. The neighbors were bewildered: Why did she have to face the sun to wind a watch?

After a day of rest, Little Leaf returned to work feeling refreshed. When she entered, the manager was sitting at the entrance smoking a water pipe. He gave her an artificial smile and said, "Have you recovered so soon? Are you sure you're all right?"

"What? I wasn't sick. I simply overslept. Really . . ." She was flustered.

"You overslept? That's okay. It could happen to anyone."

The customers hadn't yet arrived. She started her day by cleaning the dining hall. The restaurant was rather desolate. After cleaning for a while, she set the tables. The manager told her they would have no business today because there'd been a free reception the day before and the customers had all filled up then.

"It was a great day of rebirth for everyone," he said.

Little Leaf looked up: the picture of the "sail" had disappeared from the wall. In its place was a birdcage. She looked again: the other picture was also gone. On the wall was a white rectangle where the frame had hung. Little Leaf contemplated this for a long time. The silence all around seemed to be warning her of something—but what? She went to the kitchen and then to the storeroom: she was looking for Marco. In the back of the storeroom, a door led to the wasteland. Little Leaf looked out. She saw Marco bent over raking those holes.

"Are you wrecking their hard work?" Little Leaf asked with a smile.

She noticed that he had dug up seeds from most of the holes. She didn't understand why the little grayish-blue stones became black in the bright sunlight and lost their round shape. They were no different from ordinary stones. Were these the seeds the old man had planted? Marco was still digging energetically: he said he wanted to find a Holland pea. When Little Leaf asked what a Holland pea was, he said, "It's a person's heart." He kept turning over the soil, but what he found were only the same black stones. He was sweating and depressed. Little Leaf realized he never forgot his days in Holland, yet as she saw it, past events were like narrow, dark little alleys; it was hard to say where they would lead. Little Leaf felt vaguely threatened.

At last, he dug out a little round stone that was slightly larger than the others. In the sunlight it remained grayish-blue. When Marco held it up to look at it, Little Leaf heard the slight noise of an electrical discharge in midair. Marco blanched, and in a split second he became a different person. He said to Little Leaf, "I have some property in Holland that I haven't taken care of. Tomorrow I'll meet with people in the tax office. They're pursuing me all over the world. I've bought a train ticket. I'll set out tomorrow."

Little Leaf smothered her laughter and asked, "Are you an alien?"

"Yes. Even I think it's strange. Why have I stayed in this country so long?"

He threw down the stone and rake and gazed ahead. Then he clenched his teeth and walked away without looking back. He was heading to the city. Was he looking for someone else to talk to? Little Leaf detoured around the wasteland, and the sweet time she spent with Marco in the park archives kept flashing through her mind.

The manager appeared at the door to the storeroom. The smoke he puffed out from his water pipe blocked her view of his face. Little Leaf thought he was observing her. She walked toward him.

When the manager suggested that they sit beside the river for a change, Little Leaf agreed. Taking a cinder path, they reached the poplar trees on the riverbank. They had no sooner sat down than Little Leaf saw a beautiful woman dressed in a red skirt come up from the river with a sheep. The red and white color combination was very attractive.

"Who's that?" Little Leaf asked the manager.

"She's related to the old man who opened up the land behind our restaurant. I've seen her several times. Each time, she brings a sheep here and then slaughters it. Another time, I saw her sleeping on the sheep's dead body. She's really a tough girl!"

As the red and the white walked into the distance, Little Leaf still felt great admiration.

"Have you seen her slaughter a sheep?"

"Yes. She's quick and nimble. Oddly enough, the sheep couldn't seem to wait: it came over to her with its neck stretched out."

"Oh!"

Little Leaf looked at the black river with grief-laden eyes—disturbed again by Marco's behavior.

She asked the manager if it was possible for one to be psychologically transformed into another person and never change back. The manager asked if she meant the man in the river. Little Leaf saw a small boat sail past with an old and lonely fisherman on it. Little Leaf had never seen this white-bearded old man.

"He's the only one who couldn't return to his original self." The manager's voice rang out in midair.

"I've been here a long time. Why haven't I ever seen him?"

"Ah, he's always in this river, but not everyone can see him."

Little Leaf thought this was a strange day: she had seen two odd things. Were they connected with Marco's metamorphosis? In a split second, she had become fascinated with this black-colored river. It was a gently swaying world that would inhale her. She sighed deeply, and her eyes filled with tears. The old fisherman sailed past, and a strange scent blew in on the breeze. All at once, she thought of the tropical garden.

"Is he the gardener?" she asked, glancing suspiciously at the manager.

"Yes," the manager nodded. "He is. This river looks black to you, but actually it's as transparent as crystal. Have you ever seen crystal? It's exactly like crystal."

Little Leaf took her leave of the manager and walked quietly toward her box. She saw the old man's boat go past again, this time upstream. He was rowing it. After sizing him up at close range, Little Leaf thought he didn't seem as old as he had just a while ago. Though his hair and beard were white, his eyes were bright and expressive, his arms still muscular. She couldn't believe he was the gardener, because the old gardener who lived in the wooden box over there was so old that he couldn't even walk steadily. But when she took another look, she felt that this old man in the river did resemble the gardener a little. Could they be relatives?

And so it was that the two of them—she on the bank, he in the river—moved ahead at the same speed. When Little Leaf reached her wooden box, the old man was pulling the boat ashore and tying it to a tree. He rushed toward his own wooden box, and Little Leaf finally believed that this one was indeed that one. Then was he the legendary immortal? The sunlight on the river hurt Little Leaf's eyes. She burrowed into the box. Marco was sleeping on the floor.

In the dark, Marco said to Little Leaf, "How come I'm still here?"

Little Leaf started to laugh. She answered, "The manager told me that only the gardener had changed permanently into another self. But he can change his age and become young again: I saw this for myself today. He can also sail a boat: he's exactly like a young person."

"But I've bought my train ticket. I leave tomorrow."

Ignoring him, Little Leaf picked up some garlic and green vegetables, as well as cooked meat that she had brought back from the restaurant, and went out to the shed to cook.

While she was cooking, she heard Marco shouting, "I'm an alien! Didn't any of you know that?!"

Little Leaf heard rustling noises outside the shed. She whipped open the curtain and saw the old gardener. He was the same as before—a humpbacked man with glaucoma. He said something obscure and motioned several times. Little Leaf finally realized that he was asking for a bowl of food. She gave it to him, and he sat on the rock outside and ate. He was toothless so he ate slowly. He closed his eyes as he chewed, as if falling asleep. Then Marco came over, and the three of them ate together on the large rock. In the sunshine, each of them was preoccupied. For some reason, Little Leaf looked a bit distracted. She felt that at this time and in this place, she had become a lady of ancient times who was painting on rice paper. As far as the eye could see, dragon boats were racing in the river.

During the night, when the weather was vile, Little Leaf and Marco both saw a fish while they were having sex. It was an enormous fresh-water fish lying motionless on the river bottom. People said there had been no fish in this black-water river for a long time. Was this large fish real? All night, Little Leaf and Marco thought about fish-related things. The more they thought about it, the closer the fish appeared to be. Halfway through the night, they got up, grabbed a flashlight, and went outside for a closer look. The river water was black; they saw nothing unusual.

"Maybe it swam up from another place," Little Leaf said.

"I think it was native born and bred." Marco looked a little sorrowful.

They waited a long time, but the large fish didn't swim up as they hoped it would. In the river wind, the two of them embraced tightly and shivered. Something was going on inside the riverside boxes: one after another, they lit up. Did everyone know about this fish? They went back to the wooden box and lay down again. The fish was still there, but not in the same place. When they went out, the large fish also swam a short distance.

As soon as they turned off the light the next night, they saw it again—a little blurry this time. Marco called it "Holland fish." He supposed it had swum out from the dark events of the past. He told Little Leaf of an incident from long ago. When he was two years old, his foster mother had taken him to play on the beach. Then she had taken him to a large fishing boat. The people on the boat had locked him up in a small cabin that was so dark that he couldn't see his fingers. When he heard the ocean water flowing beneath him, he had a vivid sense that he was swimming. This story scared Little Leaf, and she begged him to stop talking.

On their day off, they found a boat, sat on it, and floated with the current.

"Little Leaf, Marco, what are you doing?!"

Their neighbors looked panic-stricken. Nobody here did this kind of thing, except perhaps the old gardener. They all knew this river wasn't an ordinary one.

"We're having fun," Marco answered. "We're going to Holland."

From far away, Little Leaf saw the restaurant manager smoking his water pipe at the entrance. He was completely shrouded in smoke. Next to him was a large dog, also shrouded in smoke. Flabbergasted, Little Leaf wondered how the manager could puff so much smoke. Marco asked her if she'd ever seen the manager's wife. She said she hadn't. Marco said he'd seen her once. She sat in the basement the whole day knitting sweaters. "That woman is afraid of any noise."

After a while, they sailed away from their living area. The river turned, and both shores opened up.

A strange bird dropped onto the prow of their boat: Marco said it was a cormorant. Little Leaf thought it must have come to this stagnant river by mistake, because there were no fish in the water. Yet, the bird stood alert on the prow. Wasteland lay on both banks—a few willows, each with one solitary bird calling, were scattered about. The city was far behind: Little Leaf had never come here before.

When they went ashore, Little Leaf asked what they should do with the boat. Marco said they didn't have to do anything. He'd seen it floating in the river and had pulled it to the riverbank. He didn't know whose boat it was. Marco said he would go to Holland now. He told Little Leaf to go home by herself. With that, he walked off into the distance along the path beside the wasteland. Little Leaf stared blankly, then squatted on the ground and began to cry. After she finished crying, she looked up: it suddenly began drizzling—unusual in this season. Little Leaf headed back in the rain. Soon, her hair and clothing were drenched. No one was on the bank, and the sky was dark. She felt as if she were walking at night. Just then, she saw the strangest sight—a slender young man fishing with a bamboo-frame fishing net. He stood on the bank, the net immersed in the river. Every now and then, he lifted the net up. Little Leaf stood to one side and watched him pull it up twice. Naturally, it held no fish at all.

"Are you new here?" Little Leaf asked.

"No, I'm an old hand, an old hand at fishing."

"But this river is stagnant. How could there be any fish here?"

"Hmm, I know. Different people have different ideas. And on a dark rainy day like this, I can't even get a good look at you."

Little Leaf couldn't understand him. He looked so young—how could he talk like this? She noticed, too, that he had no creel. All of a sudden, Little Leaf felt excited by her train of thought. She seemed to see a hazy way out of her impasse. Although she couldn't say what it was, her earlier dismay faded. She wanted to continue watching, but the young man urged her to leave, saying he couldn't concentrate when someone else was there.

"We'll see each other again. I come here often. My name is Roy," he said.

After walking a while, she turned around and looked again. Even when she had walked a long way, she could still see the slender figure and the fishing net. She thought he really was concentrating. She didn't know when the rain had stopped. It was still dark. Little Leaf's footsteps were lighter now. The scenery ahead was still depressing, but the stone in her heart had vanished. She wanted to hurry back to her wooden box, for she was starting to feel hungry.

After Marco had been gone several days, Little Leaf figured he wouldn't come back for a while. Although his smell still permeated the wooden box, Little Leaf rarely thought of him.

In the restaurant, the stolid old man sat across from the old woman clad in mourning clothing. Both ordered rice curry. When Little Leaf set the food down on the table, the old woman grabbed her hand.

"Sweetheart, have you lost something?" she asked with a smile in her eyes.

"Me?" Little Leaf tensed up.

"I think you've lost something, or you wouldn't look so worried."

"But I'm not—not at all."

"Okay then, that's good." She let go of her hand.

When Little Leaf returned to their table, the two old people had disappeared. A bulging handbag had been left on the chair. Little Leaf picked it up; it was heavy, as though it held stones. The manager came over, and Little Leaf picked up the bag for him to look at. He said, "Listen to it." Little Leaf placed her ear next to the bag and heard a jumble of tick-tock sounds, as if the bag contained a lot of watches or small clocks.

"Open it," the manager said, his eyes drooping.

Little Leaf unzipped it: only ordinary stones were inside.

"That woman didn't seem to be desperately ill. What do you think, Little Leaf?"

"That's what I think, too. She isn't. She's just deluded."

"Hmm. It's hard to define sickness."

The manager put the handbag away. Little Leaf thought hard, but she couldn't bring back what had been lost from her memory. She walked outside and stared blankly at the bright blue sky. The back of one departing customer reminded her of her father: they were much alike. She ran ahead of him and turned around to look: it wasn't her father. All smiles, the manager said to her, "Those two want to open up some more land for extensive cultivation. Ha."

The manager urged her to go home, and she agreed. It was the first time in a long time that she had remembered that leaky apartment and her parents' endless arguments. She had tried to find out how these two orphans had found each other, but she had quickly given up. Now she had changed her view of life: she would not deliberately try to understand anything again. She would just stay alert—that was enough.

Before she left, the manager sought her out for a talk.

"Little Leaf, what do you think of your dad?"

"He's the clown in our family, but he's also very determined. When I was a child, he kept up the act in front of us, but he felt pain on the inside."

"Was he the reason that you left home and settled down on the riverside?"

"I guess."

She thought she would stay at home no more than a day and then return.

When she was still about a mile from the apartment, she ran into her dad. He was idling away his time sitting under the policeman's umbrella on the highway. His gaze was uncertain, and his forehead more wrinkled. For a moment, Little Leaf couldn't make up her mind whether to call out to him.

"Oh, here's my Little Leaf," old Sherman said as he looked up and saw his daughter.

"Dad—oh, Dad!"

"I'm fine. Let's go home."

Little Leaf sensed that her dad was ashamed of something: he acted as if he felt inferior. No matter what she asked about the family, he simply looked embarrassed. As they walked together, he seemed to avoid being too close to her and purposely lagged behind. She had to twist around to talk with him; this made her uncomfortable.

When they were almost home, they passed by many people running along the road. One man dropped his briefcase, and Sherman picked it up and handed it to him. Little Leaf asked her dad why these people were running. He said they felt on edge. He went on to say that nowadays, people were becoming more and more nervous. As he said this, he stopped walking and crouched amid the wildflowers at the roadside. Immersed in memories, he scrutinized a small red flower. Little Leaf crouched, too, and all at once she remembered a scene from the past. She had just learned to walk, and Dad had set her down amid weeds and wildflowers. The weeds were as tall as she was: she had to trample them in order to walk, and she couldn't see the path ahead of her. She had cried.

"I'm feeling nervous, too," she said.

"Good. My Little Leaf has grown up."

As father and daughter crouched amid the flowers, their hearts were very close.

"Your mama is doing volunteer work in the garden."

"The garden in midair?"

"Hey, good for you, you guessed right the first time. Look, here's the thorn rose."

Little Leaf remembered there were roses on the riverside, too—bigger ones, and prettier.

When they pushed open the door at home, Little Leaf was shocked. On the table was a frame with a picture of an old man. The frame was edged in black silk. Sherman told Little Leaf that this was Grandfather: he had died the day before yesterday.

"I have a grandfather?" Little Leaf said.

"Of course you do. Otherwise, where would I have come from?"

Little Leaf was convinced, mostly because she was fascinated by the way he spoke. She walked to the window and gazed out at the contours of the snow mountain. She began imagining what her grandfather's family was like. She had known she had a grandfather and grandmother, but they had never appeared even once in her life, and so she had never taken their existence seriously. In the midst of her parents' arguments, she had often thought she had no relatives. Truly, her dad had walked out of the orphanage on the snow mountain and come to this small city, where he had built this dilapidated home for himself. Grandfather's home must have been a wooden house in the forest—the sort of house without electric lights and without running water. Had her grandfather been a ranger or a lumberman? A bird flew into Little Leaf's face and then fell to the floor. Ah, it was a green long-life bird; it seemed to be injured!

The two of them squatted down and looked at the bird. The bird looked at them, too: it wasn't at all afraid.

"Where is it hurt?" Little Leaf asked.

"In its heart."

Sherman found a large cardboard box and put the bird in it. He pushed the box to a dark spot under the bed and said, "What it needs now is time."

Little Leaf contemplated her dad. He had changed greatly. He had shaved his head and was wearing a gown that was neither gray nor blue. He wasn't at all like an office worker. And his gaze was bright and wild, as though he were burning inside. Little Leaf was a little afraid of the changes she saw in him. To distract herself, she went into the kitchen and cooked. She took out vegetables and scooped out rice. Next, she was going to clean the sink. What she saw in the sink stunned her—a large crab was lying there. It moved a little, then lay still.

Sherman came over, patted her on the back, and said, "It needs time now, too. You don't have to cook. We'll go over to Uncle Fei-yuan's for dinner."

Feiyuan's shop was deserted. Feiyuan was playing chess alone.

"Sherman, Sherman, they've all gone. I'm discouraged. I want my eldest son to take over this shop. As for me, I'll go away and see the world."

They ate a simple meal of salad noodles, beer, and peanuts. Fei-yuan asked Little Leaf if she had seen an old woman wearing a large navigation watch. Little Leaf said she had.

"She cheated us."

Feiyuan was ashen-faced, and his hand trembled constantly as he held his chopsticks. He put down his chopsticks, stood up, and started pacing back and forth between the tables. Little Leaf guessed that something was wrong, and she kept staring at him. Sherman seemed apathetic, perhaps because he was so accustomed to Feiyuan's situation. He looked out the window. Little Leaf followed her dad's line of sight and saw two people standing outside and spying on the shop. She was amazed. Her dad was talking softly. His voice didn't sound real: "This is a convalescence center, or you could call it a transfer center. Uncle Feiyuan can't accept this fact."

Little Leaf thought Uncle Feiyuan must have been depressed be-cause he couldn't keep certain things. When she had come to this shop in the past, it was always crowded with customers and Uncle Feiyuan was always in a good mood. But now everything had changed.

A great noise came from the kitchen: Feiyuan said it was rats. He went on to say that he deliberately ignored the rats. "It would be even more deserted here without them." Feiyuan asked Little Leaf if she had seen tramp steamers sail in the river.

"No. That isn't very likely. It's such a small river."

Feiyuan said it was possible: people just didn't pay attention. Lit-tle Leaf looked over his shoulder and saw two people outside lean-ing against the window—standing on tiptoe and peering in. When Sherman saw them, he smiled a little and then burst out laughing.

He said, "I said before that this is a convalescence center. Feiyuan, let me take over this shop."

"Okay," Feiyuan answered mechanically.

After dinner, Sherman and Little Leaf took their leave. Looking frantic and embarrassed, Feiyuan kept saying, "You aren't going so soon are you, Little Leaf? I didn't even give you a good meal. I'm sorry. I'm so down and out. All my life . . ." He slapped his forehead.

Little Leaf noticed that the two people outside had left. Nobody was on the street, and it was exceptionally quiet. Little Leaf didn't remember its ever having been like this in the past. In those days, hundreds of people had come here every day for the mutton kebabs. As he left, Sherman said, "The convalescence center is a black hole." A blast of wind blew his gown up and he took two steps back. Little Leaf stood there and thought. She decided she would leave her dad right away. Sherman brushed the dust off his gown. He looked down at the ground and said to her, "It's okay: either you stay with us or by yourself over there. It makes no difference. I'll tell your mother you came to visit."

Marco reached the border. He had been here once before and still vaguely remembered it. There were no patrols along the border, but there was a very recessed village with about a dozen tumbledown adobe houses. A ditch glistened with sewage in front of their doors. A few children played in the water with bamboo poles. The other side of the border was a large desert. Marco had to go around the desert. It was nearly dark, so he would have to spend the night in the village. When the children saw him, they called out, "Marco! Marco!" Marco was surprised because he hadn't been here for two years and yet they remembered him! He surveyed the houses for a moment, chose a sort of presentable one, and knocked on the door. Though he knocked for a long time, no one answered. Then a child passing by told him, "There's no one in this house." The child pushed the door open. Marco went in and looked at the three rooms. The furniture was simple and crude, as it was in most farmhouses. Each room had a large earthen stove for warmth in the winter. Next to the stove was a small, narrow wooden bed—barely large enough for one person. There wasn't much light.

Marco was exhausted. He set down his bag, and without taking off his clothes, he lay on the bed and fell asleep. He didn't know how long he had slept when he heard someone enter. The person struck three matches before managing to light the lamp and place it on the table, but he sat in a dark corner. Marco couldn't see his face. Marco heard him say, "Someone can't go home."

Marco sat up and said, "I'm sorry. I came in. I needed a place to stay. I'm on my way to Holland."

"Holland? Hey, that's great! People here all want to go to Holland, but they can't leave."

Arching his back, he walked around in the dark corner, as if looking for something. Marco wondered what he was looking for. He didn't expect the man to enter the closet, burrow down in it, and close the door.

Marco picked up the kerosene lamp and went into the kitchen. He saw some potatoes in the pot; probably that man had cooked them. As he ate potatoes, he reflected on his situation. He looked out the little window and saw several people walking with pine torches.

All of a sudden, in the quiet of the night, Marco heard the roar of ocean waves, but the ocean was nowhere near. The desert was in this vicinity—he remembered that clearly. When he went outside, the roar of the waves was even more audible. How strange! He walked over toward the three people with torches. Seeing him, they stopped in their tracks.

"Do you want to go out to sea? Then go around from the right side," one of them said.

"Can the ocean possibly be here? I never knew that. Yes, I do want to go out to sea."

He went back to the house and picked up his bag, and the three others also came with him. They called the landlord "Old Shao." They said he was an old fox.

"Last time when there was a tsunami, he also locked himself up in the closet and stuck his head out of a hole in the back of it. He floated to the shore. His closet is specially designed."

Marco asked, "Does old Shao sleep like this every day?"

"Yes. He never wavers. He often says he doesn't want to die for nothing."

When they left the house, they heard an upheaval coming from the house behind them. Marco heard them say that old Shao was struggling with snakes. Generally, he put two snakes in the closet with him—"in order to hang on to a kind of passion." The older person said, "You must know that the ocean is temperamental." Marco thought to himself, *Are they sending me off to sea?* They walked to the right for a while, and the sound of the ocean waves subsided. The silence of the three people frightened Marco. Their pine torches had gone out, and Marco felt that he was walking toward hell. A deep hole—or maybe a precipice—seemed to open up in front of him. He couldn't let his life end like this. He had to say something.

"I want to go to Holland. My adoptive mother still lives there. A candy workshop stands on that street. The master's skill is like a magic show."

After he had spoken, the three others stopped. Marco had a feeling that doomsday was approaching—were they about to kill him? After quite a while, the older one finally said, "Oh, son, you're at the border now."

The three of them jumped down, one after the other, and screamed desperately. Marco's legs went limp, and he sat down. He thought, *How wise old Shao is!* Just then, the roar of the waves became more audible again—attacking the stone wall beneath the deep hole or the precipice. All at once, he understood: the spot where he was standing was the safest place. He struggled hard to remember the scene when he had first come here, but that memory had become merely a blank space. Someone was wandering back and forth carrying a lamp; then he slowly came over to Marco. When he reached Marco, he hung the lamp on a small tree and sat down. Marco thought the man wanted to talk with him, but he didn't say a word.

Tired of sitting, Marco stood up and stretched. The other person stood up and stretched, too.

"Excuse me, is the ocean just ahead?" Marco asked him, pointing to the dark deep hole.

"How could it be the ocean? It's no more than a small stream. Come with me, let me take you across the bridge."

He picked up the lamp, grabbed Marco's arm, and pushed him toward the deep hole. Marco didn't struggle. He stepped down into the void with the other man.

His foot touched wood. Sure enough, the lamp shone on a narrow bridge. Marco walked in front, the other man behind. The man finally introduced himself as old Shao. Marco had been in his home just now.

"Whoever has been to my home is like family to me."

When they walked on the bridge, Marco could no longer hear the roar of the waves. The bridge went on forever; they walked quite a while without reaching the other side. Marco thought, *Why would there be such a long bridge over a tiny river?* Old Shao wanted him to stop. Marco asked why, and he said just to enjoy the fresh breeze. And so they sat on the bridge. Marco looked down and still could see no river water. Nor did he hear a current. What kind of river was this? Old Shao exhorted him not to look around and said, "We're in Holland now. What more do you want? Don't be greedy." And so Marco shrank back, calmed down, and thought about Holland.

Someone walked up from the opposite side of the bridge, also carrying a lamp. Although Marco waited and waited, the person never drew near. He asked old Shao what was going on. "How could you have forgotten everything about Holland? This is the way things are here in Holland." Marco asked, "If the man walked non-stop the whole night, would he finally get here?" Old Shao sneered and said, "He'll be gone at daybreak. Only a lamp cover will be left on the bridge."

Old Shao called Marco "cousin," and said, "Your adoptive mother is also my adoptive mother. I can understand your confusion." Then he picked up the lamp again and asked Marco if the lamp brought back any memories. Marco said he remembered many things, but he couldn't say what they were. Old Shao said, "Your karma hasn't yet run its course."

Marco felt old Shao's comment was odd, so he asked old Shao what he thought of him.

"I came to monitor you. Here we are outside the national border." He said, "I have a good impression of you. Once in Holland, everyone becomes a good person."

After a while, he suggested that Marco return home, because "You can't stay long in a place like Holland."

And so they went back. When they reached the edge of the village, Marco saw many people carrying pine torches. Old Shao said they were all villagers. "People never sleep on the frontier," he said.

Moans came from all directions. Marco looked around: old Shao had disappeared. He walked toward a bright spot on the left: a man under a tree was holding his stomach, groaning loudly, and pulling his hair. Marco couldn't bear watching and walked away. The man called out: "I've seen a lot of people like you. You simply walk away from things you detest. You shouldn't have come here in the first place."

Marco had to stop. The man moaned even louder, threw away his pine torch, and rolled around on the ground. In the underbrush not far away, Marco noticed another person tumbling, too. Surrounded by moans, Marco felt a headache coming on. It grew worse and worse, and so—holding his head—he started rolling around, too. Then he heard that person speaking above him.

"That's right. Nowadays, in our era, you have to pay attention to which way the wind blows."

The pain was driving Marco crazy. All of a sudden, he jumped up, slapping his head as he ran toward old Shao's home.

Old Shao was standing in the house. With his astonishing strength, he grabbed Marco with one hand and stuffed him into the lower part of the closet. Then he locked the closet from the outside. Crammed in and crushed like this, Marco thought he would die. But suddenly, he stuck his head out. The back panel of the closet had a large hole. Marco started panting heavily, and his head didn't ache nearly as much. He heard old Shao still in the house, and asked him loudly when the tsunami would arrive. Old Shao said this *was* the tsunami. It started underground, giving everyone a headache. He said Marco's timing wasn't very good, because this was tsunami season.

Something bit Marco on the thigh. He realized right away that it was the snake. He lost consciousness from the slight pain of the injury, and saw Little Leaf—all smiles—walking toward him.

Chapter 10

THE DIRECTOR AND NANCY

The director was close to death. Now, years after the traffic accident in the interior, its residual effects had finally shown up. As she lay in the hospital bed, the director was now experiencing what had earlier been suspected about her health. She strained to turn her dry eyes to the yellow leaves in front of the window. She was examining the conquests she had made over many years, as well as those things hidden in nooks and crannies that were waiting to be explored. She hoped that her death would simply be the fading away of her physical body while in reality she would still be the director of this massive—yet false—Design Institute. Would her subordinates be able to acclimate to this new situation? She had many subordinates, and she knew each one of them. They were all linked to her gigantic brain through their individual experiences.

She certainly hadn't started at the bottom in climbing to her position as director. Her experience was a little strange. She used to own a flower shop on a small street in a southern city. One day her father had come home from overseas, bringing a few guests with him. They had discussed some things for a long time in a back room. After the guests left, her dad told her that these friends were taking part in developing and constructing the northern frontier. They had set up a design institute in a new city there and wanted her to become its director. At first, she declined, but Father persuaded her by setting forth various reasons for accepting. As he said, it wouldn't be hard work because specialists would handle everything. As long as she established a good relationship with her subordinates, the organization would run smoothly. "Dealing with people is what this job is all about. You have a gift for this. You'll do well." As Dad talked, he smiled dubiously. A black child was standing outside. From time to time, he looked into the shop. She asked her dad who the black child was; her dad said he was his adopted son.

A pall hung in the air at dinner that night. She ate with her dad, the black child, and her female assistant in the kitchen behind the flower shop. A rumble echoed in her ears. She told her father that something was wrong with her ears, but her dad said he had heard the same sound—it came from underground. The black child said it was the sound of snow melting on the snow mountain. Dad happily patted the child on the head and said he was a great kid. He called the child "Ying." Halfway through the meal, she lost her appetite and put her chopsticks down. She felt her prospects were bleak. While they were eating, a customer showed up and bought all the flowers in her shop. He said, "There's no point in your keeping any of them." As soon as her dad and the child left, she started packing.

Although her dad told her she didn't have to take anything, she still spent the whole night packing.

When she was about to board the train, her dad rushed up with the black child to see her off. Dad joked, "My daughter is now commander-in-chief. You have to be ready for war."

The train left the city and entered an area of plains as far as the eye could see. The sky was gray, and there was no sign of human life. The sparse willows and camphors lacked vitality. It was a very long time before she saw a wild dog on the horizon. It had probably run away from its home out of fear. After looking out the window for a while, the director felt tired. She sighed and lay down on the bed.

The dining car staff were delivering boxed meals, but she didn't feel like eating. For some reason, the lights were out in the car. It was growing dark, little by little, and the people in the car were turning into shadows, all bordered in red. The moment they moved around, there were flashes of feeble red rays. A shadow approached, bent down, and said softly to her, "The snow mountain . . ." All at once, the dark plains appeared in her mind. They were so dark that not only could she not see dogs, but she couldn't see trees, either. She sat up, intending to say something to the person, but he had walked away.

The train started and stopped. Day broke and darkness fell. Some people boarded, and some disembarked. The director recalled traveling four days and four nights, one day longer than scheduled. As the train approached the frontier, her mind was filled mainly with the silhouette of the snow mountain. It was a high mountain whose peak was the only snow-covered part. Pine trees were dense at the foot of the mountain. At first, she didn't see this mountain; she only imagined it. Her train of thought walked ahead in the snow alongside the snow leopard. Then, all of a sudden, the snow mountain loomed in front of her. Somehow, she felt that it wasn't real, but more like a slide show. Sometimes she couldn't distinguish the white mountaintop from the background color of the sky.

"Hello, director. I'm the one who talked to you that night."

She looked up and saw a man who looked like a farmer. His grin revealed yellow teeth. He asked if she remembered him. She said she did: he had talked with her the night before she set out. The man smiled even more broadly. He gave a thumbs up for her good memory.

"Your father sent me to act as your guide. Large packs of wolves have recently appeared on the frontier. It's dangerous."

She thought his northern accent was very pleasant. If she hadn't been looking at his ugly face, she would have assumed he was handsome. She wanted to ask about some things on the frontier. But after casting an eye in all directions and noticing five or six people staring at her watchfully, she didn't speak.

"We have to take a small path into the city. Don't worry. Your father . . ."

Something seemed to enter his mind, and his expression turned ambiguous. He looked all around. All of a sudden, he slammed into the people crowding around him and flipped one of them over. Then he hurried to another train car.

The director could remember nothing more about that day. She only remembered squeezing into a tunnel behind that farmer. Then she walked mechanically because the darkness had robbed her of any sense of direction.

And so she became director of the large-scale Design Institute. In the dreary conference room, people walked back and forth in front of her like shadows. She believed they were the human shadows she had seen on the train because they were bordered by the same red color. She heard a burst of applause: people were waiting for her to speak. At first, she didn't know what to say. After hesitating a while, she spoke inarticulately of the rain in the south, of her flower shop, of her endless lonely waiting, of the peddlers on that street, and even of the suspicions and fears of the flower growers. She spoke softly and emotionally, and the audience was absolutely silent. She spoke for a long time. Finally, she was exhausted. She had never been so exhausted, so—to everyone's surprise—she leaned over the lectern and fell asleep.

She awakened in a strange room. She thought mistakenly that she was still in her hometown, but when she walked into the living room, she saw the farmer. He stood up and introduced himself as a flower grower from her hometown.

"You gave a splendid speech last night!" he said.

She looked him up and down doubtfully, for she didn't understand why he spoke with a northern accent. He excused himself to go to work.

It was a long time before she saw him again. By then, his intangible tropical garden had already been built, and he served as the gardener.

The first time he took her to his garden, she somehow lost consciousness. The sharp calls of the long-life bird brought her around. Although she felt suffocated in the garden—as though being interrogated by those beautiful unknown plants—she still liked being there. She talked with the gardener in the pavilion until the sun set behind the mountain. When she returned to her residence, many children were singing outside. She turned to look at the gardener, but he had disappeared—probably taking refuge behind the banana trees.

When the director had recalled this much, she saw the young nurse craning her neck outside. She shouted loudly, and the young nurse returned. The director asked what was going on. She replied that a couple outside wanted to see her, but the charge nurse wouldn't let them in. Without a word, the director put on her shoes and walked out.

From a distance, she saw Nancy's profile as a shadow vaguely fused into the darkening light of dusk. Next to her, José's figure was a little more distinct.

"Director, we miss you, so we've come to see you. We were here yesterday, too," Nancy said.

"Oh, that damn charge nurse. Nancy, you have a few gray hairs."

A large flock of sparrows settled on the ground. The director absentmindedly looked all around, and then looked again at this couple, as though placing herself in a certain setting from years ago. Just then, José said, "Director, do you have to leave us?"

"I don't know. Maybe. When I saw the two of you just now, I remembered the situation when you first came to Pebble Town. That's when I began to get sick. The charge nurse is coming."

The director walked back. When she had disappeared behind the door, José saw that Nancy's whole face was wet with tears.

"That was a devil. Just now, I saw that the back of her hand was covered with long hair," Nancy said as she sobbed spasmodically.

"You mean the charge nurse?"

"Yes."

They left the hospital hand in hand. As they walked, they recalled their association with the director. Under the soft rays of the street light, their memories drifted all around them; they seemed especially illusory. They discussed a significant topic for a long time: the third day after they had arrived here, outside the farmer's courtyard in the outskirts, the director had told José that the thing he and Nancy were looking for had vanished long ago. What had she meant? But their discussion went nowhere. Nancy said sadly, "Now there's only me. Just me."

José gripped her hand, as if to suggest "And me, too." Nancy glanced at him appreciatively, shook her head, and forced a smile. Suddenly, José realized that he could never take the place of the director in Nancy's heart. He heard Nancy saying something else, but talking so quickly that he couldn't hear what she said. Then he did catch a few words: "She's so beautiful . . ."

"Nancy, is Pebble Town beautiful because of us, or are we beautiful because of Pebble Town?" José shouted.

Nancy didn't answer. They heard someone in the stream over there: Was it Qiming? They looked and looked, but couldn't be sure. Nancy whispered to José, "It's an apparition."

Nancy thought to herself: she still had to go to the hospital. She'd go by herself without telling José. Just then, she heard José chewing something a little like a bone. José said he was eating dates from the sandthorn tree next to the road. The sound came from his chewing on the pits. Nancy hadn't seen him pick the dates, so she believed he was lying. His face was hidden in shadows. He brought his left hand up to his mouth. Nancy distinctly saw him chewing his finger. She screamed and sank into a crouch. Her stomach was churning. José also crouched down. As he put date pits in Nancy's hand, he said, "Let's go home. Let's go home."

Nancy looked at the date pits under the street light for a long time. Each one was intact; they hadn't been chewed. Why had José said he was chewing them? Was it just because the director had said the thing they were looking for didn't exist? She sensed that her husband was more tenacious than she was.

After Nancy and José had been to the hospital, the charge nurse was even stricter with the director because the director had had a flare-up after they'd left. She had lost consciousness for a day and a night. The young nurse taking care of her was fired by the charge nurse. Now, two male nurses tended to her. They stayed in the office opposite the director's room, not leaving even briefly.

The director's gaze was still fastened on the tree outside the window; its yellow leaves were gone now, and its bare limbs pointed boldly straight up to the sky. One morning, she noticed a youth in the tree. Was it her son? Her son used to love climbing trees. She gestured to him from her bed. He shook his head gravely. The way he shook his head wasn't much like her missing son, but she was still excited. Just then, one of the male nurses was about to close the curtains, but the charge nurse stopped him. The director heard the charge nurse say, "Let her look; it's good for her." They withdrew quietly. At the same time, the boy slid down the tree.

She hadn't ever gotten a good look at the charge nurse's face, because she always wore a mask. Once, when she came to take her pulse, the director noticed that her hand was all skin and bones. She blurted out, "Is something wrong with you?"

"You've got me. I don't know."

That's actually the way she answered the director. The director thought it was a novel response. She wondered if the nurse was ugly. But the eyes visible above the mask were actually unusually beautiful, though icy cold. She couldn't help but stare at them whenever she had the opportunity.

Yesterday afternoon, the director had dreamed of drowning in the stream. She had struggled hard and yelled. When she opened her eyes, the charge nurse was clutching her neck with her claw-like hand. When this nurse noticed that she had awakened, she let go and said angrily, "I was helping you breathe just now, but you wouldn't cooperate. I once had a patient who was just as stubborn as you, and he choked to death."

The director looked hopelessly at the ceiling and quietly asked the nurse if she could allow her to go outside for a walk. She was bored. She also said that the screen window was so tightly closed that not even a little insect could fly in.

"You can go. Go ahead. The main door is wide open!"

As she said this, the nurse inspected her fingers. The director suddenly noticed blood stains on those skinny fingers. The charge nurse grinned, startling the director.

After the nurse left, the director changed from her hospital gown to her street clothes. She washed her face and combed her hair, and finally left her room. In the corridor, the male nurse offered his arm, but she pushed him away. She soon reached the hospital entrance. She was surprised that everything had gone smoothly.

She stood next to the road and saw a four-wheeled carriage rushing toward her. Nancy stuck her head out the carriage window and called to her. The carriage stopped in front of her, and Nancy pulled her up and then closed the door.

"I've kept watch here all afternoon. Seeing you coming out, I hailed this carriage. We can ride around the city."

It was dark inside the carriage. Curtains covered the windows. Once more, the director felt a suffocating, drowning sensation, though it wasn't as overwhelming as it had been during her nap. Nancy held the director's icy hand tightly, hoping to warm her up. They held hands in silence, and long-ago events were resurrected vividly in her mind. Outside, the carriage rushed on; inside, the director's thoughts also sped up. Worn out, she leaned her head on Nancy's slender shoulder. Over and over, she said, "Nancy, ah . . ."

Nancy didn't know how much time had passed when she heard a noise outside and realized that the carriage had rushed into the market streets. These streets were newly constructed: they were filled with the lively scene of people and cars coming and going. The director sat up straight and tapped Nancy's knee lightly. She said, "The flower shop I opened in the south has now started selling Celebes orchids. I heard that exotic flowers are very popular. The flower growers are falling all over themselves to plant them."

"Is our gardener one of those flower growers?" Nancy asked.

Nancy's eyes wandered in the dim light: she saw the rather deserted small street. The dark stone street glistened in the rain. The flower shop was on the corner, a pot of Nippon lilies at its entrance.

"Yes. He's the one who brought me back home. Look: I'm in the north, but at the same time I'm in the south."

"It was the advertisement you put in the newspaper that changed my life." Nancy heard her own voice quivering.

When the carriage returned to the hospital entrance, the director suddenly became weak and light as a feather. She couldn't move. She needed Nancy's help to get up. Nancy was surprised that the director weighed so little. With the driver's help, she easily got her out of the carriage.

When they walked to the ward, the director kept joking, "Actually, there's no body under my clothing."

Nancy settled her into bed, and then sat on a stool next to it. The director wondered why the charge nurse and the two male nurses were ignoring her. The corridor was very quiet, as if no one could come in. The director asked Nancy to lean close and then she told her that she hadn't eaten anything for a long time, for each time food was delivered to her room, she had furtively dumped it into the bucket of swill under the kitchen sink. No one had discovered this, and the director was quite proud of herself. She emphasized, "I'm getting cleaner by the day."

She wanted Nancy to tell Grace that she thought there was still hope for her. At that, Lee's wizened figure appeared in Nancy's mind. He had died: How could there be any hope for Grace as a lonely widow? She used to have Lee and the dog: that was hope. So, back then, she always wore black clothing and a white flower. Nancy's lips moved, but she couldn't speak. The director started laughing and said, "Do you think there's hope for me?"

Nancy glanced at the director's wan face. All at once, she felt enlightened. She remembered that Qiming used to wind-bathe facing the glittering snow mountain. And so she shouted to the director: "Yes, there's hope for you! There's hope!"

A breeze blew the curtains open a little, and they saw the little boy in the tree. Suddenly, the director howled in grief, like a wolf. Nancy stood up and looked out the window. The little boy had disappeared without a trace. The two nurses burst into the room to give the director a shot. The director held out her arm obediently.

Nancy thought of Ying, the black man. Where had he gone? This was the end of his benefactor's life, yet he had unexpectedly disappeared. She had asked the director, but the director had merely shaken her head. Perhaps he'd really gone to the Gobi Desert to look for gold. Many times in the past, sitting at the desk in the office looking at the faint contours of the snow mountain in the distance, she had listened to his emotional confidences about the director. Ying regarded the director as his mother, the person he was closest to. He had told Nancy this many times. But the day they heard that the director had fallen ill, Nancy and Ying had run into each other in the corridor of the office building. As they walked, they talked of this. Ying had been jittery, saying he had to take a business trip right away and couldn't go to see the director. He didn't explain. Nancy thought this was odd. They left the office building and went to the dining hall. Ying was listening intently to something, and Nancy asked what it was. He said, "The drumbeat." Just then, José walked up, and Ying approached him and said sadly, "Mr. José, I have to begin carrying out that plan. I can't wait any longer."

José fell silent. As they walked together, none of them said anything else.

Later, Nancy and José talked about Ying. José said, "He's going to implement the director's ideas. That's a very beautiful thing to do. And someday, I will do the same thing."

"Of those who've gone there, not one has ever come back," José continued.

They were absorbed in reveries.

Still, Nancy wasn't much interested in the Gobi Desert. What she saw in her mind's eye was their hometown, Smoke City. The longer they were away from that city and the more unfamiliar it became, the more she was attracted to it.

She said, "I never could see that iron bridge very well, because the fog over the river didn't break up for years on end."

At first they went to the hospital every day, but never saw the director. Then, once they did see her, José didn't want to go back. He reasoned that since she wanted to leave them, they shouldn't disturb her again. Nancy thought José was really tough; men were very logical. Nancy felt that the director was like a part of her own body, and thus Nancy was now aware of the director every minute. So she continued to go to the hospital. She didn't even go to work. The nurses always drove her away, though, and she grew desperate. Later, all of a sudden, she ran into the director next to the main road. As it happened, a carriage also stopped there just then. Without thinking, Nancy got in.

Had the director's body become an empty shell? She saw the thick hypodermic needle prick her vein, but she saw no blood flow back into the syringe. Nevertheless, the two demon-like male nurses started the transfusion.

Many days passed. Whenever Nancy had time, she went to the places that the gardener frequented, but she never saw him. When she mentioned this to José, he said he hadn't seen him, either. After Lee died, Grace moved away. At night during this time, José and Nancy often went to look at their empty apartment. They looked inside and they looked out the window: they saw nothing. The only thing outside the window was the long-dead poplar tree. The birds' nest in it was an old one that the birds had long since abandoned. José said there were two possibilities: either the gardener was in hiding and only the director knew where he was; or the gardener had gone home to the south. One time when they were about to leave the room, they heard something like a wooden stick pounding on the skylight. Nancy started shaking, but José was calm. He said it was birds. Only one small area in this long corridor was dimly lit. The other spots were all dark. No one seemed to be living in this building, so who had turned on a light? The manager?

After they returned to their bungalow, Nancy told José she had to go to work the next day because, after seeing that once-occupied now-empty apartment, she sensed that her heart had also become empty, and that the domain of her life had contracted. She had to go out and expand the scope of her life: this was also the director's wish. She fell asleep while speaking of this decision.

When she awakened in the morning, she had forgotten what she said and once again asked José to request time off for her because she had to go to the hospital.

The director was dying. Nancy placed the director's hand on her own chest, trying to warm it. Since the director could still speak, Nancy asked where the gardener was. With a smile, the director said he'd been to see her and he was always hanging around. Just then someone entered. It was the charge nurse. She pushed Nancy away with one hand and sat at the head of the bed listening to the director's heart with a stethoscope. The charge nurse wasn't wearing a mask, and Nancy felt she was a little scary—like a cold-blooded murderer. The director kept staring at the ceiling. Perhaps she couldn't see anything. After the nurse left, she said clearly: "Nancy, did you finally see the gardener? He was just here caressing me. He was so tender! I'm dying, and he came to see me. You can't find him easily. He always plays hide-and-seek with people around him! That time in the farmer's courtyard . . ."

She couldn't go on. Her throat was gurgling with phlegm, and the whites of her eyes showed.

The two male nurses rushed in, followed by the charge nurse. They prepared to give her an injection.

Nancy slipped out quickly. Later, she found out that the director hadn't died after all.

The director revived again, just as she had many times in the past. She stared at the beautiful eyes above the charge nurse's mask. The director asked, "Do you want tulips or chrysanthemums?"

The nurse shook her head, her eyes showing distress. The director told her that she had died once: what a fabulous experience that had been! Now she wasn't at all fearful. After the nurse left, the director sat up and looked at the birds flying back and forth in the dusk. This happened time after time, and it was always the same three birds. The air was suffused with an amethyst color. It was as though time had stood still. The window screen had been removed while she was disoriented. How beautiful the twilight was, and somewhere children were singing. She stood up and looked down from the window. Everywhere, canna were in full bloom, the petals so red that they seemed to drip blood. She wondered, "Am I in the south or the north now?" Darkness fell, and a warm breeze brought the scent of tangerine blossoms. By the light of the lamp, the director looked in the mirror and saw an amazingly young face.

She bent to tie her shoelaces, for she had to go to the courtyard. When she heard someone whisper in her ear that she was a beauty, she was filled with joy.

"Do you want to admire the tangerine trees blossoming?" One of the male nurses in the corridor asked her.

"Wait a minute," he added.

To her surprise, he emerged with an old-style hurricane lamp. He took the director's arm quite naturally and amiably, and they walked to the courtyard. The courtyard was large and unfamiliar, divided into several sections by flowerbeds. The flowers in the plots looked familiar—like southern varieties. The nurse grumbled, "You never visited our garden before."

He pointed to a large expanse of trees in dark shadow ahead and said the tangerine blossoms would wither soon. It would have been much better to come here earlier. When they circled around the flower beds and entered the tangerine orchard, the director's knees started aching dully. In the south, she'd had arthritis, but after coming here—a few decades ago—it had gone away. The nurse shone the hurricane lamp on a tangerine tree so that she could see the blossoms. Such tiny white flowers—if you didn't look closely, they were invisible. The director breathed deeply: she felt she had lived a hundred years.

It took them a long time to go through the tangerine orchard. Someone was sitting in the dark on a bench next to the path, crying.

"That's the charge nurse. She's homesick," said the male nurse.

They walked over to her, and the male nurse shone the lamp on her, but she kept covering her face with her sleeve. The director thought to herself, *This poker-faced guy must be feeling embarrassed now.* And so she tugged at the nurse's clothing, wanting him to leave. But he insisted on standing there with the lamp. The director said, "I'm going south very soon."

As soon as she said this, the male nurse turned around and helped her walk back. They left the charge nurse behind. When they re-entered the tangerine orchard, the moon had already risen, and the sound of weeping came simultaneously from several places. In the moonlight, the male nurse's voice became gentle and sweet. He asked the director: Can a person die of homesickness?

"Yes. A person can die and then come back to life," the director answered serenely.

"How strange it is that the tangerine blossoms here don't wither."

The nurse shone the lamp on the flowers, and the director saw the trees laden with tiny white blossoms—so many that they hid the leaves. She suspected she might have blurred vision, because she had never seen such dense blooms on tangerine trees. Their scent reached her heart.

"Even I never imagined the tangerine blossoms would be so luxuriant this year." The nurse added, "If you can hold out for another few months, you'll see even more fantastic scenery."

"Ah, I'm so tired. What am I stumbling over?"

"It's those people who've collapsed. They're everywhere in this tangerine orchard. Listen: the charge nurse has stopped weeping. She's always like this: she cries for a while and then she's all right again. She's a shy person."

The tangerine orchard became still. Arm in arm with this gentle young man, the director felt dimly that this person beside her was her sweetheart from the long-ago time when he worked in the flower shop. She asked him his name. He said he wouldn't tell her, because it wasn't important, and besides, his name was banal. She could imagine him to be whoever she wanted him to be. As he spoke, some passion that the director hadn't felt for ages rippled in her mind.

"Then, were you once a flower grower?" she blurted out.

"Yes. When I gave you injections, did you notice my hands? My bones are big and strong."

"I sort of understand. But no, I don't. Aren't I already old?"

The nurse turned taciturn. Every time the director tripped over something underfoot, he held her more tightly. He was tall and sturdy. The director thought he was the personification of gentleness. Why hadn't she found this out until now? She used to think that he was fiendish and that there was no way to communicate with him.

They parted in the corridor. The nurse looked into her eyes and begged her not to turn on the light.

"I can signal you with the lamp. If you look up, you'll see it," he said.

As he walked into the office, the director thought he looked lonely from behind.

After the director lay down, she still felt excited, because just now, the impossible had happened. She believed this surely had something to do with the gardener, whose influence was expanding. She was so lucky that, before death, she was able to revive the passion she'd felt in her youth in the wonderland-like tangerine orchard. From the day she was admitted to the hospital, her intuition had told her that it would be hard to see her old friend the gardener again. She'd been depressed about that. But the events tonight had eased her mind and told her that the gardener had been near her all along. Wasn't that exactly right? Look: the young nurse outside was sending her a signal with his lamp. Despite having a little chest pain, she was happy. Would that young man stand outside all night?

Before she dozed off she was afraid she would die, but after sleeping a while she woke up again. The youngster was still standing out there. No, now there were two of them, each one holding a lamp that produced pleasant tangerine-colored light. A smile floated up on the director's face. She thought, finally she would die in her hometown.

Outside, some children were singing in a southern accent. She half-rose and looked briefly at her luminous watch. It was past midnight. She seemed to have endured another day. She remembered the charge nurse and started thinking about her, and she suddenly understood why this woman had such beautiful eyes. Yesterday, she had intended to leave after inspecting the rooms, but she turned and said to her, "For some people, a day is like a year."

The director hated to leave this world: she hadn't lived long enough. Since the screen had been removed from the window, the wind of death kept blowing in. She liked inhaling the wind, for this eased the feeling of suffocation. The next time she propped herself up to look outside, the two boys had vanished. Ah, day was dawning. Footsteps echoed in the corridor: there they were. One of them said, "Such a nice day . . ." They went into the office and closed the door. Their hearts were surely overflowing with great happiness. Another smile floated on the director's face, because a new day had arrived:

this was an undeniable fact. She thought of Nancy, she thought of José, she thought of Qiming, and also of Ying. She thought of Grace and Lee, and of Nancy's daughter and Haizai, and many, many others. Pebble Town, next to the snow mountain, was so vivid in her mind. Each and every path was animated, as though they would open their mouths and start talking. Above Pebble Town was that high, eternal, grayish-blue sky . . . Just then, the charge nurse came in.

In the haze, the nurse's face was sometimes large and sometimes small. It was a little scary. She wasn't wearing a mask, either. The director thought the face probably wasn't very ugly. As she was about to talk to her, the nurse turned and left.

The wind blew up, and the director wanted to sleep again for a while in the wind. She closed her eyes and tried to fall asleep, but without success.

So many years had passed since she'd been in the hospital to give birth to her baby, yet Nancy felt the hospital was just the same as it was then. There was only one notable change: the poplars, willows, and birches had grown into large trees reaching the sky. Shrubs and flowers were lush. Nancy thought this hospital was like a lovely convalescent home. After coming here a few times, she noticed there were no birds here, nor bees or butterflies. Not even ants. Only one or two mosquitoes flew past in the sky. Why did vegetation grow so green and lush, and yet there were no insects? She stayed a bit longer in the garden and felt a clammy moisture rise from below. She moved at once to the dry concrete road.

The inpatient ward of the hospital where the director was staying was particularly beautiful. Although one side faced the street, an immense flower garden inside extended straight toward the south as far as the eye could see. It seemed boundless. At the front of it were flowerbeds and a lawn; a little farther was a grove. Nancy hadn't been to the inpatient ward before. She squinted at those trees, but couldn't guess what kind they were.

Once, because the director was sleeping, Nancy thought she'd take a stroll in the garden. She walked to the edge of the flowerbeds and saw a large wooden sign with striking red letters: "Loiterers: Keep Out." A young man came up with a bulging muslin bag. He saw her hesitation and said, "The garden has been dangerous the past few days because poisonous butterflies are flying everywhere. Look: there are many more in here that have to be released. It's enough to give you a headache!" He held up the muslin bag.

Nancy looked at the colorful little things inside the bag.

"They'll die when they reach the garden, won't they?" she asked.

"Ha! You know this, too! That's right. These poor short-lived insects—the things in this garden don't suit the season."

The young man urged Nancy to leave the garden right away for her own safety. Nancy's heart was still pounding for some time after she'd left the garden. She stopped next to the hospital wall and looked at the garden through the iron fence. She was dumbfounded: there was no garden inside. There was only bare wasteland, with piles of rubble.

She told José what she'd seen. He pondered for a long time and then said, "I also think something's amiss. One thing bothers me—that Haizai: Why did he volunteer to work in the morgue? It can't have been just a whim."

Nancy wondered about this, too. The hospital was definitely a real place: she had given birth to Liujin here, after all. If the hospital also turned into a place like the garden in midair, then what was left to hang onto? She looked up and said to José as if complaining, "Life's domain shrinks more and more."

She made up her mind to discuss this with the director the next time she saw her.

The director still hadn't died. The worst attack had passed, and she realized she was still breathing. She was inhaling the wind of death.

That wind was carrying the blended fragrances of gardenias and white orchids.

After a day's rest, she felt her strength starting to return. She wasn't at all worried about the Design Institute. This institution had been run autonomously in line with her ideas. After being admitted to the hospital, she consigned any specific work to the back of her mind. Now she was preoccupied with something more abstract and more essential. She could almost reach out to touch it. The night before, the male nurse who had taken her to the tangerine orchard jumped in through the window. She had thought it was death coming for her. But instead it was the nurse; he said all the doors were closed. Only her window was wide open, so he had to climb in. In the dark, she thought of asking where he had gone, but she was too weak to speak.

"The charge nurse and I were in the garden: she sank into homesickness, so I came back alone. This place was locked up as tight as a fort. I thought to myself, there must be an opening somewhere—and sure enough, I found it."

He walked out the door and returned to the office. The director felt all of her strength rush back.

She saw some square beams and some triangles. In between were some automobile tires. She heard a stranger calling her from outside. She imagined he was her old friend the gardener; he had never used his real voice before. He was either speaking a northern dialect or else he was using incomprehensible language. At this moment, she so cherished the sunny rain of her hometown. In the rain, one could hear something growing in one's body.

The person who came in wasn't the gardener; it was Nancy. Nancy looked nervous.

"Nancy, is it because of the garden outside?" she asked with concern.

"Exactly. How strange . . ."

"You'll get used to it. Nancy, this isn't a bad thing. It's a good thing."

As the director spoke, she could see herself walking in the sunny rain: beautiful flowerbeds were on all sides.

"I'm exhausted. Nancy, I've come so far. It'll be over soon."

"Oh."

Nancy combed the director's white hair tenderly. Her long hair was lustrous, and not one wrinkle marred her round face. She wasn't a bit like a person plagued by illness. After her hair was combed, the director asked Nancy to help her stand up. She strained to do it, but she managed. Nancy was scared.

The director started walking. She asked Nancy to support her as she moved out step by step. They ran into the charge nurse in the corridor; to Nancy's surprise, the nurse ducked to one side and let them pass without a word.

At the entrance to the hospital, the director's gaze followed the pedestrians on the road. She seemed apprehensive.

"Are you looking for the gardener, ma'am? José saw him the day before yesterday in the courtyard."

"What was he like?"

"José didn't get a good look at him. He was getting on the bus. José just saw him in profile."

The director's expression turned placid. Then she told Nancy that she might die tonight, but she wasn't afraid—because she was used to it. The director stood here watching the people come and go on the road and watching the sun suspended in the sky. She was very moved. Then she uttered some curious words.

"In fact, the real director is the gardener," she said.

Then she suggested walking over to the fence. She moved slowly to the side. When they looked in through the iron bars, they saw a sky filled with colorful butterflies. Then they looked down: dead bodies of butterflies were scattered everywhere. The director said that she and the gardener had secretly bred these butterflies in the suburbs for years. All at once, Nancy remembered the strange things that had occurred years before in the farmhouse courtyard.

"These butterflies are poisonous, but they aren't a threat to human beings or small animals."

"Why did you breed short-lived, poisonous butterflies?"

"Nancy, if you look closely you'll know why. Do ordinary butterflies have such beautiful colors?"

Nancy stared blankly, as though in a trance.

"It's a miracle—an absolute miracle!" she said foolishly.

The director started to laugh. She seemed invigorated.

For a long time, even after Nancy had left, the director was still thinking of the butterflies. Since the night that the male nurse had taken her to the tangerine orchard and she'd seen the scenery there, she'd gone back to the garden twice by herself. She'd gone in the afternoon the first time and stood between the flowerbeds, for she wanted to find the tangerine orchard. She had looked and looked without success. The second time, it was morning, and she had again run into the young man who was freeing butterflies. After learning that he'd been sent by the gardener, she was exhilarated. The two of them released many butterflies, and her eyes sparkled with excitement.

Someone had come in. The director got up and saw a rather old man. He was filthy and he had a shock of messy hair. She recognized him from his expression, but for the moment she couldn't remember his name.

"I saw that the door was open, so I came in. You haven't tried that perpetual dialog yet, have you?"

He smiled, shamelessly exposing his black teeth.

The director's head slumped weakly to her chest. After a while, she finally mumbled in a low voice, "Haizai, I'm no longer able to confront you. I'm going to die soon. Did you come because you smelled the tangerine blossoms' fragrance on the wind?"

Haizai was a little panicked, but he calmed down and said, "No. You can't die yet, ma'am. We can resist together . . . We can continue this if you don't give up lightly."

But something seemed wrong with the director's neck: she couldn't straighten it. Haizai took something out of his pocket, pressed it into her hand, and left.

Not until it was time for her injection did the director relax her right hand and look at its contents. It was a crude old watch. The hands no longer moved. She shook it and then listened closely, but it still didn't run. The nurse's mouth twitched, and he took the watch away, threw it on the floor, and then stomped on it. Then he picked it up and returned it to her. The director stared at it: she saw the hands finally tremble a few times and start to move.

"That man is a hoodlum, an old one. The charge nurse and I both know him. Did you enter into an agreement with him? We both did."

"I guess so. I've forgotten."

"That's the problem, ma'am. He won't forget you."

The director put the pocket watch under her pillow. She heard the hands moving more and more energetically. Probably the whole room could hear this. Puzzled, she thought maybe this was the watch that Qiming used in the past. For some reason, she was a little disappointed. She asked the nurse, "If I play dead, will this Haizai come and talk with me?"

"Of course. The charge nurse asked him to come. He lives in the basement over there."

"Oh."

After her injection, the director was cold all over. She felt unspeakably lonely. It was very quiet in this part of the hospital. No one was here. She passed by many large wards—all empty. Where had everyone gone? She arrived outside and saw a door leading to the basement. On an impulse, she went in. Going down long flights of steps, she reached the bottom and entered a large room.

A light was on. Under the light, Haizai was working on a pistol. He had disassembled it and placed the parts on the table. Seeing the director walking in, he turned on two more lights, each one illuminating a narrow bed with someone sleeping on it. One was a man, the other a woman. Their eyes were closed.

"Ah, director! Please take a seat. I've been here several days. And these two people? They both now have end-stage kidney disease."

"Are you treating them?"

"Me? No, this is only end-stage palliative care."

He walked around the room with his hands behind his back. The director waited apprehensively.

"Do you want to lie down, ma'am?" Haizai turned on a third light in the corner.

The light illuminated another bed—wider than the first two. On it was a quilt with a black-and-white pattern of lovebirds. The director hesitated and then lay down. A tangerine fragrance came from the quilt, and the director felt joy rise within her. She was going to say something but then she fell asleep. In her dreams, Haizai was whispering to her. He spoke urgently and passionately.

Nancy spent two more days worrying, but still heard no news of the director's death. In other words, the director was still alive. But at noon, José brought word that the director had been kidnapped.

"It was that worker named Haizai," José said, looking uneasy.

Nancy sat on a small stool in the kitchen. Everything went black before her eyes.

"I often think that maybe the director's avoidance of Haizai isn't really avoidance. What do you think?" José asked.

"Of course it isn't." Nancy looked at her husband in surprise. "You knew this, too."

They walked out to their courtyard and watched for a long time. In each of their minds one door was closing little by little, and another door was opening softly. They spotted the magpie simultaneously. It was singing gleefully in a tree.

"It's a good omen, isn't it?" Nancy asked hesitantly.

The sound of a carriage drew near. Nancy listened closely, and her worried expression gave way to a carefree one. She saw Liujin's slim figure swaying at the window and heard José making noise in the kitchen. The sounds of real daily life made her even more sentimental, yet also aroused a faint desire. She thought, *A new era is beginning.*

Later, in an uncertain tone, she told José, "There's a place where poisonous butterflies fill the sky, and a shepherd boy plays a flute under the trees. Have you been there?"

José said he'd gone there several times.

"Then I won't worry about the director anymore. Neither of us will forget it, and she knows we love her. Isn't this true?"

"Yes." José's eyes glittered. "When you have time, we'll take Liujin over there. She's also very interested in butterflies."

Just then, they heard Liujin's excited voice, "Dad, Dad! The magpies are building nests under our eaves! Wow!!"

Chapter 11

LIUJIN AND AMY,
AS WELL AS QIMING

L ate at night, when that mournful song rose once more from the small house across the street, Liujin walked from the courtyard to the middle of the road. The night was so still and clear. As she concentrated to listen, the singing stopped abruptly. In the lamplight, some large cat faces seemed to be hiding amid the sandthorn leaves. They vanished when Liujin drew closer and reappeared when she withdrew. All the cats seemed to be in heat. Liujin looked to her left and saw that the house was dark. A figure stood in the open space in front of the courtyard. Liujin tensed up and headed over there right away.

"He's the sort of old man who comes and goes without a trace. When you bathe in the river at dusk in the summertime, you might see the likes of him. They stand alone in the river," said Amy, answering Liujin's unspoken question.

"Amy, did your parents know him?"

"Yes, of course. He was my mother's dream-lover when she was young, though in reality she didn't love him. Look, things are so strange. It was only after Mama died that I came to this city with Uncle Qiming."

"Uncle Qiming!? When I was little . . . Now I don't recognize him at all."

"I know, I know! He's adorable, isn't he?"

Amy leaned close to Liujin and gripped her hand. Amy's hand felt stiff and callused. In the courtyard behind them, a sheep began to bleat. The light went on in the house. Meng Yu was coughing. Amy quietly asked Liujin to crouch down with her and whispered, "We're like sisters." This warmed Liujin's heart. Liujin wanted to respond with something similar, but—afraid the sheep would hear her and start bleating—she held back. At this moment, Liujin realized from the bottom of her heart that this Pebble Town below the starry sky was not quiet at all. Human desire seethed in it. The sheep were nothing but the incarnation of lust.

Meng Yu shouted from the doorway, but not for Amy. Yet, Amy jumped up and ran in.

Liujin stayed where she was, suspecting that what had happened just now was only a dream. Why did Uncle Qiming want Amy to stay at Meng Yu's? Was this sheep dealer's home the best choice for a beauty like Amy? Liujin recalled that in the past—always early in the morning—she had seen old Meng Yu herding a large flock of sheep back home. In the golden light of morning, the old man and the sheep looked flushed with excitement. Liujin, her bookbag on her back, had stood beside the road and stared in awe. At dusk when she came back from school, Liujin would go peek at the sheep: now, all the sheep looked sorrowful.

As she walked away, Liujin kept looking back. The lamp soon went out. The sheep were bleating softly. She couldn't tell if these sounds came from their being satisfied or dissatisfied. "Oh, sheep. Sheep," Liujin said to herself.

She walked ahead along the main road, imagining the scene years ago when her parents had come here from the train station. This six-lane road had decided the layout of this small city, and had been here from the beginning. The housing and commercial districts were laid out along both sides of the road. Later, as the city grew, the road expanded to the east and west, and then expanded more. On the east, it now extended as far as the snow mountain. Why hadn't a second and a third road been built? Why hadn't a few north-south roads been built to intersect with this one? Liujin couldn't understand. All the visitors who came here were astonished at the length of this road. They said, "It's as if it connects with the ends of the earth." She stopped in the middle of the road and listened closely: somewhere, an infant was crying. Sometimes, it sounded as though the child were inside a room, sometimes as if in the open country. But it certainly wasn't two infants. When the crying stopped, a male voice lifted in song. But these sounds weren't real: it would be better to believe they were figments of her imagination. How could she hallucinate like this?

When Liujin returned to the entrance of her courtyard, she heard once more the bleating from across the way. This time, it sounded like pure contentment. One sheep bleated first, and many sheep responded. The light inside the house went out again. How long had Dad and Mama been away? Five years? Ten years? She was at a loss to answer. Back then, was the road this empty and quiet at midnight? Or was it filled with little animals running around? She had long ago taken Dad's photograph down from the living room wall, because she had realized that hanging a large photograph of him made it seem that he had died. So it was inappropriate. Liujin knew her parents would never come back here. She still loved to imagine their present life: this consoled her. Maybe her parents felt this, too, so they kept writing odd letters to each other. Every time the mailman thumped a thick letter down on her table, Liujin felt a little surprised. She sniffed the envelope and sniffed it again: it didn't smell at all like smoke. The stationery was always the same—gray-colored with a little light yellow, but why was a little person printed in the corner? It was an image of a young man holding up swords in both hands in a defensive pose, as if under attack. The living room looked quite natural without any pictures on the wall.

Liujin fell asleep before dawn. Before that, she tried hard to imagine Smoke City and its iron drawbridge. She couldn't picture what her dad would look like now. She rubbed her face sorrowfully and still couldn't guess. The budgerigar spoke from its cage: "It hasn't been ten years. It's been five years."

It was eerie to hear these words in the dark. Had she said this out loud earlier today? She had bought this bird a few days ago. The bird seller had said she would "get rich" if she bought this bird and took it home. After the curly-haired salesman had opened the cage and let the bird fly out, it had landed on her shoulder and scratched her. She had almost cried. This was a fierce bird. Liujin hung its cage in front of the living room window. She hadn't heard it say anything. Had she bought it because she had fewer and fewer little animals at home? This courtyard used to be so lively. If it was ten years ago, she must now be forty years old. The bird was right. Not ten years. Five! Looking at Amy, she could be sure of this. She was so youthful—far from being old. Two days ago, she had replenished her stock of merchandise and had encountered an unusual homespun cloth: it was snow-white stamped with black circles. Looking at it made one's head spin. People said this cloth was very fashionable. For some reason, it seemed familiar. She had definitely seen it before and then had forgotten it. Only five years had passed, many more years lay ahead of her, and her parents were still alive and well. Consoled by these thoughts, she fell asleep.

Across the street, Amy wasn't sleeping. Once again, she slipped in among the sheep and crouched there. The next day, these sheep would be driven to market, and so she wanted to spend some time with them for now. This was an exciting time for her.

Her coming to the city was a little strange, for her family had never discussed the move. It was as if they tacitly mulled over allowing her to leave the family: they wanted her to experience a different lifestyle. Just now, when Liujin had asked about Uncle Qiming, Amy had been a little distracted. She couldn't think too much about things that were happening to her. They happened, that's all. It was only afterward that she could think about them.

She raised her head a little and saw a dim light in the old woman's bedroom—it was Mrs. Meng's. She had an odd relationship with this old woman. Mrs. Meng seemed acrimonious, yet Amy knew that she genuinely cared about her. And so she said to Liujin, "It's as if the old grandma is putting on an act for other people." Her words astonished Liujin. Seeing Liujin's heavy-hearted expression, Amy felt even closer to her. In the past, before she came to the city, was Liujin like this, too? At night, Amy saw many people with double images. Sometimes one person looked like an entire squadron. But Liujin was simply Liujin—real and clear. Even so, Amy still couldn't understand her. Perhaps she was genuinely "unreal." Amy felt several sheep pressing tightly against her, looking at her bluntly—or maybe not looking at her, but rather looking at something inside her. She said to herself, "Something new should emerge on a night like this."

She knew many people were thinking of the snow leopard descending the mountain. She had seen that caged leopard at the Snow Mountain Hotel. She thought Snow Leopard City might be a fitting name for Pebble Town. Yes, it should have two names—Pebble Town as the external name and Snow Leopard Town as the inner name. Uncle Qiming didn't have double images at night, either. He and she both belonged to "the inner."

At daylight, Amy stood up and looked at the white pagoda ahead of her. The rays of light always fell first on the white pagoda. In the blurry light, the structure stood there like a giant. Just then, the street-washing truck sped by.

"Good morning, Amy. It was a really long night. I thought I'd slept a long time, but when I looked at my watch, I realized it was only a little more than an hour!"

Liujin yawned. She didn't have to go to work today.

"It's a new day, Liujin. Can you hear it?"

Liujin did hear it—a bird chirping in the white pagoda. It was a large bird, but they couldn't see it. Amy said they could call it "nameless bird." Amy grabbed Liujin's hand, and the two of them stood together breathing the refreshing air in the first glimmer of dawn. Liujin thought, *Amy is really charming. If I had a sister, would she be like Amy?*

"Amy, why do you always go barefoot?'

"It's comforting to touch the earth with bare feet. I'm afraid to look at the sheep's expressions."

"I know. I'm afraid, too. When I'm in bed at night, I tremble with fear."

Somebody pushed open the courtyard gate and entered, but he stood there without moving. He was tall, like a tree. Amy said quietly that he was her brother and that he didn't like to talk with her. "I don't know why—he falls silent as soon as he comes to the city."

He glanced at them for a while, then turned and left. In the dim light, Liujin couldn't see him clearly. Amy said he had gotten a good look at them. "He has a mountain man's vision." Liujin was curious. She wanted to know more about this tree-like man, but Amy dropped the topic.

Before Liujin left, Amy told her that it was Uncle Qiming who had given her a second life. If it weren't for him, she'd still be feeling her way in the dark. It was light when she said this. Sure enough, a bird was on the white pagoda—a large bird, but barely visible because it too was white. Its nighttime chirping seemed to be summoning something—but what? Liujin was afraid Meng Yu and the others would see her, so she hastened away. Just then, Amy began her workday. *What an energetic person she is*, Liujin thought.

"What's mountain life like?" Liujin was talking to herself as she entered the courtyard. Before this, she'd had no contact with people like Amy and Amy's brother. Maybe they were sort of like Roy, but greatly different, too. When she thought of Roy, Liujin perked up.

Amy loved city life, but she was still a little lonesome. At dusk here, she would sit and wait under the elm at the doorway. She thought Uncle Qiming might come to see her. The old woman—Meng Yu's wife—always jeered at this because she loathed Qiming. Once, she had even beat him with a steel pipe until he bled from the head and fainted. The old woman had walked away, leaving only Amy in the house with him. When he came to, Amy helped bandage his head. He said it didn't hurt at all and that he had only pretended to faint so the old woman would leave and he and Amy could be alone in the house. Amy looked at him, hoping he would say something. She stood up and peered outside, afraid the old woman was hiding there. But he just asked indifferently how she was doing, and then took his leave.

Amy pondered this question for a long time: Why had Uncle Qiming arranged for her to stay in this home? Was it merely because they had no daughter and so he had brought them one? She'd seen for herself how much the old woman loathed Uncle Qiming, and so her doubts and suspicions mounted. She wanted to ask her brother, but her brother didn't like to talk. He said the city dust had ruined his voice. In this family, the one who least liked to talk was Meng Yu. Soon after arriving, she felt she had dropped into a silent world. Of course the sheep bleated. As time passed, she learned to distinguish the sheep's bleats. Later, she started singing songs she had learned from her mother. No one stopped her, and she even thought the old couple actually enjoyed her singing. The old woman told her that singing was helpful as long as she didn't immerse herself too much in hopeless illusions.

Finally Uncle Qiming showed up. Standing next to the elm tree, he looked at the stars and said, "Amy, what's the difference between sheep and people?"

Amy trembled all over. This question frightened her, and Uncle's hand on her shoulder was really heavy. When she finally answered, she said, "I always look into their eyes. I think they know that thing before people do. I think they understand thoroughly. They . . ."

She gabbled on and on inarticulately. As she spoke, she suddenly recalled her taciturn father, who lived in the mountains. Was she perhaps in the same clan as Meng Yu? She sensed she was on the verge of discovering something. It was almost on her lips, but of course she still couldn't say what it was. Uncle Qiming had been gone for quite a while, and Amy was still trapped in thought. Something light dropped to her feet—a jade-colored butterfly. It was sliding from her foot to the ground. It was dying.

"Many butterflies have died in the nursery in the park over there. They fly and fly and then drop."

Liujin had come over. In the sunset glow, Liujin's face was radiant, like that of a twenty-some-year-old woman. Liujin asked her if her father was Han. She couldn't say, because sometimes her father said he was Han, and sometimes he said he was Yao or Hui. Her father said, "There's no way to be sure. Since your mother is Uighur, you can also consider me Uighur." Amy had asked her mother, too, and she had said her father was "a person of the mountains." Her mother explained that mountain people were those who worked for years and years in the old forests deep in the mountains. No one knew where they came from.

"Oh, I see!" Liujin stared at Amy. "The first time I saw you, I couldn't believe my eyes. I thought you weren't a real person. Now I see: you're doing well in Mr. Meng Yu's home."

They scooped out a hole and buried the jade-colored butterfly under the elm tree. Just then, the old woman came over.

"Liujin, has your relationship with Sherman cooled?" she called.

"Yes. Or it might be better to say there was never anything to it," Liujin said, embarrassed.

"That's what I think, too," she nodded.

In a split second, Liujin felt this old woman was particularly reasonable, and she was surprised that she had changed her opinion of her.

Watching her from behind, Amy said, "The old woman is like this: you look at her and you think she's talking about one thing, but no, she's talking about another important matter. In the past, I wasn't used to the way she talked. Now I am."

"Amy, you're really bright."

"Liujin, come with me to see the sheep."

When the two of them crouched among the sheep, Liujin's heart leapt with longing. She said to herself, "So that's what's been going on in this courtyard all along." Liujin observed the sheep's eyes: their expressions were vacant. She looked up at the sky; her line of sight fell on the last rays of sunset. She asked Amy, "Do you hear children singing? How strange."

"Yes, I'm listening," Amy said. "It's so beautiful. They're probably on their way."

"Where? Where are they heading? They sound far away."

"It's hard to say where they're going. When it gets dark, they stop singing. Listen! They've stopped, haven't they?"

Unexpectedly, the sheep on both sides began bleating: it was a heartbreaking lament. When Liujin noticed Amy's wooden face, she thought Amy had long been accustomed to this. All of a sudden, Liujin noticed the sheep's legs shaking. A gigantic eagle—two or three times the normal size—was flying overhead. It had begun to circle.

"What kind of eagle is it?" Liujin asked in alarm.

"Don't worry. It's okay. This eagle is a little like my dad."

Amy looked mesmerized, as if drunk. At the same time, the sheep were shaking even more; a large number of them knelt down, and a terrifying silence saturated the air. Liujin noticed old Meng Yu emerge from the house with his shoe repair tools. Indifferent to what was going on in the courtyard, he sat down to do his work as usual. Amy told Liujin that he would begin a long journey the next day, so he was repairing his shoes.

The eagle finally swooped down and grabbed a lamb just as the sky darkened. Although she couldn't see much, Liujin sensed an immediate ease in the tension. All the kneeling sheep stood up. What puzzled Liujin was that the snatched lamb had uttered no sound.

"Where will old Meng Yu go?"

"Not sure. He never says. Liujin, will you come again tomorrow? If you don't, I'll be lonely."

"I can't come tomorrow. I have to work. But you like being alone, don't you?"

"Yes. But I also like to talk with you."

Amy lit the lantern, and once more Liujin felt a surge of strong emotions. Over there, old Meng Yu was repairing shoes in the dark. He tapped calmly on the soles. Sorrow once more appeared in the eyes of the sheep, illuminated by the lamp. This was their habitual expression. Liujin's heart trembled, overcome by strong emotions. She said to herself over and over again: "Amy . . . so beautiful." The passions this young mountain woman stirred up in her were much stronger than the feelings she'd had in the past for her various sweethearts.

Liujin awakened with a start at midnight. She sensed someone entering her room. When she turned on the light, she saw to her surprise that it was Amy. Amy's hair was a little disheveled, her gaze a little blank. She held a cat to her chest: it was Liujin's tiger-striped cat. When Liujin sat up, she saw two geckoes that had disappeared for a long time clinging to the wall. And under Amy's feet, two wagtails were pecking at grain.

"When you showed up, they all came in. How did you get in, Amy?"

"You've forgotten—you left the door open. I haven't come here before. Your place is like an ancient castle. As soon as I reached your courtyard, your cat and your birds all showed up. They're starving. Were you keeping them out? Hey, your bird is pecking my feet! Does it eat meat, too?"

Amy sat down cross-legged on the bed. The two little birds squawked and rushed out the door.

Liujin asked Amy if old Meng Yu had come back.

"No. I don't think we should worry about it."

"So he won't come back?"

"Probably not. He wanted to leave a long time ago. He prepared many pairs of shoes for himself."

Amy was staring at one gecko, which was stuck to the edge of the lampshade. It looked as if it might fall any minute. The cat she held was snoring. Liujin heard sounds coming from the flowers and plants in the courtyard. Little critters were probably moving back and forth among them.

"Someone from an earlier era has entered your courtyard. Everyone thought he was gone, but he wasn't. His longevity is amazing. He's coming to your home. I never believed anyone could live that long until I saw him with my own eyes. It was he."

"Do you mean Uncle Qiming?"

"Of course not. This is a person without a body. Once upon a time in the mountains, my father told me about this. And it's in your home that I've discovered it. Your home is like an ancient castle: even the moonlight is different."

Liujin was sitting across from Amy. As she listened, she imagined seeing little critters going to and fro in the clumps of flowers, and she felt a great satisfaction. Could it be that she really hadn't closed the gate yesterday? She swept her eyes involuntarily over the scene outside the window and saw birds moving in the nest that had been abandoned long ago. Amy turned off the light, and green moonlight flooded the room. Everything looked green and lush.

First, a frog croaked in the corner to the west, and then came the responses. There seemed to be three or four of them.

"What was your life like in the mountains? I can't even imagine it. A lonely family surrounded by nothing but mountains . . . They must be under enormous pressure. If it were I, I wouldn't be able to cope. That's a little like being naked in public."

"Dad and my brother always went to dangerous places to cut firewood. Back then, we had no clock. Mama and I estimated the time by the sun's position. That kind of life wasn't at all monotonous. Right now, my brother is sitting in old Meng Yu's firewood shed. He was so quiet that I got scared and slipped over here to your place."

"Would he hurt you?"

"I don't know. I never know what he and Dad are thinking. But back then, they did agree to my coming to the city. They saw me off at the crossing, and then went back home without a word."

"Are you ready for bed, Amy?"

"Yes."

She didn't want a quilt. She curled up in a corner of the bed and soon fell asleep. She was really thin! She didn't take up much space. Her posture while sleeping made her seem very lonely. Liujin looked out the window again: it was pitch-black now with no moonlight. Recently she had remembered something: she was crying helplessly, and a man bent down and picked her up and lifted her to the sky as he shouted something. Probably it was the missing Uncle Qiming. That's who it must have been, although she couldn't be sure.

Liujin couldn't fall back asleep. It was as if Amy had created a strong magnetic field in her bed: each time Liujin was about to drift off, something startled her. She got up and walked into the courtyard. By the light of her lamp, she saw a person sitting at the courtyard gate. It wasn't Uncle Qiming. This person was much younger—maybe Amy's brother. Liujin thought he didn't want her to disturb him, and so she kept her distance as she gazed at the dark shadow. A frog croaked again—quite abruptly, frightening her a little. After a while, the person left, and Liujin promptly walked to the gate with the lamp.

On the stone bench was a sickle for cutting grass.

Amy was awake and said, "That's my sickle. I killed a leopard with it."

She said once more that Liujin's home resembled an ancient castle. She let the cat go and walked out, barefoot and soundlessly, sickle in hand. Liujin thought, *She's just like a leopard.* The two wagtails flew out from somewhere and lit on her shoulders.

Liujin got into bed, hoping to sleep some more, but Amy ran up again, gasping for breath. She said, "Liujin, my brother, he . . . my brother, he knocked Uncle Qiming down!"

"Oh, no!!"

By the light of her lamp, she saw the old man lying on his side by the fence.

"Uncle, Uncle, where does it hurt?" Amy asked anxiously.

Uncle Qiming waved them off. Liujin heard him repeating something vaguely.

"He says, his heart hurts. He can't move yet. He wants to lie down here for a while. I clearly saw my brother stab him in the back with a knife!"

"Amy, do you know how old Uncle is?" Liujin asked.

"Almost eighty. He's the oldest person I've seen in the city. I've heard that an even older person lives on the riverside, but I haven't seen him. My brother tends to be violent."

"Amy, Amy, how come there's blood on your sickle?!"

Liujin sniffed the edge of the blade and saw Amy cover her face and squat down. Her shoulders were shaking, as if she were crying. Liujin also crouched down. She wanted to comfort Amy, but she didn't know how. Below the wall over there, Uncle Qiming groaned again.

"We, Uncle Qiming, my brother, and I—we burst in here and now we have no way to leave."

Amy whispered this, as if very distressed.

"There are butterflies here, too. I noticed them as soon as I entered.

They aren't wild butterflies. Liujin, your home is more frightening than being on the mountain, so my brother ran away."

It was so dark all around, and the lamp was almost out of oil. Liujin felt cold all over. Amy's distress was infectious. What had happened to the ebullient longing she'd felt earlier? A bone-deep loneliness was spreading through her. Liujin wondered what kind of thread connected these three people. All of a sudden, she thought of her faraway parents: it had been quite a long time since she'd received a letter from them. Was this because they trusted her more? Oh, Dad! Oh, Mama! She was about to break into tears and was embarrassed to be so childish. What was wrong tonight?

Amy stood up. It was hard to breathe because the air here was a little thin. She'd been longing to enter Liujin's home. From outside the courtyard, she saw the flowers bloom and wither, and she saw the large, colorful butterflies fly in and out unhurriedly. In the daytime, the scenery at this home was primitive; at night, an intangible gate closed. When Amy stood outside the courtyard gate late at night, she felt waves of dank air pushing her backward. That's why she called this home "ancient castle." Although she had tried many times, she was unable to enter. Now she was finally inside, and everything here was novel. The gecko stuck softly to the edge of the lampshade. It made her shudder all over. The strange thing was that Liujin couldn't see the butterflies in her own home. They crowded in through the windows—they were so large, so numerous. They fluttered unhurriedly, and then after a while, they flew out again. Amy knew from Liujin's expression that she didn't see them. It was a strange selective blindness. The colorful butterflies in Liujin's courtyard must be the little creatures closest to being a mirage, because Liujin actually couldn't see them, though she was aware of all the other little creatures. As Amy held the drowsy striped cat, she felt she was holding the entire snow mountain in her arms!

"Liujin, do you think Uncle Qiming will die? He said he injured his heart. It has nothing to do with my brother. But I saw my brother gouge a deep hole in his back."

"Maybe your brother was trying to save him."

"Then, shouldn't he be happy now? He walked to your home and then collapsed. It's so dark here. Liujin, Liujin, I'm all stirred up!"

"Me, too, Amy. Let me hold your hand."

Liujin held out her hand, but what she grabbed was the edge of the sickle. Blood gushed out, making her hand sticky.

"Amy, did your hand turn into a sickle?"

"Oh, that happens a lot. Did you get hurt? I have bandages."

By the light of the lamp, Liujin wound a bandage on her hand. The lamp flame leapt a few times and then went out.

"Amy, Amy . . ." Liujin sighed ardently. "You mountain people are sometimes so far away that I can't catch up with you. You're watching me quietly from afar."

Over there, Uncle Qiming moaned softly. Amy heard him right away. She wanted to say something, but didn't. Suddenly, the parrot in Liujin's house screeched: "Not eighty years old. Seventy-nine!"

Liujin burst out laughing.

Amy gave Uncle a hand, and they walked out of the courtyard. She said they were going to Meng Yu's home to treat Uncle's wound.

It was when Liujin was measuring cloth for a customer that the man walked over: he was Amy's brother—tall, with a long beard and eyes like an eagle's. Liujin's hands trembled slightly. She folded the cloth and handed it to the woman, took her money, and quickly turned and went to the back room for a cup of tea; actually, she left mainly to avoid the man. To her surprise, her boss said, "Isn't that gentleman here to see you?" So the boss had noticed him. Liujin had no choice but to return to the counter. She was startled when she heard him speak, because he actually spoke in the standard accent of Pebble Town—not like Amy, who spoke like an outsider.

"I'm not here to buy cloth. I'm just looking. Everyone here is so guarded. Is there ever a time when you let down your guard?"

He looked puzzled and helpless. He was carrying an iron cage. Liujin glanced into it and saw a wolf cub. She blanched. He started to laugh.

"Don't be afraid. It's a demi-wolf. But in an era like this, who can distinguish wolves and dogs? For example, I . . ."

When Liujin heard him say "an era like this," she felt it was quite strange. What was *an era like this*?

The man didn't go on talking. He bent down as if to open the iron cage. Liujin decided that if he let the wolf out, she would run to the back room and bolt the door. But although he bent down a few times, he didn't open the cage.

"Sometimes, I sit here and think about your lives on the mountain, but I can't figure it out. Wouldn't you go crazy living alone on such a high place?" Liujin immediately regretted her words; she thought she was really an idiot.

"Of course not, Liujin. Of course not!"

Liujin was startled all over again, because all at once his tone had turned intimate—actually, even with a little seductive overtone. She recalled that Amy hadn't come to the market today, and asked if he'd seen her.

"No. She probably stayed at home today with Uncle Qiming and Mrs. Meng."

Liujin thought this man didn't feel guilty at all. Then, what exactly had he done to Uncle Qiming? Or had he really helped him? What kind of mental state was Uncle Qiming in—Qiming, who wandered around all day? She looked up and saw those eagle eyes looking at her brightly. He didn't hide his lust. Liujin couldn't understand, yet she was curious. What type of man was he?

"I have to go, Liujin. Don't worry. The wolf can't bite you."

He picked up the iron cage with a carrying pole and slung it over his shoulders. People stayed out of his way as he walked out with long strides. Liujin and her boss craned their necks, staring at his receding figure. The boss whispered that he was a "swindler." Liujin asked why he said this.

"Why did he bring a wolf cub here? Did he think we were little children? And since he brought the cub with him, he should have taken it out and shown it to us. I think it was a fake. It wasn't even a demi-wolf. It was just an ordinary mutt."

Liujin was surprised by the boss's indignation.

"Take the rest of the day off, Liujin. Anyhow, you're in no mood to work."

When Liujin walked out of the market, she spotted Sherman emerging from the rice shop. It was obvious that he didn't want to see her, for he immediately ducked back inside. Liujin muttered "sinister guy" to herself and walked past the rice shop with her head high. Liujin thought, *Everyone is putting on a disguise. Amy's brother is the only exception. Maybe that's the way mountain people are.* Liujin disliked his barbaric candor, and yet was helplessly attracted to it. *On the mountaintop four thousand meters above sea level, could the rarefied air affect people's thoughts?* Liujin had grown up in the city, and it seemed she would always be fascinated with the snow mountain.

She kept thinking about Amy, so without stopping at home, she went into the courtyard across the street. Eyes drooping, Meng Yu's wife stood in the courtyard. She looked unhappy.

"Amy's sick."

"Oh!"

"She's heartsick. As soon as that old Qiming showed up, she got sick. And her brother—he's a bad influence on her. This girl has no mind of her own."

Liujin could see that the old woman didn't want her there, so she left and went home.

As she tended the plants in the courtyard, she was a little anxious, but she didn't know why. Just then, Roy appeared at the fence. Liujin kept calling his name "Roy, Roy—" and her tears gushed forth.

"The snow leopard really did come down the mountain. Did you smell it?" she asked Roy.

Hugging each other, they sat on the stone bench. Roy held Liujin's left hand tightly and said uneasily, "Liujin, you mustn't leave. If you do, I won't recognize this house."

"Who said I was going, Roy?"

"It was the gecko. I saw it climb the fence the other day."

After a while, they heard singing. The white clouds drifted in the sky, and the two of them sank into memories. Liujin thought, *Amy is such a passionate woman!* Roy imagined his parents sitting in the sunshine peeling lotus seeds, and five snow leopards surrounding them. How had the snow leopards gotten there? He couldn't remember.

As soon as Amy stopped singing, Roy jumped up and said, "The train has pulled in. I have to go right now."

As Liujin watched him dashing away, she ached. Roy and Amy—she would always be separated from them by mountains and oceans. She packed up her tools, went into the house, sat down, and started a letter to her mother.

". . . Today I have some good news. A young friend told me that he could recognize this house only if I continued to live here. I think others probably also feel this way. Mama, Dad, our home will always be here, won't it? Day before yesterday, the long-life bird really came. It lit on the grape arbor. I saw it the moment I entered the courtyard. It must have flown over from your place. This messenger calmly stopped there, as if reporting that all is well with you.

"The last couple of days, it's been very windy. I heard that on the border a sandstorm buried a whole village. I can't imagine what that would have been like. Now, it's tranquil here, and the long-life bird came. I think I won't leave, because the two of you haven't left, either. This place holds your youth, and that is not a mirage. Just as Amy said, the two of you built this hidden ancient castle . . ."

Liujin stood up and sealed the letter. Some things became clear in her mind. Formerly, in front of the window in the room at the Snow Mountain Hotel, her stonecutter boyfriend had said to her, "Pebble Town is a young city." Where had that ex-boyfriend gone? She felt this had happened a lifetime ago.

It was evening before Amy came over. She told Liujin that her brother had gone back. Amy looked uneasy and kept saying, "He's certainly disappointed in me." She meant her brother. She leapt across the room and tried to grab the gecko from the wall. When she failed, she was really annoyed. She said she didn't have a clue about Uncle Qiming or old man Meng Yu. She was completely ignorant. After complaining for a while, she suddenly calmed down and said she would get over it.

"I fell in love with an old man. Can you understand this?" Amy said suddenly.

"It must be Uncle Qiming—right? Even I almost fell in love with him."

"When I was three, he took me to see the river. He didn't come to my home. He waited on a faraway slope. Mama handed me to him on that windy day. He and I stood on the riverside. He told me to stand still and shout. I shouted 'Mama.' Later, I fell in love with him. You mustn't think that I fell for this old man because I didn't have many chances to meet young men in that place. That's not true. Many young men lived in the village below the mountain. And for the most part, they were handsome, but I didn't love them."

In the lamplight, Amy's face looked rather tired. This was unusual. She was always so vivacious and lively. Liujin wondered if something was wrong. Was Uncle Qiming all right?

"Amy, you're so pretty, Uncle must love you a lot. We think you're like the sun."

"No, no. He doesn't love me. The one he loves is my deceased mama."

"Where is he now?"

"He's injured. You saw that. He's always getting hurt, and then he hides somewhere until he recovers. I can't find his hiding place, Pebble Town is so large."

"Does your brother hate him?"

"My brother also loves him. He wants to be like him, but he can't. He was sad when he went home."

Liujin turned the light off, but she didn't see the green moonlight. The cat walked past the windowsill, looking very large. And a bird was pecking at something on the floor. Amy said it was feed that she had scattered.

"I often think about coming here to hide, but this ancient castle doesn't belong to me. We can only visit."

"My home is your home. It would be great if you moved here. Little birds are coming back, and frogs will, too."

"The air here is too thin. People in your family have extraordinary lungs. That's what Uncle Qiming told me. You didn't know that, did you? And so we can stay here only a short time."

Liujin had long ago sensed what she spoke of, but she had never given it careful thought. She walked over to the window and moved the parrot to a different spot. When she turned back, Amy had disappeared.

"She loves him. He doesn't love her!" the parrot said.

Liujin turned on the light and looked closely at the floor. She saw neither a bird nor any feed.

Liujin sat down and thought back to Amy's brother's appearance. He was about forty years old, a good-looking man. His face would have been charming if he weren't so aloof. When someone like this strolled around the city with a wolf cub, it was conspicuous. He didn't seem to like cities, so why had he come here? Amy had said that snow leopards, black bears, and other carnivores wouldn't harm woodsmen, because woodsmen were in the mountains every day and so the animals thought they were one of them. A man who worked in the mountains every day was actually interested in cities and came to see if city residents "were ever off-guard." Having such a brother, would Amy be likely to feel tense all the time? Amy said her father had never come down the mountain. Was Liujin ever negligent? For example, did she write to her mother regularly?

This was the first time Liujin had seen a real mountain man. She knew there were woodsmen in the mountains and she had thought they must be like Ying—covered all over with memories and stumbling when on flat land. She was interested in Amy because of her singing and her beauty—but mostly because she was from the mountains.

That little gecko (could it be the big one's daughter?) was crawling in the light outside. She could hear animals passing through the underbrush in the courtyard. On a night like this, Liujin sensed that she was particularly good at communicating with people like Amy's brother. Of course, her thoughts held no erotic overtones. She was merely imagining visiting a snow leopard's home with him. If this really happened, maybe she would be able to solve the riddle of the snow mountain. Woodsmen were part of the riddle, and so was Roy. The little gecko crawled over to the window frame and stopped. Liujin lamented to herself: *It really is a new era.* She had sympathized with Amy's brother, and now she felt that her train of thought was flowing particularly freely. Inhaling deeply, she could even smell the smoke from Smoke City. But for some reason, she still couldn't recall what Uncle Qiming used to be like. What she remembered was still a cloud of smoke.

Outside the window, someone gasped for breath. Liujin rushed out the door and saw three neighbor boys doing handstands by the wall. Their upside-down bodies kept trembling in the moonlight. When Liujin approached, they stood up and wiped the sweat from their faces with their sleeves.

"You look exhausted," Liujin said.

"We came here to do exercises. It's hard to breathe here," the slightly older one said.

"Really?"

The three kids started laughing and ran off.

When Liujin looked down, she saw the sickle on the ground. Was Amy still here? She picked up the sickle and looked at its serrated edge in the moonlight. She felt a chill in her back and immediately put the sickle down on the windowsill. She went to the courtyard and looked around again, but didn't see Amy. When she went back inside, Amy was sitting upright in the living room.

"Did you see the sickle?" Amy asked, her head drooping.

"Yes. I didn't dare look very long. I was afraid of being cut."

"I made marks on their hands. Such well-behaved children!"

Amy said she was all mixed up. She'd like to sit up all night in the living room. Liujin went off to bed.

Liujin awakened when she saw wolves in her dream. Then she heard animals gasping for breath throughout the whole house. She turned on the lights, but didn't see any animals. She went to the living room and saw Amy still sitting next to the table, her head propped up in one hand. There were no animals in the living room, either.

"I'm waiting for Uncle Qiming. Are you waiting for him, too?" Amy asked.

"No. I was dreaming. There were so many big animals in this house."

"Unh. That's because your house is so big. Your dad and mama are broad-minded. So are my parents."

When Amy laughed in the dark, the parrot in the bedroom also laughed. The parrot's laughter made Liujin's hair stand on end. Liujin put the birdcage on the living room table, returned to her room, and went back to sleep.

Between sleep and waking, she kept hearing Amy talking with the bird. The bird responded harshly, as if in a pique. Was it possible that the bird didn't like Amy? Or that it didn't like staying in the living room? Plagued by these questions, Liujin couldn't sleep well. She awakened at dawn: it was the parrot that awakened her. The parrot kept repeating in a loud voice: "Is this it? I'm so happy! Is this it? I'm so . . ."

Rubbing her eyes, Liujin ran to the living room. She didn't see Amy. The bird had emerged from the cage and was standing on the table. One of its legs was bleeding; the bones were exposed. It stood on its good leg, and was still very excited.

As Liujin bandaged its leg, she said, "Bah! Bah!" It looked disdainful, and Liujin was amused. As she laughed, she glanced at the sickle on the chair, and so she again recalled the wound on Roy's hand.

"What an Amy!" she sighed.

"What an Amy!" the parrot sighed back.

Chapter 12

LIUJIN AND ROY, AS WELL AS A HEADLESS MAN

oy went to the courtyard at dawn and sat beside the abandoned well. Liujin must have seen him. She shouted from the house: "Roy! Roy!" He didn't answer. He was observing ants coming out of cracks in the well's granite. He wondered if the ants would build their nests at the bottom of the well. What a long and narrow, twisting and secluded path they had been crimped through! He was so absorbed in nervously watching these worker ants that he didn't notice Liujin approaching.

"This well is a legacy, built before Pebble Town. The engineers must have been highly skilled. It is said that they still live in seclusion somewhere around here," Liujin said softly.

Roy stood up and smiled appreciatively at Liujin. They went to the kitchen to eat.

"Roy, are you ready?

Roy finished the sheep's milk and set his bowl down. He said somewhat hesitantly, "I don't know, Liujin. I'm really on edge. I've never been sure of myself."

The day before, the two of them had agreed to go together to the Gobi Desert because Liujin wanted to spend her vacation "repeating the trip I made with my father." So many years had passed since

290

then, and her idea of going back had grown stronger with time, she had told Roy. After contemplating this, Roy asked her, "Will the people there remember me?"

"I don't know, but it's worth a try, isn't it?"

"Sure."

They tidied the kitchen, and the cart showed up at the courtyard right on time. It was a simple, crude cart, pulled by two black horses. The driver was arrogant and always seemed to be sneering.

They got into the cart, and Roy gripped Liujin's hand. He seemed afraid. Liujin felt warm toward him. She thought, *Roy is only a kid, after all, even though he's been traveling on his own for a long time.*

The cart soon exited Pebble Town and reached the open countryside. Roy still looked tense and said nothing. Liujin noticed they were traveling on a good asphalt road, but the strange thing was that they could see no signs of human habitation on either side of the road. After going a long way, they could still see only a vast wilderness. Wildflowers—yellow and purple—bloomed everywhere. There were very few trees. The sky was high and distant. The cart's wheels rolled smoothly and lightly, yet that didn't ease Liujin's doubts. She wanted to dilute the tension by talking, but Roy didn't want to talk. The driver had been introduced to Liujin by one of her coworkers. It was said that he went back and forth between Pebble Town and the Gobi all the time and knew this route well.

"Roy, don't be afraid. In the evening, we'll go to a hostel. I know the manager."

The driver turned and asked loudly, "Is it that headless man? It's a good sign that you know him!"

All of a sudden, Liujin's hazy memories became focused: it was a cold night when she and her father, dressed in cotton clothes and hats, reached the patio of the hostel. Something like a torch landed on the flagstones, sounding like glass shattering. Was it a meteor? Below the corridor, that person had shouted for Dad, and Dad walked over. They talked for a long time. Liujin nearly fainted from the cold.

It's true—not even once had she seen that face wrapped in a scarf. She had asked her dad about him, and he'd said that he used to be a soldier and had been injured on patrol.

In the afternoon, the cart left the wilderness and entered a small county seat. Roy finally seemed more active. Liujin and Roy got out of the cart and went to eat while the driver watered the horse.

The small restaurant wasn't very welcoming. Liujin was depressed by the two watercolors on the wall. They both depicted rocks on the Gobi Desert, the rocks illuminated like fire by the setting sun. Roy stepped closer to look at those rocks with a magnifying glass. He kept mumbling "whoa."

"We haven't reached the Gobi yet," Liujin reminded him.

The restaurant had no other customers while they were eating. Yet, the restaurant across the street was filled with people. Having nothing to do, the waitress walked over and chatted with them.

"Customers say we shouldn't hang this kind of picture here, for it puts people in a bad mood. People here don't have good taste." She curled her lips in disdain.

When Liujin wanted to pick up the tab, the waitress said it wasn't necessary. She explained that this restaurant offered complimentary meals to "friends from afar."

Walking out of the restaurant, Roy rubbed his hands excitedly and kept saying, "What kind of rocks were they? I never imagined! And then there was this . . ."

Liujin asked, "What did you see?"

"What? Are you asking what I saw? Everything."

"Do you always carry a magnifying glass? To look at pictures?"

"Yes."

The cart and driver weren't where they had stopped. Liujin sensed vaguely that something had changed. She stood next to the road to get hold of herself, and she told Roy about the time she had traveled here before. For some reason, her impression of the Gobi seemed to be changing. She struggled to talk and to remember, yet—in spite of herself—she always brought up "the headless man"—that is, the hostel manager. She couldn't help it. That black-swathed apparition who had talked with her father: she found him infinitely appealing.

"Oh," Roy said, "from what you're saying, the mystery of the Gobi lies in that hostel—right? Liujin, do you think our waitress recognized me?"

"But we aren't there yet, Roy."

"Is that what you think? Are you sure?"

Liujin couldn't answer. Something was happening: the waitress was reading a newspaper at the kiosk. But who knew if she was really reading? At the restaurant across the road, patrons were coming out all the time and standing beside the road in pairs or groups, looking at Liujin and Roy. Roy took his magnifying glass out of his pocket and peered at a small advertisement on the power pole. Liujin also took a look. It was nothing but a hostel's advertisement: the Peculiar Hostel, two hundred meters ahead, offered room and board. The ad actually used the words "Gobi style."

"Oh, the Gobi Desert!" Roy looked through the magnifying glass and gasped, "There are meteorites here, too!"

Liujin took the magnifying glass and looked, but all she saw was a large centipede climbing out of a crack in the wooden power pole. She was so scared she nearly dropped the magnifying glass.

"Roy, do you want to go to that hostel?" Liujin asked.

"Let's go. I think we've arrived."

Liujin was a little afraid and also a little relieved. *What will be will be*, she thought, as she walked ahead.

The Peculiar Hostel was a multi-leveled wooden building on a high slope. When Liujin climbed to the entrance, she was perspiring a little. When she looked down, the small county seat seemed to have vanished. Everything was blurred. Looking harder, she could dimly make out a few belt-like roads.

"It's so high here!" Liujin said.

"It's so close to the sun." Roy was glorying in this.

The hostel's lobby was desolate: only a few male staff members sat behind the counter. Liujin glanced around and saw watercolors of that rock hanging on all four walls. She felt hot all over. After she booked two adjoining rooms on the first floor, she and Roy parted ways to rest.

Liujin showered and fell asleep. She was really tired. But before long she was sweating so much that she awakened. She was too hot to fall asleep again. Liujin recalled that the hostel where she had stayed with her father was just as hot. She was amused by this. There was a fan on the table. She changed clothes and, fanning herself, went out to see Roy. Strange—Roy wasn't in his room. His bag was there, unopened. She withdrew, and a maid came up. She made an apologetic gesture and said, "I can't stop and chat with you. The moment I stop, I start to sweat. Excuse me."

She walked past. Liujin fanned herself and reflected. Some paintings also hung in the corridor—oil paintings, all of centipedes. Some depicted one centipede, some a swarm of them. Liujin gazed out from the east window and saw several people squatting in the courtyard, staring at something on the ground. Everybody from the hostel was here!

As she exited the area of guest rooms, the sun was so bright that she grew dizzy and nearly tripped. She felt pinpricks of pain at her temples. When she looked down the slope, it was a vast expanse of white. She hurried back to the guest-room corridor and stood there for a while until the pain vanished. She shouted, "Roy! Roy!" Her voice echoed in the corridor, embarrassing her. She walked over once more to the east window and looked out: those people were still squatting on the ground. There were many trees in the courtyard. It was very quiet, and everything was shaded by the trees. As she considered climbing out the window to look for Roy, someone spoke from behind her.

"You mustn't jump from the window. You think it isn't very high, but actually there's an abyss tens of thousands of feet deep below this."

The speaker was the maid. She spoke as she walked. When she finished speaking, she was far away. Liujin gave up the idea of climbing out the window and just stood there, fanning herself and watching. In an instant, she saw the black-swathed headless man. He seemed to be explaining something to the crowd of people. He was sketching directions on the ground with his walking stick. Ah, it really was he!

"Have you seen the guest staying in this room?" Liujin asked the maid who was coming over.

"He jumped down. It was his choice. The hostel takes no responsibility." The maid didn't stop walking as she said this. She was like a robot walking back and forth in the corridor.

Liujin leaned against the window, waved her hand, and shouted, "Manager! Manager!"

She heard her own voice grow feeble and weak. No one down in the courtyard heard her.

A guest came by. He probably also wanted to look out from this window. Not until he came closer did Liujin realize that it was the cart driver. He was dressed entirely in black, as if in mourning. He became more amiable.

"Some people never want to leave once they get here." The driver grimaced, "I don't think you're one of them. On this high slope, one can have whatever one wants. Someone noticed this right away."

Liujin wondered if he was alluding to Roy.

"But the Gobi is where I want to go."

"Then where are we now? Didn't you see the headless man? When you locate your companion, he'll tell you everything. I think he's a sensible person."

Everyone in the courtyard stood up. The driver wanted Liujin to take note of their faces. Liujin saw centipedes climbing over each person's face. One person even had some centipedes on his eyelids—he had to keep one eye open and close the other.

"Are there also poisonous insects in the guest rooms?" Liujin asked.

"Yes. They come out at night. You've seen the pictures. Do you think they're oil paintings? No, they're photographs! Someone went all over taking photos, including photos of all of these insects. See: one is in the corner of this wall. In the daytime, it seems dead, but at night . . ."

Without finishing his sentence, the driver left to answer someone's call. The centipede in the corner was huge. It scared Liujin. She turned around and hurried into the room.

There, she carefully inspected the bedding, the bed, the drawers, and the wardrobe, and killed two centipedes. As she struck them, she felt despair rising in her. She was afraid to sit on the bed or the sofa, so she sat on the table. She did her utmost to remember everything that had happened today. She thought about her idea of "repeating the trip Father had taken." How had she come up with this idea? Had her parents urged her to do this? Recently she'd received a letter from her mother that had mentioned desert birds. Yes, it was the mention of desert birds that had made Liujin nostalgic, and that's why she had decided to "repeat Father's trip." But this road was surely not the one she'd taken with her father when she was a child. They had rocketed straight along on the wasteland and suddenly had reached this small county seat. Now, she seemed stranded in this guest room. And then there was Roy, this young scamp, who had actually gone into hiding.

Liujin opened the curtains. All she saw was a small plot of muddy land in front. Farther ahead was a steep slope. Everything below the steep slope was chaotic. Roy's torso appeared in her field of vision. He was carrying a black umbrella and hurrying past the slope. Liujin shouted at him loudly. He jumped a few times and quickly disappeared. What had Roy discovered here? What had attracted him?

She felt very hot; her perspiration drenched her clothing and soaked the table. She remembered this small county seat as being pleasantly cool. How could it be so hot up here? Was it because "it was close to the sun" as Roy had joked?

Liujin showered again and changed her clothes. Just then, the maid knocked on the door.

"Our manager invites you to join him in the tea room on the second floor for tea. Can you come with me now?"

As she talked, the maid bent and picked up a centipede, tossed it into her mouth, and chewed and swallowed it. Seeing this, Liujin went weak in the legs and nearly fell.

The tea room was dark, closed up tightly. There was only a small green light on an inner wall. A small table and three chairs were set up below the light. The manager was sitting on the middle chair. Sure enough, he was the headless man. But maybe he wasn't really headless: it just looked that way because a scarf was wrapped around his head. His voice was low and stiff. He apparently wasn't the manager from twenty-some years earlier. After making the tea, the maid withdrew.

"Is someone else coming?" Liujin asked, pointing at the empty chair.

"Not sure yet. He's a man who doesn't make up his mind easily."

Liujin heard a metallic tone in the manager's voice as it came from the scarf. This made her suspicious.

"I'd like to talk with you about Roy. In these short few hours, this young friend of yours has become acquainted with everyone in the hostel. This is a good thing. Our Peculiar Hostel encourages the guests to get together. But I'm a little uneasy about him because I happened to see him looking at the large oil painting on the wall of my office with his magnifying glass. It's a painting of the Gobi rocks."

Liujin couldn't help laughing. But the manager writhed nervously under his black robe.

"My office has never been locked, but this doesn't mean that guests can go in whenever they please and look at everything with magnifying glasses. What do you think?"

"I'm sorry that my friend disturbed you so much. You must know that my motivation for coming here stems from my dear dad—oh, I'd better not go on. We'll leave right away, okay?"

Liujin thought she was about to cry, though she didn't know why.

"Oh, Miss Liujin, you're mistaken! I told you this, not because I wanted the two of you to leave. Actually, it's quite the opposite! I mean that I've become very much interested in your friend."

The manager rose and lit a cigarette. Liujin craned her neck to look at him curiously. Holding the cigarette, he paced back and forth in the room. Liujin wondered if a demonic face was hidden in the black scarf. Her gaze shifted to the doorknob, which someone was turning as though intending to enter. But the person never came in. When she looked again at the manager, she noticed that the cigarette had burned down to the end, but he didn't feel any pain.

He said abruptly, "I'm blind." He aimed the cigarette butt precisely into an ashtray. "The year that I was stranded in the Gobi, the sun blinded me. This place is a miniature Gobi that I've fabricated. What can a blind person look forward to?"

Liujin vaguely recalled the night that was as cold as an ice house. She recalled Dad's anxiety. For some reason, when she saw this headless man, her hair suddenly stood on end, and she nearly cried out. Who—who was he!?

The manager reached the door in one stride and wrenched it open. "It's the wind." Then he closed the door and started smoking again. The smell was rather strange, and Liujin felt a little dizzy. She stood up suddenly and rushed toward the door, opened it, and bolted down the stairs.

No one stopped her. No one chased her. There was no reason to rush. The building was quiet. Liujin walked involuntarily once more toward the entrance to the guest rooms. But she immediately drew back—the air seemed to be burning, and it was so bright that her eyes stung. When she remembered that Roy was carrying a black umbrella and wandering around, she started to worry about him.

Was this really a test? After more than twenty years? What kind of gentleman's agreement had Dad had with this man? Or had Dad betrayed this man? Liujin noticed that the maid was no longer in the corridor, and the guest rooms were all wide open and vacant. She went over to the window again to look out. No one was in the courtyard. Only a lot of centipedes were still crawling around on the cool ground.

She returned to her room. The maid was sitting on the table, crying.

"I miss my mama." She lifted her coarse face, which was wet with tears.

Not in the mood to deal with the maid's troubles, Liujin angrily assailed her, "Why on earth is your manager looking for me?"

At this, the maid forgot her problems at once, jumped down from the table, and said to Liujin, "It's because of something wonderful, truly wonderful. You'll benefit from it all your life."

Liujin watched her leave, wide hips swaying. Looked at from behind, this woman was very attractive and sexy. All of a sudden, Liujin grew interested in the maid's life experiences. She dashed to the door and called to her to stop.

"Is your mama from the south?"

"How did you know?" the maid goggled. "Yes. My parents raised flowers for a living. They were both risk-takers who chased after the latest thing. One year, they planted the whole flower garden in imported tulips that didn't suit tropical conditions. They went bankrupt. You understand flowers, don't you? I just knew it as soon as I saw you. I'd like to talk with you. It's so hot, what else can we do but talk?"

Liujin was surprised: the corridor had been empty, but the maid dragged a chair over with one foot, and she was now sitting on that chair. The maid's actions were intriguing—like a sorcerer's. Just then,

Liujin remembered all at once that the old director of the Design Institute had owned a flower shop. Was this maid somehow connected with the director? Liujin asked if she'd seen Roy. She said yes, but there'd been no time to talk with him because he was too busy scurrying back and forth all around.

"Do you know what he's doing?" Liujin asked.

"Attending meetings," she said and rolled her eyes. "Meetings are held every day here. This young man isn't afraid of sunlight. I knew this as soon as I saw his eyes. He scurries everywhere with a black umbrella. Our manager wants me to protect him."

"Are people who stay here all in danger?"

"You could say that. You can see the poisonous insects on the ground, but nobody has actually died here."

Liujin noticed something ruthless in this woman's expression: it didn't give people nearly as good an impression as the view of her back did. Evidently she was the same sort of person as the headless manager. Liujin wondered what the other guests were like. Why didn't she see them anywhere? The maid took a comb from her pocket and ran it through her thick dark hair. She said she was much better now. She stood up and kicked the chair. The chair disappeared. The move was indelicate, yet dexterous.

As soon as Liujin returned to her room and sat down, a guest came looking for her. She had gray hair and seemed to be a manual laborer. Because she was afraid of centipedes, Liujin didn't invite her to have a seat. The two of them stood and talked.

"I'm a mother," the woman said.

"Oh!?" Liujin asked dubiously.

"Put yourself in my position—I stay in the same hostel with my son, but there's no way to communicate with him. I made inquiries all the way from my hometown and ended up here. I heard that my son came here with you. Will you let me see him? My home is in the interior, and I work in a factory. But my son always says he's a mountain man and lives in a cave. He hallucinates . . . He's shrewd. We aren't worried about him. But I miss him and so I hurried over here."

"Did you ask the maid for help? The one over there. I think she can help you."

The woman's cloudy eyes brightened, and she said, "Great." When she walked outside, she stretched out her hand and plucked a black umbrella from the empty air. She tucked the umbrella under her arm and went out. Liujin stared, amazed. Then she heard that woman shout outside the room, "Woolball! Woolball! Come out! I've brought your hoop—your favorite plaything! Look: it doesn't tip over no matter where it's rolled—such a wonderful hoop . . ."

Liujin stood on the table and looked. She saw Roy below the slope. He was holding a black umbrella in one hand and waving to his mother with the other, as though imploring her to leave. His mother stood on the slope, holding a black umbrella as protection against the sun. She looked blank. Then she walked away, probably returning to the hostel's lobby. Liujin looked at Roy again: he also disappeared. The black umbrella was sticking up in the ground. She heard the maid's voice in the corridor.

"I really envy you. You have such a good son."

The mother was crying, saying she wanted to go home. Liujin craned her neck and looked out. She saw the woman's face age a lot all at once. The maid was supporting her and the mother was saying, "No one can anticipate his movements. He's always been like this. When I see him, I feel much better. Sometimes I wonder if I really do have a son or not. Of course I do. You've all seen him."

The mother wept brokenheartedly as she left. The maid wept with her. Looked at from behind, the two of them cried in much the same way. Liujin wondered if they were sisters.

The sun finally set. Someone called Liujin for dinner. She said they would "be treated to a dinner party."

The dining room was in another building. It was very large. Hanging from the ceiling were straw, tufts of cotton, beanpoles, and corn.

People were eating together at more than ten tables. Liujin thought they looked a little familiar: they were the ones who had been squatting in the courtyard. She threaded through the tables looking for Roy. A few times, she thought she saw him, but when she looked closer, it was never he.

When the manager came in, everyone stood. He toasted them. Liujin saw that he really did drain his glass, but she couldn't see his face. There was plenty of food on the table, but Liujin stopped eating after two bites. She had a headache, and it was hard to breathe, as though the dining room lacked oxygen. What was happening to her? She saw people swaying. Countless winged insects flew out from the straw and beanpoles. They buzzed and hit her in the face. Flustered, she hid her face in her sleeve. She couldn't eat. The more she hid, the more these winged insects attacked. Covering her face with a napkin, she hurried out. Not until she left the dining room could she take a breath.

There was a pavilion outside the dining room. Sitting there and looking down, Liujin was astonished. The county seat seemed to have disappeared. It was pitch-dark everywhere. The hostel had evidently become a tiny island. Or it had been transformed into several structures floating in midair. Out of curiosity, she went over to the slope, thinking she would walk down the steps. She looked and looked, but could never find the path. She felt that if she stepped forward blindly, she would plunge into a void, yet she didn't believe that there would be a void at the bottom. All of a sudden, she saw Roy walk over from below. He was illuminated by the dining room lights. He looked hurried.

"Roy! Roy!" Liujin waved and shouted.

Her voice was so feeble and weak that it had seemingly been cut off. Maybe she was the only one who heard it. Roy disappeared. Liujin thought: *He just keeps patrolling around the hostel.* Was he playing a game? Just then, the manager—wearing a black robe—appeared at the entrance. He walked toward the pavilion. His silhouette moved up and down, as though he were drifting in the dark. He was actually whistling; maybe he had drunk too much. Liujin heard him whistle a children's song. He was very good at it, and it was pleasant to listen to. A swarm of white-winged insects flew around the dim light, as if they were dancing along with the tune. Liujin could now see his head, but his face was still a blur.

"Miss Liujin, your father and I have been friends for years."

He sat on the railing of the pavilion. He sat there lightly, as though he were a dark cloud.

"Do you know how my dad has been doing recently?"

"No. There are some things in this world that one never has to know. Your young friend is pressing on with his drill. His prospects are unlimited. Look: he's flying!"

Liujin didn't see anything. Only darkness lay ahead.

"How long ago did you build this hostel?"

"A long time ago. Just think: in a place like this . . . at first it was lonely. No one came here. Later, it turned into this kind of place."

Liujin kept wanting to see the manager's face, but for some reason, the moment her gaze rested there, she began feeling dizzy. She tried to cough off the dizziness, tried every way to concentrate. For a moment, she vaguely saw a farmer's face. Smoke from burning wood seeped from his wrinkles.

He stretched out his hand and plucked a little black turtle from the air.

"Your dad has been raising this recently. Look: Aren't the lines on its back unusual?"

Liujin couldn't see the black turtle well, either. She knew it was a turtle, but whenever she wanted to get a good look at it, dizziness overcame her and her eyes hurt. She'd better give up the idea. A bird chirped in the pavilion, though: oh, it was the long-life bird!

"Your young friend has been chasing things all along. He wanted to catch hold of those things."

The maids stood at the dining room door and called the manager.

The manager immediately walked toward them. As soon as he left, the long-life bird also disappeared. In the gloomy atmosphere, wave after wave of heat streamed over Liujin. Her clothing was immediately drenched in sweat. She walked out of the pavilion, intending to go back to her room for a shower.

A black brick wall suddenly appeared at a corner. It was so long that it blocked her exit. At first, she walked left, but didn't reach the end, so she returned to her starting point and walked right, but she still didn't reach the end. She heard a bird twitter in the dark from the top of the wall. The new moon in the sky seemed to be quivering slightly in the heat. She decided to go back to the dining room so she wouldn't get lost. However, Roy's voice came from the other side of the black wall.

"Liujin, there are a lot of people here. They all recognized me!"

He seemed excited and happy.

"Roy! Roy! Do you see me?"

"Yes! You're under the sun. The sun is on top of your head! I must hurry over there. There are people there. Over there is the heart of the Gobi . . ."

When Liujin returned to the dining room, no one was there. Only a few white winged insects were flying below the lights. She wanted to go back to her room, because she couldn't stand this drenched clothing. Just then, she saw her savior—the maid came over. She still looked somber.

"Can't you find your room? As soon as night falls here, everything changes. When I was new here, I could never find my room, either. Come with me."

They left the dining room, and the maid suddenly became extremely muscular. She pushed Liujin, and Liujin fell down. Liujin thought she would die and abandoned herself to despair. But she didn't die. She dropped onto the bed in her own room. The window was still open, just as it was when she left. When she got up to close the window, she saw the manager standing outside it.

"I'm looking for your friend. This boy—it's as though he's grown wings! I can definitely use someone like him here."

When Liujin awakened in the morning, she didn't quite remember what had happened the night before. When she made the bed, she found she had crushed two insects to death. They looked a little like centipedes, but they weren't. What were they? They were disgusting. She wrapped them in paper and threw them into the trash bin.

The door to Roy's room was closed. She walked over and knocked, and the door opened. It was the manager.

"After your friend arrived here, he lost all sense of time. He talked with people all night long. He wouldn't let anyone go. Some guests were so exhausted by this that they slept on the grass. Look, this is his hand!"

The manager held up Roy's sparkling hand and snickered in the dark. Liujin almost fainted.

A long time passed before she asked, stuttering, "Is he dead?"

"Don't be silly. How could he die? He's just temporarily dismembered. Didn't you ever hear your father talk of this sort of thing? For example, my head . . ."

He didn't go on because Liujin's legs had gone weak and she was sitting on the ground.

"Are you all right? You'll get used to this eventually. We're too close to the sun here, so you might be reacting to that."

Clenching her teeth and holding onto the wall, Liujin stood up. Although everything had turned black in front of her, she felt her way back to her room.

A male servant was cleaning her room. She sat on a sofa and heard him swatting the insects with slippers. He was enjoying this, but she felt nauseated.

"Are you done yet? I'm going to throw up," she said weakly.

"It's finished, it's finished. I'm sorry!"

When he passed Liujin, he bent down and said, "You're pretty. Just now, I thought I'd like to leave one of my eyes here!"

Liujin was too nauseated to eat breakfast. She walked slowly over to the window on the east and looked again at the courtyard. Roy was standing among some small trees in the courtyard. Liujin waved to him.

"Roy! Roy! May I come over? Would that be okay?"

"No! Absolutely not! Liujin, there's an abyss below you!"

Behind Roy was a dark shadow. Liujin saw that black shadow grip him like a gigantic bear, yet he didn't struggle. Those small trees were swaying fiercely. Roy shouted, "Mama! Mama . . ."

After a while, Liujin could no longer see them. Liujin felt comforted by thinking that, after all, Roy was now with his mother.

Intending to check out, she walked to the entrance of the guest room area, and was again forced back by the burning sun. The worst part of it was that she couldn't open her eyes. All of a sudden, she thought of Roy's black umbrella. Where had he gotten it? The male servant emerged from a guest room. Liujin approached him to ask about checking out.

"Yes, it's about time for you to leave." After a pause, he added, "But you can't check out in the daytime. You know the sun is burning here. Wait until evening. Someone will escort you down."

Liujin was surprised. How did this person know that she should be checking out? Had Roy already left?

When she returned to her room, the temperature suddenly soared again. Her head was covered with sweat. The fan didn't help much. She took another cool shower. Then she emerged and heard a sharp whistle from outside. She pushed the window open and saw people standing in line in the burning sunshine. The manager was training them. He was still dressed in black. Only his face showed through: it was an ordinary farmer's face. Liujin couldn't look very long because she was dizzy. She thought, *It was probably only after a period of training that people could become accustomed to the sunshine here.* The last person she saw in that column was actually Sherman. He had changed a great deal: he was now much coarser—a lot like a farmer. Liujin closed the curtains and sat down on a chair. The shrill whistle outside surprised her.

"Do you like it here?" the maid asked her.

"Me? I don't know. Why is it so close to the sun? I've never seen anything like this before."

"It's all because of the manager."

As she swept the room, she shook her head, as though she disapproved of this aspect of the management of the hostel. But Liujin thought this woman was the manager's spy. She shouldn't trust this woman.

"I didn't know the driver before. A friend recommended him to me," Liujin said.

"There are many people we don't know, and yet they've known us for a long time. Look, he's here."

Liujin turned and, sure enough, the driver had arrived. He held a black hat in his hand—a big, tall hat. Who had such a large head? The maid was talking.

"If you cover your head with the hat, you can go out."

She peremptorily put the hat on Liujin's head and, gripping her arm, dragged her out.

The cart was parked at the entrance. The two of them pushed Liujin in, and she felt the cart tear off at a high speed. Was it really flying in midair? She wanted to look from beneath the brim of the hat, but she was too afraid. As the driver sped along, he roared as if charging ahead in battle.

Finally, the cart reached a flat road. Liujin heard Sherman speaking: "It feels so right to stay in the same hostel with Liujin."

She took off the hat and looked at the ashen-faced Sherman.

"I arrived before you did. I've always wanted to be here. That manager used to be the head of the orphanage where I stayed. Wasn't that fortunate?"

They reentered the wasteland. Liujin didn't feel like talking. She was immersed in a world of imagination that was filled with manors, and where shadows were everywhere. Liujin tried to imitate bird calls, and she really did make some sounds. Sherman looked at her in surprise. He felt he was drifting away from her. But sitting with her, observing her, was still exciting.

"Look, this is your bag," he said.

"Oh, that was thoughtful of them."

Liujin cast a fleeting glance over the wasteland. She was wondering how many people in the world could approach the sun? Who did Pebble Town belong to?

Chapter 13

QIMING AND LIUJIN

A bad thing happened yesterday evening. It happened just as your dad and I were about to sit down for a rest after we cleaned the kitchen. It's the little black turtle your dad bought a month ago at the market. We raised it in a pot. It stayed there quietly and even grew a little. But yesterday it became jittery. Who knows how it climbed up to the windowsill—anyhow, it gnawed the curtains to bits. When your dad discovered this, it was about to jump down, so your dad nabbed it and placed it in the pot again. He covered it with a lid. It was so outraged that it snapped and scratched all night long, climbing up and falling down repeatedly, splashing the water and making a lot of noise.

I turned on the light and saw cold sweat running down your dad's forehead. He said weakly, "Could the turtle have come to ask for payment of a debt? I feel as if I'm dying."

I retorted loudly, "Nonsense!"

"Then you just put the turtle back on the windowsill, okay?"

And so I did, but it didn't jump down. I went back to tell your dad, but he seemed thoroughly bored and didn't want to hear any more.

The two of us went downstairs before daybreak, intending to go to the bridge, but the streetlights were shrouded in fog. It was dark everywhere.

We couldn't see the road at all. Your dad stopped and asked if we should go on or not. I said of course we should. When we went to the frontier years ago, we couldn't see the road clearly then, either. Since we couldn't see the road, we just walked ahead. Sometimes we could tell we were walking on flat land, sometimes on rubble. Later, at daybreak, we found we had circled back to where we had started. We had gone nowhere.

This letter from Mother made Liujin rather uneasy. She kept wondering: Was this the very turtle that the manager had shown her the other day?

Three days ago, after a long absence, Qiming came again and sat at the entrance to the courtyard. He set two empty birdcages down in front of him. Liujin remembered something from the past that was connected with birds. Before she could grasp the memory, though, it faded again. She was dismayed: Why couldn't she ever remember the times she had spent with Qiming? Through her recent chat with Amy, she knew this old man had been important to her while she was growing up, but she couldn't recall anything specific. Oblivion was frightening. Were certain parts of her dying?

When she left the room again at night, she noticed a wagtail now standing in each of the birdcages. The doors to the cages were open, and the birds stood quietly inside. Liujin thought the old man was really a magician, and in a flash, she remembered her dad's black turtle. She was a little distracted.

That night, Liujin tagged along with Uncle Qiming on his way to the market. She found out that he had lived all along in a small room next to the indoor market. Liujin stood at the entrance and heard the old man say from inside, "Liujin, how can you so thoroughly forget the past?"

Liujin was really ashamed of herself and strode in. His birdcages were placed on the table, and the birds were sleeping despite the light. Uncle Qiming was fixing the spring of a toy duck. Liujin thought the duck looked familiar. Without knowing why, she blurted out, "Do you raise turtles?"

"No," he looked up at her for a moment and said, "Turtles are extremely spirited. If you raise a turtle, you shouldn't leave it. Otherwise, your life will change."

Liujin glanced around the room. She saw a narrow bed, a low cupboard, and various birdcages, but all of these things were in the shadows. She couldn't get a good look at them. She also heard a large clock chiming, but she couldn't locate it. Was it under the bed? Now this old man was speaking clearly. Why had he garbled his words a while ago in her courtyard?

"Have you always lived here?"

"This is simply my temporary dwelling."

When Liujin left, he didn't see her off, but continued making repairs. Liujin thought, *That's probably the toy duck I threw away.* She had thrown away many things.

Later, Liujin told Amy of her distress over losing her memory. Amy simply advised her not to tag along after Qiming, because he "was a person from the past era." Liujin asked what this meant, and Amy looked into her eyes and said, "You'll just be annoyed, because time can't be reversed."

Then what was the barrier between her and this old man? Liujin remembered the "long-term" relationship her parents had with him, and felt he had the air of a relic. She admired Amy because she knew Amy could communicate with him. Amy said he had lived many years at the forestry station at the foot of the snow mountain. He hadn't come to the city until recent years. He didn't have a regular residence in town, but moved from one shabby place to another.

Qiming felt that dreams were great when you were old. In his dreams, his desires were blurry, but easy to achieve. He was frequently pleasantly surprised. When he awakened, he would remember that he was retired and free of financial worries. He could do whatever he wanted. He appreciated the deceased old institute director so much. It was she who had given him a life of good fortune. The year he retired, he was curious about other ways of life. On an impulse, he went off to do odd jobs in the logging industry. He worked hard every day and felt enriched. But he left later because of a nightmare. Actually, he had never figured out whether it was a dream or reality. Back then, he and a fellow worker were resting on a slope. Someone's shouting woke him up from his nap. He looked up: a big black thing came crashing down. He took off immediately, but quickly realized there was no place to hide: on the left was a cliff, on the right was a cliff. Was he in a gorge between cliffs? He heard a thundering sound. A large tree now lay spanning the gorge, its branches twitching wildly. His legs were shaking as he walked out into the open and saw his workmate smoking a cigarette.

"I couldn't sleep, so I got up and cut down this tree. I was going to wake you up, and then I figured it wouldn't hit you anyway, so it would be better to let you sleep," he said apologetically.

"I thought I was going to die just then. Being a lumberjack is scary."

He left that very night. Recalling it now, he felt a little regret: after all, he liked the mountain life, especially the forests at night. The trees in the breeze sounded like the soft murmurs of families— so many of them. But how had the incident with the tree occurred? At the time, he was resting on the mountain slope, and his workmate was a likable person. They had always been a good team. Later, Qiming had gone back and searched for that gorge, but couldn't find it.

He pitched a tent in the woods beside the road in the suburbs. No one stopped him from staying there. He felt relaxed and even helped someone dye cloth. It was only in the last two years that he had moved back to the city. Sometimes, he returned to his old home at the Design Institute, but most of the time, he simply lived wherever he could. The strange thing was that he could always find a small room to stay in: he found places with no trouble at all. Pebble Town was truly a paradise for vagrants. Old Yuan, the garbage collector, had said to him just yesterday, "Warehouses, tool sheds, basements—one can live in any of them. I came here five years ago, and I've never had to pay rent. And I also know of a hostel that doesn't charge anything." As for Qiming, he still didn't know why he wanted to live only in these temporary places. Was it for those dreams? Each time he moved to a new place, he had very good dreams. He enjoyed these dreams very much.

It was life at the Design Institute that had broadened his horizons, so when he left there, he felt full of energy and curiosity. His greatest feeling after retiring was a certain kind of harmony. When he went walking in the suburbs, no creatures were afraid of him—not the birds, not the beasts, not the fish. Sometimes they even approached him. One day when he was enjoying the breeze as he stood in the river, dozens of little fish swam up and rubbed against his legs. And the people—everyone he ran into—understood him very well and offered all kinds of help. During that time, Qiming often said to himself, "My life has only just begun!" He congratulated himself. When he worked at the forestry station, he often went to look at his former lover's tomb. It was an unobtrusive hillock without even a tombstone. It was there that he began talking with Amy. He was resting on the grass next to the grave, and crows were hopping back and forth by his feet. Amy came over. She was still a young girl, maybe eighteen years old. Qiming saw a small brown snake hanging from her neck. She smiled at him as if they were old acquaintances.

"This is a friendly snake. It always wants to play with me. It lives near here."

The crows weren't afraid of her, either: they cawed right in front of her.

"My mama certainly can't be lonely here now. Little animals and people all come to see her."

While she was talking, the snake opened its mouth, as if to attack Qiming. Qiming thought this was great fun. The two of them sat there, not talking of the dead, because they sensed that the dead were there with them.

Later, they often met at the cemetery. They didn't arrange to do so, but it *seemed* arranged. Qiming felt that Amy had an inhuman sort of beauty: she wasn't at all like her mother. Qiming wasn't good at talking, so he didn't talk with her of past events. He felt that the dead were communicating for them. After all, the dead were from the past era, and Qiming was, too. If it weren't for the mother, Qiming couldn't have understood this young girl.

Qiming took her to the city, where he entrusted her to Meng Yu's family, and then he left. He didn't know Meng Yu well. He just had a vague idea that this family would be suitable for her. The weird thing was that this old couple readily agreed. That day, after making these arrangements, he went back to stay at the Design Institute. On the way, he passed Liujin's home and heard the merry chirping of birds filling the courtyard. He turned to the entrance to have a look: four snow leopards stood behind that young woman while she sat there drinking wine. Her face was red. It was a stimulating scene. And once more, he felt profoundly that his life was just beginning. Then, he thought of a way to use cages to tempt the birds away from Liujin's courtyard. Liujin had no idea that he was the one who did this.

Another big thing occurred in Qiming's life back when he was at the Design Institute. When Qiming was in a slump, the director was in the hospital. Feeling anxious and desperate, he wished he could find a dark hole to crawl into and break free of his insignificant life. In the middle of the night, he sneaked off to see the director. She told him to stand outside the sickroom while she talked. Her days were numbered, and her voice was so hairspring-thin that it might snap at any moment.

"Nancy came here today. She's interested in the butterflies in the garden."

"I need to avoid her—avoid that whole family. Director, do you really have to go?"

"I understand, Qiming. You can disappear. For example, I had close friends in the past, too, and then I simply disappeared . . ."

He couldn't hear the rest of what she said, for she was gasping for breath. Two big guys dragged Qiming out of the hospital. As he walked on the deserted streets, he kept pondering the director's words: "You can disappear." At daybreak, he finally understood.

He resolved to become a deaf mute. In other words, he would say nothing and hear nothing. Before long, his decision was acknowledged by people all around. It wasn't long before even his name was changed: he was called "Dummy." His colleagues at the Design Institute had bizarre memories. No sooner had the director been buried than no one remembered that he was Qiming. For some reason, they thought of him as a flower grower from the director's hometown. They said he had sought shelter with the director because he was old and handicapped. Qiming thought he must have changed greatly. How could no one recognize him?

He watered the lawn with a hose. Nancy wandered over with Liujin. She said to Liujin, "Look, this is really hard for Uncle Dummy. The last gardener disappeared, and he has replaced him."

Nancy's eyes darted here and there, never looking him in the face. Qiming felt that in the setting sun, the view of mother and daughter's backs was a little dreary—especially the child. He thought she was pitifully skinny.

With his change in identity, he could behave more freely than before. He felt he had retreated successfully. In the entire Design Institute, only José still recognized him as the same old Qiming. Still, even he called him by a different name. He now called him "Uncle Flower." José was surprisingly discerning, and he never forgot certain things from that time long ago. With his new identity, Qiming worked an additional two years before retiring. When he inquired about retirement, the person in charge told him, "You can work here until you die!"

But he no longer wanted to work here. He wanted to change himself into a fish.

The manager was a little disappointed. He said, "Go ahead and retire. If you want to come back later, you may."

This surprised Qiming. Later? How old would he be then? Was the manager teasing him? He looked up at the manager. He didn't seem to be joking at all.

When Liujin called him "Uncle Qiming," he felt a physiological response.

"My mother got better because of that turtle. I'm not kidding you. It's true."

"Your mother was wonderful. And your dad, too. I've never seen such strong people."

They were chatting in a free hostel—the kind where five or six people stayed in one room. Each person had a hard wooden bed. With no chairs in the room, Liujin had to stand. The vagrants were all staring at her. Qiming thought, *She's just as energetic as ever. With so much energy, life must be tough.*

They went outside together, Liujin squinting in the bright sunlight.

"Do you know the Peculiar Hostel?" Liujin asked him.

Qiming said that he not only knew it, he was also a shareholder in that hostel—of course, just a rather small shareholder. Liujin noticed that the moment he spoke, the years fell away. He looked only about sixty years old. Earlier, his face was always in the shadows and she hadn't ever gotten a good look at him. They stood together on the tree-shaded roadside watching cars come and go. The sunlight shone on them through the trees. Liujin suddenly felt that this old man was much like a relative to her: she had known him since she was a child, but she had ignored him. How had she made such a mistake?

"You fit very well in that kind of hostel. My friends strive to make it unique."

"No, I'm not at all accustomed to it. It's so close to the sun . . . I'm not perfect."

Liujin told Qiming she had lost her beloved young friend there.

Qiming smiled and said, "You have to believe that you can't lose anything at home, no matter what it is."

It was the first time Liujin had seen Uncle Qiming smiling. This gorgeous smile—surging like dozens of creeks!—affected Liujin deeply.

"Then where is he?"

"You'll see him soon. Look over there."

On the sidewalk across the street stood a headless man. His rectangular body was covered in black cloth. A Uighur girl was dancing in front of him.

"See how free he is!"

"Yes. It's great to be headless. But why is he like that?" Liujin was puzzled.

More and more people crowded around the dancing girl, and her moves were getting wilder. She twisted her body painfully. Liujin saw the headless man walk away hurriedly. When she looked back, she noticed that Uncle Qiming had also walked away.

Liujin wanted to cross the street, but a motorcade was passing through, one truck after another, as though there was no end to it.

She came back home, and as she cooked dinner, she thought that although she could never be as free as Uncle Qiming and the others, maybe she could still make some changes. For example, maybe she could gradually learn to be like them—calmly accept whatever came up in life.

Eating her supper under the grape arbor, she thought of Roy again and felt sad. The way he had hoisted that black umbrella and hurried off made her very uneasy. She felt his future was hanging in the balance. Maybe she was too worried—maybe he would be all right, but she just couldn't quell her concerns.

After a while, Amy came over. Liujin mentioned the Peculiar

Hostel to her. Amy beamed when she heard the name. "That's his experimental station." Liujin didn't understand.

"Who do you mean?" Liujin asked.

"Who else? Uncle Qiming, of course. He and his friends do experiments to see if people can live in that kind of place. You must have seen it: the sun there is like fire. It's an out-of-the-way place."

When Amy talked, she looked euphoric: she was waving her hands. She said she'd gone there once, but had stayed only a short time. She couldn't get accustomed to it; she'd rather save that sort of thing for her dreams.

"It's really charming," she sighed.

Rain was falling on their faces. Liujin said, "It's raining." Amy said, "It isn't real rain. Whenever I talk about the hostel, beads of water float in the air. I've experienced this twice." Her words put Liujin in a better mood.

Amy heard something at the well in the backyard. She got up and walked over to inspect it. Liujin followed and told her that a pangolin came out from there. Amy crouched down next to the well. Her pose of attentive listening captivated Liujin.

"It's seething under here." Amy said, "Was it the pangolin you mentioned just now?"

"Hmm."

"It came from my home village. At midnight, that mountain can suddenly become off-white-colored and dead. Little animals flee in all directions. People say it's a recurrent scene from ancient times."

After listening a while longer, Amy stood up and said she had to go because she had to deliver food to Uncle Qiming. "That kind of hostel doesn't provide meals. It just provides pleasures that are disappearing in the world. If I don't give him food, he'll starve just like those vagrants." She left the courtyard in a hurry.

Amy had just gone when people from the Health Bureau showed up. There were four of them, all wearing white sailcloth uniforms, pulling two dump trucks of cement into the courtyard. They said they wanted to seal the opening of the well and then dump these two truckloads of cement onto the opening to form a small cement mound.

Liujin stood in the courtyard and watched. She felt that this home would soon be destroyed. Even a long time after the Bureau people left, she was still scared out of her wits as she paced back and forth in her room. Later, she felt drowsy, and fell asleep as soon as her head hit the pillow.

When Liujin awakened, it was night. Someone was playing the flute in her courtyard. The sound was so melodious that it brought to mind the paddy fields of the south and the foothills where small trees grew. She was amazed because she had never been to the south, and yet the soft, moist blue sky appeared before her now. She dressed and walked to the entrance, and the flute music stopped. It was Uncle Qiming, sitting in his old place. Surrounding him were many animals that looked like something between cats and dogs. It seemed they had all been listening to him play the flute. Where had they come from?

He said, "They made a tremendous disturbance in the well tonight, and then they all came out."

"But the opening was sealed tightly with cement."

"So what? They have many other passageways."

Recalling the serious manner of the men from the Health Bureau, Liujin was amused.

"Have you been to the bottom of the well?"

"No. I couldn't, and there's no point in going, anyhow. Don't you see that these animals have come up? Their lives are mixed up with ours."

Liujin thought of Roy, who used to search for such creatures in the crowds on the streets. How anxious he was when he did this. Had the Peculiar Hostel perhaps put the underground world in the same place as the world above? No wonder that as soon as he arrived there, Roy felt at home. He was busy, yet relaxed. Liujin looked up at the poplar: oh, a bird was singing in the nest there! A nameless bird. Why did it sing continually? She really wished that Qiming would play the flute again, for she was sure that it was the music that called the little animals up. But he was silent, as if remembering.

"Liujin, are you happy?"

"Very happy, Uncle Qiming. Just now when I awakened and heard the flute, I felt as though I were living in Shangri-La. I've heard people say that this is Shangri-La. I never knew before that little animals could communicate with people."

The moment Uncle Qiming left, those strange little animals fled. Liujin was still feeling moved. She thought that she really was living in the most beautiful place and among the best people. How fortunate she was! And she hadn't had to work for it. It was as if good fortune had come knocking on her door. In a flash, she had developed the same love for Uncle Qiming that Amy felt for him. That bird was no longer singing; it was probably feeling peace and joy. Liujin recalled that Sherman hadn't been here for quite a while. Did he—like her—now feel fortunate? Thinking of this, she went inside and brought the rattan recliner out so she could lie down in the courtyard.

Dad used to spend so many sleepless nights here. Was that perhaps to prepare her for the independent life she now enjoyed? When he left by train, he hadn't even glanced back at Liujin. His resolution had contained such deep fatherly love. Even though she did her best to remember, there were many things that she couldn't remember, but they lay all around her, gradually unfolding. For example, Uncle Qiming's relationship with her was one of these things. Liujin had long sensed that he was very close to her when she was a little child, but she had no memory of it. Liujin heard something stirring at the well's opening: animal claws were scratching at the cement. She was amused as she remembered the white-uniformed people who had come to seal the well. The world was so funny! At this moment, she felt a light fog drifting in—very unusual in this dry season.

Unlike her father, Liujin felt drowsy after lying down for a while. Just as she was about to doze off, that bird awakened her again. Could the bird be ill? Liujin stood up and walked over to the fence, where she heard a man and a woman arguing vehemently on the other side. She looked out from the gate and saw Sherman and the young woman she'd seen before. That woman slapped Sherman in the face; he crouched down and cried. The woman stood there watching him. Liujin pulled back immediately. A while later, Sherman shouted tragically, as though bitten by a beast. Liujin had to look. What she saw was strange: the woman was supporting Sherman, and they walked intimately into the curtain of night. Liujin sighed softly, as if relieved of a heavy burden. She said to herself, "Sherman . . . the son of Mother Earth." An image appeared before her of him climbing out of the well. And once again, she remembered those frogs.

The bird in the poplar chirped again and flew out. This bird was dark-colored and had big wings. It flew around the courtyard once and stopped on the roof. It wasn't like local birds. Could it be a nocturnal bird? Might it have flown here from Smoke City? When Liujin passed beneath her window, the parrot said to her, "The good days are coming!" Liujin laughed, and so did the parrot. Her drowsiness vanished. She went to the kitchen, took a tender ear of corn out of a pot, and gnawed on it. It was still the same kitchen, still the same stove. And the hole at the base of the wall next to the stove still hadn't been blocked up. A withered garlic bulb still hung on the wall where her mother had put it. Her parents had left so hurriedly. But it was possible that this had been meticulously planned.

Liujin got into bed. She felt calm and self-assured. She vaguely recalled that someone in the past had slept this way every day. Who had it been? She remembered that person said his sleeping was like "sinking into Mother Earth's belly." Thinking about this, she drifted off quickly. She dreamed of the blue sky and of white birds flying in formation.

"Liujin, have you ever thought of moving to Smoke City?" Qiming asked.

"No, not at all. Wouldn't that be betraying their hopes?"

"Once upon a time, I thought of you as my own daughter."

"I am your daughter. I feel telekinesis each time you approach."

"Amy, too. I have two daughters."

They stood and talked under the poplar next to the stream. Qiming sighed to himself: because of his rheumatism, he could no longer go into the river. He used to derive so much pleasure from this river.

"Roy is so young. How could he leave home on his own and live here so long? I've never seen anything like it. What's so special about our Pebble Town?"

"Roy actually isn't young," Qiming said. "You can't guess a person's age only by his appearance. For example, look at that poplar across the river: Does it look very young? But it didn't grow from a seed. It grew out of an old tree's roots. Our Pebble Town is a huge magnetic field, attracting people who are fascinated with secret things. Liujin . . ."

"Huh?"

"My dad—he was a fisherman at the coast. He left me with a debt—an old watch. My grandfather took it from the body of a dead prisoner of war. In the last few days, I buried our family's watch. I thought, anyhow, no matter where I go, I can always hear its tick-tock, so there's no need to carry it with me."

"You're so determined."

"That year, I was standing in the river trawling for fish when your parents came over. I still remember how bewildered they were, because one of our people had abandoned them in the wilderness. In fact, it only looked like a wilderness. A lot of people were all around, but at the time, they couldn't see them. Later, they adapted quickly.

Your parents aren't ordinary people: you're lucky. Back then, the city was overrun with Mongolian wolves: they didn't hide as they do now."

Liujin quivered. She couldn't say anything. She was looking at Uncle Qiming, and yet she seemed to see not him, but only an illusory mask. She flung out her arms involuntarily, but she threw herself into a void: Qiming wasn't there. She looked down and saw freshly dug earth in the lawn. She bent over and listened: she heard the watch—tick-tock, tick-tock . . .

"I can't remember it. Why?" she murmured distractedly.

One time, in order to see those fish, she and Roy had come here. Roy had told her that all the outsiders who came to Pebble Town had to go through the path next to this stream. He said that the night he came here, this path had become a dead end: each end had been tightly sealed off by shrubs. He had to spend the night sitting beside the stream. He said the stars that night drove him crazy. At this point, Liujin looked up and saw an elderly white-haired couple approaching. They were supporting each other. The old man spoke to Liujin.

"Our son came here from the south. He died many years later, and it's said that he was very happy in this place. We didn't believe it until we came down here."

"I can understand that," Liujin nodded in agreement.

They were old and feeble, but you could see their excitement. They walked for a while and then stopped for a while. Remembering something, Liujin caught up with them and asked, "Was his name Lee?"

The old man looked at her in surprise, and said, "No. His name was Zhou Dashu. He had colon cancer. But is that important? His mother and I think this place makes people happy. All you have to do is look at these fish in the stream, and you know."

Leaning on her husband's arm, the old woman looked infatuated.

"I see," Liujin said. "I hope you'll be happy here."

Uncle Qiming hailed her from the bosk, and she ran toward him.

Lying on the lawn reading a newspaper was a middle-aged man with a waxen face.

"This is Zhou Dashu," Uncle Qiming said. "He's been weak all along, but he doesn't want to die. He asked me to write a letter to his parents saying that he was dead. But look: he's still very much alive."

With an apologetic glance at Liujin, the man resumed reading his newspaper.

"I even set up a fake tomb for him in the cemetery, and his elderly parents went there to pay their respects," Uncle Qiming said.

Liujin stood for a while, but she couldn't think of anything to say and so she left. As she walked, she thought about today's events. First, she had suggested that she and Uncle Qiming take a walk. She said she wanted to go to the riverside because she thought the river would help her remember the past. Uncle Qiming had smiled and asked, "Really?" She wanted to remember things that she and this old uncle had done when she was a child. Later, looking at the river, Uncle Qiming had become emotional, too. Liujin hoped he would speak of the past, but he said nothing; his thoughts were somewhere else.

What was up with Zhou Dashu? Liujin gave this a lot of thought, and then decided to try to clarify it.

When she returned to the bosk, Uncle Qiming had left. Zhou Dashu was lying alone on the ground, reading the newspaper. He kept swatting his left hand, as if to drive away mosquitoes, but Liujin saw no mosquitoes on the lawn.

Liujin also noticed a colorful lacquer box between his feet. He kept moving it with great agility—just like an acrobat. Several snow leopards were painted on the lacquer box.

Zhou Dashu rested the newspaper on his chest and said to Liujin with a smile, "This is the box for my ashes. I intend to be cremated. What about you?"

"Me? I have no idea. Probably cremated." Liujin added hastily, "I haven't given it much thought yet."

"Of course not. You have time. Qiming and I are roommates in the free hostel. I saw you the other day, but you didn't see me because I was in a dark corner."

He thumped the newspaper on his chest and went on, "I care about current events. I don't want to die uninformed. I want to understand what kind of planet I'm living on. You see how ordinary I am. There are mosquitoes and flies everywhere, even in a place like Pebble Town."

Then he stood up. He seemed quite weak. Liujin was afraid he would fall, but he didn't. After vomiting a little blood, he leaned against the poplar trunk, turned, and said, "Ordinarily, you can't see me. I'm always in dark places. What is painted on this box?"

"They're—" Liujin had intended to say they were snow leopards, but they weren't snow leopards. They were opera masks.

"You don't know, do you? Haha. You can't know!"

Liujin grew uneasy: several people were exploring the area of sand-thorn trees on the lawn in front of them. She told Zhou Dashu she had to go home.

"Bye," he said. "My friends are coming. They don't usually see other people. Like me, they always stay in dark corners. They're shy young guys. You're leaving now. Take it easy, okay?"

Liujin was shocked: she stopped in her tracks. After giving it some thought, she walked into the grove of small trees and hid among them. She saw two young people on the lawn, busy with a rope. Zhou Dashu had toppled over: Had he died? The two people knotted the rope around his neck. As they talked, they dragged him away. After a while, they reached the road, where a lorry waited. They threw him on top as if he were a bundle of firewood.

Liujin went home, still feeling nauseated. She asked herself: Had she taken all of this philosophically or not?

Suddenly, her parrot shouted, "You slut!"

She looked at the parrot, smiled slightly, and all at once recovered her energy. She shouted, "I did take it philosophically." And with that, she went to the kitchen to start cooking.

As she cooked, she murmured, "Uncle Qiming, Uncle Qiming . . ." She found she had completely regained her composure. Was Zhou Dashu an employee of the Design Institute? Ever since her parents left, Liujin had felt she, too, had made a complete break with the institute. And yet, she still felt a vague connection with it. For example, hadn't Uncle Qiming also retired from the Design Institute? She resolved that she would ask him that the next time. She made herself a pumpkin biscuit.

Liujin sat down to eat. She listened closely, thinking to herself that it was the wind—the wind in the courtyard was so jubilant! The frogs must still be there. They had very likely reproduced and formed a chorus. Back then, Sherman had been so farsighted! Her little courtyard and her house were seething with excitement: it was such delightful weather. A couple of days ago, Amy had blurted out, "Your home is also a Peculiar Hostel." Those words made Liujin's mind run wild. She couldn't help it. At this moment, she was hoping that Uncle Qiming would show up. Then they could eat together. What had he been doing? Loafing around in the city?

After tidying up the kitchen, she rested next to the hole in the wall. For quite some time she had sensed the same thing that her father used to sense: namely, that a lot of small things ran out of the house at twilight. She held her hand out toward the hole: she seemed to touch their bodies lightly. She sensed feathers, or something like feathers.

It was completely dark, and Liujin hadn't yet turned on the light. She hung the parrot's cage at the main entrance so that it could smell the flowers in the courtyard. A slender woman wearing a nurse's uniform walked over in the dark. She was carrying an exquisite lamp that shone with the patina of age. As she approached, Liujin smelled the slight scent of disinfectant.

"I could hear the noise in your courtyard from the road and walked in here without thinking. How's your mother, Liujin? Here in your home, time can run backward."

She placed the lamp on the ground and concealed herself in the dark. Liujin heard her laugh softly, and a bird pecked at the grapes in the arbor and let them fall to the ground—one after another.

"I work in the hospital that you haven't once visited for decades. I'm old now, much older than your mama. Back then, the city didn't yet exist. The hospital came first. I was the charge nurse."

Liujin thought the charge nurse had a young voice. She said she was just passing through, and now she had to return to work. She also said there were so many patients that even the basement was full.

It wasn't until she left that Liujin realized that the only parts of the charge nurse she'd seen clearly were her feet. They were such pretty feet, encased in white shoes . . . She had actually been able to hear the noise in Liujin's courtyard from the road. But in fact, tonight her courtyard had been really quiet. What kind of ears did she have? The charge nurse's words had once again proved one thing that many people had attested to. At this point, Liujin sensed an upsurge of intense emotion. Many small lattices appeared in her mind. And each lattice held rare items.

"She can do intravenous injections," the parrot said in an old voice.

"We have everything here!" Liujin said to the bird.

"Everything? That's good."

Liujin slept in the heart of Mother Earth: it was dark and firm. Sleeping next to her was Uncle Qiming. He was talking; it sounded like non-stop buzzing. Liujin could catch only one or two words—very good ones, the kind that make people's minds feel radiant. Liujin thought, *This kind of sleep is so soothing.*

Chapter 14

LIUJIN AND YING

It was in Song Feiyuan's small shop that Liujin ran into Ying. Song Feiyuan had left home, and his son was managing this shop. Liujin had finished eating some shish kebabs when she saw Ying enter. She blinked and took another look. Yes, it was definitely Ying—who else could it be?—though he looked older and a little humpbacked. He sat next to her and said softly, "Ah, it's you. Are you okay living here alone?"

Liujin didn't say she was okay and didn't say she wasn't okay, but asked, "Are you still living in the office building? I'd like to visit you. Is that all right?"

"Sure, but only after dark. I moved to the slope in the open country."

Liujin said "Oh," and then fell silent. Ying ate his mutton fastidiously, not making a sound. His face still looked young, unmarred by the scars of time. What had he been doing the last few years?

"I live behind the third office building. Will you come?"

Liujin nodded her head. Only when he left did she notice that he walked unsteadily, his movements like a puppet's.

She took the last bus out there. She planned to walk back. When she got off the bus, it was dark and there was no street lamp, so she couldn't see her surroundings very well. She knew instinctively that this place hadn't changed much. Walking with the aid of a flashlight, she soon found the third office building. Liujin wasn't a coward, but she felt a little uneasy because it was dark and quiet all around. She stood on a path in front of the building, not knowing whether to continue. These buildings were much lower than the ones she remembered. No light was on in this building, and it seemed no one was there. She wondered if people worked here even in the daytime.

Someone was shining a flashlight on the hill: it must be Ying! She turned and walked up a hill that had no path. She took one step after another on barren land. Once, she startled a bird in the weeds, but it flew off without a sound. How strange. The sky must be heavy with clouds, for not a glimmer of light appeared. She guessed it was about eight o'clock in the evening.

Ying was sitting on a large rock.

"This rock didn't exist when you were here last time. It emerged after the earthquake."

His voice was as soft and pleasant as before.

"You must want to ask about the earthquake. Each part of Pebble Town is like an airtight cabin. You couldn't have felt the earthquake that struck here."

The rock was warm. Sitting on it felt good. Liujin pressed her face against the rock next to it. After a while, she found that the rock gave off faint rays of light, much like the light from a luminous watch in the dark. In the middle of the rock was a concave surface. She touched it and got an electric shock.

"Isn't anyone in those buildings?" she blurted out.

"Liujin, it's been a long time since you last visited here. We've had an earthquake. Look: Song Feiyuan! He's been working here all along."

Liujin saw the shadow scurrying past. As he ran, he seemed to be bending down to pick something up. He quickly disappeared. In a place as dark as this, one couldn't see very far.

"Uncle Ying, why don't you tell me about the big change here?"

"It's hard to talk about. I'll just tell you about this rock. This rock didn't appear suddenly; it emerged slowly. Do you know how large it is? It borders on the neighboring county of Muye! Your mother and I walked in this wilderness a long time ago. At the time, I wanted to go back to my home—Africa. Later, I changed my mind and came to love this marvelous land. You may not know that it was the former institute director's father who brought me here."

As Ying talked, it grew so dark that Liujin couldn't see him well. She was momentarily taken aback because Ying fell silent and she thought she was all alone in this wilderness. Fortunately, he made another noise. He struck the rock with a little hammer and said he was communicating with his compatriots. He talked with them for a while every night. Liujin bent over the rock and placed her ear on it, but heard no other sounds.

"Year after year, as soon as it grows light, the scrap collectors show up. Now, the bare contours are all that remain of these buildings. They've even knocked out the windows and doors and carried them off. Even so, everything is fine at night: it's such a beautiful scene. Someone once told me that the scenery on the ruins was the most beautiful, but I didn't believe it. I've slowly discovered how beautiful this place is. Just think—I've been here for decades . . . Everything has appeared slowly. Liujin, I'll go in first. You just sit here for a while."

Ying stood up and circled around to the back of the rock wall. Liujin heard a soft "kacha" sound, and Ying disappeared. She touched that wall for a long time. The electric current from inside the concave surface pushed her hands away time and again. The rocks smelled very good, not like the usual smell of rocks. They smelled like wild-flowers. The hazy glimmer was also pleasant. Was this the home Ying had made for himself? If so, it was much different from hers. What other weird things might be here? Just as Liujin was about to sit down, she heard Ying say something from behind.

"It's a little oppressive tonight: the people of Muye County are riding up on war horses, clouding the air."

Ying handed Liujin a bunch of flowers: he said they were the sweet-scented osmanthus. Liujin had never seen them before. Actually, she couldn't see these, either; she could only smell them. The same scent came from Ying's body.

"Uncle Ying, your home should be called 'Rock Garden,'" said Liujin.

"But the people of Muye County always make war." His tone was a little distressed. "Do you want to go in and look around?"

"Sure."

"It's too late, Liujin. You don't belong there. You're a remarkable woman. It's good enough that you've come to my home on such a night. Is it pretty here?"

"Yes!"

"Yesterday, I heard the drumbeat of my hometown again. How could I bear to leave here? What do you think? This stone home is the rock garden, as you called it. I've waited for decades for it to break through the ground. It came out just for me. When I sit here, I can talk with people living in my hometown whenever I wish. Hey, look! Song Feiyuan is passing by again. How anxious he looks! He stumbled onto my home."

Listening to Ying's charming voice, Liujin thought admiringly that he was much like her mother, but she couldn't say exactly how they were alike. Could it be that they both hung onto certain things that had never existed? His appeal had nothing to do with sex. It was something much more illusory, like the fluorescent rock that emitted a wildflower fragrance. So many years had passed, and yet he had become more and more charming. Was he the man she'd been longing for?

Ying urged Liujin to place her hands on the concave surface of the rock. After she forced herself to do that, wave after wave of heat struck every pore of her body. She began to moan with pleasure.

After a while, beads of water dripped onto the backs of her hands. It was bizarre: she felt that her hands were thirsty and longing for the beads of water. The sound of an infant's chortling rose beside her. Ying leaned over to tell her: this infant was her daughter. Liujin thought: *I've been single my entire life. Where would a daughter have come from?* The chortling sound came from inside the rock. Every time Liujin moved a finger, the laughter would come out from inside, as though she were tickling the baby's chin. Liujin was fully absorbed in this game—and so overjoyed that she forgot all about Ying, who was still beside her.

It was a long time before Liujin heard Ying's voice again.

"I converted the office into a game room. The office is no longer an office; rather, it's a den of monsters! Gah gah gah, gah gah gah. I dance with African lions there . . ."

Ying was gesturing as he spoke; he was very agitated. Liujin sensed that he was a little worried: he seemed anxious to finish something. In the north, the clouds dispersed, revealing a little of the sky. Two large stars were gleaming. All of a sudden, the night had darkened. What past events was this man—this man with the seething heart—entangled in? Liujin couldn't read his mind. But this place was truly inspiring!

"Ah—" Liujin sighed deeply.

She pulled her hands out of that "den of monsters" and smelled them. She smelled the heavy sweet scent of wildflowers.

All of a sudden, a light was turned on in the attic of the office building in front of them on the right, but it was turned off just as quickly.

"Song Feiyuan." Ying said, "What an utterly evil character!"

Liujin heard the admiration in his tone. And the astonishment, too. Liujin was also surprised: this neighbor's energy had become enigmatic. Perhaps he was carrying out the plan he had once discussed with Sherman in the poplar grove. Liujin couldn't help saying, "He is the intruder of life!"

Ying applauded.

"I need to go, Uncle Ying," Liujin said uneasily. Actually, she didn't want to leave.

"Oh, yes, it's time. It's pleasant to walk at night. You didn't bring a flashlight, did you? I could give you this flashlight, but I think you'll enjoy it more if you walk in the dark. Bye!"

He shone the flashlight to point out the path, and Liujin set out. She was soon engulfed in darkness. She actually had brought a flashlight, but she couldn't remember where she left it. Behind her, Ying called loudly, "Great! Wonderful!"

Liujin couldn't see anything, not even the direction she was taking. But as she walked ahead blindly, a strange thing occurred: she wasn't stepping on wasteland, but on a cobblestone path. Really. A road underfoot! She tried walking fast, walking at random, walking sideways—and she always stayed on that road. She sat down and touched the cobblestones. She could still faintly hear Ying's voice: "Great . . ."

"Are you looking for your dad?" Song Feiyuan's voice came out of the dark.

"No, I'm going back to my own home," Liujin said.

"Although your dad isn't here, you can still find him if you look."

Liujin could hear him, but she couldn't see him. She pulled herself together and continued walking ahead. Next to her, Song Feiyuan reminded her to walk to the right. She felt light-footed. She looked up and saw the strip of sky to the north. The two stars shone brighter and brighter. The vision thrilled her: that narrow strip of sky had turned violet. Her left foot stepped on something slippery, and she nearly fell.

"Look: this is the little turtle that your parents raised over there; it crawled here," Song Feiyuan said.

This time, Liujin saw him: he was bent over, hurrying along beside her.

"What are you doing?"

"I'm cleansing my gut. There are always some dirty things there. I'm not like you . . . Didn't you catch it? It's run off again. Your parents love you so much, I really envy you."

"Mr. Feiyuan, I need to go on ahead."

"Go ahead. I'll catch up soon."

Liujin walked quickly toward her home. After a while, she heard the river gurgling. It was that small stream with fish leaping in it. When she looked up again, she saw that the entire sky had turned violet. One goose was on a solitary journey in the sky. She could see the road well now: she was walking on the blacktop road with poplars on both sides—the route her parents had taken thousands of time. When she turned around, she saw everything behind her still cloaked in darkness. Song Feiyuan's short form passed by in the dark. His flashlight was still on. The place where she stood was the boundary between light and darkness. She mused to herself that she had walked from the Design Institute to the main road within half an hour! Even in the daytime, it used to take her at least an hour and a half.

She sat on a stone bench beside the road. Once more, she heard Song Feiyuan.

"I can't match Ying, yet I also made it bit by bit."

Liujin looked all around, but couldn't see him. One person wobbled along the road: it was Sherman, whom she hadn't seen for a long time. He was wearing an ugly robe that didn't match his manner at all.

"Liujin, you'll laugh at me for sure. I can't walk steadily now. I can't help wobbling."

"Do you also cleanse your gut at night?" Liujin asked.

He started laughing, showing his white teeth. Liujin thought he was a little spooky.

"Oh, you must mean Song Feiyuan's trick. As for me, I just muddle along. The incident with my daughter taught me a lesson. Luckily, those frogs and turtles all love me. Sometimes I buy them at the market and let them go. People say I'm like a child."

Liujin watched him wobble toward the market. What would he do there at night? She compared him with Ying, and said to herself, "They're both a little like ghosts, one wandering on the wasteland, the other hiding in the crowds of people." She recalled the scene when Sherman first came to her counter to look at cloth. What a charmer he was!

When she pushed open the courtyard gate, a voice spoke to her from next to the well. "It's been autumn for some time now—don't you feel cold at night?"

It was old Meng Yu. He hadn't come to her home before. He had returned from his travels.

"I chased a lamb to your courtyard. Amy carried it back. This well of yours isn't an ordinary one. If you go down this well, you can reach Muye County!"

"Muye County? I heard of this county only recently. I heard that it's chaotic over there," Liujin said, flustered. "Muye County is where Ying often goes. I just came from seeing Ying."

"I also just returned from Muye County. I have to go home now. Liujin, you must take good care of this well."

After he left, Liujin leaned over the well—that is, over the cement—and listened. She heard frogs singing—a large chorus deep underground. Now she realized that all of them knew the secret of the underground world. She was amused to recall how affected Sherman had acted when he worked on something in her yard. Some violet coloring still gleamed in the sky, stirring Liujin's emotions. She took a deep breath and sighed, "Oh, Ying!"

She prepared a sumptuous dinner for herself and kept listening as she ate—imagining the chaos caused by the war underground. She knew this evening was extremely unusual.

When she reached the living room, she saw the letter on the table. Her mother's handwriting seemed a little shaky. She wrote that she and Dad had taken part in an activity for seniors organized by Smoke City: they had dug trenches on the farm outside town. Every day, they had been covered with mud and sweat. "Even though the era of war ended long ago, your dad and I found this sort of work very inspiring. Just think about it: so many people were involved in digging trenches. And it was raining. Frogs were singing everywhere. The triangular red flag loomed through the fog in the distance . . . Just think, when does anyone ever get to see a scene like this?!"

Liujin gave it a lot of thought. The scene her mother had described was very familiar—as though she herself had participated in that great activity of "digging trenches." But Pebble Town had no smog, and so she couldn't experience the hazy anxiety that one felt when on the edge of a great breakthrough. At the end of the letter, Mother mentioned Ying, saying that Ying was her "good friend whom I have lost forever." When Liujin read that, she was reminded of Roy. Roy was her good friend whom she had lost forever. She heard the parrot talking in the next room. It was talking very fast, a little testily.

When she went into the bedroom, the parrot was still saying, "Another day has gone—huh!"

She opened the cage to let it go to the living room to drink some water, but it stayed arrogantly in the cage and said, "No!"

The courtyard was quiet tonight, and Liujin fell asleep as soon as she lay down. In her dreams, that bird argued with her incessantly. It kept saying that her home wasn't safe because a beam had cracked.

Liujin went to the Design Institute again on her day off a week later—this time in the daytime—and people were working in all of the buildings. She went upstairs to Ying's office. She knocked lightly on the door, and Ying opened it a little and stuck out his coal-black head. Liujin heard buzzing in the room—like a toy airplane circling in the air, or like a huge fan spinning around. It set her nerves on edge. Ying hesitated before letting her in.

Ying had shrouded his office in darkness. The only light came from the reading lamp on his large drafting table. The noise was coming from skulls—more than a dozen of them—hanging from the ceiling. There was no chair, so Liujin stood next to the drafting table. She had never understood those blueprints, and they held no interest for her.

Pointing to the skulls, she asked, "How come these things make noises?"

"What? You hear noises? I guess I'm used to them, so I don't hear them. These were my buddies, long ago. They lost their lives during a malaria epidemic. Do you feel ill?"

"Yes. Uncle Ying, I'm dizzy." Swaying, she gripped the table.

"Let's get out of here. Right away!"

Ying supported the trembling Liujin out to the corridor, and then downstairs and outside. They sat on a bench under a tree. Liujin couldn't say anything for a long time.

"Oh, I'm so sorry," Ying said.

"But why aren't you feeling even slightly indisposed?"

"I got along well with my buddies. Of course, it isn't that I'm not stressed at all, but I got used to it a long time ago."

They walked slowly to the wasteland, and Liujin noticed that huge rock again. It wasn't at all conspicuous in the daytime. It was covered with ash and other dirty things. Some little black-colored birds were pecking at worms there. When people passed by, they flew away. Ying said there was no sound in the daytime. He asked Liujin to try, and she planted her ear against the rock. It's true, she heard nothing. Ying went on to say that this huge rock was dead in the daytime, coming back to life only at night. Liujin thought to herself, *This mysterious rock brings Ying so much consolation.*

"There's something that always puzzles me: Is the war in Muye

County going on now, or did it happen a long time ago and we've just learned about it here? There's a time difference."

"Do you still agonize over past events?" Liujin asked sympathetically.

"Maybe it isn't agonizing, but instead a certain kind of recreational excitement. Do you think that the events I'm entangled with belong only to the past? No, it's not so."

Liujin asked Ying: Why did they still have to go to work on the weekend?

"Ever since the old director died, work has turned into a hobby for everyone. This institute of ours hasn't had a leader for a long time: it's more a concept that's leading us. The institute is still in good shape."

As they sat there, dark clouds drooped from the sky, and the ground began to take on the dreariness of autumn. Liujin saw this on Ying's face, too. She thought of Song Feiyuan. Was he also working here because of a hobby? What could that hobby be?

"Song Feiyuan? Unh. He took on the job of janitor for the main building. He also has an office there. Do you want to see it? Our employee Old Gu died, and Song Feiyuan took over his office."

When they approached the No. 3 office building, many people opened their windows and leaned out to look at them. Liujin thought Ying must really be somebody important here.

Song Feiyuan's office was large. Files were strewn in disarray on his desk. Two little chickens walked back and forth amid the files. Ying said that Song Feiyuan was freer than he was. Song spent hardly any time in the office. He stayed ten minutes a day at most and then left. He had never locked his door. He pointed out the shish kebabs on the tea table and said, "See? This is freedom."

After standing in the office for a while, Liujin's head began to hurt again—the same feeling she'd had in Ying's office. Although this place didn't have that buzzing sound, it had a sort of evil wind that was nearly undetectable. She didn't know where it had blown in from. Bit by bit, that wind was eating away at Liujin's willpower.

"Uncle Ying, I'm dizzy." Everything was turning black in front of her. She gripped the desk.

Ying steadied her, and the two once again walked out of the office and stood in the field.

"But my parents worked in the building for decades," she said uncomprehendingly.

"That's true. I remember well the first time your mother came to the office. Back then, there weren't many people in this building."

As they sat on that rock, Ying seemed depressed. His head drooped. Liujin stared at his hair, noticing that his short curls were all spirals that seemed to be screwed deep into his brain. Liujin was nauseated and hurriedly averted her gaze. She had always felt this black man was unique. Now she seemed to understand him a little: he was melancholy because he had never been able to identify his desire.

Liujin looked ahead: in the misty distance, the area of shrubbery, Song Feiyuan was struggling with a boa constrictor. He was very agile, jumping around like a monkey. Finally, he clutched the lower part of the boa's head. She wanted to continue watching, but man and snake tumbled into the shrubbery.

"Feiyuan is addicted to this romantic life," Ying said. "On this barren slope, people can exhibit all kinds of audacity and imagination."

Two office buildings were over there. Many people were watching, craning their necks from the windows. Maybe they were watching Feiyuan fight the boa, or maybe they were watching her and Ying. Liujin felt uncomfortable. She wanted to hide behind the rock and complained to Ying, "How can people in the Design Institute be so curious?"

"It's true, they are. But you mustn't think they're watching you. No. They aren't."

"Then who are they watching? They certainly aren't watching themselves, are they?!" Liujin said angrily. "Look, someone's even using a telescope!"

"Oh, I saw that. Yes, someone is using a telescope. Her name is Tulip. She's adorable. Haha!"

"She's watching us through a telescope, and you actually feel good about it? Who is she?"

"Why not? We should be happy! This girl can see the shadow of her own lungs."

"Then why doesn't she look at herself, instead?"

"Can't you see that's exactly what she's doing?"

Liujin looked closely at Ying's kind expression, and her inner anger vanished all at once. She remembered the bottomless spirals of Ying's hair.

Ying took a telescope out from a hollow in the rock and began looking back at the people in the office buildings. The way he was using the telescope was just like observing the surface of the moon. He looked for a long time, and then apparently tiring of it, he put the telescope away. He told Liujin that he and his colleagues had to look at each other every day.

"Uncle Feiyuan, are you looking for those snakes?" Liujin asked Song Feiyuan.

"Yes. Without them, I feel uneasy. Have you seen Sherman lately, Liujin? I was thinking about the old days when the two of us were together. The more I thought, the more confused I got. That's why I've ended up with these snakes."

As he stood in the wasteland, he looked young and refreshed. In the past, Liujin had always thought he was a little wretched.

As he walked away, Liujin noticed Ying staring at Feiyuan's receding form and said, "One night in the poplar grove, I walked into a trap that this man set. He's quite amazing, isn't he? I like him a lot!"

"I can imagine that scene. You're amazing, too," Ying said.

That day, Liujin and Ying circled around the office buildings time after time, and the people in the buildings kept observing them. Ying joked that their "eyes would soon start bleeding from overuse."

At dusk, Liujin saw the pageantry of the birds returning—so many birds, darkening the sky. The birds lit in the weeds and disappeared without a trace. Liujin asked Ying where they went. Ying said they had gone to Muye County.

It was just like the time years ago when Ying had seen Liujin off on the bus and had run after the bus waving at her. Liujin saw the full moon gradually rise behind him: it was actually bigger than his dark form. How strange: Shouldn't it be a new moon tonight? After she took a seat on the bus, she looked up, and saw a man on her right ogling her. He seemed to recognize her and smiled. But Liujin didn't know him, and this made her uneasy. She avoided his eyes and looked to the left, but the woman on the left was ogling her, too. So Liujin bent her head, propped her forehead against the back of the seat in front of her, shut her eyes, and rested.

When she got off the bus, she heard someone behind her say: "She keeps going back there time after time. Our Design Institute can reshape anyone who comes in."

Chapter 15

SNOW

Liujin went to replenish her stock of piece goods at a place at the foot of the snow mountain. She bought calico cloth with the peculiar design of white flowers shaped like corkscrews. The pattern reminded her of Ying's hair, and she felt a little sentimental. When she left there, it was snowing. She went through a vegetable plot to get to her jeep, which was parked next to the main road. An assistant pushing a wheelbarrow filled with piece goods headed over there with her. All of a sudden, she heard the sound of a large animal coming from the mountain—shrill and brutal. She was too afraid to move. The man shouted impatiently, "What's wrong with you? Never mind the snow leopard. It's a long way away from us!"

She pinched her thigh, but didn't feel anything. Her legs didn't seem like her own. Her head didn't clear until the driver leaned out of the car and waved at her. By then, the snow leopard had stopped howling. The mountain looked different with snow, but it was still arrogant and aloof. All around the foot of the mountain, those tall buildings were like jesters craning their necks to gape at it. Liujin thought the snow leopard must be inside a grotto. This household and the path between these vegetable plots were somehow linked with her—and had been for years. Not many households wove and dyed cloth now. Why hadn't this family ever given it up? Just now, when she had gone to pick up the cloth, the owner hadn't shown up. It was his daughter who had received her. She said her father had gone up the mountain. Liujin had stared blankly for a moment. Now she remembered this incident—and connected the snow mountain, this household in the foothills, and her coming here for years. A new picture appeared in her mind. It was a little murky, but it wasn't insignificant. Just before getting into the jeep, she glanced again at the snow mountain. As the snowflakes fell more densely, the silhouetted mountain looked misty.

When she returned to the market, she discovered that there'd been an accident in the shop: the rolling door had slipped down and hit the manager in the leg, and he was lying in the back room. Liujin urged him to go to the hospital, but he refused. As Liujin turned to leave with a sigh, he stopped her and wanted to hear in detail about her trip. So she talked about the howling sound of the snow leopard, as well as the cave, the lonely night, and the bright full moon she had seen from inside the cave. As she went on and on, the manager closed his eyes slightly, as if bewitched. "Liujin has now become truly amazing. The snow leopard—wasn't it calling for us?" He waved Liujin away. He wanted to enjoy a certain memory in solitude.

Not until seeing her mother's letter on the table did Liujin gradually relax. Appreciation for her parents grew from the bottom of her heart.

In her letter, Mother said that she and Dad were still digging trenches on the farm every day. This physical work made them "feel they were being renewed from the inside out." They also took that turtle to the farm. In the daytime, the turtle walked everywhere in the open country, and at night it returned to the dormitory. The old couple were overjoyed to see how fast it was growing.

Your dad says we're willing to dig trenches all our lives. The volunteers all around us give us confidence. Straightening up in the trench, we can see the red flag through the fog and hear the birds singing sadly in the forest. At this, your dad says, "This is truly a bloodless war." All of us volunteers are silent, because through silence we can broaden our horizons greatly.

Liujin, have you fertilized the grapes? In the suburbs of Fan City in the south, people sell yellow bananas. You have no idea what the scene is like in the flower market in Huadu in the winter. We've changed a lot, but compared with our turtle, we're still far behind . . .

Mother's letter broke off abruptly, as though she were too grief-stricken to continue.

While Liujin was reading the letter, Amy quietly entered the house and sat down next to the door.

"I just came back from the market, too. You didn't see me, did you? The way you looked then—you had just come back from picking up goods—worried me. Now you look much better. Oh, that calico cloth is really beautiful. I can't imagine how it's made. People tend to daydream on snowy days, don't they?"

Liujin smiled at her in embarrassment and told her about the snow leopard.

"It's probably dying," Amy said, widening her beautiful black eyes.

They stood at the window and looked at the snow. Liujin looked and looked, and felt that the snowflakes were changing into individual vortexes, much like the pattern on the calico cloth. Amy tugged at Liujin's sleeve and said, "Listen. People are talking everywhere. Liujin, it's really lively here."

They smiled at each other, feeling fortunate.

"What about your young friend?" Amy asked.

"He's still in that place close to the sun, but I think he'll come back here from time to time. Amy, has your brother ever come back? What does he do on snowy days?"

"My brother is loitering in the city now. In the morning, I saw him plop down on the snow in the plaza and imprint his body in the snow. Deep down, he's thinking the same thing I'm thinking."

They reached the courtyard, and all of a sudden Amy pulled Liujin down. They fell to the ground together. Their cheeks sticking to the snow, they listened quietly without moving. They didn't hear anything, yet they seemed to hear everything. Amy felt that life in Pebble Town was seething: this was what she liked best. Liujin glanced sideways at Amy's red skirt and immediately thought of the red flag Mother had mentioned in her letter. Lying on the snowy ground, Liujin finally sensed the charisma of the red flag.

Only after a long, long time, when they were about to freeze to death, did they get up. A little black dot jumped in the snow and then jumped up to the steps: it was a tiny wagtail. Perhaps because it was starving, the bird had shrunk. Liujin ran into the house and got some bird food, which she then scattered on the ground. The wagtail began pecking at the food. Although the bird was very small, its feathers were still shiny and bright. It didn't look at all malnourished. Liujin conjectured that perhaps it lived in the crawl space under the floor.

Amy looked excited. She kept saying, "It is I. I'm this bird."

After eating, the bird flew away: it disappeared into the air with snowflakes swirling all around.

They changed out of their wet clothing and went to the kitchen to cook. Liujin took stock of Amy, who was wearing clothing she had lent her—and suddenly she saw another self turn toward herself. She paled in fright.

"Relax. I'm playing a prank. I'm imitating your expression."

The voice seemed to be coming from far away. Liujin's mind was in chaos.

It wasn't until Amy brought the food to the table that Liujin could see the real Amy. She said in embarrassment, "What's wrong with me? I'm confused. I saw that it was you, but it was also I."

Watching Amy gnawing mutton kebabs like a little animal, Liujin was stunned again.

"Pebble Town and the mountain used to be connected by an invisible path," Amy said breezily. "Across the street, I used to watch the little animals coming out of your courtyard, and I knew instinctively that you were the kind of person I would like. I would have come here much sooner, but I was afraid I couldn't stand the grim atmosphere in your courtyard."

That night, Amy said she'd like to stay overnight in Liujin's parents' room, and Liujin made up the bed for her. Both of her parents had slept in this room. Later, Dad moved to the study because of his awful insomnia. Amy lay down, turned off the light, and admonished Liujin not to stay up too late.

When Liujin returned to her own room, the parrot kept grumbling. Liujin couldn't understand what it was saying. This was the first snowfall of the year: Liujin stood at the window, and by the light of the street lamp shining on the courtyard gate, she saw the snow falling. The snowflakes gave off a faint blue light. She felt that in this instant, everything all around contained a certain clue. Then she recalled that Amy was sleeping in the next room, and happiness once again washed over her like a tidal wave. The snow fell directly on her heart, covering up all the shadowy spots. She became light-hearted and content.

Just as she was feeling a little drowsy and was about to go to bed, Amy came in. She was trembling all over. She gripped Liujin's arm in order to steady herself. She told Liujin that her dead mother was talking in the other room.

"She won't leave. Oh, Liujin! Do you think Uncle Qiming has died?!"

"Of course not, Amy! He's so strong and he loves you so much!"

"When I was little, he walked off with me one time. We stayed in the forest, and then it began to rain. We ran back and forth in the forest. I've always remembered this: it was genuine happiness."

Liujin heard Amy crying. Why was she so despairing? Liujin asked Amy where she had last seen Uncle Qiming. Amy said it was at the market entrance. He was running—moving clumsily. He waved at her and disappeared into the crowd.

The two women sat on Liujin's bed, and Amy haltingly related the story of her time with Uncle Qiming. As she listened to Amy's story, some of Liujin's memories were resurrected. She felt more and more that she was the one in Amy's story. She loved Uncle Qiming, too, didn't she? When they first met, she'd felt she already knew him. How could she have forgotten him so completely over the years? Maybe in the time that she had forgotten him, Amy had all along been helping her remember him? Hadn't she seen herself clearly in Amy's face?

At dawn, beads of water fell on their faces.

"Amy, Amy, did you dream of the Peculiar Hostel?" Liujin shouted excitedly.

"This door is broken. He's stuck, unable to go in or out."

Amy's voice was thin and weak, as though floating in from far away. Liujin saw that she wasn't awake yet.

The snow had stopped, and it was deathly still all around. Happiness once again surged up in Liujin's heart. *Oh, how I wish Amy were as happy as I am,* she thought. She bent and looked at the snowflakes under the steps. Once more, she saw the vortexes that had made her dizzy. So many of them, and so deep! It seemed they would inhale her! She turned her gaze to the sky. It was gray, and it too had many vortexes. Liujin felt sure that something was growing in her heart—it was the thing that she found most exciting. She called out softly, "Ying, Ying—Ying—Ying . . ."

She closed her eyes and visualized the scenery in Muye County. The sound of African drums arose, far away at first and then just outside the courtyard. Liujin turned and smiled at Amy.

"I saw him. We ran into each other but didn't talk. From now on, we can meet only in that place. I finally understand."

While Amy was talking, her expression softened a lot, and Liujin was happy for her.

"Look—what's that?" Amy said, pointing at the snow.

Liujin noticed that the vortexes she'd seen before were moving—and a tiny black dot had spun out of one vortex. Oh, it was a wagtail! With a flapping sound, it shook off the suction and flew out. It flew around the courtyard once and landed on that old nest in the elm tree. All kinds of birds had lived in that nest.

"This is a guest from Muye County," Amy said again.

"I think so, too. I was calling to someone just now. Did this happen to call the birds out?"

"Liujin, did you call the one you love so much?"

"No, no. Oh, maybe so. He is so beautiful, as beautiful as the dark night, as beautiful as animals, and like a cloud. When he's keeping vigil on the rock, drums rumble in the distant west. Can you picture that?"

The snow began falling again. Liujin and Amy broached the subject of the Design Institute. They knew for sure that they were both children of the Design Institute, even though one lived in the Institute and one lived outside it. What kind of organization was this huge Design Institute that took up more than half the space in Pebble Town? Liujin thought back, trying to catch the faint shadow of the old director. Her narrative was choppy. She felt she couldn't express herself to Amy as much as she wanted. Yet she had to continue. If she didn't speak, the Design Institute would be even less focused, even more transient. Amy listened sympathetically, quietly adding a word or two every now and then. Of course she understood. Finally, they fell silent. They heard snowflakes falling lightly to the ground. Amy said a little hesitantly, "Early in the morning, I can see the activities of the Design Institute in the sheep's eyes. And my mother's eyes, too, when she was near death."

Liujin's train of thought widened instantly. She said, "Your parents and my parents, you and I . . . The torch has been passed to us! That's true, isn't it?"

"Yes! Yes! And also the wagtails!" the parrot said.

Wagtails lit on the windowsill—three of them altogether, all the small variety. They were a little wet. Liujin thought, *They probably struggled out from those vortexes. They're Ying's soul.* All at once, her feelings for Ying intensified greatly.

"We love only the people of the Design Institute. I've known this since I was little," Amy said.

"But I figured this out only recently. I'm not as pure as you. Something's always covering my eyes, or you could say that in the past I looked without seeing. I'm ashamed of myself."

Amy had been gone a long time, and yet Liujin was still thinking of Ying. She even felt that she lived in this elderly man's body. Now she sort of understood why her parents had wanted to leave back then. The boxes in her memory that were always kept separate were now fusing. Obstacles were vanishing. Before her appeared the barren hill under the golden-yellow full moon, but it was no longer a barren hill. It was now overgrown with a garden of tulips.

Carrying an umbrella, Liujin trod through the snow to the outside and headed for Song Feiyuan's grilled mutton shop.

From a distance, she saw that the shop had been enlarged and its business was thriving. She went in. It was steamy inside, and people's faces were all blurry. She sat at a corner table. Song Feiyuan's son came over immediately, as though he had noticed her the moment she entered.

"Liujin, you hardly ever go out in the snow, right?" he said.

"Unh. It's great to be here—even better on snowy days. Why is it so steamy in here? I can't get a good look at anyone."

"I boiled water in three large pots to produce steam. The customers all appreciate it," he said. Lowering his voice, he added, "Because no one here wants others to get a good look at each other's faces."

Liujin complimented him on this and said he was managing a very good business—better than his father had.

"Oh, I just did a few things to help those of you who feel uneasy.

No way can I be compared with Father! I can tell you—my father is my spiritual mentor. Even though he has left home now, we have a closer relationship than ever before. You ordered noodles. Nothing else?"

Liujin ate slowly. The faces floating in the steam seemed novel and elegant to her, and she couldn't help saying something that startled her: "It's like Africa here."

"This is Africa," someone answered.

It was Sherman who had spoken. He was sitting at the table to her right. He didn't intend to join her. Speaking from there, he looked relaxed.

"I come here every day, Liujin. Junior Song is quite creative, isn't he?"

"Will Feiyuan ever come back?" she asked.

"No. He wants to live a more adventuresome life. Liujin, how about coming here more often? That way, I can see you often. This is a great place. No one should feel bashful here. Will you do it?"

"Okay."

Some dogs moved back and forth under the tables. Liujin had seen them before. The expressions in their eyes were heartbreakingly mournful, the same as the expressions in the eyes of Amy's sheep. Now they were hidden in the steam, like animals troubled by worries. They were crying softly. Liujin thought, *They must miss their homes.*

When Liujin left the shop and went to buy flour, she noticed two large dogs following her. After she bought the flour and headed home, they still followed her. When she got home, they stayed at the courtyard gate and didn't enter. At first, Liujin took no notice of this and busied herself with housework. While she was resting in the kitchen, she recalled her mother and father's conversation from years ago.

"Why is the flower garden in the dog's eyes?" Mother had asked.

"Dogs are the recorders of history," Dad had replied.

Liujin stood up at once and ran to the courtyard. The two large dogs had apparently been standing there for a while: they were covered with snow. When they saw Liujin approach, they wailed in unison and ran off. Liujin felt she had been remiss again; this had happened numerous times in the past. She sat down and did her best to comb through her memories of the flower garden. For many years, she had heard this person or that person mention in dark tones the tropical garden that was, in reality, non-existent. No one had ever explained this clearly to her. If the mutton shop hadn't been steamy, would she have been able to see the garden in the dogs' eyes? What Junior and Sherman were meticulously covering up were the exact things that she kept neglecting. She thought again of when she was buying flour: a middle-aged woman in line behind her had said to someone: "The old gardener must have a hard time on snowy days like this . . ." She had heard this remark, but hadn't dwelled on it. Liujin was always like this. At this point, she felt that she was sort of approaching the stuff of legends. Perhaps the dogs had barked because a certain old person's life was ending. Liujin's good mood began to be transformed: snowflakes couldn't hide those frightening ditches and ravines.

When Liujin walked into the bedroom, she discovered something even stranger: the parrot repeatedly and rather crazily kept saying something Ying had said: "You mustn't think they're watching you. No, no, that isn't it. You mustn't think they're . . ."

Liujin took the cage down and hung it at the front door.

She walked into the study and opened the cupboard. She bent down and took out the framed photo of her father. Then she saw the remains of five little geckoes stuck to the glass. Her father's face on the lower part of the glass was contorted in pain. Liujin wondered why Dad had had such a large photograph taken just before he left, and why he had framed it. Looking more closely, she felt that this person wasn't Dad, but a relative who resembled him.

Using a screwdriver and a small spatula, she tried to remove the geckoes' remains as whole pieces from the glass. She worked on this for a long time without succeeding. She crushed two of them and found their shapes had sunk into the glass. She realized that the little things were actually joined to the surface. Liujin despaired. She couldn't get a good look at Dad's photo, but she didn't want to throw out the glass along with the geckoes. Annoyed with herself, Liujin wiped the glass clean and wrapped up the frame. She put it away. She began to imagine the way the five little geckoes must have looked as they were dying on this frame. Would Dad's appearance have changed then? In the past, when Dad sat alone in the kitchen, he must have communicated frequently with those old geckoes. What was going on just now? As if possessed, she had actually destroyed the remains of two geckoes! Even now, she was still thrilled to see the geckoes stuck to Dad's picture frame.

Meng Yu's wife came over in the snowstorm. She stood on the steps and shook off the snow.

"Have you seen our ewe? It disappeared yesterday. A lot of things have been stolen in the last few days."

Mrs. Meng was dressed all in black, like a spirit. She didn't intend to come in.

"I haven't seen it. This didn't happen much in the past, did it?"

"No, never. The end of the world is coming. I'm worried about Amy."

When she turned to leave, she looked solemnly into Liujin's eyes, making Liujin nervous. She had no sooner left the courtyard than Amy's sad, shrill singing came from the little house across the street. The sound almost broke Liujin's heart. She kept trembling even long after Amy finished her song.

As she cooked, Liujin thought of things that were even less focused. This helped her calm down. Just now, from Amy's singing, she once more experienced Amy's inner frenzy. No wonder Mrs.

Meng was worried about her! Amy must be disheartened. How could she catch up with Uncle Qiming—this spirit of the past era?

Liujin had a dream in which someone kept calling her. She answered again and again until she ran out of patience, but the person wouldn't stop and even scolded her, saying she was pretending to be deaf. Enraged, Liujin woke up. She looked at the clock: it was only one in the morning. She turned on the light and went to the living room to drink some water. There, she saw Uncle Qiming. He seemed to be looking at the snowflakes in the sky.

"The cart is waiting at the courtyard gate. Let's go," he said.

"Where?"

"You've forgotten again. We're going to the snow mountain, of course."

"Then I need to change clothes."

When she left, she was wearing a coat over a padded jacket, as well as a pair of fur-lined boots. Qiming glanced at her and said, "Look at you. You're dressed as if you're ready to die on the battlefield."

It was actually a passenger carriage. They sat down in it. It wasn't very comfortable: the seats were hard, and wind blew in from all sides. Liujin was glad she was wearing warm clothes, and noticed that Uncle Qiming was wearing only a thin overcoat. He wasn't even wearing a hat. As soon as the cart started, wind blew in their faces. It was painful, and tears spilled from Liujin's eyes. She told herself it would be okay after her face became numb. After a while, her face finally numbed and she didn't feel the pain. She leaned against Uncle's broad shoulder, and he hugged her lightly. Liujin couldn't talk because of the numbness. She heard Qiming say happily, "Even death can be so pleasant!"

The carriage went fast, and they were jostled back and forth as the road became rugged. Liujin wanted to laugh, but she couldn't. They could do nothing but endure and struggle in the dark.

They seemed to have traveled a long time, and yet it wasn't light yet. It was actually even darker.

Suddenly, the carriage stopped, and the driver stood in the snow and began to curse. They couldn't tell if he was cursing the weather or cursing the two of them. Liujin thought his words were very obscure. Cursing and cursing, the driver left them and the carriage behind and walked off alone. It was then that Qiming said, "We've arrived."

As they emerged from the carriage, Liujin saw the two black horses standing, unmoving, in the snow. They were much like sculptures. She sighed inwardly, "So calm." The sky was a murky gray. The mountain ahead seemed to want to hide itself. They could see only a dull shadow. Liujin asked Qiming how long it would take them to reach the snow mountain. He replied, "It depends on the road under your feet."

Liujin opened her eyes wide to see what kind of road it was. In fact, there was no road. They were standing among sparsely scattered bushes. Qiming said, the snow mountain has a bad temper and tends to stay away from people. For example, they were now circling around the foothills, and yet it wouldn't even show itself.

"Then, where are we going?" Liujin asked.

"We're going to see a dying old man."

They entered a frame house. By then, it was dawn. Wind pierced the frame house from all directions. The old man was lying in bed in a corner. At intervals, he moaned loudly, "I can't take this anymore."

At first, Liujin couldn't see clearly and felt terrified. Later, she mustered her courage to approach the old man and saw that he looked spirited. This was a handsome old man. His eyes were clear, and he looked healthy. He certainly didn't seem to be on the verge of death. Did he really feel ill? Maybe he looked healthy because he was confident he could conquer his physical illness.

All of a sudden, Liujin noticed that Uncle Qiming had disappeared. Besides her, the only one left in the house was the dying old man. Motioning with his index finger, he indicated that he wanted her to move closer to him. Liujin took hold of his right hand. Though it was stiff and cold, it was still strong. How could he be dying? Could this be a prank? But Uncle Qiming definitely wasn't the sort of person to play a prank like this.

"Is it snowing outside, Miss?" As he spoke, he began breathing more rapidly.

"Yes, sir."

"Is it really snowing?"

"Yes, really. It's white all over."

"I'm dying. The holes in my body can never be patched up. It hurts a lot!"

He began moaning again. Liujin went outside and looked up. She was stunned—the mountain was right in front of her, and animal footprints were everywhere on the snow-covered mountain path. Memories of past events surged up in Liujin's mind. She felt an urge to walk into the mountain. But she couldn't leave the dying old man alone. Just then, she heard a conversation.

"Some people die, and some people are born. On this mountain . . ."

"We aren't afraid of anything."

The speakers were Uncle Qiming and Amy's brother. They were walking over from the mountain path. Amy's brother nodded, unsmiling, to Liujin, and went to the kitchen. Liujin realized then that this was Amy's home. Uncle Qiming stooped down and whispered a few words to the bedridden old man. The sick person actually began to smile, and the atmosphere in the room lightened instantly. Liujin spotted a door in the wall and guessed it was probably Amy's room. She walked over and pushed the door open, but it was dark inside.

"Go inside," Uncle Qiming said.

Liujin tripped over something and dropped down into a small bed. She heard an infant crying.

"That's Amy. When Amy was little, she cried a lot. She wasn't one bit like a mountain child," Qiming said.

"People said that I was like this, too, when I was little. This room is full of memories. Was it Amy's idea to bring me to her home? Her dad is dying, yet she didn't want to come back!"

"That's it. She wanted me to bring you here. What do you think about that?

"She has stopped crying. She's here in this room, isn't she? Ha. One is in the city, one is here!"

Liujin touched the infant's tiny hand. The hand gripped her index finger, making her intensely sentimental. Choking with sobs, she called, "Amy—"

Just then in the outer room, Amy's dad moaned loudly again, "I'm really in pain!"

Amy's room smelled of animal fur, a smell that made Liujin think of Roy. It was such a similar smell: Were Amy and Roy brother and sister? The infant's tiny hand glimmered in the dark, just the way Roy's hand used to do. Liujin sensed that Uncle Qiming had seen everything. He was standing next to the door watching her. It was strange: it was windy in the entire front room, but Amy's room was warm. Liujin was perspiring. She removed her coat and stood in the center of the room. She thought, *Something must be about to happen.* She waited.

Before long, she heard Amy's brother singing in the kitchen. Liujin couldn't tell what he was singing: she thought it was like a cavalryman planning to jump from a cliff. Liujin emerged from Amy's small room and saw Uncle Qiming looking out the window. Amy's dad was delirious.

The song became more and more upbeat. Liujin and Uncle Qiming saw two snow leopards, one male and one female, squatting in the snow of the foothills.

"Is that brother's leopard?" Liujin asked softly.

"Yes," Qiming answered. "Look, more are coming."

Sure enough, Liujin saw two more descending. The two new arrivals stood opposite the others, and the two pairs of leopards looked at each other. In the kitchen, Amy's brother finished singing. Liujin sensed that he had jumped down and was falling from midair.

"Brother will never move to the city, will he?"

"Of course not. You can see how fortunate this old father is."

"I see. That sort of garden is everywhere. Snowy weather is wonderful."

Liujin and Qiming left in the carriage. From far away, they could still hear Amy's brother singing. He had started another round. Liujin felt deeply moved. As she listened attentively, some knots vanished from the bottom of her heart. The June sunshine leapt in her heart, and she said sincerely, "Thank you, Uncle Qiming."

"Liujin, I've fixed your toy duck. Do you want to take it to the stream?"

"Oh, Uncle Qiming!"

She bent over the old man's shoulder and sobbed uncontrollably. The wind pouring into the carriage had become a warm spring breeze. The lively silhouette of the snow leopard flashed through the bosk.

They parted at the entrance to Liujin's courtyard. Qiming didn't get out of the carriage, and his voice sounded feeble, "I'll give all those chicks and ducklings back to you . . ."

The carriage quickly vanished into the snowy landscape.

It stopped snowing. She heard the persistent calls of little creatures in the courtyard—the voices sounded like cicadas, or birds. They came from the mouth of the well. Liujin walked over to the cement mound, but she couldn't locate the source of the sounds. From the entrance to the courtyard, the mailman called to her, saying, "You have a letter from Muye County!"

Liujin took the letter and stood there, dazed. It was strange: this thin envelope made of gossamer tissue was so large. She had never seen one like this. Looking at it closely, she could see a vague design of a wolf. Oh—there really was a Muye County. Why had it never shown up on a map? "Ma, No. 4 Zhongshui Street, Muye County."

Someone surnamed Ma had sent her this letter. The handwriting was nothing unusual.

She tore the envelope open carefully and withdrew the letter. Both sides were stamped with a pretty, pale green leaf design. It looked familiar. Why was there no writing?

"When you aren't thinking of him, he shows up!" the parrot said.

Had Roy sent the letter? The wagtail stood in the wind tunnel and suddenly called out like a cicada. Amazing—a bird could call for so long in one breath! It was only one-fourth the size of ordinary wagtails. Its feathers were black and shiny. It was so tiny and its voice wasn't at all like a bird's. Maybe it was "the thing" that had invaded the world of the living. At last, it tired of calling and retreated into the wind tunnel.

When Liujin walked into the kitchen, she saw dinner on the table. It had to be Amy—how nice and warm she was to her. Liujin was so touched that she nearly wept. Recently, she'd often been emotional like this.

When it grew dark, she placed that letter on the windowsill and saw a glimmer of the pale green color. She said to herself, "That's Roy's handwriting. So many people care about me."

She sat in front of the window and once more heard snowflakes falling lightly to the ground. Silhouettes of her parents pressing ahead came to her mind. When she considered that, even in their old age, they could still join the seething collective cause, her heart was filled with admiration for them.

She sat there until deep into the night. She simply gave up thinking and enjoyed the touch of the cool evening air. Bit by bit, her mind became luminous.

The boss reclined in a cane chair with his legs crossed. He still couldn't move his legs, but he didn't seem to be in pain.

"I had no sooner placed the spiral-patterned cloth on the counter than it sold out," Liujin told him.

"Ah, Liujin," the boss sighed, "how many years have you worked for me? In this market, only us, you and me. This is . . . is . . ." He was unable to go on.

Generally, the boss was composed. Liujin was surprised that he could be so emotional.

"That's right, boss. When we stand on this spot, we can hear voices from all directions. We . . . oh, boss, I chose to take this job just because I wanted to hear the voices that come from crowds."

"Liujin, you're very smart."

The boss leaned over to look for something under his chair, but he couldn't lean down far enough. Liujin asked what he was looking for. Glancing at her, he said meaningfully, "The turtle." That little thing, he said, always appeared and disappeared mysteriously.

Liujin's customers were a little strange. When they interacted with her, their eyes drooped and they didn't look at her, as though embarrassed about something. Liujin wondered if there was something on her face, and walked to the back room to look in the mirror on the wall. She saw a gecko on her forehead—the translucent remains of a tiny gecko. She wiped at it with a handkerchief—wiped it several times without getting rid of it. She grew restless. Touching her forehead with her bare hand, she couldn't feel anything at that spot, but looking again in the mirror, she saw the little gecko embedded right in the center of her forehead, as if it were an ornament. She recalled the geckoes on her dad's picture frame, and her heart pounded.

"Ah, Liujin, there are some things you shouldn't take too much to heart. Just let them go."

When her boss said this, Liujin calmed down. She turned back to the counter.

"On snowy days, one's field of vision widens," she said to one old woman.

Taking her cloth, the woman nodded her head and replied, "I love buying cloth here. This kind of cloth is made in the snow mountain."

Liujin noticed a crowd gathering in a corner of the market. At the same time, cicadas' voices were rending the hall, as if it were a summer day rather than a snowy day.

A crowd of young women came to the front of her counter. They touched the cloth and spoke softly. Liujin's eyes swept over them, and then she stopped in amazement: embedded on the four young women's perfectly white cheeks were tiny coral snakes, as though the vipers were growing out of their flesh. In a quavering voice, she asked, "Are you buying cloth?"

"We're looking for that local cloth printed with a bamboo-leaf design. The little snakes on our faces are called 'green bamboo snakes,'" one of the young women said calmly.

Liujin was gazing at the backs of these pretty young women. She sighed to herself, "How dramatically this world is changing!"

All of a sudden, Ying appeared. He was so tall and his face so dark that you knew from far away that it was he. But he didn't come over. He was craning his neck looking for something. Liujin thought, *Could what he wants to find possibly be here in the market?* Just then, her boss spoke loudly from behind her, and Liujin spun to face him.

"Has that masculine man arrived?" the boss asked.

"Do you mean Ying? He's in the market."

"Yesterday at dusk, I saw him from this window. He looks a lot like our ancestor. He was fetching water from that well." Her boss recalled, "He's really black."

Liujin didn't think her boss was recalling what happened yesterday, but rather was remembering long-ago events.

Her boss opened up the back door, and leaning against the bamboo chair, he watched the snow filling the sky. His face was alight with charm. She had never before realized how handsome he was.

After leaving work that day, Liujin didn't go straight home because she ran into Mrs. Meng on the way. Mrs. Meng told her that Amy had been missing for two days. Now she, Meng Yu, Qiming, and Amy's brother were all looking for her. Liujin was frightened when she heard this. The snow was heavy—more than a foot deep. Liujin remembered the white pagoda—the one she and Amy had once gone to.

When Liujin walked into the park which held the white pagoda, it was difficult to move through the deep snow. She stood at a loss in the vast white world. Just then, she saw human forms imprinted in a line on the snow—probably more than ten of them. Liujin felt as if her heart would jump out of her throat. She walked along the row of imprinted forms and thought, *This must have been left by Amy. She flopped down here on the snow and tried to disappear from the face of the earth.* She stood in the last human shape and saw no more signs of Amy ahead. So, then there must be a crevasse. But where was it? Liujin turned and walked back. She left the park and came to the main street. Mrs. Meng's shouts reached her: "Amy—Amy . . ." Liujin touched her face and felt some ice crystals: they must have been her frozen tears.

Mother Earth was no less charming without Amy. Human shadows were still drifting and floating above it. Liujin strode decisively toward the opening.

Translators' Acknowledgments

We are grateful to publisher Chad Post for his steadfast support of Can Xue's works and of our translations; editor Kaija Straumanis for her thoughtfulness and collegiality in copy editing; art director Nathan Furl for his spectacular cover design; and intern Hannah Rankin for her attention to the page proofs. We also thank Porochista Khakpour for graciously taking time from her pressing schedule to write the perceptive introduction. Most of all, we thank Can Xue for once again entrusting her work to us.

Karen Gernant & Chen Zeping
August 2016

Can Xue is a pseudonym meaning "dirty snow, leftover snow." She learned English on her own and has written books on Borges, Shakespeare, and Dante. Her publications in English include *The Embroidered Shoes*, *Five Spice Street*, *Vertical Motion*, and *The Last Lover*, which won the 2015 Best Translated Book Award for Fiction.

.

Karen Gernant, professor emerita of Chinese history at Southern Oregon University, and Chen Zeping, professor of Chinese linguistics at Fujian Teachers' University, have collaborated on more than ten book translations and about sixty translations for literary magazines.

OPEN LETTER

**OPEN
LETTER**